DRAGON ROGUE

RIDERS OF JADE & FIRE
BOOK THREE

MELANIE ANSLEY

Copyright © 2025 by Melanie Ansley

All rights reserved.

Join the author's reader club on www.melanieansley.com/subscribe to receive free books, exclusives, and giveaways.

No part of this book may be reproduced in any form or by any electronic or mechanical means, including information storage and retrieval systems, without written permission from the author, except for the use of brief quotations in a book review.

Dragon Rogue is a work of fiction. Though certain characters such as Empress Wu did exist, this is very much an imagined version of them, and set in a distinctly alternate Tang dynasty. The author has taken liberties with exact dates and court language to better fit the story and its world. All other likenesses to people living or dead are purely coincidental.

Cover Design: Get Covers

For Cecilia Sutton.
Thank you for being there for each and every book!

CHAPTER 1

A pounding sound. Scraping. Jin could barely breathe from the dust that clogged her throat.

Rayshan!

A dim hum, as if coming through water.

Rayshan!

The hum came again, and Jin tried to open her eyes. Her head felt tender—had she fallen?—and the light hit her like a mallet.

Light. Why was she surprised that there was light?

Because the Well had collapsed—right on top of her.

She had been buried in darkness. How was there light?

Jin forced herself past the painful throbbing and blinked. There was definitely a crack in the dark, like a seam in a blanket. It was widening, ever so slightly, until she sat up and realized she was looking at a break in the cavern.

She crawled toward it, her hands cutting on unseen rock as jagged as the shards of memory returning to her, but she needed to get to the light. Her swimming thoughts and queasy insides told her she wasn't getting enough air. And where there was light, there was air.

Then something moved behind her.

"Jao?" she called. "Panshalar?" Her wing mates had been with her, she was sure. They'd been here to do something, something important . . .

Kill Mengkhis Lai.

Her stomach roiled in a hot wave, and she retched, wiping the mess from her lips with a scraped hand.

But he was supposed to be asleep. It was supposed to be easy! Instead—

A guttural sound cut into her memories, and despite her splitting head, she moved toward the source, pulling at rock and debris until her fingers brushed an arm. Then a shoulder. She dug more frantically until she had unearthed Jao.

"Where is the bastard?" Jao asked. His words were slurred, and Jin dimly made out a nasty split in his lip that had swollen to a plum's size.

Jin didn't answer. Instead, she peered around, seeking Panshalar. "Panshalar!"

The sound reverberated off the rock and stabbed her head, but she tried again. A muffled grunt came from the other corner.

She scrabbled toward the sound, drawing on her blood bond strength to pull at the rocks, even when her arms screamed and her head throbbed. Jao joined her, trying his best to help, though he was severely hurt. She smelled blood. Lots of blood.

They eventually unearthed Panshalar, and Jin cleared as much rubble as possible to make sure he didn't have any broken limbs.

"We can't move him," Jin said.

"I don't think anything's broken," Jao responded.

"No, I mean we don't have the strength to move him," Jin said. "He's heavier than an ox." She looked around. "I'll have to squeeze out of that rift and get help."

"Why you?"

"I'm the only one small enough!" She glanced outside. "I'll get water." Dragons. Rayshan and the others had been outside. "And find the dragons." She forced her mind to think through the pain, to remember. "Nakkalan can help move the rubble, and one of the blacks can pump air—" She remembered words that sent an icy finger tracing her back.

Are you sure I'm the one who was meant to die here? Mengkhis Lai's question came back to her.

"What's wrong?" Jao asked, his words sounding strange through his lips.

"If Sanjin or the others come without me," Jin said, "be on your guard."

He looked confused. "What? Why?"

"Just—" Her head protested at the effort of making sense of the pieces of memory skittering at the edge of her mind. "Just don't go out unless your dragons are there."

Jao closed his eyes. "Hurry."

She didn't need the reminder. As she moved to the slim crack and squeezed her way out, a thought besides survival surfaced.

Nothing had gone according to plan. Or at least not hers. Then whose?

A memory rushed back, clear as a summer brook, at how easy this had all seemed a mere week ago, when she left Changan.

TO JIN'S MIND, killing a man in his sleep was not a reason for city-wide celebration. But clearly, many disagreed.

Her ears rang from the shouting in the streets and the rhythmic drums pounding a war beat. Colorful flowers showered her and Prince Tai as they rode on horses down the Avenue of Vermillion Birds, the main thoroughfare that ran north to south from the capital city's main gate at the south to the imperial palace at the north.

Throngs of cheering crowds choked the avenue, waving banners woven or painted with the words "Long Live the Dragon Princess and Dragon Prince" and "Slay the Traitor." Children waved sticky crabapples and sugar blown into the shape of dragons, their parents shouldering them to give a better view of the departing heroes.

She was off to murder a man in his sleep. And being called a hero for it.

He murdered many more, Rayshan growled in her mind.

She glanced up to the skies to see his reassuring emerald bulk against the clear blue, circling lazily to keep pace with her slow gait on the gleaming chestnut mare she rode. The mare felt like a fragile toy beneath her, ears flicking at the surrounding tumult.

How much simpler it would have been to have flown on Rayshan with the rest of the Dragon Class team at daybreak and avoided all this ceremony, this public display of might and purpose. But, no, Empress Wu had not been able to resist a show of strength for the people: she was sending the Dragon Class and the blood-bonded rider Jin to Mengkhis Lai, the most dangerous man in the empire. The one who had brought on the Age of Chaos over twenty years ago, terrorizing everyone with his powers to turn himself, and others, invisible.

But no more.

Jin would go with a company of mages and kill Mengkhis in his magic-induced sleep, as only a blood-bonded rider could kill another. Mengkhis Lai was, besides Jin, the only blood-bonded rider in the world. Therefore, only she could kill Mengkhis, and he her.

A pang struck her. He was the only one like her, the only one who might be able to explain to her what powers and dangers lurked in the blood bond. But she would have to end his life, for her empress demanded it.

Do you not want him dead? Rayshan asked.

She saw again the bodies at Jimo. Through the Firesong, she had witnessed via Mengkhis's and Baikalan's eyes what he had done to the village men and seen that Mengkhis was indeed the monster of legend.

I do. But like a coward, I don't want it by my hand, or while he is defenseless.

Next to her, Prince Tai seemed at ease on his favorite steed, Leiyu. He beamed his usual disarming smile, and the crowds seemed to relish it all. He waved his hand, the thousands of gold-plated pieces sewn into his armor as regal as his movements and aura. A beautiful work of art to be sure, but like everything here, it was for show. The clothing was so heavy that Jin was surprised his horse could carry him.

"You may want to try smiling," Prince Tai shouted. With the roar of the crowd, there was no chance anyone would hear him. Jin, because of her blood bond, would have heard him if he whispered, but didn't bother to enlighten him.

"Smiling to go kill a man?"

"One who deserves it."

Jin kept silent. Just because a man deserved death didn't make it a reason to celebrate as if it was the New Year. Such displays struck her as grotesque.

They made their slow way down the avenue, the drums still going strong as the one hundred drummers kept time and the soldiers cleared the path of overenthusiastic celebrants. Jin spotted the southern gate to the city, where she would leave the capital, Changan, and mount Rayshan. She looked forward to getting off this mare's back.

A hum of agreement came from the great green beast above. Riding a horse and being pressed on all sides felt like the opposite of flying: restrictive and prison-like.

Jin was just passing an intersection when she spotted a face in the crowd. Something about the woman in her fur-lined cloak was both strange and familiar. No one else was reacting to her, despite her distinctly foreign features and her garb, which was not only from a faraway northern land but also definitely not suited to summer.

A phantasm.

Rayshan's reaction rippled with hers. *Who is she?*

I don't know, Jin said. Rayshan, as a jade, had manifested his unprecedented power as an ability to summon the dead, or what was known as "flaring." And though they had gained control over most of these summonings, the stronger souls occasionally pushed through even when Rayshan was not flaring. Often these were strangers. But this woman was so out of place here, yet so eerily familiar, that Jin was unnerved.

She stared at the woman, trying to think where she had seen her before. The *huren*, or foreign, eyes and light hair meant she was from the west, and possibly north. Bactrian? Too fair-skinned, Jin decided.

"What is it?" This time Tai's voice was lower, and though his smile remained, his eyes showed concern.

"A ghost," Jin answered.

Tai looked around but clearly didn't see what she saw. "Someone you know?"

Jin deliberated. "No."

The woman turned and walked away, disappearing into the oblivious crowd. The dead, Jin had found, were sometimes like that—unseen by any but "flames," those who could draw the dead, like Rayshan.

A thread of ice slid down her nape. Though she had summoned thousands at the battle of Bohai, she would never get used to the appearance of the dead. The empress's most skilled bards and poets had made sure to sugarcoat Jin and Rayshan's dark abilities in songs, serials, and plays, convincing the empire that Jin's gift was divine, a blessing from the Boddhisattva herself. But Jin saw the truth in many eyes: her gift was dark.

She glanced back at Tai and saw that behind the smile, his eyes were distant.

"Are you alright, Your Highness?"

He blinked and looked back at her. "Just . . . it's nothing."

She sensed it all the same.

"Is it hard, not knowing the truth?" she asked.

He raised an eyebrow. "About what?"

"Peilah?" Tai's first infatuation had died by the empress's order, if one believed the rumors. The talk of ghosts had no doubt reminded Tai of when Jin had inexplicably summoned Peilah before Tai and his mother.

The prince continued to smile, though not so broadly. "I can't decide." He leaned in a little closer. "Would you want to know for certain who your parents were? What is the truth worth to you?"

She stilled and raised a finger to the scar behind her right ear. It had been there since birth, Haitao had told her. Haitao had found her, or bought her, she was still unsure which, on the day she was born, or shortly after. He had seen the word "Kway," or "precious," branded there behind her ear and named her Kway Jin, or "precious gold," in the hopes she would bring him and his thief clan a fortune. Which she had. But that same fortune had also killed them, and the thought of everyone who had died made her throat constrict.

"Well?"

She realized Tai was waiting for an answer. In fact, she wondered why he seemed so keen. "Why care about a truth I'll likely never know?" The lie was easy, but she doubted the prince was fooled.

"Sometimes, knowing is not worth the price. You are a warrior. Strong. And like your jade dragon, occurring only once a generation."

She shot him a questioning look. "Are you mocking me, Your Highness?"

"You offend too easily," he said. "I just mean that perhaps the past is just that: gone and buried. What counts is who we are now."

Jin rode in silence, the mare twitching beneath her as a fresh wave of cheering greeted them. Was he right? Should she forget trying to find out her birth and who her parents were? Perhaps it didn't matter that she was a criminal's child, as Sanjin and the now-dead Minister Gao had claimed. Certainly Emar, her master trainer, had told her it didn't matter. But then why did she feel this hole in her? A hole that only this knowledge could fill?

The woman's face lingered in her mind even as the gates were pulled open by rows of soldiers straining at ropes as thick as their upper arms. The gates led through a wall fifty paces deep, and Jin was grateful for the dark that hid her expression as she rode through it to the outer areas of the city, where thinner crowds from the surrounding lands had gathered to see their heroes off.

She mustered a dignified expression by the time they were visible again, but she relaxed a little when they reached the roped clearing where the dragons, each the size of four horses from nose to tail, waited, along with her wing mates, Panshalar and Jao.

Aadan should be here.

Rayshan's sympathetic hum met her from where he stood next to the other dragons, their ridges gleaming in the summer light and their wings stretched as they readied for flight.

He will return.

Yes, but when? Aadan had been gone two months now. It felt like a year.

Stop.

Rayshan was right. There were many things to do today, and moping wasn't one of them. Especially as moping never changed anything.

"Jin."

She turned to see Prince Tai had dismounted beside her. "I'm sorry you are doing this on your own."

"I'm not alone, Your Highness," she replied. "I have them." She indicated her wing mates, Panshalar and Jao. They cut an interesting pair, for Panshalar was from the north and large as a bear, while Jao was small and compact like most southerners. She had fought against them and with them, which had sprouted a strange sort of friendship. They still grated each other often, but they would also die for each other. And that was what made clans.

"I mean I am sorry I am not going."

"The Minister of War cannot go to every skirmish," she said.

He grinned, though it was less happy. "As I always say, just come back. The people will miss their Princess of Dragons. As will I."

"There are no crowds here to win over, Your Highness," she replied. Jin chafed at the charade of their relationship, but she had no say over it, being a mere dragonrider.

He regarded her as if about to say more, but then nodded. "May the winds be at your back."

Jin sensed a simmering nervousness in the prince. "Don't worry, Your Highness. I will kill him."

The prince swallowed, then clasped one hand over his fist and bowed ever so slightly. It was a gesture no prince made to anyone but their parents, and Jin was struck by the knowledge that hidden so cleverly under all that poise and charm was a fear that Mengkhis Lai, the man who had tried to kill Tai on the day he was born, would one day return and finish the job.

She bowed in turn and walked away, toward her wing mates and the dragons. Nakkalan the bronze, who was puffing as his limbs began to expand, was preparing to grow to three times his size. And Panshalar's dragon, a gold named Bayan, was nervously creating a little whirlwind of metal shards in the earth.

Jin nodded a greeting to each of them in turn, then stiffened as Sanjin approached.

Sanjin's name meant "three brilliance," but the words were a homonym for "three pounds," and this nickname stuck. The macabre joke was that Sanjin left only three pounds of anyone he interrogated. Those invited to the "tea rooms," as the interrogation rooms were euphemistically called, rarely came out. He served the empress with an iron fist when he was in a good mood, and a red-hot poker when he was not. Today, he was leading the expedition against Mengkhis Lai, even though Prince Tai had tried to take the role.

"If the parade is over," he said coldly, "then let's get the real business started. We have blood to spill."

CHAPTER 2

The journey south brought hotter weather, humidity, and what seemed like blizzards of mosquitoes.

The dragons were the only ones undisturbed by the insects, protected by their thick hides. As the group prepared to mount and fly the last stretch to the Champa capital to pay their respects to the Champa king, Jin absent-mindedly slapped one on her bare arm, noting that her chrysanthemum powder didn't seem to work against these insects. And she could do nothing about the heat. Even the light cotton riding suits their new commander, Oyang Kang, had ordered for them still clung to them in the moist air, and stripping down any more would leave her naked.

Panshalar suffered the most, being a northerner who was more used to snow than heat. His meaty face had turned a constant crimson, and the humidity seemed to sap him of words.

Jin moved over to Rayshan, who was busy cleaning a strip of moss from his tail.

I hate the weather here, he growled in her mind.

Not long now. We'll kill him and return home heroes.

We're already heroes, he said. *Everyone loves the Princess of Dragons.*

She grimaced. He knew she didn't fancy the nickname.

As they rode, Jin acutely felt the gaps in her wing. Ezho. Emar. Aadan. She said a quiet prayer for Ezho and Emar, hoping their scattered energies were at peace in the world. Did Ezho's parents blame her and her wing mates for his death? For not bringing his body back to be buried in his ancestral home after the Khitan ambush?

She would never know. Communication with fallen wing mates' families was actively discouraged in Dragon Class. There were too many to mourn.

Despite her better judgment, she let her thoughts stray to Aadan.

Where was he now? Was he even alive? Did he ever think of her?

Her anger at the empress for banishing Aadan still simmered, but she knew it served no purpose, so she bottled it.

Something flickered in Rayshan's bond. It had been there occasionally, and Jin had simply interpreted it as irritation at her thoughts about Aadan, but somehow this felt different. It was more primal, edged with a longing that was smothered, like a spark ground underfoot before it could blaze.

What is that?

It is nothing.

This alerted her. *What are you hiding?*

He made a reluctant noise, his ears flattening, but then with a great pump of his wings, he gave in. *It's the mating year.*

It took her a while to understand his words. *Mating year? What do you mean?*

Every three years dragons are called back to Nine Claw Mountain for the mating season. It's called the Song of Scales. The queen sings to us, and we answer.

Then . . . you will go?

Uncertainty fanned through Rayshan, and his wings beat faster. *I would, but our blood bonding makes it . . . complicated.*

How?

I am not sure whether those who have broken a taboo will be welcomed.

Of course. He had broken the age-old rule of blood bonding with a human, and this meant that going back would be risky.

What will they do?

I don't know, Rayshan admitted. *Kill me, perhaps.*

Jin's heart went cold. *Then you can't go.*

No, he answered tightly. *I can't.*

Once the initial fear wore away, however, Jin suddenly found herself shouldering guilt. If Rayshan had not saved her life that time in the desert by blood bonding with her, then he wouldn't have this dilemma. He'd be free to go with the other dragons, without fear of retribution.

This means you won't have young, she said quietly.

I have you, he answered. *I told you, we dragons are not sentimental when it comes to offspring.*

Despite his words, she sensed the loss in him, the yearning to fly to Nine Claw Mountain. *Is that what you feel like when the queen sends the song?*

It will grow stronger, Rayshan confided. *It will keep calling and more frequently. But I can resist it.*

She rested a hand on his neck. *Thank you.*

He huffed like it was nothing, but deep down she ached at the notion she had robbed him. She had never considered having children of her own, for she hadn't known whether she would even live that long. But it had never occurred to her that it might be taken away from her, which was what Rayshan was facing—a future where his line would end and he wouldn't even get the choice, because he had chosen to save her instead.

She glanced at the other dragons around her—Nakkalan, Bayan, and others.

Do they feel it too then?

They will. Our blood bond makes everything more acute, so perhaps the Song feels stronger for me.

When will they go? she asked.

They choose different times—many choose to go early, in hopes of less competition from other males. He let out a small burst of fire. *Let us not dwell on these things,* he said, ending the conversation, and did a small dive in the air in the way he knew she relished. She loved the rush of air and the flutter in her stomach, and the sense of freedom flooding her veins. She and Rayshan would get through this. Together. At least they were alive and had each other, and that was all that mattered right now.

That, and killing Mengkhis Lai.

THEY FLEW OVER lush jungle that rang with the sounds of exotic birds and strange beasts. Jin had decided she detested the jungle after one night where they had landed and Jin had woken up with a python the size of her arm writhing in her bedroll. She still had nightmares about it that rivaled those of the dead she saw.

Seeing the dead had become easier, if still not pleasant. Her dreams were filled with those who wished her to communicate for them, to talk to the living and intercede. But she knew better than to fall into that trap too often. The dead would suck her dry given half the chance, and she had to conserve her energy. Especially for what was ahead.

Mengkhis.

She suppressed a shudder at the memory and leaned close to Rayshan's neck, grateful for his warmth despite the hot air. This kingdom of Champa was unlike anywhere she had been before. Stone cities with wooden huts huddled on impossibly steep terraces, where emerald pools sheltered delicate rice shoots beneath the venomous sun. Clouds of insects swarmed, and the birds here screamed rather than chirped. The people gazed up, faces slack, at the dragons passing overhead. No doubt they had rarely seen *one*, let alone so many. Though the king of Champa had one dragon, as per his agreement with the empress of China, Jin heard that he rarely rode it or let it out of the capital, Simhapura.

When they reached it, Jin studied the capital's architecture, her curiosity stirring. A city wall encircled the capital, where clumps of residences built out of bamboo, wood, and thatch spread around tall temples with curving roofs. The palace gleamed at the center, an expanse of golden tiles over smooth stone walls.

They landed in a clearing outside the palace. A large contingent of soldiers marched out, banners of blue and yellow waving in the heat. The soldiers wore helmets with long points on top and held spears topped with feathers, their faces as imposing as the stone statues that towered over the avenue to the palace.

Jin missed Aadan anew. He would have known all the artwork and been able to explain the different figures. As it was, she only had Tai's brief explanation that the Cham people were Hindu and worshipped a multitude of gods.

The dragons huffed and snarled, tails whipping. Besides Jin's wing, there were five others, along with three wearing the "zheng" emblem for Sanjin's Royal Veil. One of them, a tall man with a gold dragon, struck her as particularly haughty, as if he knew something she didn't.

Sanjin descended from the carriage strapped to a bronze transport dragon. The new head of Dragon Class, the renowned hero Oyang Kang, dismounted after Sanjin.

The soldiers bowed, and their leader, a stocky man in bright gold armor, stepped forward. "His Majesty King Haptuma the Third welcomes you to his capital and invites you in. The grooms will take care of the dragons."

Jin didn't see much in the way of where dragons might be kept but noticed Oyang Kang shading his eyes to scan the hills that sloped up from the palace. There was evidence of an area having been cleared, and stone turrets and long walls wound their way up the slope face, apparently having been laid for the dragons' benefit.

"Come, the king awaits," the soldier said.

Oyang Kang strode over to Jin and her wing mates. "The king has asked for you to come as well. He wants to meet you."

Jin still hadn't grown used to her reputation traveling faster than dragons' wings. Having been a thief all her life, she found attention of any kind unnerving, but attention now seemed to find her. She gave strict instructions to the wide-eyed groom who came forward to tend to Rayshan, and then to the dragons in her wing.

No harming the grooms, understand? They have little experience with dragons, so try to be patient.

A result of her blood bonding was her ability to communicate with all the dragons, but it didn't mean they necessarily liked her for it. She felt distinct pushback from Nakkalan and some of the others.

She followed Oyang Kang into the palace and immediately relished the cool air inside. The stone palace was airy and open, allowing airflow while also keeping shade.

They walked a long stone walkway where ferocious statues and carvings of *apsaras* loomed above them. The soldier marched with them up the long avenue, over flagstones carved with snarling beasts.

He led them past giant doors, then up a staircase and into a spacious chamber.

The audience hall stretched to a throne of elaborately carved wood on a dais with steps, and a panel overhead showed brilliantly painted sculptures of Hindu gods. A herald waiting there struck the floor with a staff, the sound echoing off the chamber walls. A strapping, towering man of thirty strode in, and Jin wondered at the king of Champa. But then followed an old, wizened man who looked as if death walked at his heels.

He sat down gingerly, his gnarled hand gripping his staff, while the strapping companion stood to one side. The old man waved his fingers, and when his voice came it sounded like a child's, it was so reedy and soft.

"Welcome, Lord Sanjin. I don't believe we have met, but the people of the Tang court are always welcome here."

"It is an honor to meet you, Your Majesty. The empress sends you her best wishes and thanks you for cooperating in this matter."

The man sighed. "We have always cooperated with the Tang. But once Mengkhis Lai is killed, we will have to renegotiate our treaties."

"Yes," Sanjin said. "I will be able to have that conversation with you in a short time. For now, we need to reach the Well of Fire as soon as possible, for we wish to accomplish our mission soon."

Again, the king waved dismissive fingers. "You young, always in a rush. When I am the one closest to death. Do you see me hurrying anywhere?"

Sanjin cleared his throat. "Your Majesty, you wished to see the female dragonrider?"

The man's eyes sparked. "Ah yes, the girl. Let's have a look at she who will kill Mengkhis Lai."

Jin stepped forward, fighting her annoyance at being treated like a showpiece. The king's eyes raked over her, a soft snort escaping his lips.

"She is barely past childhood. It's a good thing Mengkhis Lai is in a magical sleep."

"This will be an easy mission, Your Majesty," Sanjin said. "A quick operation. And once we are done, you will not need to fear his rising and destroying your kingdom again."

The king harrumphed. "Something we should have done years ago, in my opinion. But your empress doesn't always do things that should be done, does she?"

Sanjin smiled, though Jin thought it hid a thousand blades. "She has her reasons, even if others don't agree with them."

The king frowned but then leaned forward. "My troops will accompany you to the edge of the Well of Fire, but no further. I trust you do not need my mages to do your work."

Sanjin bowed. "We have brought our best mages for the task, Your Majesty, you need have no worry."

"Good," the king said. "Just don't make a mess of things. Like you did in Khitan."

〜

THAT NIGHT, the palace treated their guests to singing, dancing, and foods that Jin had no names for but that were greatly satisfying. A childhood where she'd been strategically starved meant she relished food now, and the blood bond had increased her appetite. She ate enough to feed three men, which the king commented on repeatedly.

As Jin was facing off with the hundredth question about Mengkhis and her experiences in Khitan, her wing mates, Panshalar and Jao, managed to save her by appearing at her elbow and saying they needed her help with their plan to enter the Well.

She followed them to an open courtyard with a wide moon-drenched pond, the quiet sticky night interrupted only by the steady croaking of bullfrogs and the splash of a fish.

"Are you nervous?" Panshalar asked her.

"About killing a defenseless man? Strangely, yes." Jin tamped down the flicker of unease. Sanjin had briefed them on the specifics, and everything seemed easy. Which was exactly what bothered her. Her years as a thief had taught her to be wary of easy prizes. "But at least you two will be there."

Panshalar nodded. "But we won't have our dragons."

The Well was too narrow for dragons to enter, and so only Panshalar and Jao would accompany her.

Jao cleared his throat. "Which makes us nervous."

Jin looked from one to the other. "Is there something you're not telling me?"

Panshalar folded his thick arms. "Are the rumors about you and Tai true?"

She startled. "What rumors?"

"That he's your lover."

She turned to him, expecting to punch a grin off his broad northern face, but instead she simply found his brows knit, his expression serious.

"That's none of your business. And has nothing to do with this."

"Jao and I were kind of hoping he is." Panshalar rubbed the back of his neck.

Jin tried to absorb this, looking from one to the other. "I don't follow."

"Well, something doesn't sit right," the northerner muttered, glancing at Jao. "You want to tell her?"

"Nakkalan glimpsed what he was transporting," the smaller man said tightly. "There's black powder in there."

"Fireworks," Panshalar added.

Jin's mind worked over this. "Why would we bring fireworks?" The goods were expensive, used only for festivals, and dangerous to transport long distances. They also reminded Jin of the disastrous attack on the Parhac ships in the battle at Bohai, where fireworks had decimated them.

Panshalar's meaty shoulders shrugged. "I asked Oyang Kang, but he told me that was the Veil's order and to not question instructions." He looked both nervous and sheepish this time. "After what happened in Khitan, well, Jao and I are just . . . more careful."

She sympathized. They had walked into an ambush in Khitan, where the king had lured them in and then slaughtered their soldiers, including Ezho. "Perhaps they're taking precautionary measures. Again, what does any of this have to do with my relationship to the prince?"

Panshalar looked exasperated. "If you two are playing the clouds and rain together, then he wouldn't send you off on a dangerous mission, am I right?"

Jin snorted. The logic did make strange sense. Though that hadn't saved Peilah. "I hate to disappoint you. But there's nothing between me and Prince Tai."

Panshalar looked crestfallen. "By the eight levels of hell. So the leaders aren't as confident as they seem."

"Looks that way," Jin said. "Keep your wits about you, and hopefully there will be no need to use the fireworks."

Panshalar nodded, glancing at Jao. "Was hoping we had some extra leverage, that's all." He sighed. "Very well, it's wagering our lives as usual. Want to grab more of that spicy fish stew? It's amazing."

Jao snorted. "It makes you belch like a pig. Stop eating it."

She watched them return to the banquet hall, still bickering.

The knowledge that Sanjin had brought fireworks

nagged at her. If they were for celebrations, he would have presented them to the king of Champa already. And if not, then what did he think might happen at the Well of Fire?

What could go wrong if Jin, Jao, and Panshalar were truly facing a defenseless, unconscious man?

CHAPTER 3

Dawn brought no gentle easing into the heat of the day, but rather blasted the land with pounding rays as soon as the sun slipped over the horizon.

Jin's arms were slick with sweat by the time they reached the cleared area that she instinctively knew was the Well of Fire.

Should have called it the Well of Lead, she commented. She smelled the metal in the earth and sensed the dragons did as well. The lead would cut off their abilities to speak to their dragons, which only added to their nerves. Riders and laborers had already stripped to the waist and begun clearing the marked area, their shovels working in rhythm to a taskmaster who beat a drum. It was like watching a ship's galley.

"Remember the plan," Sanjin said as he gathered Jin, Panshalar, and Jao together. "There will be a small chamber, with a door that leads to Mengkhis's prison cell. Once down there, you will signal us."

"Why do we need to signal you?" Jin asked.

"We will know you are near the chamber, and our mages will remove the protective spell on the door so you can enter."

"Perhaps they should come with me," Jin suggested. Panshalar's comment about the fireworks still rankled at the back of her mind.

Sanjin shook his head. "There is not much room down there. Too many people will deplete the air quickly, and then we'd have to have the black dragons pump air in. This way we keep it simple."

Jin pushed her palm at Rayshan's snout, which was cold. It only grew cold when he worried. *I won't take long.*

Rayshan huffed, but didn't speak.

The mages placed stones around the perimeter and began chanting, walking first one way and then another, their feet crushing grooves in the grass.

Shovelfuls of earth flew as they dug through the topsoil. Within the hour, they had broken through to a thick wooden cellar door in the ground, the size of two carriages across, with ancient writing carved into it. Jin read the words: "Well of Fire."

She tried not to think of how a year ago they had been at the Well of Ice, and how Baikalan had been freed. This was different, she told herself.

This time, there was no enemy to ambush them.

They were with their own people, and the Champa troops had stayed well back, unwilling to accompany them through the last of the jungle that led to this place.

The fireworks were a gift to the Champa king. It didn't mean that things would go wrong.

Jin took a calming breath. The mages chanted for another hour, the words indecipherable to Jin, and then gave a nod. The apprentice mages pulled open the doors, revealing a yawning well that coiled deep into the earth. Damp, rotten smells rose out of it, coupled with the tang of lead and other metals.

The well was as wide as Panshalar was tall but would be impossible for a dragon to navigate. There were no footholds going down, nothing but a black emptiness into rock and earth.

Sanjin motioned to one of the attending mages, who whistled. A team of soldiers came forward and threw a thick roll of hemp rope down, with no sound of it landing.

"It is a *li* deep," the mage said to Jin and her wing mates. "We built it exactly that length. When you get to the bottom, you'll find another chamber with a closed door. Release this bird when you get there, and when the bird flies out, we will unlock that door."

Jin took the small cage, peering at the twittering, long-plumed bird inside. It flitted from bar to bar, trying to escape, its bright gold tail feathers like a flare. A mage helped her loop a scarf through the cage's circular handle, before putting it over her shoulder so the scarf lay across her chest and the bird cage rested on her hip.

They allowed the soldiers to equip their belts with loops that hooked on to the rope, and then they descended, the group of soldiers watching from above, the dragons lined behind them. Bayan, Nakkalan, and Rayshan were most restless, the growls from their throats sending birds scattering.

Jin's hands gripped the rope, and she tried not to think of the drop beneath her. More disturbing, however, was the slow fading of Rayshan's thoughts from her own.

Can you . . . hard to see?

I can't hear. What?

Soon she had to give up hearing Rayshan altogether, and tried to assuage the unease she felt. She wasn't the only one, at least.

"I can't hear Bayan," Panshalar said. "Can you hear Nakkalan?"

"No!" Jao called, then reached out to touch the walls. "It's almost solid lead in here."

It made sense to bury the nation's most notorious dragonrider in a lead mine. There was no way his dragon, Baikalan, could find Mengkhis. Even if Baikalan himself wasn't currently buried under the sea.

Buried, but not dead, a little voice whispered in Jin's mind. It was so like Baikalan's voice that she had to shake her head, and she thought she heard laughter.

"Jin. Now's not the time to crack."

She looked down to see Panshalar's worried face upturned.

Jin shook her head. "Just eager to get this done."

"You're not the only one," Jao muttered.

"Cheer up. This will get us into the war banner for certain," Panshalar argued. "We're about to go kill the most notorious dragonrider in history. Mengkhis Lai, Jao!"

"Thank you, I'd forgotten his name." Jao's sarcasm might have cut rock.

They continued down, the bird emitting panicked squawks as they went. The light grew dimmer as they descended, until Jin held up the lantern they had tied to the rope.

With her blood bond ability, she made out what the others couldn't.

"I see the bottom," she said. "We're halfway."

"Halfway?" Panshalar groaned.

They continued down, Jin's arms beginning to shake with the strain. She knew that if she was feeling tired, then her wing mates were doubly so, for they did not have the advantage of the blood bond.

She sighed gratefully as her feet touched the floor of the well, and Jao and Panshalar dropped down next to her. She held up the lantern while Panshalar took the caged bird, ready to set it free.

Jin raised the lantern. There in front of them, as the mages had said, was a great round door, wide as

Panshalar's arm span. Etched on the door were ancient mage symbols, clearly there to seal the occupant inside.

"Well, here we go, eh?" Panshalar said. Jin gave a nod, and he opened the bird cage. The bird bolted out, hitting one wall and then another in its panic, but then found the light. It flew like an arrow toward the pinprick of sunlight they could just make out above them.

Jao and Panshalar each pulled out their swords.

"How will we know the door is open?" Panshalar whispered.

A loud hiss emanated from the door, dust and cobwebs sloughing from it like a discarded coat.

"I think that's the sign," Jin said softly. Though she knew Mengkhis was unconscious, she instinctively kept as quiet as possible.

Jin crept forward. Her own heart beating drowned out other sounds except for the quickened pulses of her two wing mates.

She cautiously pushed the door, then shoved harder when it didn't budge. It creaked on what sounded like rotted wood hinges. She held up the lantern, revealing a stone cavern about twenty paces across and the same wide. It was devoid of anything except for a sarcophagus in the center. Carvings ran around the walls, again in an ancient mage script indecipherable to Jin.

"Ready?" Jao whispered. The sweat on his lip had nothing to do with the heat, for down here, the air was surprisingly cool for something named the Well of Fire.

Jin hefted her sword and looked to Panshalar, who nodded.

Jin motioned to Jao. He and Panshalar stood on either side of the sarcophagus and pulled. The lid didn't budge at first, and the two men strained, until there came a screeching of stone, and the lid crashed to the ground. The sound shattered the silence but also their nerves.

Jin cautiously peered into the tomb. A man lay there, thin lips slightly open. He had the high cheekbones of a huren, and his sand-colored hair lay in a messy tangle around his head. His eyes were closed, his face scarred, and great giant hands lay at his sides, strangely peaceful.

Jin readied her sword. Next to her, Panshalar and Jao tensed but nodded encouragement.

She drew a breath. She had never killed someone in cold blood before, someone who looked like they were simply sleeping. But then, sleeping people didn't have their eyes open—

He was on her in an instant, his hands closed over her throat. Panshalar and Jao shouted, but then the whole world was cracking and shaking. A chunk of rock fell square on Panshalar's shoulder, felling him, and the shaking made Jao stumble over the open tomb lid. He sprawled under a rain of stones and earth.

Mengkhis Lai momentarily lost his grip on her, and

Jin darted away, trying to see through the dust and earth. She raised an arm to cover her nose and mouth but then felt a hard push from behind and went crashing into a pile of rubble.

And that's when she noticed it.

The door was blocked. A new mountain of broken stone had sealed the entry, trapping them. The lantern snuffed to nothing, leaving them in pitch darkness.

She felt around her, trying to make sense of the jumbled rock and floor, when she stopped at another sound.

Laughter.

She froze.

This chilled her more than the dust or the thought of her friends buried. It started low and quiet, then grew into a high, rolling laugh that seemed to suck the very dust out of the air.

"Stop!" she screamed, but dust clogged her throat.

The laughter ceased. "Why deny a man his laughter when he's been dead and buried for decades?"

She focused, letting her blood bond do her sensing. She could just make out his outline across the room.

"So, you were sent to kill me, little fledgling?"

She didn't bother answering, instead homing in on his voice. She crept slowly to where his silhouette sat, hunched. She saw him now, his bulky shoulders hunched over something in the rubble.

His leg was trapped!

She hefted her knife and sprang.

Her blade hit stone, and with a sickening flash of insight, she sensed him too late. He was on her, and though she blocked his first punch, his other hand twisted the knife from her and turned, pressing it to her throat.

Mengkhis's face was mere breaths from hers now, and she had her first long look at him. He was not what she had expected. Beneath the matted blond hair and thick beard, she detected a face that might have been handsome. Was, she realized. He stank, and she tried to hold her breath not just because of the smell but because his blade—her blade—was much too close.

"Not what you expected, I imagine," he said.

She swallowed. By the eight levels of hell, this was how she ended?

He smiled, the teeth a flash in the darkness. "Before I kill you, I am curious—do you know who was really meant to die here?"

Her mind reeled.

"Oh, innocent little fledgling," he clucked, and the blade nicked her this time. He must have felt her flinch, for he shifted the weapon. "You haven't yet put the pieces together? Rock doesn't cave by itself."

His words sank in. What had caused the collapse? And right when they had released Mengkhis Lai?

She took a sharp breath, and Mengkhis chuckled. "They meant to kill both of us. You would kill me, or I would kill you, preferably at the same time. But if not, the explosion would bury both of us here until someone decided to kill us off in twenty years' time." He grimaced. "Even now, the mages are working to seal this place. They'll need an hour at most."

"No," she said, but the word didn't quite stick true. Something in what Mengkhis said made all the pieces fit, when nothing else did.

"You are such a naive little thing," Mengkhis sneered. Something rumbled above them, followed by the clatter of rock falling to the ground. Jin tried to twist free at the distraction, but the hands holding her only tightened.

A sliver of light pierced the gloom from outside, where the falling rocks had created a small chasm. She blinked as the light hit her face and lit up Mengkhis's, revealing dust-caked skin, a thick beard, and eyes that seemed to suck the soul out of her. "You're a half blood," he said.

She tried to bring a hand into play, but he easily shifted his weight so that even with her dragon bond strength, she couldn't escape. He examined her closely, and something changed when he reached her eyes. He hesitated, his grip slackening, and she pushed him off her with a great heave.

She reached for a fist-sized rock nearby, but he placed a boot on it. She backed away, wary.

"Who are your parents?"

The question threw her, but she kept an eye on the blade in his hand.

"What does it matter to you?"

"Ah, so you don't know."

Was that—disappointment?

"Come with me," he said.

If the first question threw her, this did even more. "What?"

"I can get us out. But you have to come now, leave the others. Are you with me?"

She thought of Jimo, the men lying on the beach. Even now she saw every face, every cast-off shoe or hat those men had left on the beach when Mengkhis Lai had killed them. Or made them kill themselves, rather. Besides, Jao and Panshalar were here somewhere, though whether dead or alive she had no idea.

"Never."

His voice came from right beside her. "Don't say I didn't offer."

Something blunt and hard smashed into the side of her head.

No, nothing had gone according to plan, Jin thought as she clawed her way out of the tunnel opening and blinked against the searing light outside. Or at least not *her* plan. Then whose?

Jin stood up on unsteady legs, then bent, hands on her knees, and let the nausea have its way. There was nothing to give, but her stomach didn't seem to know that. And her head felt cloven.

She leaned against a nearby tree, cradling her belly and willing her eyes to focus. Why hadn't Mengkhis killed her? Had he tried to but failed? He had offered to let her live. Why? It only added credence to his accusation that the throne had intended to kill them both today.

She gritted her teeth. Find Rayshan. Save her wing mates first, then worry about why the Well had collapsed.

When she found her bearings, she started up the hill toward where she figured the entry to the Well of Fire would be. As she walked, she called out mentally to Rayshan until she finally heard his reply, and her heart soared.

Where are you?

I'll be there soon.

Soon was not soon enough, even in the short time it took him to reach her. She half leaned, half fell on him, then said, *We need to get Nakkalan and the others. Jao and Panshalar are still down there.*

How did you get out?

There was a crack in the Well. Mengkhis escaped through it, and I came up.

Mengkhis is alive? Rayshan went rigid.

She nodded, climbing on. The movements made her head throb. *Nothing went as planned.*

I know, he growled, taking to the air.

The well collapsed. What happened?

Rayshan's anger rolled from him like a tide. *The*

mages said you were taking too long, something must have gone amiss, so Sanjin ordered that the fireworks be dropped. His emotions turned venomous. *We tried to fight, but the mages had put binding spells around us.*

She called to Nakkalan, Bayan, and the others as they reached the gathering of dragons and men, shouts of welcome floating up to them as they landed.

Nakkalan and Bayan paced anxiously, snapping in answer to Jin's assurances that Jao and Panshalar were alive. They clearly wanted to see for themselves.

Jin dismounted, and Sanjin strode up to her.

"You took so long we thought we had lost you," he said. "Mengkhis?"

"Gone."

Sanjin's face slipped into a brief mask of terror before he resumed his usual stony expression. "Oyang Kang, take your wing and spread out. He can't get far. Jin, you go with him."

"But Panshalar and—"

"I have others who can do that, but you're the only one who can kill Mengkhis," he barked. "Now go."

She said nothing, suddenly very conscious that it might be best to keep her anger, and Mengkhis's theory, to herself.

"Yes, Marquis Sanjin."

CHAPTER 4

The sun withered the slain men in the sands, heating the blood until it stank and mixed with the smell of horses, urine, and sweat.

Aadan surveyed the scene with a bitter eye, his hand on Wanli's ridge tightening into a white-knuckled fist. This was the third battalion they had come across. At this rate, the Persians would be wiped out before they had a chance to reach the gate of Messina.

"They are fleeing, and that is a good sign."

Aadan turned to see his cousin, Gah'med, ride up on his bay horse, his helmet glinting in the sun. Behind him rode Gah'med's brother, Jahmid, whose lanky build and easy-going face contrasted with his sibling's dark, bear-like stature.

"They flee, but they are killing us as they go," Aadan said.

The prisoners had been alive but days ago, and Aadan cursed his own lack of speed in finding them.

"You and your beast should head them off at the mountains. If you make good time, we can flank them and trap them at the base," Gah'med said.

Aadan shook his head. "How many more do we have to lose, Cousin? The men are too weary, and besides, we have lost enough blood."

Gah'med looked displeased but made a conciliatory gesture. "Then what do you suggest?"

Aadan sighed. He still needed to adjust to the different ways of his new countrymen. He had never met Gah'med until a month ago, but the man was clearly used to command and expected Aadan to be a mere figurehead for the troops. The returned prince was here to show off his dragon but was little more than a symbol. Gah'med led the troops, decided on battle tactics, and barely consulted Aadan at all. He was only agreeing because he didn't want to cause Aadan embarrassment before the soldiers, and Aadan saw the truth in Jahmid's eyes.

Aadan didn't fully blame his cousin. Gah'med had been fighting this war for years, while Aadan had grown up in the Tang empire, with comfort and peace around him, bonding with Wanli and learning the ways of dragons. Meanwhile, Gah'med had been embroiled in brutal resistance efforts against the marauding Arabs, launching skirmishes against the forces and losing men along the way—as well as two of his own

fingers, which Gah'med made sure to display promi-
nently at every opportunity, a reminder of his own
sacrifice toward the cause.

Gah'med was also ten years Aadan's senior, and
never lost a chance to mention that as well. He was
shorter than Aadan but made up for it in width. Like a
wall, anyone going against him would be wise to bring
a battering ram. His brother, for one, almost never
opposed him.

"We will bury the dead and make camp. I will think
of bleeding the enemy in a different way."

Aadan sensed the sullen disbelief welling in the
men. Gah'med remained stone-faced, and Jahmid
cleared his throat.

"How, Cousin?" Jahmid asked. "Your dragon is
mighty, but we will need at least five more to quell all
the Arab battalions."

"I don't have the exact answer," Aadan said. "But we
have seen enough bloodshed, and it is time for a
change."

Gah'med favored ambushes, but Aadan doubted
their effectiveness, especially as the Arabs seemed to
have learned their ways. This last ambush they had
made had cost them these men that now lay strewn
across the sands. And the one before that had only
driven the enemy around them, delaying them but not
stopping them from taking a village that only weeks
ago had been in Persian hands.

Aadan sighed and glanced toward his father, sitting

astride his war horse some ways back. The man had insisted on coming on this far-flung campaign, leaving his mother at home in the base of Makana.

He climbed onto Wanli's back. The dragon comforted him with the reassurance that things were bound to change.

At the cost of how many men?

And, Aadan felt, what then? What happened once he took back Persia? Already his Persian had grown thin. His parents, having been away for so long, spoke a Persian that was outdated. The Persian the men here spoke was more rolling, less languid, and faster. Born of war and strife, the language sounded harsher and more brittle, whereas his own sounded soft and anachronistic, even to his own ears. He had heard the men mocking his and his family's accents more than once, saying the princes of past had forgotten their roots.

He had expected this to be a homecoming. Instead, he was again an outsider. Only this time, he was an outsider in the world meant to be his home. A home at war, a home he was expected to win back. And yet, the people seemed not to have made up their minds about whether they wanted him or not.

He thought longingly of China but stopped himself angrily. Thinking of China led down dangerous paths, and to thoughts of Jin. Thoughts he could do nothing about. He needed to stay in the here and now.

Aadan walked to one of the basins of water a soldier

had set up and splashed his beard and face. Like many, he had stopped trimming his beard, and it now grew long and ragged, curling. His hair had likewise grown, reaching down past his shoulders. Unlike the Chinese, who believed cutting hair was disrespectful to one's elders and so let it grow, he had regularly trimmed his hair in the Persian quarters of the Tang capital, Changan, but now without a barber, he was growing unkempt. Not that it mattered, when life and death hung in the balance here.

A hand clapped on his shoulder, and he turned to see his father.

"The men will accept you. You'll see."

His father had been saying that for over a moon now, and Aadan suspected he said it almost as much for his own benefit as for Aadan's. The king was no king, for Gah'med treated the king very much as he treated Aadan: a visitor here to lend a face and a figurehead, but no more.

"I know. Everything takes time."

His father nodded. "A new shoe always creates blisters. But they appreciate you and Wanli."

More like they appreciated the fear that Wanli instilled in the enemy. That, at least, had been a positive. The sight of a dragon flying at their lead had emboldened the men and cowed the Arabs. Wanli's fire, and his water skills, had been a tremendous advantage. Even now, the full basins of water everyone enjoyed on the war path came from Wanli, who every night used his powers to pull water from the ground, creating pools where there had been none. The men were now used to having plenty of water to drink and cook and wash, where before they had been trackable by their pungent scent alone, as far as Aadan was concerned.

Aadan reached into his saddlebag and pulled out a map of the surrounding area. His skills had never been in hand-to-hand, but in strategy. And using resources to get what he wanted. What kept the Arabs strong? What would make them weak?

As his eyes roamed over the map, he traced the rivers, the thin lines that plotted out the trade routes. The Arabs were organized and had luxury goods that everyone wanted. But what if . . .

He stood back, teasing the thought into shape. He pulled out another map, unrolled it, and searched again. This one had more detailed roads, and he traced a finger along one of the thick meandering lines. Dunhuang. Kuchar. Bactria. No, too large. But Samarkand . . .

His brows were still furrowed when Jahmid approached. "The priests are ready for you." At Aadan's frown, Jahmid added, "The *dakhma*. It is finished."

A knot of shame formed. He had been so preoccupied, he had forgotten about the preparations for the dead. As he folded his maps and shrugged on his coat, he noticed Jahmid waited to follow.

His cousin gestured toward the west side of the encampment, where Aadan spied groups gathering around freshly dug earth and blazing torches, despite sunset being some hours away. Fire would purify the area and protect the living against the harmful forces of *druj nasu*, or the contamination of the dead.

"Is it true, that the girl dragonrider can raise the dead?"

Aadan glanced over, not in the mood to discuss Jin. Though at least Jahmid spoke with genuine curiosity, whereas Gah'med reminded Aadan of a rat, constantly digging for gossip to leverage against Aadan. "Yes."

Jahmid gave a low exhale. "A witch then." At Aadan's look, he raised his palms. "Sorry, just—how do you explain that?"

You don't, Aadan snapped silently, and pushed away the familiar worry. Jin could take care of herself, as she had proven time and again. Though that didn't stop him from wanting to be next to her for every breath he had left, and if that meant time spent with the dead, then so be it.

The pit was at least three lengths of a man, and just as deep. The men had worked hard. The inside was lined with stone as ragged as the faces gathered around, and Aadan tried not to count the shrouded bodies laid inside the pit. Or look at the swords in a pile, waiting to be purified by fire before being given to new owners.

The priest, or *mobed*, had a beard as white as the cotton *kusti* tied around his waist. Aadan looked around at those already gathered: his father, Gah'med on the mobed's right, soldiers whose faces and hands were scrubbed but whose clothing still bore the mud and splatter of battle. All fell silent as the mobed began his prayer.

When the prayers were finished and the men began loading stones on top of the pit, most of the men dispersed. Aadan stayed watching and glanced up when his father appeared next to him.

"We will come back for them."

Aadan nodded. The dead needed to be given a proper burial in a Tower of Silence, where the scavengers would pick them clean. He knew one of the soldiers had been assigned a map where every burial pit was marked, so that when they won the war they could return and properly dispose of the bodies.

"Gah'med tells me you and he disagree on how to defeat the Arabs," his father commented.

"He's come complaining to you, has he, Father?"

The king made a disapproving sound. "You are my son, and I will always support you. But he has the support of the men. Don't forget that. We need him."

Aadan sighed and followed his father to the basin of water provided to purify the hands before leaving the burial site. "I do have a plan for defeating the Arabs. And it involves less bloodshed."

His father looked from him to the burial pit. "Let's hope it works, then. We are running out of men."

CHAPTER 5

The search for Mengkhis proved worse than fruitless.

They failed to find even a footprint, much less the man himself, even though they searched the jungle in widening circles, combing the underbrush on foot, beating through dense shrubs and braving the insects and snakes in their search. The man who could turn invisible had, it seemed, disappeared into the air.

Jin thought of trying to use the Firesong to track Mengkhis, as she wondered if his memories would already be there.

It won't work unless he's with Baikalan, Rayshan explained. *The Firesong is accessible and imprinted through dragons, not humans.*

When Jin visited Jao and Panshalar in their tents after a full day's searching, she grimaced at the sight of their wounds in full torchlight.

"Does that mean I shouldn't visit the song houses tonight?" Panshalar gave a mirthless grin.

"You both look more like eggplants than people."

Jao's lip was still an ugly black and purple where two teeth had cut straight through, and bandaging around Panshalar's mid-section and shoulder spoke of cracked bones. A swollen left eye made his face look even larger than usual.

Jin sat down gingerly on a stool. Her own head was still throbbing, though her stomach had decided to settle.

Jao's eyes darted to the tent flap, making sure they were alone.

"Why'd you tell us to not trust Sanjin?"

Jin strained to hear any close footsteps. But no one lingered, and she heard no approaching feet. "Mengkhis said he thought the plan was for him and me to kill each other," she said softly. "Then have the mages bury our bodies under a binding spell. If we survived, then we'd be entombed. If we didn't, we'd still be dead and buried. End of blood-bonded riders."

"That's absurd. They'd never sacrifice their strongest rider, Jin," Panshalar grunted. Jin wasn't sure whether he truly believed that or was just trying to comfort himself.

"True," Jao said quietly, his voice laced with bile. "Us, they'd kill. But not Jin."

"I'm not convinced," she said. "Watch your backs. Just in case."

AFTER FIVE DAYS OF SEARCHING, Sanjin called off the trackers. He ordered Oyang Kang's wing to patrol the Champa borders for another week, with strict instructions to the Champa king to ransack his country if need be, but to find Mengkhis Lai. He also sent almost all their accompanying mages, along with two of the bronze dragons, to the abandoned seaside village of Jimo, where Baikalan lay under the sea. No doubt, Mengkhis's first priority would be to seek his dragon.

Jin's journey back to Changan was full of bad dreams. Images of Mengkhis about to kill her plagued her nights, where he'd plunge a blade into her neck to carve a mark.

She woke in sweat and often took walks to calm her pulse. The first night of the journey back, she decided to pry some answers from Sanjin, for the whole mission at the Well of Fire felt rotten, and Panshalar and Jao's reassurances did little to assuage her doubts.

Jin approached his tent after camp had been set and she had seen to Rayshan.

"I trust you are healing?" he said once she had announced herself and entered. He sat at a desk with multiple scrolls before him, along with an inkstone and brushes, surrounded by piles of letters.

Jin nodded. "Nothing that will kill, at least. Panshalar and Jao have suffered more."

He inclined his head. "I thank Buddha that you are all alive."

"What happened back at the mine? Why did it collapse?"

Sanjin laid down his brush and folded his hands. "No doubt Rayshan told you about the fireworks. We intended to use them only if things became uncontrollable. We couldn't risk your dying and Mengkhis escaping. It was a backup plan." He paused. "Fortunately, you escaped."

"Mengkhis was awake when we arrived," Jin said. "Why?"

"I'm still investigating. My theory is that the mages, in unsealing the door to the chamber, may have also accidentally broken the spell keeping him asleep. And when things took longer than we expected, we feared the worst. So we decided to destroy the mine."

"While we were in it?"

His look never wavered. "It was a price we had to pay."

She swallowed at his unapologetic tone. Strictly speaking, it could have been a mistake. Yet her gut was that Mengkhis had known the truth, and she had learned that her thief's gut kept her alive almost every time.

"What if you had killed me, and he was let free?"

"Fortunately, that is a situation we'll never know, is it?" Sanjin said smoothly. "Now I recommend you stop spending your time thinking about the infinite possibles of the past and start thinking of the future. The empress will be most displeased at this outcome. I have already instructed everyone to do with the mission not to speak of Mengkhis's escape. We have gone from having the advantage to having a distinct problem of magnificent proportions, which I am in the process of dealing with."

Is the problem that Mengkhis is loose, or that I'm not dead? "And what is in the future? What happens now?"

"I can think of a few things, but that is ultimately for the empress to decide," the marquis said. "Now, I asked you before and I'll ask again. Do you remember anything that Mengkhis said or did that might help us find him?"

"No." This was the truth. Everything that Mengkhis had said related to whether the empress wanted her dead and who her parents were. None of that would lead to his whereabouts, even if Jin was inclined to share that information.

"Then you may step down," Sanjin said.

Jin bowed stiffly at the dismissal. "Yes, Marquis Sanjin."

She had gone to find answers but left with only more questions, and a cloying sense that she was meant to be hundreds of feet underground in a lead tomb.

CHAPTER 6

The scales tipped, along with Tai's concentration.

"Better," Mage Situ Han cackled. "But not by much."

Tai sighed, smoothing his hair and focusing again on the bucket of water and the feather. The summer heat pressed through the palace doors, which they kept closed to practice his magic in secret. Tai's study was spacious, with a convenient open space in the center where officials came to call on him. But today, as with every day that he trained, the gold-and-purple carpet with the dragon motif had been pulled back to reveal the rosewood floor beneath. It was easier to connect to one's magic, Tai had found, when one was closer to the ground.

But even so, he had never tried to make a feather

heavier than a bucket of water, and it was proving difficult.

This was partly because his thoughts kept straying to the knowledge that a dragon from the Champa contingent had returned with news.

Tai shelved his curiosity for later and focused on the feather. He started the slow, even steps around the scales that would harmonize his *mai*, or his pulse, in order to change the feather's mass.

"Excellent, Your Highness," Mage Situ urged, his cheerful smile ever pasted to his face. The rotund man always exuded good humor and had a disarming way about him that hid much of his mage abilities. "Now bear harder on that. Feel the power of weight as you move slowly outside in."

Tai did, his steps narrowing in their circular path, and soon the feather's side of the scales moved down while the bucket of water hovered above the floor. His own feet and blood turned heavy with the effort, until sweat broke his brow. The feather lowered further, then a breath more, before the exhaustion overwhelmed him and the bucket crashed down, spraying water all over the floor.

"Well done, Your Highness," the mage said, clapping. "Soon we will have a true mage of you. Your mother will be most impressed." He paused as he casually threw a cloth on the floor to absorb the water, clearly catching Tai's expression. "Your mother still does not know of our training?"

Tai shook his head, wiping the sweat from his forehead with a kerchief. "I will find the right time."

The mage nodded. "I think that's wise. Do you fear her reaction?"

"I do not fear my mother," Tai said, hoping his retort was not too sharp. "I simply feel there is a right time for everything."

The mage grunted. "True. The slow drip of water wears a stone faster than any torrent. And though I look forward to the day the people know you have special skills, I feel times must grow darker before revealing them."

"You speak as if dark times are inevitable."

"Nothing lasts, Your Highness, good or bad." The mage shrugged. "But ultimately, the people will need a hero. You."

The pealing of a bell reached them, and Tai tensed. A summons for a cabinet meeting.

"Go," the mage said. "I will see you for lessons tomorrow."

Tai was used to praise and lofty expectations. Yet he sensed in the mage's predictions of a hero an undercurrent that made his skin crawl—as if what mage Situ Han said was not a message of hope, but an omen.

WHEN HE REACHED the audience chambers, Tai found his mother not in official garb, but in trousers, boots, and a loose tunic whose gold and russet weave was splattered with mud. She had clearly come from the polo field, not bothering to change. In fact, one hand gripped a scroll as if it were a polo club, as if given the chance, she would smash something with it.

Tai bowed, bracing himself. "Ill news?"

"See for yourself." The empress held out the scroll to him, and Tai took the muddied message. His eyes scanned it, his stomach plummeting.

"By the eight levels of hell. We are lucky Jin is alive."

"That's what you think of?" his mother snapped. "Mengkhis is loose, and you are happy a dragonrider is alive?"

Tai bristled. He could argue about the value of human life, but he knew that carried little weight with his mother. And he was barely willing to admit the depth of his relief at her safety to himself, much less his mother. "She is our only hope against Mengkhis."

His mother looked like she tasted something sour. "Clearly our hopes are misplaced, if she can't kill a man in his sleep."

Tai tapped the scroll. "The spell broke by accident. The fault is ours, not hers."

The empress rounded on him, coming close enough to dig her gold-painted nails into his arms. "I will find who is at fault and punish them. But that is nothing compared to what we must do. We are in grave danger, my son."

The prince saw fear in the waver of her eyes, stoking his own anxiety. "You think he will come for us?"

"As surely as I know winter follows autumn." She let go and strode to the windows overlooking the imperial gardens. "And when two tigers fight, one must fall."

The frailty in her shoulders caught him off guard. Ever since he could remember, she was the strongest force in his world, a might that even the greatest of men in the empire feared. And though they had their distrust, she was still his mother. He couldn't imagine a world without her, or one where she lived scared of another.

He thought of telling her of his mage powers. Perhaps it would comfort her, knowing her son was capable of defending himself and her?

She wiped viciously at her eye and then turned around, and all trace of the scared woman was gone, replaced by the iron warrior he knew as the empire's ruler.

"Don't worry, my son. I defeated him once, and I will defeat him again." She strode to him and pulled the scroll from his grasp, then dropped it in a vase filled with water and peonies. "We must control who learns this news. The War Ministry, the Veil, the censorate. The people cannot know."

Tai stared. "News like this will leak sooner or later."

His mother began washing her hands in a basin of

water, scrubbing the mud from them. "Then let us make it later. Besides, the line between news and rumor is very fine. We will make sure the censorate monitors all letters and communications, and inform only the ones who must know. We don't need an empire-wide panic on our hands. Besides, there are enough wolves at court who might turn on us if they knew Mengkhis was at the gates."

This was true. Tai watched a dragon and his rider wing by in the distance. "I miss having Emar here to ask his opinion."

His mother's face looked pinched. "As do I."

"There are many things I wish to ask him," the prince admitted. *Why did you never talk about growing up with my mother? Why did you never want to discuss my father? What was the real reason you always refused promotion, preferring to stay in Dragon Class?* He had thought he'd have time enough to ask these questions, never imagining Emar would die so soon.

His mother's hand brushed his shoulder. "You know you can always ask me if you seek advice."

"Of course," he agreed, though inwardly he was suspicious of all her advice.

"In the meantime, we have much to do."

TAI'S HEAD felt like it might burst.

The advisors in the war cabinet all belonged here, he thought wryly, for they fought amongst themselves as if they were in an actual war, rather than players on the same team with a common cause. For the first time in his life, Tai sympathized with the former minister, Minister Gao, even though he was the one responsible for the visible scar running across Tai's neck.

". . . delays will make us lose our chance!"

"We are stretched thin as it is, and if we tax the people further, we will have unrest. Whereas a war with spoils . . ."

"What are you suggesting, then, Chancellor Li?" Tai asked. Li Yifu was not unreasonable, but he had earned the nickname "Chancellor Profit" because of his reputation for backing strategies that somehow always ended up being advantageous to him.

"In such times, a war rallies people, Your Highness," Li said, his thick lips pursed. "And the people are feeling a victory over Mengkhis. What better follow-up than to attack Khitan now, as punishment for their involvement in releasing Baikalan?"

King Ulagan's ambush and allying with the Parhae forces against the Tang had certainly fueled anti-Khitan sentiment. But a war was the last thing the empire needed.

"Mengkhis is loose. We all understand that, don't we?"

There was silence, for even the mention of the name sent nerves fraying. The news of Mengkhis's escape had prompted a flurry of frantic emergency sessions amongst the various ministries. Tai was not the only one who felt the chill of fear, though he might fear his adopted uncle the most.

"Therefore, all our focus should be on Mengkhis," Tai reasoned, "and not on waging another war."

Chancellor Yirong, a man with an egg-shaped head and a wide mouth that reminded Tai of a toad's, bowed low. "Your Highness, a war will douse the firewood under Mengkhis's pot, so to speak. For where will he go now that he is free? Straight to his allies. He will soon learn of the Khitans, and they, for their part, will welcome him should he seek their help. They'd like nothing better than to destroy us for killing their king and taking their princess."

"As long as we have their princess, they won't move against us," Tai rebutted.

He sensed the chancellors Li and Yirong had their doubts. Admittedly, the Khitan princes seemed to care little for their young sister, Nobu, whom Tai's soldiers had taken after the Battle of Bohai. But loved or no, she was a princess of royal blood, with two dragons, and such a prize would not be sacrificed lightly.

"They will still scheme behind our backs, like snakes in the bed," Li grumbled.

"Perhaps," Tai admitted. "And I want Mengkhis dead more than anyone. But we should avoid open war." His sentiments were unpopular, judging by the expressions, and he flashed his most disarming smile.

"Your wisdom is great, Yirong and Li, and I know you have the best interests of all at heart. You will agree with me that if we can save our forces, we should. Besides, our army will take some time to rebuild after Gao's siphoning of funds."

This ended the conversation, as he knew it would. The empress's very public execution of all who had been involved in Gao's graft had put everyone in the War Ministry on edge and extra careful to scrub their books of anything that hinted at financial wrongdoing. No one wanted to be seen condoning or siding with Gao, and disagreements with the financial state of the War Ministry was a sensitive topic.

"Thank you for everyone's contribution," Tai said, standing. "I think that is all for today, and I will report our consensus to the empress, that for now we will not move toward war."

THE MEETING with the ministry reminded him it was time he paid the Khitan princess a visit. It would be useful to keep the princess on side, even better to know what she was thinking. Besides, it would keep his mind off the news of Mengkhis.

As he walked the halls to his horse and mounted for the short ride to her suites, he wondered if the girl held a grudge. She had lost her father and new husband during the Battle of Bohai, thereby made a widow and hostage all at sixteen.

He had sent a message to her quarters and was amused to arrive and find her dressed in Tang clothing, but with a smudge of dirt on her neck that her collar didn't hide. She clearly disliked the revealing cuts of the Tang court, as she was used to the northern modes of dress with high collars and thick, lined robes and trousers.

She dipped in a bow as he arrived, her Tang maidens doing the same. He felt a twinge of pity for her. Nobu had none of her own people here, as she was a hostage and not allowed anyone who might aid her in smuggling messages or items to her brothers in Khitan.

"Your Highness," she said. "You honor us."

"The feeling is mutual," he said. "Would you walk me around your gardens? I wish to make sure we haven't been neglecting you."

"Nothing would give me greater pleasure," she said formally, and he noted that she must have been practicing her Chinese. Whereas he remembered her accent being rolling like the Khitan speech, she now clipped her words much more in the Tang manner, each syllable distinct but fitting together in a more musical way. As they walked, he slowed to match her gait, though he was careful to make it seem like his natural pace. A childhood illness had left her with a limp, though he had never had the chance to ask.

"You must miss home," he said instead, after they

had done a round of the gardens where pavilions sat amongst chrysanthemums and peonies.

Nobu shook her head. "I am well cared for here. And I have all the family I need: Shafeng and Satu."

It took Tai a moment to realize she was referring to the dragons she had inherited from her father. The two had been gifts from his mother to the former king of Khitan for his service in keeping the dragon Baikalan in his Well of Ice. But then the king had betrayed them.

"I thought his name was Shatang?" Tai said lightly.

Nobu reddened. "It hardly seemed diplomatic, Your Highness. He has accepted his new name."

The words Shatang were a homonym for "kill the Tang," and Tai had no doubt that the king of Khitan had deliberately chosen the name. But now the king was dead, his plans lying on the bottom of the ocean, and Tai was relegated to care for his daughter and negotiate her release back to her brothers in Khitan. A task he had no stomach for.

"What will you demand of my brothers?" Nobu asked.

"I am not sure," Tai admitted. "But we cannot have Khitan betray us again."

Nobu nodded, biting her lip. "My brothers will wish to avenge their father."

Tai stopped walking, surprised by her candor. "You are saying they cannot be trusted?"

"Yes."

He regarded her. "I would have thought you'd be on their side."

"They only have their own side," Nobu said. "They are prideful, like my father was, and put revenge before peace."

"Is this your way of trying to tell me that you are a worthless hostage?" He had his fair share of negotiating experience, especially with Nobu's father, Ulagan. Hard bargainers often downplayed the value of what they wanted. He was surprised to find the meek, quiet Nobu that he remembered from his trips north now employing such negotiating tactics. The Khitan king had made sure Nobu was at every diplomatic meeting with Tai, in hopes of arranging a match. She must have listened to every word all those times she sat in shy silence by her father.

"I think I am worthless to my brothers," she answered, "but not to you, Your Highness."

He had enough experience with girls as well as diplomacy. He recognized the telltale flush in her cheeks. She might have been speaking pure politics, but her words were colored by other emotions. "I am sure the Lady Nobu is worth more than a thousand stars from the sky to a thousand love-struck men," he said. "But I assume you mean politically?"

She flushed a deeper shade, though he also detected bitterness in her expression. Perhaps he'd been too forward with the love-struck men line and came across as mocking. "Yes, politically. You have a female ruler here in China, who has brought peace and prosperity. What if Khitan had the same?"

He glanced at her sharply. "My mother has no desire to rule Khitan." Ruling the vast expanse of China was challenge enough, and his forbears had learned that ruling through vassals was a much more efficient way of securing borders.

"The Khitan would never accept a Han ruler," Nobu said. "I am speaking of myself."

Tai raised an eyebrow. This was definitely unexpected.

"I will swear allegiance to the Tang, and I have two dragons who obey me. They will be my mandate to rule, and with the Tang's blessing, I can persuade my brothers to step aside for me."

"Forgive me, but I think you underestimate your brothers," Tai said. He had only met them briefly on one of his many diplomatic missions to the north, but the three were as fiery and prone to fighting as their father. They would rather cut off their manhoods than give up a single *liang* of power to their younger sister.

"I can persuade them," Nobu said firmly. "If given the chance."

Tai didn't answer immediately. The idea had merit, but involved significant obstacles that would give even the greatest optimist pause. "You can understand why I cannot simply send you back to Khitan in the hopes that your brothers see things your way? If you fail, then we will have given up a very valued . . ." he searched for a word other than *bargaining chip* ". . . friend, and opened ourselves to possible attack."

Frustration wrinkled her brow, before she smoothed it and bowed. "Your Highness knows best. But I beg of you not to dismiss my proposal outright."

"I would never dream of it, Princess Nobu." He bowed and took his leave, wondering when the shy young girl from Khitan had turned into a politician.

CHAPTER 7

When Jin and the retinue returned to the palace in Changan, Jin thought they would fly straight into the Imperial City. But instead, the wings spiraled down well outside the outer walls, where a retinue of horses, grooms, and officials in black-and-grey robes waited with parasols along the shaded road.

Jin glanced at Sanjin, unsure why they would ride through the thoroughfare. Was the empress going to parade her shame?

But when the main gates opened and they rode through, the dragons winging above, the welcome was ecstatic, and Jin's confusion turned to a sickening rage as understanding dawned.

"They don't know," she murmured.

Next to her, Sanjin said, "We told them you're a hero. So act like one."

The shouts and cheering only made Jin want to hide, her stomach already knotted with anger, but now shame as well. This was perhaps worse than being paraded through the city as a failure. She would be forced to endure an agonizingly slow display as an imposter. She wrestled the scowl off her face, envious of Jao and Panshalar. Because of their injuries, they had won seats in the carriage behind her.

Banners of "Victory" and "Long Live the Dragon Princess" flew from every roof and window, thickening Jin's discomfort.

She had expected a summons to the audience hall on her return, but was surprised when the staff guiding her took her instead out of the palace grounds, where the empress waited for her in a carriage. Clearly, the empress wanted to leave the court clerks behind so their conversation would not be recorded.

Jin and Sanjin boarded, before the carriage took off. It swayed as it traveled at a fast clip over the cobbled stones of the palace roads, and though it was cushioned and luxurious, Jin felt ill at ease.

The empress was resplendent as usual in robes edged with pearls and jade. Her headdress beads hovered over her smooth, almond face, and her eyes were unreadable.

"You failed. How?"

Jin related how Mengkhis had escaped, how there had been a collapse of the cave.

"A misunderstanding, Your Majesty," Sanjin said.

"We had thought Mengkhis killed Rider Jin and so collapsed the caves as a precaution."

The empress flicked her gaze between them. "Then we should be grateful that all our riders survived."

"Indeed," Sanjin concurred. "Especially Rider Jin, as her survival gives us a second chance. Though we cannot ignore the fact that the task is much harder now than when we started."

Indeed. You have two blood-bonded riders alive now, Jin thought. *Where you'd hoped to have none.*

The empress let out a breath. "Have there been any sightings of Mengkhis?"

Sanjin shook his head. "He has vanished for the moment. The king of Champa has promised to alert us if he finds him."

"No doubt he's trying hard," the empress said drily. "I'm sure he's thrown open his borders in hopes Mengkhis will come straight into Tang lands."

"Won't he go looking for Baikalan, Your Majesty?" Jin said. A rider and dragon were bonded and would do anything to seek each other out. Being blood bonded meant that despite Baikalan being at the bottom of the sea, he was still alive and could be drawn forth by his rider. Mengkhis just had to find him.

"I've ordered extra troops to Jimo, in case Mengkhis does go there. But he would need an enormous amount of strength to help Baikalan resurface. He is weak from decades in the Well of Fire and would need time to recuperate."

"Good." The empress tossed both of them cold looks. "Now all we need worry about is how you will kill Mengkhis Lai, when you failed while he was a trussed goose, imprisoned and waiting slaughter."

"There was a complication with the spell, Your Majesty. He was not awaiting slaughter." Jin swallowed her temptation to outright accuse Sanjin of sabotage.

She watched the empress's face for any trace of guilt or a telltale lack of surprise. Had she known that would happen? Had that been her intention?

But the empress's expression held nothing but angered annoyance as she turned to Sanjin. "So the marquis reported. You've dealt with the mage responsible?"

Sanjin nodded. "Of course, Your Majesty. An unacceptable error on the senior mage's part, and he has been stripped of office and all his titles. I also accept responsibility and will submit to Your Majesty's will."

"Good." The empress regarded Jin, face stony. "I once knew Mengkhis Lai well. He is more clever than any demon and knows ways to get under your skin that you didn't even realize were there."

A chill slithered at the back of Jin's neck. Mengkhis had certainly gotten under her skin.

The empress's eyes bore into Jin's. "He will tell you things that you want to hear, speak so persuasively that you end up doubting the sky is blue or that fire burns."

Jin remained silent while the two regarded her.

"Did he say anything to you before he escaped?" the empress asked.

Jin weighed her words. "Only that he knew I was blood bonded."

"That's all?"

Some instinct told Jin to reveal as little as possible of the conversation. "We were in a fight for survival, Your Majesty, not just against each other but against the collapse of the mine."

The empress sighed. "Now we must decide what to do to contain this mess." Sanjin bowed his head in agreement.

"Your Majesty," Jin started, "would it not be best to tell the people the truth?"

The empress's lip curled. "The truth? That you failed and that Mengkhis Lai walks the lands unseen and unhindered? What exactly do you think that will achieve? Besides humiliating me, you, and the throne in one move?"

"Your Majesty, I—"

"Don't waste your breath," the empress snapped. "Let's each do what we were meant to. In your case, that's killing Mengkhis Lai. You will train to be the most lethal weapon this empire has ever seen, so there will be no failure next time." She turned to Sanjin. "I entrust this to you."

Jin's insides went cold as Sanjin bowed, for she sensed something unpleasant was coming.

"She will join the Royal Veil," the empress said. "Our

toughest people come from the Royal Veil. Let's make her one of them."

"I will see to it, Your Majesty," Sanjin said.

"Your Majesty, may I point out that this was not due to lack of training. It was—"

"Regardless, now you may need more than just your blood bond to kill Mengkhis Lai," the empress said. "You have failed. And though you both deserve to be punished, I don't see what that would achieve. What matters is that we cannot afford for you to fail again." The ruler's eyes hardened. "We cannot have another Age of Chaos, where parents turned on children, husbands turned on wives, and friends butchered each other in the streets." The empress leaned close to Jin. "You have a duty to the empire to kill him, but you also have a duty to yourself." She sat back. "The Veil is the only way we can prepare you for Mengkhis."

CHAPTER 8

Fireworks screamed across the city, and it seemed that the whole of Changan had come out to choke the main public squares, eager to watch the plays depicting Jin slaying Mengkhis.

The performance at the palace would be the most luxurious of all, complete with giant models of dragons made of bamboo and colored wax paper, hundreds of dancers to portray the dragonriders, and one of the empire's most famous opera singers to play Mengkhis Lai.

"We paid for it. Besides, if we cancel, people will talk," Tai's mother had said when he'd suggested they pull it from the festivities.

The last thing Tai wanted to do was sit in finery to celebrate a victory that never happened. Yet it looked like it might be the only chance he'd have of talking to Jin and getting her account firsthand.

His mother had refused to elaborate much when he had met her and Sanjin after their talk with Jin, but he had caught the quiet undercurrent of tension between the two. His mother blamed Sanjin for something—Mengkhis's escape?

As he changed from official robes into elaborate silk trousers and sashes, a familiar dread pooled at the thought of where Mengkhis was now, what he was doing, plotting. How did a man Tai had never met instill such fear in him, even twenty-two years later? He regarded himself in the mirror, examining the scar on his neck, the cheekbones and nose that his mother said were his father's. All his life, his mother had told him of this monster who had tried to kill him, from whom his mother alone had saved him. Mengkhis Lai had cut down the emperor's personal guard, fought his way into the private chambers to kill Tai's father and Tai himself to gain the throne. And now one of Tai's greatest fears was here. Mengkhis was back, an invisible terror who might literally slip unseen into any room. An unkillable demon from nightmares the empress had done nothing to assuage.

No, not unkillable, Tai reminded himself. There was one who could kill him.

Did the thought of Jin comfort him because she was their one hope against Mengkhis? Or because he often remembered what it was like riding back from Bohai with his arms at her waist, or hearing that rarest of sounds—her laugh?

"Your Highness?"

He turned. His valet bowed from the doorway. "It is time, if you would not be late."

Tai checked his reflection one last time before following the valet out and mounting his horse, Leiyu, to ride to the courtyard outside the Hall of Virtuous Kylins. He handed Leiyu to a groom before entering. Crowds of nobles, ministers, and minor officials already overflowed the benches that lined the courtyard. A raised wooden stage had been erected in the center, where a dozen musicians worked their zithers, gongs, drums, and bamboo flutes to flood the night with a rousing song.

Tai made his way through the crush of officials and nobles offering congratulations, but his eyes strayed to the royal seats. His mother's was empty, but Jin was already seated at the place of honor next to his. He watched her in the light of the courtyard lanterns, noting the tension in her jaw, the intensity of her hazel eyes that were so unlike those of purely Han Chinese. Her mix of Han and huren blood was not unusual, especially in the capital where foreigners abounded, but somehow she was unlike any he had met.

Tai at last managed to extricate himself to reach his seat. Jin stood in greeting, stiff in formal dragonrider regalia: leather pants and vest, with a silk cloak emblazoned with the silver-and-scarlet Dragon Class insignia. Her hair, that unique shade of tan, was braided with a slash of red silk through it, and though someone had been careful with her makeup, Tai noted the dark smudges beneath her eyes.

"Welcome back, Dragonrider Jin."

"Your Highness." She bowed, and he spied the key hanging from her neck. It had been a gift from him, a key to his private library as a sign of his trust.

As they sat back down, he felt the eyes of hundreds of nobles on him and Jin, so he faced forward as he spoke. "One of the mages broke the spell by accident. Is that true?"

"The spell broke, yes," Jin said. After a pause, she added, "Though I'm not sure it was by accident, Your Highness."

He frowned. "What do you mean?"

When she remained silent, he chanced a look at her. She seemed to be debating whether to continue. "You once said you might prefer not knowing the truth."

"That was when it came to Peilah," Tai said. "Not regarding your or the empire's safety." When she hesitated, he leaned forward. "Please."

"Do you know the story of the first blood-bonded riders, Your Highness? During the first emperor's reign?"

Being head of Dragon Class while loathing flying had meant he spent a great deal of time learning dragon history. "Which part? How they formed?"

"How they died."

His mind worked, trying to figure out what Jin was

saying. "You mean when the remaining two were given bows and arrows and forced to choose?"

Jin nodded. "They could have spared each other. But they killed each other instead."

He regarded her. "You think someone wanted you two to kill each other?"

"Am I right, Your Highness?"

Tai digested this, trying to find accusation in her voice. "I would never allow that."

"I did not say it was you."

He was about to reply when drums and cymbals crashed, heralding his mother's entrance. He followed Jin's example and got to his feet, turning her words over in his mind. Did she think Sanjin had tried to have her killed? Or even . . .

His mother ascended the steps to the seats, her hair dripping with jade and gold. An elaborate paper phoenix had been pasted to her forehead, the exact same shade of gold as the paint on her lips. She gave Tai a smile and Jin a polite nod of acknowledgement before sitting down on her throne and motioning for the festivities to begin.

A herald in cobalt blue and midnight black stepped forward, unrolling a scroll. "In the name of Her Majesty, the Empress Wu of Celestial Light, we welcome you to the Hall of Virtuous Kylins as we celebrate the death of the notorious traitor and menace, Mengkhis Lai! In her generosity and benevolence, Her Majesty shall share with you how the Princess of Dragons, with Her Majesty's blessing and might, slayed our enemy and saved our glorious, illustrious empire. Let the night's celebrations begin!"

A flurry of appreciative cries and cymbals greeted this, and the musicians bowed off stage as the actors came forward. The dragons had been intricately carved from thin strips of bamboo and decorated in fine silk, with puffs of smoke from the mouths eliciting squeals from the crowd. Tai recognized some of the more famous actors in the empire, but his mind still clung to what Jin had said.

His mother was ruthless. But try to kill Jin? She was their only hope against Mengkhis, especially now. He chafed as the play wore on, wishing to talk to Jin alone, without gossip-hungry courtiers and servants hovering over every gesture and word. Regardless of his own feelings toward her, they needed Jin now more than ever. If she believed that the throne wanted her dead, why would she help them? Why wouldn't she flee and find some remote island, never to return?

The audience shouted cries of recognition as the actor portraying Jin entered the stage, waving a prop sword and circling Mengkhis with long, dramatic strides.

He leaned closer to her. Gossip he could handle. Her leaving, he could not. "You know I am your friend?"

She turned to look at him then, her eyes darting to

the empress before she quickly faced the play once more. "I know you are a good man, Your Highness."

"That's a start." He was about to say something else, when the singer playing Mengkhis Lai burst into song, making conversation impossible. And when the song finished, so did the play, and as the prince, he was obligated to present the actors with tokens of appreciation.

By the time he had worked his way back to his mother and the viewing box, Jin had somehow managed to disappear from the crowds, her light brown huren hair a distant spot in a sea of black.

CHAPTER 9

Aadan's first view of the city of Samarkand gave him the notion it was a diamond in the desert.

It shimmered in the merciless sun, the towers gleaming dove white and an azure blue that rivaled even the color of the sky. Minarets on the corners emitted reedy calls to prayer, and soldiers armed with curved scimitars at their waists patrolled the city walls.

Aadan landed just outside the city's outer perimeter and again tamped down the frustration of waiting for his fellow Persians.

What's the point of flying, hey, Wanli?

His silver dragon huffed in sympathy and focused on a spot in the sand by the road. Soon, the sand darkened, then bubbled, as the dragon pulled any available water in the ground up to the surface. A few moments later, Wanli had separated the water further until it turned from a muddy brown to clear.

Aadan thanked Wanli as he squatted and dipped his palms in, splashing his face and curly beard and then slicking his hair.

He didn't bother looking at his reflection, as he knew he would be unsatisfied. Such little water with no soap and the constant winds meant his dark brown hair was still rough with sand, his Persian features only slightly less dusty.

By the time the rest of his party caught up with him, the water had dried from his face, and his hair lay in a damp layer over his neck and to his shoulders. The water in the sand had disappeared, and Wanli didn't offer to replenish it for Gah'med and the others.

"They know we're coming," Gah'med said.

"It's hard to hide Wanli," Aadan replied drily, looking over at the silver beast who could have filled a palace courtyard.

As if proving his words, a dust cloud bloomed on the horizon near the city, and soon the soldiers wearing the cloaks of Samarkand emerged.

Aadan looked to Gah'med. "You ready?"

Gah'med nodded. "Let's hope your idea works, Cousin."

THE KING of Samarkand seemed most impressed with Wanli, marveling at his wings and scales, and asking Aadan multiple times to make the creature breathe fire, until Aadan had to soothe the disgruntled Wanli that he was indeed not a performing dog.

"Marvelous!" the king said, clapping a ringed hand against one thigh. He sighed, longing. "If only countries other than China had dragons."

"It's a jealously guarded secret for good reason," Aadan remarked as he pointed toward the king's gardens. "Shall we walk? I would love to see the famed hanging gardens."

The king seemed reluctant to leave the dragon, but apparently remembered expected hospitality. He had a swarthy face ringed by a dark beard that had been oiled and shaped precisely, which made his jaw look unnaturally large, like some predatory cat, Aadan thought. Gah'med trailed them, and though Aadan wished to leave his relative behind, he knew Gah'med would outright refuse.

"I hear you were banished from China," the king said. "Such a shame."

"Perhaps it was a blessing," Aadan replied in what had become a rote response. Especially with the king of Samarkand, he wanted to appear as an ally, and not as a fleeing prince begging for help. "The Arabs have had Persia for far too long, and it is time to reclaim it."

The king gave him a sidelong glance. "Yes, I am sure you want your birthright back. But the Arabs are not to be trifled with. And I certainly don't have the men to spare."

"I'm not asking for your men."

"Oh?" The king stopped walking, eyebrows raised. "Then what are you asking for?"

"Taxes."

"Taxes?" the king repeated, as if he had never heard the word.

"I'd like you to tax all Arab goods coming through here."

The king grunted. "Here I was thinking you'd come asking for an old-fashioned war. I didn't expect something so banal."

"Well?" Aadan pressed.

The king frowned. "If I were to cut off trade as you ask . . . well, it would be disastrous for Samarkand."

"Not if they are defeated," Aadan said. "And they may have a mighty army, but a mighty army without supplies and food is simply a group of disgruntled mouths who will turn on the hand that fed it."

The king stopped at a small pond with flowing water, where lake flowers bloomed. Aadan felt Wanli's senses heighten, and he, too, wondered how expensive it was to keep running water in this dry, harsh desert.

"My dear prince," the king murmured, "try to understand. Samarkand is in a difficult place. We rely on both the Arabs and the Chinese to keep our kingdom safe. We are strong, but that doesn't mean we should wake the giants around us. I would be wise to keep the peace and ensure trade runs smoothly. Trade is what makes all this possible and keeps my people happy and fed. What would they think if I asked them to gamble it all away and turn against one of our greatest trading partners?"

Aadan tried on his best smile. In these situations, he wished he had his friend Tai's charm. He would have to hope his wits were enough. "You would be gaining a more powerful ally. Persia."

The king chuckled. "My dear prince, you are a wonderful fellow, and I have heard of your bravery at the Battle of Bochai."

"Bohai."

"Yes, Bohai. But you have been far from home your whole life." He paused. "Some say you are not Persian anymore, but Chinese."

"I will always be Persian," Aadan said, reiterating a phrase his father had drilled into him. He was, after all, versed in all the Persian ways. Outside of growing up in Persia, he was as educated on Persian language and history as anyone in the kingdom. Perhaps more.

"You certainly have the fine looks of one," the king admitted. "But do you know how to fight a war? Lead a Persian army? Keep the fractious Persian nobles from tearing each other apart? And even if you could, I'm afraid you underestimate the Arabs. They are organized, and there are no . . ." he glanced at Gah'med, Aadan thought ". . . internal disagreements, shall we say, as to hierarchy or power. The sultan is law, with no one to dispute it. It makes for good trade."

Aadan drew a breath. "I am the rightful heir to Persia, and my people expect to go home after this long absence. The sultan may be organized, he may be powerful, but he still sits on a throne that is not his. It is a Persian throne."

The king regarded him once more. "And what can you, Prince, do for me that the Sultan cannot?"

Aadan looked around him, and at Gah'med, who seemed just as interested in what Aadan would come up with. He clearly wasn't going to lend Aadan a hand, and Aadan thought he detected a hint of enjoyment at Aadan's discomfort.

The trickling of the water fountain drew Aadan's eye. "I can give you water."

The king looked as if he had misheard. "Water? And what would I want with water? I have plenty of water."

"Do you?" Aadan countered. "What does it cost you to bring this water forth? With my dragon Wanli, I can draw on water below ground, whenever you want it and however much you want. I can make oases appear from nothing. I can make water systems that will never dry out. Your people will never starve even if trade wanes, for they will have their own food."

The king's eyes narrowed, contemplating. "You really could do this?"

Aadan nodded. "You know the power of the drag-ons. They can do this and more. I will do this for you if you will support me against the Arabs by taxing their trade goods."

The king fiddled with a strand of his oiled beard. "Very well. Build me an oasis in the Sands of Sulfi, and you will have what you ask."

Relief flooded Aadan. "Thank you, King Talkund."

The king held up another hand. "That is not all, however. I want to have your word that you will help us and take our side in any border or trade negotiations with China."

Aadan schooled his face to hide his reluctance. The web of conflicts the king was inviting him into was murky and decidedly sticky. He would have preferred to keep his options open, as he knew confronting the empress would only widen the chasm between them, and it felt wrong to go against one he had sworn to protect, even if that person had betrayed him.

He bowed his head before Gah'med's and the king's searching gazes. "As the rightful prince of Persia, as well as a dragonrider who has been raised in the Tang court, I will always try to negotiate peaceful outcomes during disagreements."

The king grunted. "That is very diplomatic, but I think I will expect a firmer commitment. Come, let us celebrate our cooperation with some wine and food."

"Good catch back there, Cousin," Gah'med murmured, raising a wine goblet to toast Aadan. "But you cannot appease the eagle so easily every time."

Aadan chewed on a date before replying. "What do you mean?"

Gah'med sighed, as if he were a child. "At some point you will have to prove to the people that you are Persian and not Chinese. You must choose a side."

"I thought I already did," Aadan replied. "I'm here, feasting and drinking with you and making a pact with the king of Samarkand, aren't I?" He gestured at the dancing hall, where girls in sheer shawls, their faces obscured by beads, danced in fluid motions that reminded him of grass in water. Servants in voluminous pants and beaded vests moved amongst the court nobles, many of whom had come to pay respects to Aadan's table. He had tried to remember half their names, but stopped after a while, noticing that Gah'med seemed to have a much better memory for such things. Tai would have remembered too. Aadan's shortcomings irked him more than they should, but perhaps that was also because Gah'med was goading him.

"This is not committing to being Persian," Gah'med scoffed.

"I am of the faith, and I am fighting to win back the kingdom. What else do you suggest?"

"Say outright that you will support Samarkand against the Chinese, for one," Gah'med replied, helping himself to a large haunch of goat as a serving platter came by on the hennaed hands of a young servant. Aadan didn't miss Gah'med's admiring eye as she passed.

"Do not ogle our host's women."

Gah'med laughed. "To be honest, Cousin, you might consider more ogling. That would certainly help your cause, and at some point, you are going to have to do it."

"Do what?" Aadan asked. He found it hard to imagine that ogling was part of diplomacy.

"Marry a Persian," Gah'med replied, swallowing a mouthful of goat. "It's a pity your sisters are dead. One of them would have made a good wife."

Aadan just managed to keep himself from relieving his cousin of some teeth. He had never been able to shake his aversion to the Zoroastrian custom amongst nobles to marry one's siblings, which Gah'med brought up to needle him, he knew. But worse was his cousin's casual mention of his sisters' deaths, casualties of the great plague ten years past, and a reason his father had been so determined to see him regain Persia.

He recalled all the conversations with his friend Tai about the empress planning to marry Tai off like meat at market. They had joked about it often, and Tai seemed to accept his lot that his mother would have control over whom he married. Aadan had sympathized, but with all his Dragon Class training and studies, he had never really thought about who, or even if, he wanted to marry.

But now he knew.

"Political alliances can be forged in other ways," Aadan said, and immediately hated how childish he sounded. But it was true, for he had just negotiated help using his and Wanli's powers alone.

Gah'med snorted. "Yes, good thinking on your part. And that will work to some extent. But in this case, blood truly is thicker than water, Cousin. And my sister is of our blood. Our family would welcome the match." At Aadan's silence, he added, "Your water tricks will only get you so far. If you want that throne, you will have to pay a blood price, either in becoming blood kin with someone powerful, or spilling blood on the Persian side fighting the Chinese. It's your choice."

Aadan disliked his cousin, but even more so when he feared his cousin was right.

CHAPTER 10

Lost in thought after the day's events, Jin retreated to Meipin's quarters where she usually lived, but found the apartments nearly deserted, with none of Meipin's usual pipa music or laughter in the air.

A maid, not the usual Ahlu, came out and bowed in apology.

"Mistress Meipin is visiting friends in the city and won't be home until tomorrow," she explained. "Shall I ask the cook to return and prepare a meal?"

Jin shook her head. She didn't want to drag the cook from her time off simply to cook for Jin, so she decided to head to the Dragon Class mess hall to grab a quick evening meal.

When she arrived, she instantly regretted her decision to eat dinner at all, as all eyes seemed to slide to her. One table was filled only with women recruits, a new development since Jin had first entered Dragon Class and proven that dragons didn't just bond with men.

Shock rippled through Jin at how young they looked. Some were only eighteen, though others must have been her age. Yet to her they all looked like children, fresh-faced and eager. Especially as they seemed to abandon all conversation to stare.

She gratefully ducked away when Jao and Panshalar spotted her and motioned her over. She sat down, feeling the eyes still on her. Jao looked even more dour than usual.

"What's wrong?" Jin asked.

"He's sore about the play," Panshalar answered, sliding an empty bowl toward her while a kitchen hand came with a pot to ladle out rice. "Didn't even have Jao and me in it!"

"Well at least you're not training with the Veil."

Panshalar sucked in a breath, then winced from the pain in his ribs. Jao frowned as he said, "Why? They already chose their allotted five."

Unlike Jao, Jin hadn't kept track of which banner or department took the most Dragon Class second-year students.

"They're going to make you go after—" Jao stopped himself just in time. "They're training you for another chance. Is that it?"

Jin glanced around, trying to see if anyone had heard. But, no, all the whispers were quietly envious, admiring, or downright jealous. But just then, a group of riders approached to congratulate her on killing Mengkhis Lai, making Jin wish she had the man's powers of invisibility.

"Rider Jin, did you really kill him in one blow?"

"No," she replied curtly. At least she wasn't lying.

"It was an easy target."

The retort was two tables away, but Jin stiffened, recognition turning her stomach cold. "Killing a man in his sleep, how brave. Next are we going to admire her for killing the dead?"

A few laughs rippled out at this, and Jin's head whipped around. She knew that voice.

Madu.

When she caught his smirk, she turned back to Jao and Panshalar. "What is he doing here?" Being nephew to the traitorous War Minister Gao had earned Madu exile, but Jin disliked him more for his vendetta against her, which had taken root the day they met. "Wasn't his sentence for life?"

Jao shrugged. "A friend in the messenger banner said that practically every able-bodied rider has been called back to Changan."

The three exchanged looks, not needing to say what they all thought. With the knowledge of Mengkhis roaming free, the empress was trying to fortify the capital, even if it meant calling home disgraced riders like Madu.

Jao shoveled rice into his mouth. "I hear his cousin

will be married to some noble as well, as a show of forgiveness."

Jin steeled herself as Madu strode up to the table.

"So, hero of the hour," Madu said breezily, putting both hands on the table and leaning into Jin's space. "And blood bonded. I guess murdering my uncle came with a lot of rewards, didn't it?"

Jin didn't answer, making Madu lean in closer so that only she could hear. "I hear you can't be killed. Is that true?"

"Want to find out?" Jin asked, refusing to flinch. He bore the signs of a hard year in remote regions. His once unlined face had been carved by the sun, his skin having lost any last pale shades from his time as nobility. But the eyes were the same.

Madu grinned, his mouth stretched like a blade. "I wouldn't be so bold as to challenge the empire's most favored rider. Everyone here would tear me down."

"Not to mention she's a member of the Veil now," Panshalar commented, picking a piece of millet bread from his teeth.

Jin shot him a look, but he shrugged.

Madu's grin widened. "Congratulations. Rumor is, most who enter yearn for death." He cocked his head. "Though maybe Sanjin just has you in there because you're perfect for his sick nighttime fetishes."

Jin was out of her seat before she knew what she was doing, and her fist connected with Madu's jaw.

Gasps rippled across the hall, and it seemed like everyone was watching.

The rider rubbed his chin, glowering. "I'm going to break that hand, Rider."

"Stay away from me," Jin said, flinty.

Madu gave her a malicious smile, then turned and headed back to his table, leaving Jin's stomach cold. Murmurs erupted all around as people watched but slowly went back to their meals.

"Turtle turd," Panshalar muttered after he'd left, and let out a belch that seemed to hurt his ribs. "But seriously, is that why you joined the Veil?"

"Not by choice," Jin replied. She made herself eat, for her appetite was still hefty even if her stomach churned at the memories of the day. She glanced at Madu sitting deep in conversation amongst his cronies, then back at them. "Thank you for that. I can handle him. But it's nice to have help."

Panshalar's head bobbed. "Well, after tomorrow you'll have to handle him on your own."

"What's happening tomorrow?" Jin asked, trepidation forming.

Jao's voice carried a tinge of pride. "Panshalar and I were accepted to the warrior banner. We leave for our post at Hainan tomorrow."

"I thought everyone had been recalled here?" Jin said. Hainan was the southernmost end of the empire, nearly back into Champa.

Panshalar spoke through a mouthful of rice. "Not

all. They're keeping a line of defense along the south, in case Meng—I mean, in case there's trouble there."

"Congratulations," Jin said, trying to find a sincere smile. She knew Jao and Panshalar had wanted to join the warrior banner, as so many did, and she was glad for them. But at the same time a small seed of disappointment sprouted in her. She was losing her allies one by one, it seemed, at a time when she desperately needed them.

The bench next to her creaked as a wiry man, Bo Tan, sat down, a broad-shouldered woman looking awkward in dragon leathers following suit.

Bo Tan looked more confident, Jin noted, than the man she had saved from freezing on Ice Beard Mountain during their first Dragon Class test. Then, he had been so scared of failing, but now he moved with a self-assurance born from having finally graduated.

"This is Rider Wei Ru," Bo Tan said. "Wei Ru, may I introduce Panshalar, Jao, and, of course, Rider Jin needs no introduction."

Rider Wei Ru dipped her head, her words surprisingly soft for such a large woman. "It is an honor to meet you, Rider Jin. A really true honor."

Jin searched for a polite reply, but Bo Tan didn't give her the chance.

"Did I just hear you joined the Veil?" the new arrival asked, pulling his bowl of rice to himself and dumping in a saucer of pickled fish and turnip.

"Yes," Jin replied.

"I hear people die every day in their training."

Jin's expression must have changed, for Jao slapped Bo Tan on the back of the head and Panshalar gave him a withering look. Rider Wei Ru's eyes watched Jin's every move.

"By the eight levels of hell, I apologize," Bo Tan muttered, reddening.

"I'd rather speak of other things," Jin said curtly. Her bite of lamb stewed in spices and onion suddenly tasted foul.

"Why did they put you in there, anyway?" Bo Tan asked.

"Did you ask to join?" Wei Ru asked, a tinge of awe in her voice. "To prove yourself?"

"You'd think that as the slayer of Mengkhis Lai," Bo Tan said, "you'd receive a mansion in the northern wards or something."

Though lying had been second nature as a thief, she hated lying about this. She had never had to lie about something so great that an entire empire would have to swallow it.

"I will never know the minds of the rulers," she said instead.

"Why aren't they training us as well?" Panshalar asked carefully. "We were there."

Jin understood what he didn't say in front of others. Sanjin had sworn them and the entire force to secrecy, on pain of an extended visit to the tea rooms. Why had she alone been chosen to train, if they would be sent back for a second chance with Mengkhis?

Jin shook her head. "Consider yourselves lucky."

"Lucky indeed," Bo Tan said. "Everyone views you as heroes, greater even than Oyang Kang."

Panshalar's eyes lit up, though he halfheartedly tried to downplay it. "Really? You think so?"

Jin left them arguing with Bo Tan and Wei Ru about how their exploits compared to Oyang Kang's and searched the crowded tables. She finally found the one she was looking for, where several riders in the messenger banner sat. Each member had the messenger insignia sewn into their *paos*, the thick jackets assigned to all riders.

The six riders gave her welcome smiles and polite bows of the head.

"Excuse me, esteemed riders, but do you know where Rider Mao is?"

It was a slim chance, but she'd always hoped that Mao might have stumbled across news of Aadan, since he was a messenger and a close friend of the Persian's. She had developed the habit of asking for him at every chance, in case he was passing through the capital.

The dark looks on the riders' faces, however, gave her pause. "What is it?"

"I suppose you haven't heard, then?" A short rider with small eyes drilled into a pockmarked face coughed into his fist.

"Heard what?" Jin asked.

"Mao is dead," another rider said, voice gruff. "His dragon died, so he followed a week later."

Jin let out a breath. "How? Who?"

"Song of Scales," the first rider said. "His dragon died there, and Mao's white disease set in."

"Died at the Song of Scales?" Jin asked, not understanding.

"It happens," the gruff rider said. "The dragons say it's a brutal fight for the females, and some lose their lives. Mao's dragon got unlucky."

Another rider nodded, taking a sip of his wine. "Mine barely made it back. Scarred terribly, but alive. As many as a tenth that go die there."

Jin tried not to let her mind spiral. A tenth. *You never told me this, Rayshan!*

You have enough to worry you.

You cannot go.

He growled in reply, though it felt torn between protest and agreement.

"May time heal your loss," Jin murmured to the riders, turning to leave.

She exited the mess hall, her heart heavier at Mao's demise, along with her one possible connection to Aadan. She dreaded the days ahead, and even Rayshan's reassuring hum in her mind did little to keep her anxiety at bay.

CHAPTER 11

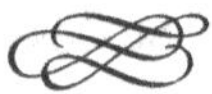

The smoky scent of mugwort greeted Tai as a servant ushered him into his mother's apartments.

Lanterns blazed from the carved ceiling, and in the center of the room stretched a long *kang*, a raised and heated platform, on which his mother lay on her stomach. Her smooth back was marred only by the hair-thin needles protruding from them, while a young mage in the purple robes of the Crane class bent over the needles, testing them with his forefinger. The empress hissed, and the mage bowed low in apology.

"Is that you, my son?"

"Forgive the late intrusion, Your Majesty," Tai said.

The empress's fingers fluttered. "Leave us."

The mage bowed out, closing the doors behind him with a whisper.

"I hear it has been a long day," Tai said, walking

toward a chair next to the kang. He sat as his mother turned her head to look at him, her usually ornate hair now coiled in practical braids and pinned to her head to not impede the mage's work on her back. Each needle glimmered in the lamplight, as did his mother's dark eyes.

"I sense you are about to make it longer," she answered, sighing. "If this is about more funds for Dragon Class to feed the returning riders, I'd rather you work it out with Treasurer Gong."

"I already have," Tai said. "He's approved the extra funds."

"Well, that's one problem solved," she sighed.

"Only because we have lost a dozen dragons and their riders thus far," Tai said tightly. Not having to feed and pay those fallen riders would help fill the gap for all the ones who had been commanded to return, but already the dorms were at capacity, as was Dragon City, where the dragons were housed. Not to mention the surplus of game they had to find for the hunting grounds to feed the extra beasts. But his mother had been adamant: trying to defend the vast coastline from an invisible rider would spread them too thin. Best to have all their defenses around Changan, where Mengkhis would be most likely to attack.

His mother pursed her lips. "The Song of Scales has started early this year, it seems. At the worst time."

"True," Tai agreed. "Which is why we need as many advantages as we can find."

His mother glanced at him. "Out with it."

Tai leaned forward. "Why did you put the rider Jin in the Veil?"

His mother's eyes sparked with a mix of disappointment and amusement. "Because you don't send a lamb to kill a tiger. Emar tried and failed. If we want her to kill Mengkhis, she'll have to be the fiercest rider we have ever had. Only the Veil can make her that."

Tai swallowed. "Have you considered that the Veil might turn her against us? I know you've always said their methods were necessary, but they don't make men. They break them. What happens when you break Jin?"

"If she can't survive the Veil, she won't stand a chance against Mengkhis," his mother said, eyes cold.

Tai straightened. "She already thinks you wanted Mengkhis to kill her."

The empress propped her chin on her hands, contemplative. "I can see how it looks that way."

"Is she right?" Tai asked.

"Why are you so concerned with her, my son?" the empress asked, exasperated. "She is not another Peilah, is she?"

Tai stood, because he suddenly didn't trust himself not to hit his own mother. "And if she is, would you kill her?"

His mother's expression turned stony. "If I say I didn't kill Peilah, then I didn't. I am looking out for you, and the last thing you need is to be infatuated with a dragonrider, of all people."

"What you call infatuation, I call being concerned. We are making an enemy of the only person who can kill Mengkhis Lai." He paused, marshalling his thoughts. "She already thinks you betrayed her. What happens when she has to suffer through the Veil?" He had been sheltered from the Veil's practices for most of his life, but Sanjin's tastes for cruelty and pain were legendary. "I am trying to make sure these methods don't turn a friend into a foe."

"And I am making sure she's not simply a mantis trying to stop a chariot wheel," his mother snapped. "You would rather I let her ride a dragon all day and eat honeyed lychees all night? Mengkhis would be delighted."

Tai's anger boiled. Growing up, his mother had never spared the rod, forcing him to face his fears and do whatever was repugnant to him, because she believed coddling did more harm than good. "Must the methods always be extreme? There are many other ways of training Jin that don't involve her joining the Veil."

"Remember the legend of the hostage king Goujian. You would not be the strong prince you are today if I hadn't made you taste pain growing up."

But I would despise you less. The shock of this new feeling sat sour in his gut.

The door opened, and the mage entered, bowing in

apology. "Pardon your lowly servant. It is time to adjust the needles, Your Majesty. May I?"

"Yes," the empress said. "The crown prince was about to leave. Remember, my son, a pot is worthless mud until it tastes fire. If you truly care about Jin, then help her grow stronger."

Tai bowed, carefully bottling his frustration and anger. "Peace upon your evening, Mother."

CHAPTER 12

The next day, Jin headed to the royal library despite her exhaustion. The question that had nagged her throughout the journey back still hovered over her, and she didn't know when she'd be able to find time once the Veil had her in its clutches.

The library was deserted at this time, and Jin replaced her key over her neck before lighting a lamp. This was Tai's private library, restricted to just him and now her. She briefly wondered where he was, whether she was right to have told him her suspicions. She didn't think Tai capable of condoning any plans to kill her, but did she have any basis for it? Even Aadan, his best friend, had warned her that Tai always put the throne above all. What was to say he hadn't even suggested that Jin and Mengkhis kill each other off? This would solve all his problems, eliminating the nightmare Tai had lived with his whole life. Yet somehow, she had shared her suspicions with him. Something in her, despite her most ingrained habits, trusted him.

"Fool," she muttered before forcing her mind to the task at hand.

She pored over the few old scrolls she found that mentioned Mengkhis and the Age of Chaos, trying to piece together some hint of why he had spared her. And why had he asked about her parents? Was it simply because she was half huren? But half bloods were not uncommon in the empire, and Mengkhis would have no reason to be sentimental about that.

When her head began throbbing from the effort, Jin replaced all the scrolls and blew out the lamp. Her frustration at coming away empty-handed dissipated, however, when she reached Meipin's courtyard and heard the familiar pipa music and her friend's voice.

"You're back," Jin said when she entered their shared foyer.

"Of course! Everyone has been talking about the return of the victorious Princess of Dragons!" Meipin said. A flicker of worry crossed her face. "Your brows have grown wild. Is that the new caterpillar look?"

Ever elegant in her favorite colors of peach and rice shoot green, Meipin wore a gauzy scarf over her shoulders that trailed to the floor, along with a pleated skirt with swirls of peach and dark emerald. Perfect almond-shaped eyes completed a plump, smooth face.

Her silks and luxurious accessories would have once been an affront to Jin. But now, she welcomed Meipin's ostentation, her color in an otherwise grey world. Color she would miss, she suspected, once she entered the Veil.

The two held each other's hands tightly in greeting.

"I have missed you," Meipin said. "Being away from the empire's greatest heroine has meant no one invites me to parties anymore."

Jin smirked. "You will never let me forget that, will you?" She had suspected Meipin of befriending her only for her own status at court, and Meipin loved to bring it up.

"And give up my leverage?" Meipin asked. "Keep dreaming." She surveyed Jin. "You've lost weight."

Jin sighed inwardly. Most girls would care that they were not the ideal plumpness. To be told one had lost weight was the equivalent of being told one was ugly, though she knew Meipin said it out of concern rather than malice. "The last month has been hard." Jin didn't think Meipin needed to know the truth about Mengkhis. Though Meipin kept secrets better than anyone, Jin didn't want to burden Meipin. Not yet.

"And still no news? About Aadan, I mean?"

Jin shook her head.

"I heard about rider Mao." Meipin sat down opposite her. "Listen, perhaps I can help. Maybe I could send a letter."

Jin had never written Aadan, not wanting to risk his

whereabouts, and had assumed that was why he never sent anything himself. "Safely? How?"

"The new secretary to the Minister of Law has her ways, after all."

Jin's eyes widened, making Meipin laugh. "You've been given a position?"

Meipin nodded. "A secretarial position, but, yes, I am officially an official." She made a formal bow.

Jin squeezed Meipin's shoulder in congratulations. Her friend had longed for ages to join government, and it seemed she had realized her first step. "When?"

"While you were off killing Mengkhis Lai."

At Jin's frown, Meipin took her arm sympathetically. "There are rumors that he's not dead. Are they true?"

Jin said nothing, and the flood of emotions she had had in the cave rushed back. Shock, anger, betrayal. Though it now simmered rather than raged, she still had no answers. And she hesitated about telling Meipin. Why dampen Meipin's joy over her new position?

"Well, that's answer enough." Meipin sighed. "His Highness is keeping up a good face."

"But if I can't kill him when he's in an induced slumber, what chance do I have with him at the height of his powers?" Jin asked. *Not to mention, the empress and Sanjin tried to bury me anyway.* This was what she had to find out. For if Sanjin and the empress wanted her dead, then her only leverage now was the fact that she alone could kill Mengkhis.

But what happened when she did? Would they entomb her like they had Mengkhis? What if they didn't keep their word?

"Jin, you look so scared." Meipin hugged her. "If there's anything I can do . . . "

"Do you have any idea where to find a forbidden book?"

Meipin pulled back, looking puzzled and amused. "You need only ask. I can take you tomorrow."

"How about now?" Jin asked. Once she joined the Veil, she didn't know how her movements would be controlled.

Her friend laughed. "It's been a while since I made a midnight visit to a bookshop. But why not?"

Everything in Jin's life seemed tethered to Mengkhis and his past. A past that had been burned away with many books. Jin managed to pull out some men's pants, a tunic, and boots she had kept in her rooms. It was not unusual for women to wear men's clothing in the city, as the attire was much more suited to riding horses and walking than the traditional women's dresses. Meipin, however, had not abandoned her feminine attire even at this late hour and wore a shimmering, pinc-colored robe over a light, cherry-colored dress, with matching boots trimmed in silk. The palanquin bearers returned with a large sedan, and

Jin noted that they didn't seem surprised. Meipin's night jaunts were not unusual, clearly.

Meipin and her trusted maid Ahlu mounted and sat on one side, and Jin clambered in to sit on the other.

They swayed through the inky city streets, the second curfew drum having sounded. The occasional lanterns dotted the avenues, signaling night patrols or those on their ways to taverns, song houses, and private parties. Even from within the palanquin, Jin heard the trailing notes of zithers, the clink of wine cups, and the flute-like laughter of women in the song houses.

They stopped at one of the ward gates, where Ahlu showed the guard their passes. Meipin smiled at Jin. "Being an official has its benefits."

The guard waved them through, and the palanquin bearers heaved the sedan with a mighty "hai" and ran through the streets.

The smell of nuts drifted in, and Jin's mind immediately flew to Aadan. He had given her problem-solving nuts before he left, a traditional gift that apparently solved one's worries if one ate them. She had wished for his return, but so far, they hadn't delivered.

"You still haven't told me what kind of book you're looking for," Meipin interrupted her thoughts as the palanquin bearers trundled onto the ring road bordering the north-south canal. Jin was almost glad for the overwhelming smells of fish, silt, and the spices plied in the wet markets that drove the smell of nuts away.

"I'm not entirely sure," Jin admitted. "I'll know when I see it."

"Very mysterious," Meipin murmured, smiling. "Well, whatever it is, I'm sure Jianming can find it."

"Who's Jianming?"

"An old friend. Likely knows of every book ever printed."

Jin peered through the window curtain at the wards going by. Her home city, and many others around the empire, were designed like the capital: grids comprised of roughly the same number of households or buildings. She noted they were entering the neighborhood of papers and books. Even at night, Jin made out the signs proclaiming the finest bamboo for scrolls, pure ink, and paper from mulberry, and coarser fibers like jute or hemp. The palanquin wound through several smaller streets until Meipin leaned out and called to the bearers to stop.

"We must go forward on foot."

Jin wasn't sure why, given the streets had not narrowed to prevent the palanquin from proceeding, and wondered if Meipin was trying to keep their destination secret.

At Jin's look, Meipin flashed her a smile and pulled a scarf over her head. "I have a reputation to protect. Even at night. We're almost there."

She followed Meipin and Ahlu down an alley, onto

a wider street, and then through a crooked laneway, where Meipin led them into a nondescript shopfront with a few banners at the door proclaiming it to be an antique book dealer. Meipin motioned for them to follow her around the side, and they did, stepping over pools of household refuse that had been shoveled into piles for the city's regular collection.

Meipin knocked softly on a narrow door at the shop. At first there was no answer, but then came the sound of cloth slippers moving across the floors.

A servant opened the door and eyed them, brows raised.

"I came as soon as I heard about Cousin Li," Meipin said.

The servant motioned for them to enter, and Jin was amused that the nobles had passwords like common thieves.

Inside, the shop was much bigger than it looked from outside. Even in the dim light from the one lantern the servant placed on a table, Jin saw it stretched deep toward the back and even had a staircase leading up to other floors.

A bird in a cage trilled from a corner, and a middle-aged man in clean cotton robes appeared from behind a towering desk, holding up a lamp. "Ah, the lady Meipin," the man said. "A pleasure to see you. You must be most eager for the new arrivals if you are coming this late at night."

Jin glanced at Meipin, who tossed her a smile.

"Teacher Jianming is an old friend." She leaned in. "One who is very good at keeping secrets. Thank you for opening your store to us at such an hour. We couldn't come during your business times."

Jianming bowed. "Anything for the lady Meipin. Let me fetch your order."

He bustled away toward the back of the shop, and when he came back, Meipin motioned at Jin. "As you can see, I'm bringing new clientele. My friend would like to ask for something on the rare side."

Jianming glanced from Meipin to Jin. "Rare, or banned?"

"Banned."

The man didn't bat an eye. "In the vein of what you usually order then, Meipin?"

The girl shook her head. "No, I don't believe Jin is of our sisterhood."

That's when Jin noticed the books Jianming had brought to Meipin. They had flowery titles, but all clearly hinted at female romantic relationships. She glanced at Meipin and Ahlu in a whole new light. Meipin smiled. "A girl can't be reading legal treatises all the time."

Jin suppressed a smile at how she was learning new things about her friend all the time, and turned back to Jianming. "I'm looking for anything you might have on Mengkhis Lai."

"Ah." He eyed her. "I have a few. And one particularly rare one," Jianming said, bustling to the back of his shop. "Wait here."

Jin looked around the shelves at all the scrolls and roughly bound books held by hemp. "He doesn't fear being shut down?" Jin asked.

Meipin scoffed. "Of course. But some things are worth risking one's life for."

Jianming came back with two books. "Here is a long unprinted version of Mengkhis Lai's life, and this is a popular one—" He held out the second. "An anonymous satire of Mengkhis Lai and the Empress Wu herself." He chuckled. "It makes for entertaining reading."

Jin shook her head. "You have nothing else?" She didn't fancy delving into fictitious rumors. She needed facts.

Jianming regarded her with an uplifted eyebrow. "My dear lady, anything about Mengkhis without an official Ministry of Education approval was burned. These copies were meticulously hand copied, and I only have two of them left. When you leave, I will have to find someone to make a new copy, which will be costly."

Jin sighed. "I'll take the personal history."

"Are you sure you don't want this one as well?" He waved the one with a plain cover. "It's pure salacious gossip, but it makes for very ripe reading. You'll understand at the end why every copy was hunted down and burned."

At Jin's hesitation, Meipin broke in. "I'll pay for it. A present from me to you, Jin."

Jin wanted to protest that she didn't want the book, but Jianming was already bundling both titles in string and paper, and Ahlu had already brought forth Meipin's purse.

"Now if anyone asks," Jianming said, "you do not know where you got these books, is that understood?"

Meipin pouted. "Teacher Jianming, how long have you known me? I'll guard my mouth like a sealed bottle."

"I meant your friend." He glanced at Jin. "One can never be too careful."

As they wove their way back to the carriage, Meipin's arm linked through hers, Jin asked, "Does your family know? About you and Ahlu?"

Meipin's grip tightened slightly on her arm. "No."

"What of your marriage to the prince?"

"What of it?"

"Don't you wish . . ." Jin's voice trailed off.

"Marriages aren't for love, and certainly not the prince's or mine," Meipin said. "You think I don't want to spend the rest of my days with Ahlu and simply not marry?" Jin glanced at Ahlu, who looked up and smiled. Meipin made a dismissive sound. "That would be a missed opportunity. A husband in the right place will help me change the system from the inside, and Prince Tai is a good man." She glanced at Jin. "Even if you did marry him, you can't expect him to not take concubines. And you don't strike me as a woman who would get along with concubines."

"Marry him?" Jin scoffed. "Heaven and Earth would have to collide."

Meipin grinned. "Don't tell him that. He'd start working on moving Heaven and Earth." They climbed into the carriage, and the sedan bearers began the long route back to the palace.

Meipin watched Jin run a hand along the books they had bought. "Tell me truthfully, do you care for him?"

Jin looked up, taken aback. "You know as well as I do that all of the rumors are just for show . . . He encourages the people to think of us together." She thought she saw Meipin wince, and said, "What's wrong?"

Meipin plucked at an imaginary thread on her gown. "I am in a position to become empress, Jin, and I don't want there to be any negative feelings between us."

Jin digested this. "You once said you didn't care about marrying Tai, it was all politics."

Meipin nodded. "It is. I can't expect the prince to not have romantic interests. But it's . . . different, if those interests are you. You're my friend. I don't want you hurt, and . . ." she searched for words ". . . I don't want to hurt you."

"You won't. I've known from the first day I met you that you two were being groomed for each other,"

Jin said. But then why did the thought still bother her?

Meipin abandoned her thread and looked at Jin. "Forget that he is the Son of Heaven and you are a rider in Dragon Class. And I know you and Aadan are close. But do you also have feelings for His Highness?"

Jin thought on it, trying to tread carefully. "I care for him. But not the way you think." *Not the way I feel for Aadan.*

Meipin had none of her usual humor now but seemed to be observing her intently. "Are you sure?"

"Of course I'm sure," Jin said, though she wondered at the intense relief on Meipin's face. Jin took Meipin's hand. "You have nothing to worry about with me," she assured, though part of her felt a tinge of sadness, and she realized it was for Prince Tai. She sensed many secrets beneath the charm, one of them being that he secretly longed for a marriage that was more than a political chess move.

Meipin smiled. "Good. That's such a relief, and a weight off my mind. But now I have one more favor to ask."

"Anything."

Meipin took a breath. "If I'm to marry Tai, I don't want the people hating me."

It took Jin a moment to understand what Meipin was saying. "You mean . . ."

"The people chant your and Tai's name when you make appearances," Meipin said slowly. "The toymakers sell statues of you two together. It will be difficult if they want you but he marries me."

The thought had never occurred to her, but she suddenly saw it from Meipin's eyes, and she was at a loss.

"See if you can talk to Tai about it," Meipin said. "I'd broach it, but I think he'll listen more if it comes from you."

Jin nodded. She had always downplayed the prince's fanning of the people's hailing them as the Prince and Princess of Dragons, but it had never occurred to her that Tai's charade was hurting Meipin.

CHAPTER 13

The day after their trip to the bookshop, Jin found out just how well the empress would enact her threat to make Jin's life one of pain. Jin barely had time to see Rayshan, come back to the Oval, and say a brief farewell to Jao and Panshalar before a message from Sanjin arrived, telling her to pack a single bag of essential belongings before reporting to the Royal Veil training grounds on the northwest of the palace complex before the hour of the snake.

Meipin rose early to see her off, giving her a tight embrace. "You are the strongest person I know. And you are welcome here anytime."

Jin hugged her back, grateful for the confidence. She pulled a sealed scroll from her pocket. "Here. If you could get this to Aadan . . ."

Meipin took it, nodding. "I will see what I can do."

Jin arrived at the Veil's offices in her rider leathers, where the men waiting for her took her to a tiled room with buckets of cold water and plain blue robes. Both were burly northerners but had none of Panshalar's humor or gentleness. One was taller than the other, with a bushy beard, while the shorter one had hands that reminded Jin of hammers. Both had eyes devoid of emotion, and Jin shivered, for she had seen some of the Veil soldiers in Gaosho in her day, and they all had that same soulless look.

"Get changed!" one of them barked as they turned their backs.

"Leave me and I will."

"Sanjin's orders are that we are to stay while you are inducted into the Veil. Clean yourself, then change."

"I don't need a bath," Jin said.

The tall one turned then, his eyes full of warning. "Clean yourself. Or we have orders to do it for you."

Jin debated, then with a sullen glare motioned for him to turn around. He did. Reluctantly, she stripped down and splashed the water on herself, her flesh prickling at the cold.

Everyone feared the Veil, but thieves even more so. She remembered the day Haitao had told her of the Veil, had shown her the silent black cloaked men with their insignia of "zheng," or "righteousness," who moved through the town streets when there had been a killing. The thieves from a rival clan had panicked after a botched heist and killed an official, which was a death sentence.

"There are the police," Haitao had said, "and then there is the Royal Veil. The police are like lambs when it comes to punishments, and the Royal Veil will strip the flesh from you alive."

She almost laughed at the phrase. She was about to enter training with the most feared man she had ever known. Mengkhis might be the nightmare of every citizen in the empire, but Sanjin was the nightmare of every thief in every city.

Even if he wanted to, he couldn't kill her. But he didn't have to. His favorite weapon was pain, not death.

True to their word, the men didn't turn around until she had knotted the robes around her. Everything was scratchy, as if she was wearing clothes made of ants rather than fabric, and she longed to pull them off. But then she would be naked, and that was worse.

"Come," the taller one barked, motioning with his hand.

She followed once she had tied the last knot in her jacket, sliding her feet into the black cloth shoes waiting for her at the door.

He led her through an austere courtyard where the Veil symbol "righteousness" was emblazoned everywhere. The air was still, deceptively peaceful for a place renowned for cruelty.

The man led her into another courtyard, and this one had benches lined around the perimeter. Sanjin was pruning a plant in one corner, his silken robes luxurious in this bare space.

"Welcome, Person of Nothing."

Jin frowned.

Sanjin turned. "You have been cleansed and entered the Veil. You will now be known as Person of Nothing. For that's who you are within these walls. You are no one."

Jin didn't reply, and Sanjin walked forward. "You must repeat it. I am a person of nothing."

Jin saw no point in fighting this soon. She would save her strength for more important battles. "I am a person of nothing."

Sanjin smiled. "And when your training starts, you will actually say that and believe it."

Jin tried to keep the glare out of her eyes.

"I don't know what you have heard of the Veil," Sanjin said, "but you might as well forget all you know. I will show you what the Veil really is."

Sanjin motioned at the expressionless tall man, and he bowed and disappeared.

"Are you a Buddhist?"

Jin wasn't sure there was a correct answer, so she shook her head. "No, Master Sanjin."

"A pity. Much of our philosophy here will be based on Buddhism, and it would help your progress so much if you'd already had some training. But no matter. You will become more than yourself and become part of something."

The tall brute re-entered the courtyard, this time with a man who was blindfolded and gagged, his hands tied in front of him.

"Ah, here we are," Sanjin said. "Put him here."

The tall Veil guard pushed his prisoner down onto the courtyard steps. The man tried to speak through his gag but failed.

A cold dread started in Jin's neck. Panicking or pleading would not help the man's case, and she had a feeling that nothing she did would prevent what was about to happen.

"Kill him," Sanjin said, and held out a sword to her.

"Why? What has he done?"

Sanjin picked up the sword and with a motion faster than Jin would have believed, cut off the man's hand. The prisoner screamed through his gag as blood flowed, and Jin's stomach churned.

"Kill him," Sanjin said again, holding out the sword.

"No." Jin shook her head. *I am not a murderer.* Though she knew what would happen next even before it did. Sanjin stepped forward and stabbed the man through the leg. The man had fallen to the side and was taking ragged breaths, sliding into shock.

Jin steeled herself. She knew what Sanjin was trying to make her do, and she wanted no part of it. "I am not a murderer."

"You are what I say you are," Sanjin said. "Now kill him."

"No," but this time it was a whisper. Jin tried to tell

herself that his pain was Sanjin's fault, not hers, but the blood had seeped to her shoes, and she stepped back, sickened.

"Ah-Kun!" Sanjin said calmly.

The shorter man who had accompanied Jin entered once more and bowed low.

"Yes, Master Sanjin."

"Kill this prisoner."

The shorter man bowed, took the sword from Sanjin, and severed the man's head from his body. Jin stifled her bile. It was not the first time she had witnessed a beheading, for she had seen Haitao killed exactly that way, by Gao, in front of her. Also to prove a point. But it still sickened her, and she knew it would live with her, like the dead she saw, until she died. If ever.

She turned a look of hatred on Sanjin.

Sanjin held her gaze. "Well done." He turned to Ah-Kun. "Now, can you tell this person of no worth what the first law of the Veil is?"

"Mission first. Life last. Empire always."

The marquis nodded. "Very good. Now prepare to kill yourself."

Jin's head snapped around to Ah-Kun, but his deadened eyes didn't change. Instead, he bowed low, then took the sword and expertly flipped it so that its tip was pressed under his ribcage, at a precise spot he had evidently practiced.

"I die at your command, Master Sanjin," Ah-Kun said, eyes downcast.

"What say you, person of no worth?" Sanjin turned to Jin. "Do you believe he will do it? Shall I prove it to you?"

"I believe you," Jin said, throat tight.

"Are you sure?" Sanjin pressed.

"Yes!"

There was a long pause.

"An exemplary member of the Veil, Ah-Kun," Sanjin said. "I would be sad to lose him." Sanjin nodded to Ah-Kun, and the man re-sheathed his sword. If he was relieved, he showed no sign.

Sanjin turned to Jin, whose stomach had still not settled. "To be a Veil member means you will kill anyone, including yourself, without asking any questions. And if you fight me, which I expect you will, then we will learn our lessons through pain." He smiled. "I expect you are dreading these lessons, but you will be stronger for them. Now, shall we start your training, or do you have questions?"

Jin shook her head. She wasn't sure she could speak anyway.

"Good. You are learning."

CHAPTER 14

For the rest of the day, Jin forced her mind away from the body in the courtyard, for she worried she would lose all control if she dwelled on it. Rayshan's consciousness prowled at the edges of her mind, demanding to be let in and to share her pain, but she wanted to spare him. He had sensed what had happened, and similar unease boiled in him.

Jin wasn't sure what shocked her more: the scenes that kept surfacing or the fact that the empress condoned it. And really, why was she shocked by that?

The empress allows all of this, she said to Rayshan. *Doesn't she?*

I can't imagine she doesn't know.

A worse thought struck her. *And Tai. Does Tai know? And condone this? That prisoner, had he done anything wrong? And what of the guard? He was ready to kill himself on command, for no reason.* Her stomach plummeted. *Simply to prove a point on Sanjin's whim.*

There was good reason you feared the Veil.

And now I'm part of it.

No, you're not part of it unless you allow yourself to be, Rayshan said. *Survive. You are still Jin. You are still you. Survival is all that matters right now. Once you survive and kill Mengkhis Lai, we will be free. Focus on that.*

Will we be free? When they had first been assigned to kill Mengkhis Lai, Sanjin had said they would enter the Messenger Banner, and then hopefully they would leave all this horrible training and death and intrigue and lies. But if the empress had wanted her dead back at the Well of Fire, what was to say she wouldn't put Jin into the Well of Fire once they killed Mengkhis?

You could ask the prince to intervene, Rayshan suggested.

Jin debated. Would Tai do that? The empress wouldn't agree, Jin knew deep down. No matter what Tai said or threatened, the empress had promised to make her life bitter, and she was doing it.

There is no way but through this, Jin whispered, remembering the dead men in the courtyard, the way Sanjin had casually sliced through the man's hands as casually as one sliced tofu for dinner. Besides, where would she go? How would she and Rayshan hide in an empire where everyone would hunt them down?

In the afternoon, Sanjin introduced her to the other Veil members in her squad. There were four others, making a total of five, like a Dragon Class wing, she realized. All wore identical robes and hair plaited in the same style, with blue head cloths, and all looked around twenty-five years of age. The tallest looked too skinny to withstand even the slightest push, but ropes of muscle stretched beneath his blue tunic. Another, shorter and stockier, had a nose so broad and flat it reminded Jin of a mushroom. The third had wide eyes and high cheekbones that made her suspect he was from the west, while the last one was muscled and solid, his face tapered and calculating like a fox's. A fifth man stood to one side, at attention but keeping to the shadows.

"Welcome your new addition. Like you, here she is a person of nothing," Sanjin said. "I trust you all to control yourselves around a feminine presence, because transgression will mean I'll mete out swift and very memorable punishment." When he had made sure everyone bowed in acceptance, he continued, "Ah-Ming will be your tutor here, show you your room and have your things brought. I will see you at the end of the week to assess your progress."

The shadowed man, supposedly Ah-Ming, stepped forward. He was older than Jin had first thought, nearing fifty. His long sleeves didn't cover the various scars visible around his wrists and lower arms, nor the ridged burn scar that ran from his grey hair down the side of his neck, its color resembling the wrinkly skin of a newborn rat.

Once Sanjin had left, Ah-Ming turned a stoic eye on them. "We shall begin with our morning meditation."

Jin cautiously followed the others in taking thin reed mats from the wall and placing them in the courtyard in a circle.

She sat, unsure, until Ah-Ming motioned. "Have you never meditated, person of no worth?"

Jin shook her head.

Ah-Ming's eye twitched. "Follow the others."

She glanced around. Everyone had closed their eyes.

I thought it would be knives and torture, she commented to Rayshan.

Perhaps that comes later, her dragon rumbled back.

Yet despite this ominous promise, Jin was surprised that the entire day consisted of Zen Buddhist teaching.

The initiates barely spoke to her throughout, and the rest of the hours passed in meditation. Jin began to chafe at the quiet time, for then she was alone with her thoughts. The only change came in the afternoon, when Ah-Ming bade the men strip off their tops while allowing Jin to keep her undergarment.

She tried to focus on her breathing, on the sounds in the courtyard and the smells of the gingkoes growing nearby, but her mind refused to cooperate, instead recreating the sight of the sword descending on the prisoner, the precise moment his severed hand flew from his wrist, the blood . . .

The deep tolls of a bell sounded, pulling her out of

her memory. The other novices stood, and she followed their example of folding away their mats. Everyone bowed to Ah-Ming, who then motioned for Jin to follow him.

"Is training over?" Jin asked.

"It is just beginning," Ah-Ming said as they passed through a moon gate and into a large courtyard where more initiates were training, only in combat.

"But it is ended for the day?" Jin pressed.

Ah-Ming considered her. "You expected more?"

"Not more, no," she said carefully.

Ah-Ming grunted. "As Marquis Sanjin says in his texts and teachings, the body follows the mind as surely as the tail follows the dog. Regardless of what you've heard, our training here focuses on the mind."

I have a feeling things grow rougher from here, Jin said.

One cannot cross a river one has not yet seen, Rayshan advised.

Though she was given her own room, Jin wasn't sure whether this was for her comfort or the others' protection. She had no doubt Sanjin had heard of her fights with the men in the dorms when she first entered Dragon Class, and he likely hoped to keep brawls to a minimum.

She had therefore been assigned a small storeroom off her wing's courtyard. One courtyard, she found, housed five wings, with the men sleeping together in groups of ten to a room. Her storeroom had been quickly converted at the last minute, with pieces of straw from brooms still dusting the floor, and nails on the walls showed where brushes were hung. Her bed was little more than a long wooden bench with a pallet thrown on, the simple clay pillow uneven compared to her smooth porcelain one in Meipin's apartments.

I've grown soft, she commented to Rayshan via their connection. *I've come to like comforts and silk sheets and lychees.*

The only other interaction she had was at the evening bell, when all initiates were required to report for the head count in the courtyard. A severe-looking man presided over the proceedings, which consisted of announcements about work shifts, new dorm rules, and laundry duty.

Standing next to the tall initiate from that morning and the one she guessed was from the west, she heard a soft chuckling and looked over.

"What's amusing?" she asked.

"You," the westerner replied. "Is it true you can't die?"

She braced herself in case it was a challenge. "Wish to find out?"

The westerner snorted. "No. You'll be Sanjin's favorite. He can do whatever he wants to you without remorse. I'm grateful not to be you."

"What a mouth," the tall one on Jin's other side muttered. "Ignore him. He's from Kwannay. Those bastards are all uncouth dogs."

Jin looked away. "I'm from Kwannay."

The westerner's shoulders shook with stifled laughter. "Whose mouth is worse now, Bean?" he hissed.

Bean reddened. "I didn't mean the women. I've known Kwannay women. All good stock and worth every *fei* I paid."

"I think you'd better stop, Bean," Jin said coldly.

"Bean's not my real name, you know. No one uses real names here."

"So who chose your name?" Jin asked.

"The squad," Bean answered. "You're Skyworm."

Jin glared at him, trying to see if he was jesting.

The warden rolled up his scroll. "That concludes today's announcements. What is the first law of the Veil?"

The courtyard echoed with the shouted answer. "Mission first! Life last! Empire always!"

The words sent ice down Jin's neck, and she hoped no one had noticed her subdued voice.

The warden barked for everyone to return to their dorms, and line by line the initiates marched toward their rooms. Jin noticed that everyone wore headbands that were either blue or grey.

"What do the different colors mean?" Jin asked Bean.

"Year level," he whispered back. "Blue for first years, grey for second."

"Is there a third?"

Bean gave a malicious chuckle. "Thank the heaven

and the earth, no. If you live to second year and pass the test, you enter the Veil."

"What's the test?"

"You're new, but did they tell you nothing?" the Westerner turned slightly.

"Just that I was going to be in a squad with dimwits."

Westie glared at her. "Eat what you please, but don't just speak what you please. You'll never pass the Iron Mind."

"What is that?"

"The final test," Bean answered, and his voice wavered. "A day-long interrogation."

"Which you won't have to worry about, skinny boy," Westie said. "Seeing as you won't live that long."

Bean pulled a face at their squad mate, who grinned before turning back to the front. They waited in silence. Jin chanced a glance back at Bean, who tried to turn his fear into a smirk.

"Must be nice to not fear dying every day."

Jin swallowed. "There are things worse than death."

"I guess that's true," Bean said. "And the Veil knows it."

CHAPTER 15

Tai sent an early message declaring that he would call upon the Royal Veil that afternoon at the hour of the rooster, with strict instructions that the Crown Prince wished to see the rider Jin.

As he suspected, a reply came, but he set off for the Veil grounds before the messenger entered his quarters, and once there in the reception room, the attendants were clearly flustered at his unexpected presence, as well as his charming protests that he had not received the message asking that he come another day.

The sight of Jin was both welcome and wrenching. She looked harder edged than even three days ago, when he last saw her at the performance. Her wide huren eyes had regained that suspicious gleam they had when he had first met her when she had stolen Rayshan's egg. He swore she had several more strands of white in her hair, and the lines around her eyes had deepened, which strangely gave her a refined look.

"Rider Jin," he said.

Her eyes darted to the Veil attendants standing by. "Your Highness troubles himself needlessly."

He swallowed. He knew of the Royal Veil having strict policies, but most were kept secret, with very few knowing the exact training that went on behind these walls. He sensed that Jin worried his presence would bring her unwelcome punishment.

He turned to the Veil guards. "You are dismissed. I wish to speak to rider Jin in private."

"We cannot. We are under orders to guard her at all times."

"As Minister of War, I outrank Marquis Sanjin, and if that doesn't persuade you, then might I remind you I am the crown prince. I order you to step outside." Protocol could go to the eight levels of hell.

The guards glanced at each other, until the head guard seemed to make a decision and bowed. "Yes, Your Highness."

They retreated, leaving Tai and Jin alone in the austere reception hall with its tiles that formed the word for "righteousness."

"How bad is it?" he said quietly.

Her eyes flicked to the door. She was strong, but wary, and Tai was reminded of a bow string pulled taut. Powerful, and capable of doing great harm, but also likely to snap at the slightest excess pressure.

"Not bad, Your Highness," she replied. "So far it's mostly meditation." A slight pull of the mouth told him that was not all, but that she didn't want to speak of it.

"I am trying to get you out." He gave his best flippant smile. "Unfortunately, my charm doesn't work as well on two women at court; you and my mother."

She shook her head. "There's nothing you can do, Your Highness. Only the empress can order Sanjin to let me out. And besides, if I don't go through with it . . ."

"What?" he asked when she trailed off.

"If I don't go through with it, the worst is yet to come." She paused. "Besides. They can't kill me. Not yet."

The little boy who feared Mengkhis worried that she would turn on him and his mother. But the grown-up man who was trying to resist her—and failing spectacularly—was hurt by her insinuation that he, or his mother, would dispose of her once Mengkhis was dead.

"I can get you out of here," he promised. He wasn't sure how—his mother seemed immovable, and openly defying her about Jin would embolden the empress's enemies, he knew. No matter what differences he had with his mother, turning against her would weaken both of them.

"Don't," she replied. "They'll punish me for special treatment by punishing my squad mates. I must get out of here on my own, or not at all."

He walked to a window. "You must hate my mother."

"I could never hate Her Majesty; she is the Celestial Ruler."

He turned. "Of course. Do you hate me?"

"I could never hate you, Your Highness."

Tai gave a humorless smile. "I hope to hear you mean that one day." At her starting to protest, he held up a hand. "Why don't we make a pact. I will not push for special treatment, but you agree to meet me once a week. And if you need this all to stop, you will tell me immediately."

She hesitated.

"I won't leave without your agreement," he said.

Jin nodded. "Agreed."

TAI SOUGHT out Sanjin's offices immediately, and a secretary scurried off to find his master. The head of the Royal Veil came in an admirably short time and bowed low, hands before him.

"Your Highness graces us."

"I wish to speak of the rider Jin."

"Ah yes," Sanjin said smoothly. "I understand Your Highness saw her just today. You found her in good health, I trust?"

"She could be in better."

Sanjin smiled. "Couldn't we all? Age has taken its

tithe, and I often envy Jin's health and immortality. It's no wonder you have a special interest in her."

There was no mistaking his meaning. "She is currently one of our greatest assets. I want to make sure you are treating her as such."

Sanjin's calm never faltered. "The War Minister honors us with his concern. But rider Jin cannot die. We can heal any injury she has."

"No doubt you can heal her body," Tai said, "but I think you overlook the mind and heart. Have you considered what happens if she breaks?"

"Not if. When. Breaking is part of the plan, Your Highness," Sanjin said. "How else can we put her back together the way we want?"

Tai wrestled his revulsion into his most charming smile. "What if you can't put her back together at all?"

"Your mother and I have much faith in our blood-bonded rider," Sanjin said. "Your Highness should as well."

"You're right," Tai agreed lightly. "Though my faith would be helped if I saw her privately each day, to ensure she is not being mistreated."

"I'm afraid that's not possible, Your Highness." Sanjin coughed. "Besides, surely your Prince and Princess of Dragons act is a show?"

Tai ignored the bait. "We need our weapon against Mengkhis Lai to be of sound mind and body."

Sanjin's lips pressed into a falsely obsequious line. "I must respectfully decline, Your Highness. That would be much too disruptive to Jin's training. And your mother specifically said I was to have full control of this matter." Sanjin paused. "Perhaps His Highness would like to take it up with Her Majesty?"

Tai gave an amiable smile, though he cursed Sanjin silently. The man knew very well that he had already discussed it with the empress, and was smug in his power. "Perhaps I shall."

CHAPTER 16

J in thought she wouldn't survive the first week of Veil training, despite her assurances to Prince Tai, and his offer grew more appealing each day.

The easy period of meditation ended on the fifth day. When she entered the morning's usual meditation routine with the others, she noted a conspicuous bamboo rod leaning against the courtyard pillar. Once everyone had retrieved their mats and sat down, the usual meditation practice began.

"Fill your minds with emptiness," Ah-Ming intoned, and Jin tried. She ignored the faint wisps of the dead hanging about in the corners, brushing the edges of her mind, and reached out to Rayshan.

A cane landed against her back, making her bite her tongue.

"You are not emptying your mind," Ah-Ming said tonelessly, as one would assess a chess move by an opponent. "Separate yourself from your body, and you will learn to do this." Ah-Ming moved to the one who looked like a fox, and whipped the bamboo across the initiate's shoulders, making a bright crimson welt rise like dough from the skin. Foxface shuddered slightly, a bare flicker of muscle.

"Choose your Zen place, and go to it," Ah-Ming said. "It is a fortress. A place where pain cannot enter. What is your safe place, person of no worth?"

Jin almost laughed. She had no safe places. From a young age she had been taught to fear and suspect everything and everyone. Everyone had an agenda, everyone would stab her in the back, there was a danger behind every corner, a poison in every bite. No one to trust.

That's not true.

Rayshan's voice in her head calmed her, and she reached out, grasping on to that. Rayshan was her safe place. Rayshan was her haven. As long as her mind touched Rayshan's, she would be . . .

The bamboo bit her again.

The searing pain made her hiss, and she had to clench her fists to keep from striking back at Ah-Ming.

"Better. Whatever you have created, it's better," he said. "But not perfect. Think of it, envision it, then let nothing distract you from it."

She reached out to Rayshan, who hummed in welcome, trying his best to support her from where he was. She envisioned him curled around himself, wings folded, and that warm spot just behind his foreleg where she liked to curl under his wing. The way she had slept in the Singing Sands when they had burrowed together after blood bonding, when she had been protected and safe.

He hummed in agreement, and she almost sensed him nestle closer, his warm scales against her face . . . something stung her, like a wasp, but she ignored it, nestling further into him, smelling the sun on his wings and scales . . .

"Good," Ah-Ming murmured. "Now stand."

Jin reluctantly left the haven she had created with Rayshan and stood. Immediately pain lanced her back, and she gritted her teeth as she reached behind her to feel blood sticking her undershirt to her skin.

"You didn't cry out at the three lashes I gave you," Ah-Ming said. "You are learning one of Marquis Sanjin's first rules: pain is only in your mind."

Ah-Ming repeated this exercise the next day, and the next. "Name the pain. Box it for later."

Jin's back was soon a crisscross of welts, though she noted Ah-Ming was skilled in delivering blows that would pain but not scar.

On the ninth day, Ah-Ming had desks brought in, with paper, brushes and ink. Each had a set of equations, and as they sat at the desks, Ah-Ming pointed at a water clock on his own desk.

"Work out the answers as quickly as you can. My assistant will count out to twenty, when you will receive a lash. You have managed to bear lashes without flinching, but now you will need to bear them while also using your mind. Your mastery of your own haven is only half of the test here."

Jin looked down at the equations and recoiled. As a thief she had a rudimentary understanding of additions and subtractions, could work out quick sets of multiples, but that was all. Numbers, especially into the thousands, had never been necessary. She forced a calming breath and did not think of how long this next test would feel. Or how painful.

"Begin!"

Jin picked up her brush and dipped it in ink.

"One! Two! Three!" The assistant's voice was surprisingly strong for one so reedy.

Jin quickly did the simplest equations, willing her hand to not shake in anticipation of the coming lash.

"Four! Five! Six!"

Four tenths of one hundred. Four tenths of one hundred.

One hundred was ten tenths.

Four tenths were forty. She wrote this down.

"Twelve! Thirteen! Fourteen!"

Ten thousand coppers, two thousand ingots, and three thousand fei made . . .

"Fifteen! Sixteen! Seventeen!"

Ten thousand coppers were more than fifty thousand *fei*, which would be—

"Eighteen! Nineteen! Twenty!"

She heard the rod land on Westie next to her, then across her back, and the sting made her hiss.

Rayshan's voice rumbled through her head.

Ignore the counting. It's there to distract you.

He was right. The miserable little assistant had been chosen for his distracting voice.

Knowing when the lash would strike only built dread, rather than preparation. Ignoring her time limit would free her mind.

Jin drew a breath and closed her hearing to ignore the assistant, then looked at the equations again. Ten thousand coppers, fifty thousand fei, two thousand ingots . . . she wrote her answer.

The lash landed again, drawing another sharp hiss from her and tears to her eyes, but she forced herself on until she had finished the page. When she straightened, her back on fire, she saw everyone else had completed theirs already.

"Too slow," Ah-Ming commented. "We will do this until you can calmly complete the equations within a *ke* on the clock, even with the lash." Ah-Ming held out the bamboo rod to his assistant. "That is enough for now. And, Jin, I think you'll enjoy tomorrow's session much more, as we will have dragon company."

Jin wasn't sure whether this was a comfort or not. Being with Rayshan would make it better, but Ah-Ming saying she would enjoy it only made her think the opposite.

As she joined her squad mates in the dorms for the

evening meal, Foxface motioned toward a servant in the doorway striding toward them. "Looks like the marquis wants you."

The messenger was indeed there for her, telling her in clipped tones that she was to follow him. Jin tamped down her hunger pangs and followed the man to the ornate office the Marquis occupied in the north wing.

This was the first time she had entered his Veil offices, and she noted the sumptuous, though eccentric, décor. Buddhist statues stood at each corner, and the floor's mosaics were a shocking white. Most people disliked white floors because of white's association with death.

Probably why he likes it, Rayshan remarked in her mind.

"Congratulations on your first week with the Veil."

Jin spied Sanjin enter from an adjoining room, his robes immaculate and the faint smell of soap wafting from him. She wondered whether he had come straight from tormenting someone.

He regarded her for a time before sitting at his desk. He folded his hands in his sleeves. "So, will you be asking the prince to save you?"

Her blood chilled. Though she had feared unseen ears at doorways, it was quite another for Sanjin to so boldly confirm it.

He leaned forward. "I highly advise against it. There are those at court who wish for the prince to openly defy his mother. She placed you here in my training. If the crown prince removes you without permission, it will be tantamount to rebellion. And the punishment for rebellion is death."

Jin swallowed. Though lying was second nature to Sanjin, it was logical that the prince had enemies.

"No mother would kill her own son," Jin replied.

Sanjin folded his sleeves back. "She might not have a choice, if the evidence was presented so starkly. Any sage advisor would tell her to execute him for open defiance."

Jin's back prickled all along her fresh welts. Though she had tried to shut the thought down, she had occasionally wondered if he would keep his word. Not that she would ask him to, but it had been a welcome safety net, helping her face each day.

"The prince is popular and loved by all," Jin said. The naivety of it made her cringe even as she said it.

"As head of the Royal Veil, I know exactly how many plots there are against the crown prince, and who will be whetting their carving knives should he fall." He sat back, regarding her. "The prince has asked to meet with you once a week. As he is the crown prince, of course I happily agreed. But I thought you might wish to know, he is not as invincible as you may think." Sanjin watched her. "And frankly, even if you do not wish to protect the prince, I think we share a common goal. A goal that requires Veil training if you are to attain it."

"And what is that, Marquis Sanjin?"

"Killing Mengkhis Lai and keeping the empire safe." He leaned forward. "Despite what you might think, you are not here for punishment." Though she kept her face emotionless, he seemed to sense her disbelief. "Few know what I am about to tell you."

She waited as Sanjin poured another cup of tea.

"Mengkhis Lai is a graduate of the Royal Veil."

Jin blinked. "He was a prince. Why would he be—"

"An adopted prince," Sanjin corrected her. "He was not the finest student, but certainly the most brutal. Some might say that this place . . . created him."

Jin digested this. Somehow, it made perfect sense that the man who had slaughtered so many at Jimo would come out of a place like this, a place that Sanjin loved and nurtured. Her stomach churned. "So . . . you're making me into Mengkhis Lai?"

"No. We would never wish to do that. But we are giving you his training, so that you can understand how he thinks, what his strengths are. By making you understand what he went through, we are giving you the best chance of defeating him once you find him. One must fight poison with poison, after all. As difficult as it may be to believe, this training is to save you, not torment you."

The torment is simply the embroidered lining on the robe, as they say, Jin thought bitterly. A thought occurred to her.

"Did Mengkhis choose to train here? Or did someone make him?"

"A very astute question, person of no worth. He chose it. He knew that out of the hottest fire comes the strongest steel." Sanjin cocked his head. "A lesson I hope you believe."

During her walk back to her dorms, Jin mulled over Sanjin's words. He had no reason to lie about Mengkhis Lai's time at the Veil, and she had to admit that it made sense. If Mengkhis had been forged in this crucible, then he was truly a hardened and formidable enemy, even more of a threat than she thought.

Anyone who chooses this training must be sick.

People choose paths for different reasons, Rayshan rumbled back.

Her Dragon Class training had made her into a honed fighter, but as much as she hated to admit it, she recognized the weaknesses as well. There was less emphasis on hand-to-hand combat, no training in how to withstand pain or think through it—because their dragons' protection meant that riders seldom experienced capture or torture, unlike the common Veil member.

And as for the crown prince, by all rights she should not worry for him so much. He had played political games all his life and could take care of himself. What business of it was hers if he and his mother were at odds?

If she does execute him, then we are back where we started, Rayshan reasoned. *With the prince's death added to the tally.*

True, she said. *Not to mention I can't do that to Tai.*

He's been nothing but kind, I admit.

Only because he wants me to slay his enemy.

Rayshan's snort was half contempt, half amusement. *That's not why.*

Jin made a gesture to slap Rayshan's flank, but realized he wasn't physically there.

Then the only way through this is to survive the training, she sighed.

That, or find and kill Mengkhis Lai, Rayshan mused.

Doubt slithered through her mind.

What if they don't let us go after? What if the empress and Sanjin are lying?

I trust the prince's word, but not theirs.

In this, as with most things, she and Rayshan agreed.

CHAPTER 17

The next day, a Veil attendant escorted her to Dragon City, where she greeted Rayshan, and he nudged her gently on the back, making her wince.

They will heal.

Yes, she said, gritting her teeth. The Veil kept a specially assigned mage to heal the initiates, and even now her wounds were entirely closed and fading.

Jin mounted Rayshan and wished the flight down to the Veil training grounds would last forever. She didn't want to dismount. This was only her tenth day training with Sanjin, but it felt like an eternity. And once more she'd have to assure the prince she was fine.

When they landed, another dragon and rider were already waiting. The gold dragon stood next to a tall rider with coarse black hair that he wore in a top knot. Jin recognized him as the haughty one from Champa.

Sanjin stood to one side, a table with a tea set already prepared. The sight of Sanjin with tea always set Jin on edge, for there was a reason being invited to tea with Sanjin was synonymous with torture. Going to the tea rooms was a euphemism for interrogation.

She reached out to the gold, but he snarled when he felt her mental touch.

"Leave Ganmu alone," the rider growled.

Sanjin smiled. "Jin is a special rider, as you can see, Tulang. She can speak to your dragon, and we will get to that. But today, I want to train you in other things." Sanjin smiled at Jin. "Are you ready?"

"For what?" She asked, wary.

But then a nausea took hold, and Jin doubled over. This was familiar. She had known this once before, back in Khitan. "Ganmu . . ."

The rider smirked as Sanjin said calmly, "Yes, we've been practicing the art of drawing metal out of a person's body, and I'm happy to say Ganmu shows great talent."

The feeling eased, and Jin slowly rose, clutching her stomach. King Ulagan of Khitan had done the same to her with his dragons, for he had trained them to draw the metals out of a body using their powers.

"This is against the rules, Emar said," Jin accused Sanjin.

Sanjin shrugged. "Emar is dead. And I make the rules. The empress agreed with me, after everything that happened in Khitan, that we would be remiss to not train our own dragons to use such powers."

A thought occurred to Jin. "Then what about the other dragons?"

Sanjin's eyes lit up. "Oh yes, we've been working on those as well. My favorite is what the water dragons can do. It is quite something to watch the water being drained from a human being, so they desiccate before your eyes. Rather like a grape in the sun, though much faster, of course. Would you like to see it?"

Jin didn't want to see anything less. But she decided not to give Sanjin the satisfaction.

"Time enough for that," Sanjin said, sipping his tea. "I think we should start our practice. Rider Tulang's goal will be to break you. Of course, your goal is to not break, and use whatever abilities you can to make him stop."

The words were barely out of his mouth before Tulang, clearly an eager pupil, gave his gold the command again. Jin went to her knees, and she felt her insides would rupture.

Rayshan's roaring brought her back. *We have to flare!*

Jin focused on her *qi*, her inner energy that was linked to all the energies of the universe, living or dead. For energy did not disappear, it only scattered, like wood turned to ash. The trick with summoning the dead was a little like turning ash back into a log—taking the transformed pieces that had fractured into numerous tiny motes and putting them back together in their unique way. A woman stood in the courtyard between her and Tulang.

"Stop this, Tulang," the woman said, and the rider's eyes widened.

The pull on Jin's insides immediately halted. Tulang slowly approached the woman, disbelieving. "Sister?"

The woman smiled and put out a hand to hold Tulang's. She had the same cheekbones and eyes but was at least a head shorter. "Elder brother?" Her eyes widened. "What is this place? Is that your dragon?"

Tulang seemed too stunned for words. Jin slowly stood. She had seen reunions like this before and knew they would be short-lived.

But she didn't know how short.

Sanjin moved forward like a ghost and brought his hand smashing into the woman's face. She crumpled to the floor and then dissolved into ash, while Tulang cried out.

Sanjin rounded on Tulang, his gaze cold. The rider looked stricken, but at last pulled himself in and stood straight-backed, tense but unprotesting.

"I am glad to see your conjuring abilities are becoming more precise," Sanjin said to Jin. "But in a battle situation, you should have run through Tulang when you had the chance." He turned to the rider. "And you would have been a pig at slaughter if Jin had been the enemy. Now again."

Tulang and his gold renewed their assault on Jin,

but this time she was ready. Instead of summoning the dead, she thought of her haven, the crook in Rayshan's body where she was safe.

She locked the pain away in a small, tight box, giving it no room to move or expand and fill her. She advanced on Tulang, willing her feet forward. Normally her blood bond strength would give her enough power to overcome him, but even when she ignored the pain, the pulling of metals weakened her. Her limbs felt like a stranger's and didn't obey her. She took one step toward him, then another, until she felt she would collapse, and still the bands around her insides tightened.

Darkness pressed in, and though she summoned, only shadows of the dead appeared. She and Rayshan were in too much pain, unable to focus enough to manifest the dead properly. Bile rose in her, and her hands shook, until Rayshan managed to blast a torrent of flame at Ganmu.

The gold dragon screeched in agony as the flame hit his tail, and the pain inside Jin immediately eased.

But relief was short as everything went dark.

THE WOMAN STOOD in the corner of Jin's room like a waiting maid, only she was no maid.

Her clothes were too foreign, and completely

unsuitable for the weather. Jin recognized her—she had been in the crowd at the farewell, when she had left for Champa. Fur lined her vest and long skirt, where an elaborate brocade panel stretched from belt to floor. Her hair, the color of burnished copper, was braided into thick plaits that framed a hauntingly delicate face with wide, tapered eyes.

There was something familiar about her, something elusive. Jin knew she was a phantasm, not the flesh and blood that came from intense concentration. Rayshan was flaring in his sleep.

The woman turned her back on Jin. The room around them dissolved into a white, wind-swept tundra. Jin followed.

They walked for what seemed an eternity, until a dim fire glowed out of the distance. There was a cave, Jin realized.

And sitting there was Mengkhis Lai, sharpening a blade over the stones, the flames of the fire lighting his dead eyes.

Jin screamed.

She woke on the cold floor of an apartment, the tundra gone.

Were these her apartments? Meipin's? No, the tile was different. She pushed herself up and saw she had fallen from a bed. It was a very ornate bed carved in serpents and flowers, the silken sheeting askew and spotted with blood.

Her blood, she knew instinctively. She reached out for Rayshan and nearly cried when she heard his reassuring hum.

What happened?

You fainted.

I gathered that.

I fantasize about killing Sanjin slowly.

I'm not sure I care about the speed. Just that we get to do it.

Rayshan growled his agreement.

She remembered Sanjin's look, the pride in Tulang's eyes. Emar said using a dragon's power on people was not allowed. And she understood why. It meant torturing people. She was sure Sanjin would argue that the people he used were criminals, but in Jin's view that made no difference. Jin, after all, had once been a criminal. Her best friends had been criminals. It didn't mean they deserved that.

The empress knows he uses these methods, she thought bitterly. Meipin is right: the empress's beauty hides beastly cruelty.

Jin stood, though her bones protested. The welts on her back were nearly gone. She had been asleep for more than a day then. She remembered that yesterday was when Tai had meant to visit. Had he come? Or had he forgotten?

Jin went to splash her face in the basin of water next to the bed. She felt she should know who the woman was, yet she also knew without a doubt that she had never seen her before. Why did she keep appearing?

The door opened, and a maid entered, bowing. "I brought you soup and rice. Marquis Sanjin says you must eat."

So she was in Marquis Sanjin's rooms. The thought was repulsive.

The maid came forward and put the tray down, transferring delicate porcelain bowls of a fragrant broth and steaming rice to the table. She reached into her sleeve and pulled out a letter, holding it out.

"For you, from the crown prince."

Jin took the letter, and Jin noted the crumbled clay seal. Clearly, Sanjin had already read Tai's message.

To the Esteemed Rider Wang Kway Jin,

I called on you as agreed, but was informed you were indisposed. I am most concerned, as your safety and well-being are paramount. I await word from you that you are well and will call again next week.

Respectfully,

Crown Prince Tai

Knowing he had visited comforted her more than she expected.

As she asked the maid to fetch a brush and paper for a reply, her thoughts circled back to Rayshan's advice.

The only way out of this was to find Mengkhis and kill him. The prince would make sure Sanjin didn't break her, but she would have to pass the Veil.

WHEN JIN next flew with Rayshan, she let him burn off energy for the first hour, then suggested they land near one of their favorite spots, Splendid Jade Mountain, a short flight south of the city.

Today the mountain was shrouded in rain clouds, and only the odd Buddhist monk from a nearby temple occupied the lake's shores, selecting rocks. Rayshan preferred the high granite cliffs surrounding the placid lake, and they sat there together for a time, watching the surroundings below.

You are debating something.

As usual, Rayshan knew her thoughts better than she did. *I thought we'd use the Firesong. It may show us recent memories from Baikalan, and if it does, then we'd know if Mengkhis has found him.*

Rayshan lashed his tail. *I dislike Baikalan's memories,* he growled.

I know. I dislike Mengkhis's just as much. She had seen things she never wanted to see again. But if it was her one way to find Mengkhis Lai, and end her current life with the Veil, then she had to try it.

Very well, Rayshan huffed. It took him a little longer to enter the Firesong, for beneath his calming thoughts, Jin still heard the Song of Scales, pulling all the time.

Her worries for Rayshan eroded as she homed in on the Firesong. It was like a rich tapestry of music, just underneath the sound of Rayshan's thoughts and emotions, until the music became colors, many of which had no name. She remembered the first time, when Rayshan had explained that dragons saw in more colors than humans.

She leaned into it, letting the Firesong flow around her. She had learned to let Rayshan be her guide in this, and so she waited, patient.

The colors and sounds coalesced into a pulsing light, and she followed. As the light enveloped her, it slowly eased into shapes, a sound. The sound of wings. Dragon wings.

She tried to focus, letting Rayshan home in on this part of the Firesong. Let it be a Baikalan memory. She needed a clue as to Mengkhis's whereabouts.

Images formed, and the sound of dragon wings faded. She was in a room, dominated by a great ornate bed carved with dragons. She frowned, then realized she had seen this room before.

She stepped toward the bed and recognized the empress—or rather, a younger version of the empress —sitting tangled in the sheets, her skin shiny with sweat and her hair disheveled, cradling a baby whose face was still blotchy with childbirth.

"Precious child," the empress said softly.

A figure entered the room, and like last time Jin had seen this in the Firesong, his face was hidden.

"He's on his way. He wants to see the prince."

The empress's mouth contorted, and Jin wondered if she would be pulled out of the Firesong like last time, when the force of the empress's emotions had seemed to sever Jin's focus. She held on, and the memory flickered but stayed.

"Stall him," the empress whispered.

"I cannot, Lady Wu," the figure said. "You must do it. It's now or never."

Jin's heart stilled. She couldn't see the face, but she thought the voice sounded familiar. She just needed to hear him speak again—

Bone-numbing cold wrapped around her like a fist, and the colors all withered into grey, then black, then blinding white. Jin leaned her palms against the ground as her real vision returned, and took deep breaths as Rayshan tucked a protective tail around her.

Are you hurt?

She shook her head. *Why does seeking Baikalan always take us to that memory?*

I do not know.

Another thought occurred to her. She had seen Mengkhis's experience at Jimo through his eyes. Was she seeing this scene in the Firesong in a similar way? In which case, Mengkhis had been at Tai's birth, yet the empress and the figure who entered had not acknowledged his presence at all.

That left only one explanation: Mengkhis had been spying on the empress and Tai within the palace the night of Tai's birth. Perhaps he had used his powers of invisibility.

But why? Jin wondered.

Regardless, it gives me the shivers, Rayshan snarled.

CHAPTER 18

A royal summons came to Jin during morning meditations, with instructions to report to the Blood Oval.

At first, she was puzzled, but then she remembered. It had been a week since she'd sent the prince her response, assuring him she was well and that he needn't check on her weekly.

It seemed he had ignored her, and part of her was dangerously glad. At least he had moved their meeting to outside the Veil's walls, given Sanjin's spies.

When she arrived, she found Prince Tai already in riding gear, no royal insignia or hint of imperial yellow to be seen, waiting with two other dragonriders and their black dragons.

Tai's easy expression slipped, and she knew he had seen a new mark left by one of Ah-Ming's more careless swings of the bamboo. He usually left anything that might be publicly visible unscathed. "What happened last week?"

"Nothing I won't survive," she said simply.

She thought she detected a wince and an apology forming, but then he smoothed it over with a glance at the other dragonriders.

"I thought we'd ride. If Rayshan is willing."

Evidently glad for any chance to fly, Rayshan barely protested Tai's wanting to mount as well when she broached it. Jin headed toward Dragon City, Tai walking with her. Today, he smelled of resinous agarwood and a hint of myrrh.

"Where are we going?" she asked.

"To fetch Rayshan."

"No, I mean after," Jin said. She would have been impatient if it was anyone else, but Tai managed to make his playful levity seem unforced.

"I was in the mood for the best noodles in the empire," Tai replied.

This time, Jin gave in to an exasperated look. Having to resist his offer of help was one thing. Having to do it while he jested chafed her.

"Very well. I wanted to talk about something. Away from palace ears. Is that better?"

She nodded but decided to leave further questions for later. Once she had prepared Rayshan's saddle and adjusted it so Tai could ride behind, she mounted and reached down for Tai's hand.

He pulled himself up but had barely gotten his legs

in place when Rayshan bounded forward and leapt out of the cave, spewing fire in a defiant halo.

Tai clung to her, and Jin made sure he was safely strapped before turning to focus on the flight.

The other two dragonriders rose into the sky next to them, and Jin asked Rayshan to follow.

Where are we going? the dragon asked her.

I don't know.

Rayshan growled but then chuckled. *Actually, I do not care.*

Jin agreed. The feeling of flying would never dull, and since the last week of Veil training had meant limited flying time, both she and Rayshan were thrilled with the freedom.

Rayshan even pulled high and then dived, making Jin whoop with delight until she caught a glimpse of Tai's green face behind her and felt his knuckles digging into her belly.

"I'm sorry, Your Highness!"

She cautioned Rayshan to be gentler. *I forgot. He fears heights.*

Then he shouldn't have climbed on board a dragon! Rayshan answered maliciously. He twisted midair, his wings curling ever so slightly into a plunge, until Jin worried Tai might actually be sick. Rayshan's playfulness was tinged with a reckless spite that felt unlike him, and Jin suspected it was the frustration of resisting the call to Nine Claw Mountain.

Easy, Rayshan.

Rayshan defiantly did a few more, eliciting a stream or two of fire from the other dragons, until Jin begged him to stop, and gradually they evened out. Though Tai didn't complain, his tightly locked hands hinted that vomiting was still a distinct possibility.

"What did you wish to speak about?" she asked over the wind. Conversation would distract her passenger from his stomach.

"I needed to get away from the palace. All this talk of war with Khitan depresses me."

"A Minister of War who doesn't like battle?"

"That's why I'm most qualified," Tai replied. "If we never go to war under my term, I'll consider myself a success."

"Sometimes it's necessary to fight," Jin said. "Some men don't understand any language other than violence."

"Tell me, then, would you advise invading Khitan?"

"I am but a person of no worth, Your Highness. I cannot advise you," she said.

"That's the Veil talking," Tai said sharply. "I'm asking Jin, my crow's mouth, who will tell me the truth."

She was silent, letting his words sink in. She had explained to him the concept of a crow's mouth—the bird's cry was ugly but spoke truth when it heralded unwelcome news: death. Had she said she was a person of no worth because she wanted to avoid Tai's question, or was she really starting to lose herself to the Veil? The thought shook her.

She drew a breath. "In my thief days, we faced many rival clans. But we never took over a clan. We always found ways of negotiating, because killing a clan boss and taking their men just opened us to being stabbed in the back." She paused. "The Khitans will never love the Tang and will only resent you more if you invade or crush them. Especially if they must kneel to a woman."

"What would you propose?"

Jin thought on it, watching the lands below. "You'd have to exterminate them. Which isn't realistic. Or give them something they want, in exchange for absolute loyalty."

Tai was so quiet that she thought she had offended him, but then he shifted closer.

"They want greater lands, which we are loath to give them."

"Why not ask for Nobu's hand," Jin replied. "A blood tie would avoid war."

"Wise counsel," he said. "But you're forgetting one thing."

"What's that, Your Highness?"

"What's to say that Princess Nobu would agree?"

Jin shrugged. "She might not. But you have much to offer, being crown prince."

"Ah, a marriage for power," he said drily. "That always leads to a happy union."

She didn't bother pointing out that most marriages

were not arranged for happiness. "It may not be purely for power. You have your attributes."

"Such as?"

"You are fair. Compassionate. Not to mention charming, Your Highness. You charm the birds from the trees."

"Please. Don't stop there."

She bit back a curse. He was toying with her. She wasn't used to censoring herself up here on Rayshan's back, for she was usually alone, free, with only Rayshan to converse with.

His hands loosened, though it seemed his body pressed closer. "Was that a compliment? You may become a true court lady after all."

"I doubt it, Your Highness."

"Good. I'd hate to see you turn into everyone else."

Just then, Rayshan dove again, and though it silenced Tai, it also made him grip her tighter, until it was hard to breathe.

The dragonriders ahead signaled for landing, and Tai muttered something that sounded like a prayer of thanks.

The dragons banked, then spiraled down, and Jin spied a small village sitting in the middle of pine-green rice paddies. Flat, low-roofed houses with brick walls lined clean-swept streets, but the town was otherwise nondescript. It certainly was not large enough to have a Dragon Class garrison, and Jin wondered at what attraction this place held for the prince.

They landed in a field behind a two-storied tavern with wooden benches and stools, and the village children gathered in doorways and behind walls to gawk.

"Where are we?" Judging by how long they had flown and their direction, Jin guessed they were somewhere outside Luoyang, the second-largest city in the empire.

"The best noodle seller this side of the Yellow River," Tai answered, sliding down from the dragon and doing an impressive job of looking strong-legged. The other dragonriders surveyed the area, looking for threats, before nodding to Tai to go ahead.

Jin glanced back at Rayshan.

I am fine.

But the way he eyed some of the nearby oxen gave Jin worry. Oxen were a family's main way of tilling fields and, hence, valued. Few ate beef, even in imperial circles.

No eating the livestock.

Then don't be too long, Rayshan advised, lashing his tail.

"Are you coming or not?" Tai called.

Jin turned from Rayshan reluctantly, for his new churlishness disturbed her. She would have to think of ways to ease his mood later. She followed Tai into the tavern, where only a few patrons sat. Some of them glanced up, but none stared, and Jin wondered if this was a frequent stop for dragonriders on their way to Luoyang.

A burly woman in her early sixties came out of the back, her plump face breaking into a surprised but delighted smile at the sight of Tai.

"Your—"

"Yes! I'm back," Tai hastily cut her off, and the woman flushed. The crown prince was not meant to travel with so few people, let alone incognito. But Jin sensed the woman knew Tai's identity. "Good to see you, Grandmother. It's my fellow rider's birthday, so I thought I'd bring her for a bowl of your longevity noodles."

Jin frowned. "It's not my birthday."

Tai raised an eyebrow, as if to say, "Are you sure?"

This brought Jin up short. She didn't know, but it was sometime in the fifth month, as that was what Haitao had said. And it matched the birth document from the prisons. But Haitao had never told her what day and had certainly never once celebrated a birthday with her.

The plump woman was already ushering her and Tai to a seat outside, however, and before long she found herself sitting opposite Tai.

"How do you know her?" Jin asked.

"She's my nursemaid's mother," Tai confided. "When my nursemaid died from the plague, I promised I would take care of her family. So I do what I can to bring customers."

Jin doubted very much that was all Tai did to help the woman, judging by the new roof beams, fresh paint, and finely crafted furniture, all of which made this the finest tavern on the village street. But her questions died in her throat. She knew Tai to be kind, but this was an act of great respect that she would never have predicted.

The elderly lady returned with two bowls of steaming noodles, each heaped with a generous serving of pork knuckle, crispy cabbage, and scallions.

"Eat," Tai said. "They're not good cold. And remember, don't break them."

Long noodles were traditional for birthdays, symbolizing long life, but Jin had never eaten them. Jin took the chopsticks, then put them down.

"Why are you doing this?" she asked quietly.

Tai looked at her in surprise, the noodles hanging from his mouth like a waterfall. He shoveled them in, unhurried, and Jin marveled at how he made even this motion seem regal. "I said I would check on you."

"Why not come to the Veil, see me, and leave?"

"I thought you could use a birthday."

"Thank you. But honestly, why do this, Your Highness? For me?"

He swallowed, seemingly debating his words. "You may not realize, but you're not the only one missing Aadan." At her look, he said, "He was—is—my best friend. So now that he's gone, I took the liberty of imposing on you for some company." He smiled. "It then occurred to me that you had never celebrated a birthday, and I thought, why not today?"

The mention of Aadan pressed a bruise in her but also brought the sting of shame. She had always assumed that Tai's interest in her was due to her ability to kill Mengkhis Lai, but sometimes, as now, he seemed to genuinely care. Besides, he was perhaps the only one at court, besides her, to truly miss Aadan.

"I hadn't realized you had only him as a friend, Your Highness."

Tai didn't look up from his noodles. "Someone once told me that I have allies, not friends. And I suppose that's true."

His words made her think of Sanjin's hint at plots against the prince. Had he been telling the truth? "At least you don't have any enemies. Besides Mengkhis."

His glance at her sharpened. "I have had enemies just for drawing breath."

Jin hadn't expected the steel in his tone, and looked away.

"Why do you bring up Mengkhis?" he asked.

She debated telling him about Sanjin's theory. But what would that achieve? If he knew about his enemies, then what she said wouldn't be news. Besides, if she killed Mengkhis, she would solve her own problems, without adding to his. But what if he had allies to come to his aid? What if in a political skirmish with his mother, he won? An empire ruled by Tai sounded better than one ruled by his mother, where Jin would be forced to endure the Veil until Mengkhis Lai surfaced.

"Just that many seem to love you," Jin said, sticking to truths. "You will make a good emperor."

He swallowed a mouthful of noodles. "Multiple compliments in one day. Careful, Rider, you are losing that hard exterior you have cultivated for so long."

"I'm not the only one with a carefully cultivated exterior, Your Highness."

He gave a convincing look of innocence, then, at her expression, bowed his head in agreement. "I'll admit I try to please when I can. But I would like to think that we are truthful with each other and can put aside the masks." He took a breath. "Which is why I'd like to ask you again, do you want me to take you out of the Veil?"

Jin carefully poked at a piece of shredded egg in her noodles. "I don't think that would be wise."

"I didn't ask if it was wise," he said evenly. "I asked if you wanted me to."

"It will cause a rift between you and your mother, Your Highness."

She hadn't expected the storm of emotions that flickered across his face, some gone so quickly she missed them, but some plain between the cracks: hurt, shock, and for just a heartbeat, anger.

"My relationship with my mother is my affair, Rider. You are this empire's best defense against Mengkhis Lai, and we need you. As a rider, an ally, and —" he paused, as if something had caught in his throat "—a friend."

"I thought Aadan was your only friend."

"Let's say I'm working on another one." He rested his chopsticks against his bowl. "You don't have much faith in me, it seems."

"If the empress crushes you, I will have no one else to speak out for me."

He smiled. "Then it sounds like we need each other."

She sipped her broth, watching him over the bowl. "If I kill Mengkhis Lai, then I will be freed from the Veil. And you won't have to cross your mother."

"We are doing everything we can to find him." He regarded her. "And I am sure you've been going over the libraries again. Any luck?"

"No," she admitted.

"Will you tell me if you do find something?" He had a way of making one want to agree to anything he said. A dangerous trait and one that Haitao would have delighted in if he'd ever gotten his clutches on the prince.

"Yes, Your Highness."

"I almost believe you. You're very good at lies, you know."

"A thief doesn't survive on truth."

He regarded her thoughtfully. "I suppose not. Here's a truth. I didn't have anything to do with the accident at the Well, and I would never condone it. Do you believe me?"

"I believe you." He visibly relaxed. "But I can't say the same of Sanjin."

"And by Sanjin, you mean my mother." At her look of denial, he shook his head. "You needn't play cautious with me. I know what she is capable of, and you have every right to dislike her. I hate her sometimes, and she's my mother."

The shock of the words said aloud sat between them. To say one hated one's parent was tantamount to inviting hell to open.

"Your mother and I . . ." Jin started, but then stopped. To say anything would be treasonous, and so she swallowed her resentment and opted for something that was still true. "For what it's worth, she loves you greatly. I know that."

He regarded her. "Because of what you saw in the Firesong?" She had told him of the vision once, when he had admitted that sometimes he felt the empress was disappointed at not having a daughter.

Jin nodded. "I was trying to enter Mengkhis's memories to find anything that would help us. Somehow, we keep ending up at that memory."

Tai's features darkened. "I guess time has not dulled his urgent desire to kill me. At least I'm not a helpless babe in arms now."

"No, you're not," she said. "And I intend to get to him first."

At this, he chuckled. "If you kill him, that'll be twice you've saved my life. I'll have to marry you."

She winced.

"It was a jest," he said. "Though I sometimes wish you lied a little better about your feelings. Some people do consider me a catch, you know."

She sipped her soup. "I'm wondering if it's wise to keep up the charade of the Prince and Princess of Dragons."

"What is it with you and doing what's wise today?" he said, leaning back and crossing his arms. "But do tell me what is so unwise."

"It sets up an expectation," Jin said. "An impossible one. And it hurts others."

He raised an eyebrow. "Who?"

"Meipin." In this, Jin decided to not mince words. She had to make the prince see sense.

"Meipin is a wonderful woman," Tai said. "But she has no love for me. As a matter of fact, between the two of us, I think *you'd* have a better chance of pleasing her." At her narrowed eyes, he continued, "Yes, I know of her and Ahlu. So she won't be heartbroken if I don't return her courtship."

Jin pushed her bowl away. "Your Highness, it's about more than emotions. She has been groomed for this part and hopes to become your empress one day."

"First you want me to marry Nobu, and now Meipin," he said tersely. "Anyone else you wish to put forward?"

Jin sighed. "I hope Meipin becomes empress, because she would be good. But will your subjects, and the court, accept her if we've been promoting the Prince and Princess of Dragons?"

He leaned forward. "Did she ask you to say this?"

"No."

He leaned back. "You're lying again."

Jin cursed inwardly. Her skills as a thief were clearly slipping. Either that, or the prince was getting to know her too well, and that was even more disconcerting.

"I admire your loyalty to your friend," Tai said, standing up and placing a bag of coins that was far too generous for noodles on the table. "But I have other considerations in who to marry."

"If it's about other women, Your Highness, you can take concubines," Jin argued. "Meipin would never oppose you."

"What if I didn't want concubines?" he asked. "And just wanted one wife?"

"Then you'd be the first in China's history," she replied. "It would be . . . scandalous."

He seemed to like this thought. "It's worth doing for that alone."

CHAPTER 19

Tai returned to the palace both invigorated and restless, making him only too eager to lose himself in Mage Situ Han's training.

His trip with Jin had stirred many concerns he usually kept under control: his anger toward his mother, his deep unease about Mengkhis being loose, his increasing resentment over the fact that the Son of Heaven commanded armies and dragons but traditionally had little say over his own marriage.

"You are unsettled," Situ Han remarked as Tai bent over, panting and streaming with sweat, after making a rock float on water for a full *ke* on the water clock. The mage held out a kerchief, which Tai took.

"Just engrossed," the prince replied, wiping his face.

"Your skills are improving greatly, Your Highness," Situ Han said. "I hope your mother can be pleased when she finds out."

Tai regarded him. "What makes you think she wouldn't?"

The mage spread his palms. "She favors the Buddhists over the Ministry of Mages, that's all. And who can blame her? The Buddhists do not value men over women. Unlike the traditionalists."

"And mages ban women from their ranks," Tai said.

Situ Han nodded. "It's natural she should lean toward Buddhism. But many feel the Buddhists are becoming avaricious."

"You want me to speak to her?" Tai asked. He had never been able to completely shake the suspicion that Situ Han was trying to groom him.

Mage Situ Han bowed. "I do not want anything of you, except for you to follow your own counsel, Your Highness. But I think a wise ruler understands what every parent does: favoring one child too much will embitter the others."

"Is the Ministry of Mages bitter?" Tai asked.

The mage grinned. "Not yet. Just watchful, Your Highness."

When Tai had finished training, he bathed and dressed for his afternoon duties, which included the monthly court assembly.

The audience hall resembled a mountain and sea of people, as the saying went. Official black and grey silk rippled like a dark tide, with jade pendants or flashes of imperial yellow breaking the monotony. Ministers filed in, murmuring greetings as they found their places before the empress entered.

As Minister of War, Tai had a special designated seat on the right-hand side, looking over the attending ministers.

He spied Sanjin looking composed as usual, and Tai wondered at how he appeared so serene yet ordered the torture of so many. He sensed Jin wasn't telling him what really happened, whether out of some unspoken code of honor or because she was too proud, he didn't know. But he had heard the rumors, the whispers, glimpsed the aftermath of the Veil's tactics. He always had other pressing matters to see to, the fates of thousands to answer to, versus the hundreds in Sanjin's grip. Like a wound one knew should be seen to but never directly looked at.

The gong sounded. As Tai pulled his gaze away, he swore for the hundredth time in as many minutes that he would abolish the Royal Veil once he was on the throne.

But abolishing the Veil wouldn't happen easily, for Sanjin would fight with everything he had. And those who accused his mother of being a faithless, disloyal serpent didn't know how deep her loyalties sometimes ran.

His mother had told him several times that she owed the throne, and even her life, to Sanjin. He had hidden her in the palace when Mengkhis Lai and Baikalan stormed in, searching for her, the emperor, and their newly born son. When Tai had broached it with Emar, the man had refused details but confirmed that Sanjin had defended the empress through some of her darkest hours.

Tai had also heard the whispers about a possible affair between Sanjin and his mother, but he didn't believe those. No one, least of all his mother, would find Sanjin attractive, even if he had saved her life. The man had never married and had no children, and many thought he was completely uninterested in the opposite sex—or the same sex. His sole passions seemed to be the throne and the Royal Veil.

"The Empress of Celestial Light enters; may she live ten thousand years!"

Tai stood and joined the gathered nobles in repeating the phrase.

His mother walked in, blinding in her usual gold attire. A gleaming silk gown flowed to the floor, covered in scales of gold that made her look like a dragon from the waist down. A gold-threaded bodice hugged her chest with a swathe of black silk to offset it underneath. Her hair dripped with the precious metal, the tresses piled high and pinned together with elaborate combs the length of a forearm, delicate latticed decorations swaying from them to brush against her face and eyebrows.

Once the official greetings were over, the regular business began. The Minister of Laws droned on about various new measures to streamline the judicial process while weeding out corruption, and then the Minister of Infrastructure launched into a detailed outline of what works had been completed and what had been delayed. The dozens of clerks seated along the wall wrote down every word.

The empress dealt with these in her usual fashion before calling on the Minister of Rites, which surprised Tai. He had attended these since the age of ten, and though this was his first time as the Minister of War, he knew he usually preceded the Minister of Rites.

The minister reminded Tai of a squirrel. He had a contained nervousness to him and always held his hands before his hunched shoulders like a forest animal protecting its kill. A bushy moustache, very uncommon for Han men, hinted at northern blood.

"Your Majesty," he started, "we all know that with the recent great victories you have secured for the empire, including the Battle at Bohai, the suppression of the vicious uprising by Gao, along with the recent execution of Mengkhis Lai," here he paused for the rest of the court to murmur their appreciation, "we at the Ministry of Rites feel it is time to recognize Your Majesty's incredible contribution. Such a contribution speaks of divine favor, and we at the Ministry of Rites have consulted several sources that confirm Your Majesty's divine blessings. We have drawn up a proposal, unanimously voted for with hearty enthusiasm by all in the Ministry of Rites."

Tai contained his inner sigh. He knew celebrating

victories was part and parcel of politics, but celebrating lies, like the death of Mengkhis Lai, did not sit well with him. He resisted the urge to glance at his mother to see her expression.

"The Ministry of Rites," the minister said, reading from a scroll his assistant passed to him, "proposes the following. That Your Majesty be addressed henceforth as Your Divine Majesty. Second, that a sutra be commissioned, to be written by select Buddhist monks, extolling Your Divine Majesty's virtues and declaring to the public what we know to be true: Your Divine Majesty is a reincarnation of the Boddhisattva herself."

Tai inhaled, and knew he was not the only one to do so, even though the ministers tried to keep their reactions quiet. To claim to have Buddha's blessing was one thing, even to be the Son of Heaven was a title every emperor bore. But to be a divine reincarnation of the Boddhisattva, the Goddess of Mercy, was, in Tai's mind, blasphemous.

"And with the declaration, the Ministry of Rites proposes the building of a grand statue, to be placed in the middle of the Avenue of Vermillion Birds, in the likeness of Her Divine Majesty, to remind all in the capital and in the empire to whom they owe their good fortune."

Tai did turn to his mother then. Reject it, he urged silently. The lack of surprise in his mother's face told him that she had known all along this proposal was coming—had perhaps even initiated it.

"We thank the Ministry of Rites for their suggestions," the empress said smoothly, "and though we are humbled at this unexpected honor, we cannot accept."

Tai knew it for the show that it was. The minister bowed once more.

"Please, Your Majesty, we entreat you to accept."

Only on the third time, as dictated by tradition, did the empress agree.

"Please let it be noted that these changes shall go into effect immediately."

The scribes' brushes moved furiously over paper.

"Your Majesty, who is to pay for this statue and this sutra?" Tai asked. He knew he would be the only one who could ask the question without losing his head.

A deep silence fell as the empress looked over at him, eyes flinty.

"The Minister of War asks a good question," she said instead of reprimanding him. "Perhaps the Minister of Rites can outline a proposal."

The minister bowed. "Of course, Your Divine Majesty. Funds for these works will come directly out of a new tax on those with property within the Changan city walls."

A ripple of disquiet passed through those gathered, though subtle. One minister dared to speak up. Tai recognized Minister of the Interior, Chen Gurong.

"Should it not come from the War Ministry, Your Majesty?"

"Your Divine Majesty," the empress corrected him. Minister Chen hesitated and then bowed.

"Of course, forgive this unworthy minister, Your Divine Majesty. I only wish to point out that given the Parhae rebels have been soundly defeated and their king has died, and the Khitans have similarly been defeated, with our forces holding their princess and their dragons, and with Mengkhis now dead, should these funds not come from the War coffers? After all, we have no need of war now."

Tai could almost hear his ministers clamoring that this would have been avoided if they had pretended to mount a war against the Khitans.

"And," Minister Chen continued, "Gao was the one who depleted the war chests to begin with. Surely that department should shoulder the costs." He glanced toward Tai as he said this, and Tai suppressed an ironic smile. The man was trying to save his own money by hoisting the responsibility on Tai, even though Tai had in fact nearly lost his life to the traitor.

"The War Ministry cannot be taxed further," the empress said. "As you say, the traitor Gao depleted the funds so much, we cannot bleed the ministry any more, or we risk opening ourselves to attack."

By the loose and very much alive Mengkhis Lai, Tai added.

There were murmurings amongst the nobles, but no one seemed brave enough to contradict the empress.

"If there are no other objections," the empress said, "then the throne approves the Ministry of Rites' proposals."

"Please reconsider."

His mother adjusted an earring with her fingers, the gold-painted nails catching the candlelight.

He had tried to get an audience sooner but was told the empress—no, the divine empress only had availability over the evening meal. Even now, the array of quail, braised water lily, and stewed bitter melon sat on the long dining table, untouched.

"I am guessing you speak of the Ministry of Rites' proposals. Which one?"

"All of them."

She grimaced. "Need I tell you that I am not one for ostentation, except for when it becomes necessary for the throne. Throne above—"

"All, yes, I know," Tai snapped. At her expression, he reined in his annoyance. "But we both know Mengkhis is out there, alive. We need every *fen* to pay for weapons and defense, not build statues. And besides, did you see the nobles' expressions? They are even now plotting how to avoid the payments. They already pay the Buddhist temples a seven percent contribution, and now you wish them to pay for a statue and a sutra proclaiming your divinity?"

"We are about to confront Mengkhis Lai," his mother said quietly. "Do you think the people will be reassured by anyone but a god defending them? You have not seen as many battles as I, my son. Men need hope. I'm a woman, and men won't fight for a woman. But they will fight for a god."

Tai leaned on the table between them. "Is that really why you are doing this?"

His mother avoided his gaze, but he thought he detected a stillness in her back. "What other reason might there be?"

"Vanity. Pride." *Delusions*, he added silently.

She looked up, her gaze distinctly cold now, with a hint of disappointment and defiance thrown in, he thought. "You insult me, my son."

"I won't apologize for putting throne above all in this case, Mother."

She stood, her gown rustling around her, and Tai again glimpsed her ring with the "kway" on it. "I do nothing but what is good for the throne, as you keep reminding me." She arched her brow. "I was, according to you, even going to sacrifice my son for it. So I don't think you'll understand that this is also pure politics. If the men view me as just a woman, they won't fight when Mengkhis comes to the gates. They will run and hide, or simply turn me over to him. Likely turn you over, no matter how much you think they love the Prince of Dragons. And what will you do then?" She paused, her expression hardening and her nails gouging into the wood of the table between them, like talons. "But they will fight for a goddess. A reincarnation of the mighty Goddess of Mercy. Because only the Goddess of Mercy can defeat someone like Mengkhis."

"And what will they think of their goddess who lied to them?" Tai countered. "The goddess who said that Mengkhis was dead? Is he resurrected?"

"We will say we were mistaken, that he is a demon."

"You will say *Jin* was mistaken," Tai amended, putting the pieces in place. He cursed himself for not seeing the truth earlier. "You'll blame her and set yourself up as the saving goddess."

"I never said it was fair, or ideal," the empress said. "But the throne must be devoid of blame. It's for the good of the empire."

Tai didn't have words. What was the point of berating his mother? She would hide behind the excuse of the good of the throne until the end of her days, and perhaps she even believed it. He had once believed it. But now he doubted. And doubt was an insidious thing.

"Aren't you staying for dinner?" she called as he turned and strode toward the door.

"You're a goddess now," he answered. "Goddesses don't need to eat."

CHAPTER 20

Jin entered the training courtyard with her squad mates, expecting the usual morning meditation exercises followed by pain control. Ah-Ming, however, stood with hands clasped behind his back, and motioned for everyone to remain standing.

"Today we will train your other senses with a Scorpion Dance." He held up his fingers. "You have all had fight training, as I know Jin has. But a Veil agent's single finger must be more powerful than all the fingers of an ordinary person. You will face enemies not one by one, but sometimes in multitudes." He closed his fingers into a fist and clasped it behind his back. "Which is why you will each take turns fighting solo against the others in your squad."

He turned to Foxface. "You, person of no worth, will be first."

Foxface bowed and took one of the sturdy poles

leaning against the southern wall. At a signal from Ah-Ming, Jin, Westie, Bean, and the one with a flat nose that Jin had learned was nicknamed Mushroom each selected a pole as well.

Foxface took up his stance in the middle of the courtyard, his expression bordering on eager, and within a few heartbeats, Ah-Ming barked, "Begin!"

Mushroom rushed first, his arms a blur as he swung the pole in a figure eight motion. Foxface was agile, though, and easily blocked the onslaught with several sharp cracks of his own pole.

"What are you waiting for?" Ah-Ming snapped at the rest of them. "The Spring Festival?"

Westie and Bean jumped in, sweeping their poles at Foxface's head. The man ducked, narrowly missing their swings, before jabbing Westie in the stomach with one pole end, and treating Bean to a flying kick that sent the taller man stumbling. Foxface closed in on Bean with a punishing blow to the back, then whirled around and kicked Westie in the face, resulting in a flow of curses.

"Are you afraid, or just know when you're beaten?" Foxface called to Jin.

Ah-Ming turned to her. "Well?"

Jin gripped her pole and stepped forward. His taunts helped her overcome her reluctance to fight. Her blood bonding gave her speed and strength, so it was but a few strokes of work for her to dodge his pole and trip him with her own.

Ah-Ming nodded approval at Jin as Foxface stood up, sullen. "Jin wins. Now it's Jin's turn."

Jin took Foxface's spot in the center, tuning herself to the others.

Don't worry, this should be quick work, Rayshan assured her.

I feel a bit bad, she admitted. *I have the advantage.*

As if he heard her, Ah-Ming pulled a black linen cloth from his pocket and wound it around his fist as he approached her. "Sometimes we may have to fight injured. Or blind. Or both. And we can't rely on our special skills." He strode behind Jin and tied the blindfold around her eyes twice, wrapping it so tightly she truly saw nothing.

"This will even the playing field," Ah-Ming said, and quick as a snake, his hand clamped on hers. Something cold slid across her palm. The blade was so sharp that at first she felt no pain, only warm blood.

"Begin!" Ah-Ming's voice barked.

Jin gripped her pole and hissed at the pain in her cut hand. She heard the feet behind her but turned too late, and a bone-jarring hook from the pole butt struck her in the shoulder. Someone delivered a hard punch to the gut that brought her to her knees, gasping.

Use your other senses! Rayshan growled.

Flaring? But—

You have other skills, Rayshan huffed. *Use them!*

Rayshan was right. She would fight this, but

without her flaring abilities. She focused on what she had: smell and touch.

She heard the footsteps again on her right, and this time rolled.

She quickly sorted her squad mates by their different scents. Bean smelled faintly of onion, while Westie carried an aroma of aniseed soap. She also smelled pu-er tea, which must be from Ah-Ming—none in the Veil would have access to such fine-grade tea. Someone—Foxface?—made a sniffing noise just before every attack. Which left Mushroom—he had a distinct, earthy but sour smell.

She received several more knocks, all sending her to the ground, before she locked on all the smells to track them. Bracing against the blows raining on her back, she thrust her pole out and swept hard to the right, putting all her strength into her hands and ignoring the slice in her palm.

Two of her squad fell, and she blocked Westie's blow before standing, staff at the ready.

This time she managed to beat them all back, sensing their movements by their smells.

Westie's pole smashed into her arm before she swung wide and heard the satisfying crack of wood against jaw. Mushroom's pungent odor assailed her from behind, and she drove her elbow backward. The crunch of his nose was followed by the crash of his pole to the ground and gurgled curses.

But then something connected with her ankle, and she was on her back, a staff pressed to her throat.

Someone ripped the blindfold from her, and she looked up into Foxface's triumphant grin.

"That will do for today," Ah-Ming said. "Tomorrow, I expect you to be able to defeat them all. And in half the time."

JIN'S one respite from the Veil, besides her weekly meetings with Tai, came with the slivers of time where she was allowed to fly with Rayshan, who craved open air and exercise.

The summer leaves were just starting to curl and turn yellow. Though Foxface's look of triumph still rankled Jin, she forced the memories away to bask as much as possible in the rushing air and freedom, along with Rayshan's clear happiness at being aloft.

She had seen worse, she told herself, in the thief world. Hadn't Haitao made her best friend, Lu, betray her when she'd pocketed a coin on one job? She had earned a harsh lashing for it, and Haitao's words still rang in her ears.

Trust no one, for a thief must look out for oneself.

But Lu had snuck to her room and tended her with salve for her back, and kept her entertained with stories to distract her from the pain. A knot in her throat made her swallow. Lu, like Ah-Ming, had helped her control pain. But Lu did it for her, whereas Ah-Ming and the Veil did it for the empire.

Jin swallowed the hatred in her.

I need to leave the Veil.

Rayshan hummed in agreement. *Are you rethinking the prince's offer?*

No. Jin gritted her teeth. As much as she wanted to leave the Veil, she also didn't want to endanger the prince or call his loyalty into question. She needed to graduate herself, unless the empress freed her. Or she could kill Mengkhis.

Not knowing where Mengkhis is makes that difficult, Rayshan grumbled.

Shall we try the Firesong again?

We will not stop trying, Rayshan said. *But in the meantime, perhaps someone from the dead would help us.*

Who?

Emar would not approve of you being in the Veil, Rayshan said.

Jin wasn't too sure. Emar disagreed with the empress on many things, but that didn't mean he ever outright opposed her. *We said we wouldn't call the dead for our own benefit unless absolutely necessary,* Jin argued. And others had certainly tried to tempt her. There had been countless letters, offers of reward from those wishing to see a dead relative or loved one one last time.

Rayshan growled back, his neck dipping as he sped through a low-lying cloud and snapped it in his jaws.

This is about defeating Mengkhis, who threatens the empire. Only a strong Jin can defeat Mengkhis and defend the people, and the Veil is weakening you in mind and spirit.

The words hit home. Perhaps that was what scared her most about the Veil. The physical acts of cruelty were all superficial, a show to distract from their ultimate purpose. The true terror of the Veil lay in their mental sabotage, their grinding down of her soul until she was as dead eyed as Ah-Kun.

As they wove through the low cloud cover, Rayshan's suggestion hanging between them, a smudge emerged in the distance.

Are those . . . ?

The rumble in Rayshan intensified, and he shifted so that they pulled away.

Dragons.

As if to prove him right, a roar floated back to them.

Jin swallowed. *They're headed to Nine Claw Mountain, aren't they?*

Rayshan grunted, and dove, as if he could shake off the Song of Scales and his creeping frustration with wingbeats alone.

She leaned over him, glad she had had the foresight to pilfer some oranges from the Veil kitchens before leaving.

Rayshan grunted again, but she had piqued his interest. *When we land.*

Jin relished the moments of solitude with Rayshan. Here, in the late summer sky, she could truly empty her mind and enjoy Rayshan beneath her, the way the sun dappled his scales and the wind whipped her face.

They had performed several rises and dives when they spotted a group of riders in the distance, and before they could move away to preserve their peace, the riders had caught up.

It was Nobu's two dragons and an entourage. Though *entourage*, Jin realized, was not quite the right word. They were more prison guards, for the riders from another wing were there to ensure Nobu didn't escape back to Khitan and her brothers. Jin hadn't checked in on Nobu since they had returned to the capital after the battle at Bohai, and guilt nicked her.

"Rider Jin!" Nobu shouted over the wind, and Jin did a double take. Nobu was not in a carriage, as Jin would have assumed, but riding one of the dragons—the bronze, which Jin had "gifted" Nobu's father in a forced choosing.

"You ride," Jin commented as they drew abreast, the dragons adjusting to each other's speed to fly at a leisurely pace next to each other.

Jin nodded to the guards in a sign that they could trust her to not let Nobu escape.

The guards seemed to relax at this and fell back a few wingspans. They were of an older year, and Jin didn't know any of them, for none had been at Bohai or at training.

They rode through the dusk for the good part of an hour, before Nobu motioned for a landing to rest. Jin was tempted to leave them there, but the girl seemed eager to have Jin join her, and so Jin asked Rayshan to follow.

The dragons landed in a bamboo grove that surrounded a field of stubbled wheat.

"Riding days are my favorite," Nobu said, her cheeks flushed.

"You are not being ill-treated?"

Nobu shook her head. "No, the prince and his mother are very kind."

Kind was not the word Jin would have used for Tai's mother, but she kept silent. At least Nobu was safe.

"You know, I once wanted to be like you," Nobu said after she had loosened her dragon's saddle.

Jin tossed Rayshan his promised oranges, which he devoured, then glanced at the Khitan princess, waiting. She had heard such things before and had always shied away from the compliments or the fishing for advice. She had enough troubles figuring out her own problems, never mind advising on someone else's.

"But I think your path is quite lonely, as mine is," Nobu said.

"You will return to your kingdom someday," Jin reassured her.

Nobu smiled and patted her gold's neck. He snapped at the air and flared his nostrils before stalking low through the wheat field for hidden prey. Nobu watched him, then looked back at Jin. "I hope so.

And I have been trying to convince Prince Tai to consider making me queen of Khitan."

That was not what Jin was expecting. Khitan did not have ruling queens, for one, and two, Jin's memory was that Nobu had a long line of brothers who would kill her before they let her take control of the kingdom.

"I know," Nobu said, as if Jin had spoken. "There are certain obstacles to this. But I also think it's a good option. The best, even. It assures peace with China, for I'm the only one who doesn't wish to avenge my father's death. To be honest, my brothers don't either. It is simply their ingrained sense of honor, I suspect."

"And what did the prince say?" Jin asked.

Nobu smiled. "Prince Tai is a consummate diplomat." Was it Jin's imagination, or was there more than just admiration in Nobu's eyes?

"So he said no."

Nobu's smile faltered, and she looked at Jin, hesitant. "I was hoping you might help me persuade him."

Jin tensed. She watched Rayshan twitch his tail in response. "Whatever rumors you have heard, they aren't true."

Nobu nodded, and Jin was sure she saw relief. The girl clearly had feelings for Prince Tai. Jin wasn't too surprised. She had meant what she said about his charm, and though she had suggested he marry Nobu to ensure peace, Jin didn't imagine the empress would agree easily.

"Still, Rider Jin," Nobu pressed, "you are my only

friend here. Well, only friend besides my dragons." She glanced over at the two, and Jin caught the wistfulness in the girl's face. Despite herself, a flash of pity swept her. Widowed, fatherless, and now a glorified prisoner, she was a political asset to her brothers and a valuable hostage for the empress. Nothing more. And being the daughter of the man who had not only killed several members of Dragon Class but also freed the feared dragon Baikalan and tried to free Mengkhis himself, it was no wonder the Dragon Class riders had nothing but hatred for the girl. In fact, Jin thought it a miracle the girl hadn't met with some supposed accident before now.

Jin tried to find words that might comfort. "I am sure he will try to do what's right, while also making your case if he can. But, yes, if you'd like, I can mention that it seems an idea with merit."

The girl's relief was palpable, and Jin squirmed inwardly. The tears in Nobu's eyes only made it worse.

A thrumming sounded in Jin's head, and it wasn't Rayshan's. It was a sense of gratitude.

Jin's head snapped around toward the dragon in the wheat field. It was the bronze she had been forced to gift to Ulagan, Nobu's father, when he wanted to punish Jin for stealing Rayshan.

"Your dragon's thoughts are . . . clearer."

Nobu grinned, proud. "I know. His feelings are more distinct every day."

When Jin had first reached out for the dragon's

mind last year, there had been nothing but discordant noise. Noise that rose and fell, intensified or lulled, but nothing that came close to a singular, definable emotion or distinct thought. Because their bond to Ulagan had been a forced one, the dragons had lost much of their ability to communicate as other dragons did.

Jin turned to Nobu, true awe in her this time. "How did you do it? For that matter, how did you bond with them?" She hadn't even thought to ask the question before, for they had been dealing with Emar's death, Baikalan's sinking to the bottom of the sea, and their return to Changan. There had been no mage bonding with Nobu, yet the dragons and Nobu clearly communicated in their own way, and the dragons seemed to protect Nobu as if she was their rider.

Nobu bit a thumbnail. "I don't know, to be honest. I never thought about it. When Father was alive, I always snuck out to see Shafeng, and Satu. But it always seemed like we understood each other, even without words or clear thoughts. And it used to be silent, but more and more I hear their distinct feelings. They can even tell me to do something specific."

Jin looked back at her. "I didn't know that was possible."

Love mends even the most shattered of minds, Rayshan said quietly.

Jin looked again at the other dragons and said to

Nobu, "You have done something no one else has, do you know that, Princess Nobu?"

The girl again rolled her shoulders, clearly pleased but also not as impressed as Jin. "I simply loved them. That's all."

Another thought occurred to Jin, and she waited until the dragons were distracted again before broaching it.

"Have your dragons been . . . restless? Due to the season?"

At first Nobu stared blankly, but then understanding dawned. "You mean the Song of Scales?"

Jin nodded.

"It doesn't seem to have started with them yet, but we have a concoction we give them, to suppress the longing."

"You drug them?" Jin asked, not sure whether she was aghast or hopeful.

Nobu nodded. "Of course. They'd be wild and dangerous otherwise." She glanced over at the other riders and their dragons. "I know the Dragon Class dragons are allowed to go freely, but it carries risk. And I know what it is to be—lacking." Nobu's voice hitched, and she shifted on her bad leg. "The females would kill Shafeng and Satu on sight because of their difference. I would rather keep them safe."

Jin watched Rayshan snap at Shafeng, who had wandered too close to the jade.

"If you'd like," Nobu said quietly, "I can make you some."

Jin, too, wanted to keep Rayshan safe. Drugging him felt wrong. But so did letting him suffer as the song grew stronger.

She watched Rayshan in the field, rolling in the stubble to scratch his limbs, and wondered. She would never do it without his consent.

"Thank you, but, no."

"It is no trouble at all," Nobu said, and Jin realized Nobu thought she was refusing the traditional three times to be polite.

"I do not wish to take what you should save for Shafeng and Satu."

Nobu looked a little crestfallen, and Jin understood she had been hoping to offer Jin something of worth in exchange for speaking to the prince.

"But if you have any extra once you have seen to your dragons, perhaps you could gift me the remainder."

Nobu smiled, pleased. "It would be my honor."

CHAPTER 21

Mage Situ Han's training seemed to double in intensity, so that sometimes Tai felt he would fall asleep during his War Minister meetings. Already some of the advisors had noted it, asking concernedly whether he was ill. One, who was known for his insolent humor, went so far as to suggest Tai was having romantic meetings with Princess Nobu.

After a particularly brutal training session where mage Situ Han insisted Tai make a grain of rice weigh down a single sheet of paper without the benefit of walking his usual circles, Tai's patience snapped. He was drenched in sweat, and his *mai* refused to cooperate.

"Patience, Your Highness," the mage said, cracking melon seeds in his teeth and flicking the shells. "The smaller the object, the harder it is to reverse its weight.

Make this grain of rice weigh as much as an elephant, and you will have mastered a skill even some of the more advanced mages struggle with."

"Can you do it?" Tai said.

Mage Situ Han grinned. "Of course, Your Highness."

"Then perhaps a demonstration is in order." Tai had seen the mage's powers, but he desperately needed a rest, and some willful part of him wanted to challenge the flippant man.

Mage Situ Han seemed to know this. He pinched the grain of rice and placed it in a porcelain bowl on the floor. "Step back, Your Highness," he instructed.

Tai backed several steps and crossed his arms, waiting.

Mage Situ Han turned toward the bowl. His body, usually corpulent and soft, seemed to transform and harden before Tai's eyes. Within a blink, the porcelain shattered in the middle, sending jagged pieces of crockery flying. Tai ducked just in time, and when everything settled, the bowl was a mess of powder and shards.

"You have your example, Your Highness," Mage Situ Han said, smiling. "Now it's your turn."

THE DEMONSTRATION HAD IMPRESSED TAI, who had frankly been astounded by the show of power, but it had also tickled a nagging question that he had ignored until now. He knew nothing of the mage's background or what the other mages thought of him.

Tai determined to change that.

When Head Mage Yao agreed to meet, Tai suggested the royal hunting grounds, and ordered the stewards to fetch his hunting horse, along with his bow and arrows.

He took only two of his most trusted valets, whom he knew would not be overly prying, for some instinct told him he didn't want Situ Han knowing about this meeting just yet. They made their way through the palace to the private hunting gardens on the western side, far away from the dragons' designated hunting grounds.

Ministers, officials, and members of the noble family were allowed to hunt here if given special passes, which were paid for or gifted by the empress, depending on how favored they were. Tai wanted to avoid prying eyes and wagging tongues. After all, it would not be so unusual to see the crown prince talking with the head mage at the hunting grounds, where members of the nobility and government often ran into each other during outings.

Tai entered the grounds and made his way to the small pond that ran north and south near the southern entrance, where he had invited the head mage to rendezvous.

He let his horse wander around the edges, getting

rid of some of his nervous energy, before he spied the head mage on a dun-colored mare approaching, a falcon on one gloved arm.

"Your Royal Highness," the Head Mage Yao said, bowing his head. "What an honor and pleasure to meet you here." Roughly sixty, he had once clearly possessed a fine physique, now rounded and thick.

"Thank you," Tai responded. "What game would you like to hunt today?"

"I'm not sure yet," the mage replied. "Perhaps His Highness can tell me what his quarry is, and I can lend my services?"

Clearly, the man sensed that he hadn't been invited just for a casual hunt. "I am not much of a hunter," Prince Tai said smoothly. "And you are the one with the mage skills and the falcon. Perhaps I can take your advice on this."

The head mage laughed. "Very well. Why don't we start small. With rabbits."

"That suits me," Tai said, pulling his horse away from the pond and following the head mage on horseback through the trees.

"I hope mage Situ Han has been serving Dragon Class well," the head mage said. "Your Highness has no complaints?"

The slight nervousness in the mage's voice made Tai curious. "No. Should I?"

The head mage seemed relieved. "So this is not about him, then?"

"I simply wanted your opinion of him, not to complain."

The old man bowed his head. "Ah! That is good. Former head mage Gu Ben appointed him, somewhat to the ministry's surprise, and since Master Gu's unexpected death, I have been so busy that I haven't yet reviewed all appointments."

The last head mage had died in Khitan during the ambush, and Tai thought there had been plenty of time to go over affairs, but decided to let that slide.

"I wanted to thank you for allowing him to tutor me."

The mage looked puzzled. "Tutor you, Your Highness?"

"Yes," Tai replied. "In the mage arts."

Yao looked blank, and then he broke out in a laugh. "Your Highness is full of humor today."

It was Tai's turn to look puzzled. "You did not assign him to teach me magic?"

Yao's expression turned serious. "Your Highness, only eunuchs can be taught the arts of mages."

Tai digested this, but his smile faded. "No wonder it's not working, then, despite all my efforts."

Yao chuckled. "Situ Han is known for his jests, Your Highness. Highly cheeky of him to suggest you learn the arts."

"Quite," Tai agreed. "But I find his sense of fun a nice change."

They emerged into a clearing, where Mage Yao

prepared his falcon for the hunt. He stroked the bird briefly before thrusting his arm, and the bird took to flight.

"Do you know why he was appointed to Dragon Class?" Tai asked.

The head mage frowned. "Presumably he wanted to be close to you, the crown prince, and Gu Ben granted him that great favor."

From the man's tone, Tai surmised that even the head mage himself resented Situ Han for winning this plum role. But had the head mage known of Tai's training? Had it been Gu Ben's idea, with no one in the ministry any wiser to Situ Han's plan?

"Tell me, how long have you known mage Situ Han?"

The head mage's face crinkled in a tight smile. "A long time. Though he has been away for much of it."

This was news to Tai. "Where? And why?"

"He was a hermit for over twenty years but returned last summer and asked for his post back. Master Gu Ben graciously accepted him. As if he'd never left. But he has quite the reputation."

"Does he?" Tai asked, interest piqued. Why would mage Situ Han suddenly return? "He said he believes in the fabled mage king."

Yao shot him an enigmatic look. "Ah. He told you that story?"

"Yes." Tai loosened his reins, allowing his horse to graze.

The head mage shielded his eyes, searching the sky for his bird. "That is an obscure legend."

"What of the ministry?" Tai asked. "Does the ministry not believe in it?"

The head mage snorted. "I suppose some do. But most of us live in this harsh reality and don't have time for such things. The seasons change, and so do emperors. Just as the seasons are inherently the same, so are the emperors. The ideal mage emperor is a myth, Your Highness."

"So you've never decided to train one to become a mage emperor?"

"What emperor would agree to give his manhood to become a mage? No one."

Tai smiled in a practiced look of agreement. "Indeed. And you've never broken that rule?"

"It's not a rule for me to break," Yao said, his eyes still locked on the skies. "A man who hasn't sacrificed his manhood can't become a mage. This is a time-honored tradition, unshakable as a mountain." He gave the prince a cautious look. "Your Highness is not considering . . ."

"I am very attached to my manhood," Tai reassured him.

Yao nodded, whistling for his falcon, but Tai's mind churned. Why had Situ Han lied about the ministry approving his training?

"Ah! Here she comes," Yao said as he raised his arm

and let the bird land. "Looks like we are empty-handed. Shall we try again, Your Highness?"

"Perhaps next time," Tai said. "There's someone I need to see."

HE FOUND mage Situ Han at the Blood Oval.

The plump man had his usual bag of melon seeds as he stood on a balcony overlooking the training grounds. There, two assistant mages were cautiously creating binding spells on a young silver dragon, who lay in a wary crouch with his rider next to him, trying to soothe him.

"That's it, never try to rush a dragon binding!" Situ Han called. As Tai walked up the steps to stand next to him, the mage bowed. "Ah, Your Highness! Did you have a good hunt with the head mage?" Situ Han asked, his usual smile unfaltering.

"The ministry never assigned you to teach me the mage arts," Tai said without preamble. How did the mage know his movements already?

"I like it, Your Highness. Open the door straight onto the mountain, as they say," Situ Han said, dusting the melon seeds off his coat. "No, they don't know I am teaching you magic. Only you and I know." He bent over the balustrade. "I said don't rush—oh dear."

A roar shook the oval, and the mages scrambled back as the silver shot a tongue of flame at them. The rider stroked his dragon's snout and pressed his hands to the scaly hide.

"Why did you do it?" Tai asked.

"I've told you, Your Highness," Situ Han said. "I believe you are the mage emperor foretold. Just because no one else knows that doesn't mean it's not true."

"I do not like those who lie to me."

"Then you dislike ninety-five percent of the empire."

"I am thinking I'm being tutored by a madman," Tai said.

"Or maybe I'm the only sane person in an empire full of mad people," Situ Han countered. He motioned at the two mages to try again. They cautiously crept forward once more, while the silver snarled and thrashed his ridged tail.

"Where were you in your years as a hermit?"

"In my mind, Your Highness."

Tai forced a tight smile. "Give me a straight answer, Mage."

"Straight answers can lead you in circles. If you're speaking of where I was physically, then I wandered. Everywhere. Persia, Nihhon, Parhae, Khitan, Champa, Bactria. I saw it all. I ate things I'd never heard of and learned languages I didn't know existed. I begged on the street one day, and the next I was pleasuring a king's favorite concubine. Is that what you wanted to hear, Your Highness?"

Tai struggled with the images this conjured, but realized the mage was simply trying to distract him. "Why did you take that journey?"

Situ Han paused, as if choosing his words with care. "It was a time of chaos. People killing each other in the streets, an emperor so self-absorbed and willful he became a curse to his people, and the capital teetering on ruin. I didn't see how dying would help anyone."

"And so you fled?" Tai asked.

"I survived," mage Situ Han said gently, as if speaking to a child. "To come back another day, with answers and solutions. As I am now."

Tai smelled a lie. A very artfully buried lie. He looked out at the oval, where the dragon seemed to have subsided to a disgruntled rumbling, and the mages walked slow circles one way, then another as they built their spell.

Tai leveled a gaze at the mage. "Is that the only reason you left?"

Mage Situ Han smiled. "You are very astute, Your Highness. One of the reasons I think you will make a good mage emperor."

Tai waited, ignoring the flattery.

"I did not leave entirely of my own volition, no."

"You were exiled?" Tai asked. "By the Ministry of Mages?"

Situ Han shook his head. "By your father."

Tai took this in. Situ Han's expression was guarded,

as if he hoped Tai would not ask further but knew he would. "Why?"

"I insulted him."

"How?"

"I suggested he was infertile."

Tai swallowed. "That is a dangerous remark to make to an emperor."

"I didn't make it to him. But, yes, it was a dangerous remark. Especially as it's true."

He searched the mage's face for a hint of pity, humor, or malice. But he found only a placid, open face. The mage's expression was that of one who had simply made a comment on the weather being warm, rather than one who had set flame to the prince's entire life.

Rumors. How he hated them. He had not expected mage Situ Han to dabble in such gossip, especially malicious gossip.

"I am living proof that you were wrong."

The mage said nothing, which infuriated Tai more than if he had presented a long litany of arguments.

"I have heard these types of accusations before, and there is not a shred of proof," Tai said, his voice even.

"My proof was in my exile."

"That only proves my father's heart was soft. You're lucky he didn't behead you," Tai said.

"It was not your father who asked for my exile," mage Situ Han said. "But one of his favorite concubines."

A thin needle of unease worked its way into Tai. "My mother?"

Mage Situ Han shook his head. "Another. Your mother's rival, Concubine Liang. But the fact that she banished me proved she already knew the truth, she just wanted to hide it."

"And so you are here to wreak your revenge on me?" Tai said, a picture forming. "You are angry that you were banished, and came back to gain influence with me?"

"If that were true," the mage said, chuckling, "would I be telling you all this? Why not lie? I am quite skilled at lying, you know."

Tai's voice held disgust. "Clearly."

The mage bowed. "I only wish to make Your Highness the best emperor he can be."

"I thank you for your service," Tai said coldly. "But you are dismissed."

The mage showed absolutely no disturbance at this abrupt severance and instead bowed low. "As you wish, Your Highness. I did not realize the truth disturbed you so."

Tai paused on the stairs, stone still. This time he felt the roar shaking his world hadn't come from the dragon in the Oval, but from within himself.

～

THE HORSES THUNDERED down the field, their riders waving wooden mallets as the assembled onlookers cheered them on.

His mother wasn't playing, for a change. Though this was her favorite sport, she had insisted on a palace match that started with men's games, to be followed by women's. Currently, it was Marquis Sanjin's team against Interior Minister Chen's.

Tai and the empress sat beneath a silk canopy, applauding each goal. But Tai's mind wasn't on the game. He kept thinking of the mage's words about his father, and his eyes kept wandering to his mother's ring.

Tai let a servant refill his wine vessel and gestured to the players. Many of them had stripped to the waist in the heat. "You have a favorite?"

His mother glanced at him. "You're in a betting mood?"

"Why not. I'll take Interior Minister Chen's team, as I presume you favor Sanjin's."

She flicked him a suspicious look but didn't protest. "Stakes?"

"You win, I take you boating."

She snorted. "You should do that for your mother any day. But very well. What if you win?"

"You give me that ring with the word kway on it."

Her eyes narrowed. "That's a strange request."

He shrugged. "I didn't know it meant that much to

you. You said your sister gave it to you, and I didn't think you loved her much."

His mother sipped her wine. "I don't recall. Why the interest?"

"I thought of making a gift for Meipin. A ring seemed a good idea."

She regarded him. "She expects to be empress. She'd slap you for giving her a concubine's ring, and rightly so."

"Yet you keep yours?" he ventured.

Her look then took a sharp turn, and he knew he had likely revealed too much. She put her wine down, the game apparently forgotten. "What is this about?"

A loud cheer rose from the stands as Interior Minister Chen's team scored a goal.

Tai leaned closer and lowered his voice. "Someone was insinuating that my father was unable to have children."

The empress tapped her gold-painted fingers against the chair. "You know how I feel about these discussions."

"Yes, but situations change, raising new questions," Tai said. His mother had always firmly insisted that she would answer all questions he had but once. Once a discussion was over, she argued, it was in the past and should be left there. "As a child, I did not have access to certain facts. In all fairness, Mother, you should agree."

The empress's face looked pinched. "That's ridiculous. The Concubine Liang bore him a son before I entered the palace."

Tai knew the story. His half-brother, the heir Ruzong, had died on his fourth birthday, a year before Tai's birth. His mother seldom spoke of him, except that his tragic fall off a horse had made Tai's father spiral into paranoia about palace intrigues and plots. He also knew the story of how his mother had fired the stable hand, and slit the offending horse's throat herself, earning his father's deepest admiration.

"And yet Empress Wang had no children, even after many years."

"That was to do with the fact that her face resembled a dog's backside," his mother said.

"That's hardly kind."

"Your father's words, not mine. People will always say whatever they think will discredit you and me, my son." She smoothed an invisible wrinkle from one sleeve. "Why this sudden concern? You haven't been rattled by rumors for years."

Because I never thought you would lie to me. "Did you have any other children besides me?"

She was so still that he wondered whether the game had distracted her, whether he had missed the announcement of another goal. But, no, she turned her eyes to him, her face wooden. "Have you heard some new rumor?"

"I always felt there was a wistfulness in how you

looked at me. As if . . . as if you were seeing someone else."

"Can't a mother look at her child and imagine what he will be like as a grown man?" She sighed. "Every prince will be plagued by talk of his mother's chasteness. If you do not bury these thoughts, they will eat at you, my son."

"Wise words, Mother," he agreed. "It's just that I've seen that mark on someone, and I thought it a coincidence."

"A mark?"

"The word on your ring."

She sipped her wine. "Who?"

Some instinct made him lie. "One of the maids in my household. I thought it strange that she should have a mark about the size of your ring."

The empress smiled, though it felt shallow. "And this made you think she was my child?"

He spread his palms. "Far-fetched?"

The crowd roared their approval. Sanjin himself had scored a goal, and held his mallet aloft, looking toward the royal tent for approval. The empress stood and clapped as Sanjin's team returned to their positions.

His mother sat back down and picked up her wine. "This sort of ring was given to favored ladies all the time. And after your father's death, I married off all his concubines to start new lives. Perhaps the girl is one such offspring."

Tai nodded. "Yes, perhaps."

But as he watched the game, the doubts still lingered. Only very favored concubines would be given a ring bearing the word *kway*, meaning "precious"— usually the most favored. And his mother had famously been the most favored of all.

Was his mother lying? If so, then he had a sibling. And if that sibling was indeed marked with the word *kway*, then might his sibling be—No. He rubbed his temples. That was beyond ludicrous. The word *kway* might have come from a merchant—for they often marked their finer goods with the symbol—or a low-level concubine having an affair. The alternative was . . . unthinkable.

A clash of mallets and then a roar of victory brought him back to the polo field. Sanjin's team had won.

His mother turned to him and smiled. "Never bet against Sanjin, my son. I look forward to our boating trip."

Though the loss disappointed him, he wasn't sure whether he wanted to push on and find the truth of that ring, and Jin's scar. For the truth was destroying everything he had taken to be his foundation.

OVER THE NEXT DAYS, Tai was so busy with War

Ministry meetings and official functions that it took him a while to notice the change in his rooms.

He didn't understand exactly what had changed until he realized he didn't see a single familiar face amongst the maids sweeping the apartments.

"Are these maids new?" he asked his valet.

The valet bowed. "Yes, Your Highness. The Ministry of the Household ordered a health check on all staff a few days ago."

"Was there a reason?"

"A palace infestation of lice, Your Highness," the valet answered. "Do not worry. We have changed all your bedding, clothing, and hats and treated the rooms."

Tai digested this, then thought of something. "All the staff, or just the maids?"

The valet looked surprised. "All the staff, Your Highness. It would hardly be effective to check only maids."

"Of course." But he suspected the examination was tied to his conversation with his mother about her ring, and the scar behind Jin's ear. His mother was hiding something.

This drove him to practice the mage arts ever harder. It had become his secret defiance, he realized, and he relished it as such. It was one thing his mother did not have her hands in, one area in which she could not outmaneuver him. And though he had lost his tutor, he was determined to continue his training.

And so, he trained. He visited his personal library and read everything he found, and ordered books brought from the official library at the Ministry of Mages. He doubled his training time each day, rising early and practicing his circular walks and controlling his *mai*, doing ever harder weight-changing exercises until he could lighten his chair enough to lift it with one arm. And with each success, a sense of power surged through him. A sense that he had new purpose, new strength, a skill he could wield along with his charm.

For what exact purpose he wished to master the mage arts, he didn't know. After all, he didn't fully believe Situ Han's prediction of a mage emperor. But something told him he would be glad for his mage abilities, and soon.

CHAPTER 22

Ah-Ming drove Jin and her squad ever harder. Lessons sometimes stretched into the night. On another day, he forced Jin to summon the dead for hours on end until she fainted.

When she woke, she was again in Sanjin's apartments, and if possible, this time she was even more revolted than before.

She pushed herself from the bed and sat up. A bowl of soup and another of rice with dried fish and black beans had been laid on a nearby table. But she didn't feel hungry.

Instead, she stood and stretched, delicately feeling all her joints and muscles to see if there were any breaks or injuries.

None. Though she hadn't looked at her back.

Spotting the mirror over a sideboard, she approached it and froze.

A long streak of silver lanced through her brown hair along the left side of her face. She had another streak that ran on the other side, as if someone had run a comb dipped in white wax along the length. But this was accompanied by more lines on her face, crinkles around the eyes that were not there yesterday.

She reached up to touch her hair, her cheeks. She looked as if she was thirty, not twenty-two. She had never been vain—who could afford vanity when every day was a survival in the streets and all you thought about was avoiding a beating from Haitao? But she felt robbed all the same. As if her soul had been sucked from her, never to return.

She caught a low, animated muttering from the adjoining room and quickly recognized the voices. She strained to hear what Sanjin and the empress were saying.

" . . . disobedience."

"I know what I am doing, Your Majesty."

There was a pause. The empress's voice lowered further. "I have let your personal fetishes run unchecked. But those tastes are overcoming your caution."

"A ruler must be harsh to be kind, Your Divine Majesty."

"Do not overstep yourself. Already she looks like she's aged five years."

"No one knows the secrets of blood bonding, Your Divine Majesty."

"Then find out," the empress said. "I believe in making her strong, but the prince is right. We can't have her deteriorating."

"You fear what happened to Emar will . . ." Sanjin's voice lowered until his next words were incomprehensible, despite Jin's hearing and her stepping closer to the wall.

"There is much to consider, and I will not be pressured into hasty decisions. But I expect you to keep her healthy, and not turn her against us," the empress said in a voice so low that only Jin's blood-bonded ears could have heard. "She may be stronger than Emar."

Jin's heart pounded, and she strained to hear Sanjin's murmured reply. Jin heard the whisper of the empress's gown and the shuffle of many footsteps as her waiting entourage outside apparently followed her out the gates.

The mention of Sanjin's fetishes made Jin's stomach feel like it had sprouted hair. It confirmed her suspicions that Sanjin delighted in tormenting her. And what exactly was the empress considering? Why was she suddenly so concerned about Jin deteriorating? What had happened to Emar that they didn't want to repeat? Perhaps they just meant his defeat with Mengkhis. Was the empress finally worried that Jin would be too damaged to face him?

Jin didn't know if Sanjin intended to really find out the secrets of blood bonding, or whether he was only placating the empress. But if he did go after information, she knew who he was going to target.

The summoning, she whispered to Rayshan. *Is it aging you too?*

Yes. But it's not as noticeable, as dragons live a long time. Or at least, dragons without riders. On you, it's much more visible, he sighed.

If this continues, I'll look like a crone in a year, she said. *Is this the blood bond?*

I cannot say. But the summoning certainly seems to accelerate it.

Jin swallowed. She raked her hair into a bun, but the silver still showed, and pulling her hair back only made the lines on her face more prominent. How was it that her body healed from all manner of injuries, but not aging? It didn't make sense. And there would be no asking the only other blood-bonded riders she knew, Mengkhis and Emar. Emar hadn't been blood-bonded long, which meant he likely didn't suffer the effects.

There's someone else who might have answers, Rayshan responded.

You're right, she agreed slowly. She would have to make a trip into the city, and soon.

She pretended to sleep all the rest of that day, lying limp and unresponsive whenever a maid entered. When she heard the gong for the hour of the dog, and all the sounds nearby settled into evening rhythms, she pulled herself silently from bed and scrounged for her shoes and clothing. Slipping out proved easy for a seasoned thief, and despite her body's aching reluctance, she managed to swing herself onto the roofs and creep over the courtyard walls, out to the city streets and the one who might answer her questions.

THE FORTUNE TELLER'S market was surprisingly busy even at this hour, perhaps because it was so close to the city's night curfew.

The streets thronged with all manner of clientele and curiosity seekers. No matter what someone's rank or business, people always hoped to find divination, Jin knew. And here, the streets were lined with all types of shops willing to sell it to anyone with coin who wanted to know. Serrated flags bearing the character *ming*, meaning "fate," flew from most shops, where lanterns had already been lit. However, some opted for more poetic names to draw the refined: Hall of Clouds and Stars and Iron Palm Court proclaimed their skills at astrology or palm reading. Statuettes in every workable stone or wood known to the empire crowded the shelves and tables, in the images of Buddha or the Goddess of Mercy. Rosaries, incense, and charts covered other walls, some with complex details of planets and stars and the hours of the day.

Women with swollen bellies pulled toddlers along, asking for predictions on whether they'd bear sons. Others holding babes peered into shacks offering to take the child's birth date and time to come up with a lucky name.

Jin shook off wistful thoughts of whether her parents would have done the same for her, had they lived. She used to imagine what it might have been like, having a mother fussing over her name, instead of Haitao naming her for the scar behind her ear. She cursed under her breath. She was far too old to still be missing what she didn't have, she thought angrily, and focused on her task.

Jin wove between the thinning crowds, glancing at various tents and dismissing them. All dealt with the living. She needed the ones who dealt with the dead.

At a corner where the shops crowded closer together, however, she realized she was on the right track. The crowds here thinned, and there were visibly fewer women. Especially pregnant ones. No one wanted to draw ill luck from the darker fortune tellers, she presumed.

She glanced at the signs and then chose one hawking oracle bones. There was only one person in front of her, and when he had finished, she sat down at the table. A reed-thin man with a wispy beard sat on the opposite side, his puckered lips wrapped around a pipe.

"Good man," the fortune teller said, using tongs to turn over some heating bones in a corner stove that glowed red, "what is it you wish to know from your ancestors?"

"Excuse me, Uncle," Jin said, "but I am looking for a woman said to conjure the dead. Would you know where I can find her? Her name is Yuli."

The man stiffened at the name, and he fumbled the bone back into the fire.

"Get out."

"Excuse me?" Jin asked, surprised.

The old man glanced behind her, then along the street for good measure. "She's down the lane, to the right. But no one goes there, and I don't know her. You hear?"

Jin nodded and left. A bell sounded down the lane, and she cursed under her breath. With no pass to be out after curfew, she would have to make sure she returned to the palace before the next bell.

She followed the man's instructions, heading down the lane past increasingly silent and brooding stalls, some with heavy wooden doors. She reached one with a sign that had but a single symbol on it: a white chrysanthemum.

If she was in another neighborhood, Jin would have assumed this was a funeral organizer. But the door was too small, and this was not the district for funerary supplies. This was the fortune-teller district. She pushed at the door and found it locked.

"Appointment only!"

Jin suppressed a smile at the familiar voice. "I hear you are the best, Lady Yuli."

There was a moment of silence, before a window cracked open, revealing a pale face and suspicious eye.

"It's me," Jin said. "Rider Wang Kwei Jin."

"I know who you are," Yuli said. "No one calls me Lady Yuli."

Jin sighed. "May I enter?"

"What for?"

"I need to ask you something."

The eyes peered around the street, taking in the stray dog trotting to investigate a pile of scraps, and an older matron sweeping the outside of a nearby stall.

The windows banged shut, and then the door was unlatched and swung open. Jin entered, and Yuli immediately shut the doors again.

"Does he know you're here?" Yuli asked, her voice barely above a whisper.

Jin turned to face her. She knew who Yuli meant. Jin didn't blame Yuli for fearing the marquis. She looked the same, with the face that might have once been pretty but that now had a crisscross of scars across one cheek. A souvenir from Sanjin years ago.

"No."

Yuli eyed her, even more fearful. "Then why are you here?"

"Business is slow, I take it?" Jin said instead, looking around. The cramped room was dark but tidy. A table in the middle was clearly for clients, surrounded by four crouching stools. An altar against one wall held offerings for the god of the dead, and a shelf held various vases and drinks. Otherwise, the room held no indication of Yuli's powers.

"No one wants to come see the one who Sanjin took to the tea rooms twice. Unless they're desperate."

Jin nodded sympathetically. "Do you need money?"

Yuli sniffed. "Everyone needs money."

"Then I would like you to advise me." She took out her coin purse and sat at the table, motioning for Yuli to sit.

"I taught you everything I know," Yuli said, though she eyed the coin purse hungrily.

"Tell me, how old are you?"

Yuli regarded her quietly. "Ah. I wondered when you would notice." She brought a pot of tea from a back room and set out two small cups. She poured, then sat down. "I am forty."

Jin sipped her tea, trying to hide the shake in her hands. Yuli looked fifty, and Jin had put that down to a hard life scraping a living together. A hard life made harder by her run-in with the head of the Royal Veil. Jin still marveled that Yuli had thought to blackmail the most feared man in the empire.

"You didn't tell me that flaring ages you," Jin said quietly.

Yuli sighed. "You didn't ask. Besides, would you have stopped doing it, knowing what you know?"

Jin was silent.

"Exactly. You don't refuse Marquis Sanjin." Yuli peered at her and took her chin in her fingers. She made a soft noise in her throat. "By the heavens, you have aged faster than anyone I know. I heard you summoned over a thousand people at the Battle of Bohai. Is that true?"

Jin nodded.

Yuli gave a dark chuckle. "Well then, anyone else would be dead."

"How do I stop it?"

Yuli snorted. "There's no stopping it. You are dealing in life force, girl. You go and pull on the life force that has already scattered as what we know as death, but when you do that, you give up a little of your own life. There is no taking without giving, no action that has no price. You have been summoning and rebuilding people to an extent that I never imagined. It's no wonder you have some wrinkles and grey hair."

"So . . . will I die? Or just . . . age forever?"

Yuli shrugged. "If it were me, yes. For me, even drawing phantasms costs me. But you clearly have your dragon's power. You can manifest thousands and still be sitting here breathing today. But whether you'll die sooner, I don't know. You are blood bonded, so who can say?"

Who indeed. Jin had found some answers, but she was disappointed to not find them all. She was in uncharted territory; no one had been blood bonded *and* had such a dark gift. There was no one to ask, no one to learn from. That in itself was terrifying.

"Is there anything else I should know about . . . this gift?"

"It weakens you after you use it," Yuli said. "But you've probably already learned that. Make sure you don't become so weak you can't defend yourself. That's why I always say, don't flare unless you must."

Another thought occurred to Jin. "Do the dead lie?"

Yuli laughed. "What, you think death makes someone honest and talkative? Of course they lie."

A loud knock sounded on the door. Jin caught a whiff of oiled leather, boots, and a distinct metallic smell. She clamped a hand over Yuli's mouth, shaking her head.

Yuli's eyes widened.

"Royal Veil, open up! Yuli is being summoned to the palace."

By the eight levels of hell. Jin had known Sanjin would come here for information, but she hadn't thought he'd be so quick. She nodded for Yuli to go toward the back rooms and hoped that there was another entry somewhere. The soldiers would have no reason to think Yuli would run, so hopefully they hadn't thought to station anyone there.

Once Yuli was safely gone and the pounding grew, Jin threw open the doors.

"We're seeking—" The guard paused, catching a good look at Jin. "Aren't you—"

"Rider Jin," she said, "yes."

The guard blinked, then narrowed his eyes. "What are you doing here?"

"The same as you, I imagine," Jin said. "Looking to have my fortune told."

The man shot her a scowl, but she opened the door wide. "She wasn't here when I arrived. You're free to search."

The Veil agent barked an order to the three behind him and moved past Jin into the house. Once they were satisfied the place was empty, the others left and fanned through the streets. Jin believed Yuli would be smart enough to know where to hide. And she hoped the woman still had some friends left.

"I think Marquis Sanjin will want a word."

Jin said nothing. No doubt he would, and no doubt there would be consequences for her leaving the palace without permission.

But it had been worth it. She had a little more information, and if the empress wanted her to stop deteriorating, then they would have to stop training her with the Veil. Or at least stop demanding she flare all the time.

THE TEA STEAMED on the table while a bird flitted on its cage bars, fluffing its feathers and turning its bright orange beak in sharp little movements.

Jin watched Sanjin behind the desk, his movements

unhurried as he poured the tea and let the leaves swirl. His hands, she noticed for the hundredth time, were smooth. Such strange skin for a man who inflicted such pain. She thought back to what Haitao had told her, about the man with smooth hands who had sold her to him.

"I understand you went to see Lady Yuli. Why?"

"I thought to visit an old friend. She and I became quite close during training."

He frowned, and she wondered whether she should have left that part out. Sanjin didn't need to think Yuli had allies. He would only go after her all the more.

"And did you see her?"

"As I told the guards," Jin said easily, "she was gone when I got there."

"The guards heard speaking," Sanjin said.

"I was trying to see if she was at home."

"Two voices?" Sanjin asked.

"I summoned someone," Jin said.

Sanjin narrowed his eyes, but let it lie, apparently tired of trying to catch her out. "You still seem unaware of what a privileged position you are in. You have the empire's respect and trust, and we need you."

"Can I trust the empire?"

He raised an eyebrow. "Do you deserve it?"

"I believe that trust begets trust, Marquis Sanjin. I sought Yuli because my flaring is aging me and weakening me."

Sanjin poured a cup of tea. "A blade's edge comes

from sharpening, and a plum blossom's fragrance comes from winter's bitter cold."

"My poetry is no match for yours, Marquis Sanjin," she said tightly, "but I know that swords struck too hard will break. And plum wine, once frozen, loses its flavor." If he feared the empress, then it was time to see if the fear of breaking her would work.

Sanjin's expression remained stony, his eyes narrowed. "Well then, you may be gratified to hear that the empress shares your view. I am pausing your flaring until further notice."

Jin bowed. "I appreciate and thank you for the concern. However, I would like to make a further request. I wish to graduate from the Veil as soon as possible."

Though Sanjin watched her impassively, his very silence spoke of his surprise. "Graduate? You would have to pass the test first."

"The Iron Mind, yes," Jin said evenly.

This time a ghost of a smile appeared. "You know of it. Do you know what it involves?"

"A day's interrogation."

He leaned forward, folding his hands in his robes. "That's right. If you can survive without giving up the information you've been tasked to protect, then you pass."

"If not?"

"Then we continue your training. Harder, because you severely misjudged your abilities."

Jin's skin prickled at the thought. But she needed to leave the Veil, and kill Mengkhis, before she aged further. If this was her way out, then so be it.

"Then I respectfully request to complete the test as soon as possible."

The marquis regarded her. "I cannot agree."

"If you are truly making me go through this so that I can beat Mengkhis, then all that matters is that I can pass the test," Jin said. "If I can pass, then I am ready."

His eyes narrowed, and she knew she had hit home.

"The longer you keep me here, the less time I have to hunt down Mengkhis," Jin said.

"I will speak to the empress," he conceded.

It was only when she was nearing her dorms that she realized there had been no punishment for leaving the palace without permission. But she refused to celebrate just yet. Her instincts told her that Sanjin wouldn't let her leave his claws without a fight.

CHAPTER 23

"Today's lesson will be a little different," Ah-Ming said as Jin and her squad mates noticed that no mats were available. "We will be training in the city."

Jin knew better than to ask, and followed the others' lead as Ah-Ming took them through the courtyard to the outer perimeters of the Veil walls, where a cart with an awning awaited them. They climbed in, Ah-Ming bringing up the rear, and with a "yah!" the driver set the horses to a quick gait through the palace and out a western side door.

Soon they were bouncing along the outer canal amongst throngs of people, joining the busy first ring road that encircled the palace walls.

The jolting ride brought back memories of her life as a thief, when she spent entire days in a bustling city, combing the streets and picking all manner of pockets.

A stifled groan rose next to her. She looked over and saw her squad mates with their hands out, different fingers outstretched.

"Why do I always lose?" Foxface hissed under his breath, but even so, Ah-Ming heard and glared. Jin understood what was happening.

"You'll be assigned partners," Ah-Ming said gruffly. "Complaints will earn you nightsoil duty."

Foxface looked relieved, while Westie and Mushroom cast Jin wary looks. She gazed back out the window. There was a time when the small-framed Jin would have worried about having to hold her own. Now, with her blood bond, she knew she was stronger than any of them, and their disdain for her only seemed petty.

The cart trundled up to a ramshackle inn with a worn banner sporting the character for "wine." Jin recognized the signs of a paid network inn immediately. The tables were just filthy enough to discourage real discerning customers, and if the smell of the inn was anything to go by, the wine was watered down so that those who did come in didn't stay for seconds. Like many taverns, it had seats out the front and private back rooms where more prestigious patrons could imbibe sorghum or rice brews in privacy. An innkeeper led them to one of these, pushing aside a musty curtain and waiting for them all to file in before dropping the fabric behind them and taking his leave.

"We will be testing your teamwork today," Ah-Ming

began. "As Veil agents, you may sometimes be tasked with working together to find targets."

Jin glanced at her squad mates. This would be preferable to pain exercises, that was certain, but she also had little faith in their abilities to work together, especially considering how none of them wanted to partner with her. Outside of some quick grunted comments, none of her squad mates seemed too eager to converse.

"Your target is an envoy disguised as a musician," Ah-Ming said. "All we know of him is that he is somewhere in the eastern market, and he has a scroll with the names of ministers who are passing sensitive information. Your job is to find him and secure the scroll. First team to bring the scroll back here will win a day's holiday."

Even Jin's excitement picked up at that.

"What kind of musician is the target, Master Ah-Ming?" Mushroom asked.

Ah-Ming snorted. "I have given you all the information. The rest is up to you. Now for teams." He nodded to Mushroom, Foxface, and Westie. "You will be the red team." He turned to Jin and Bean. "You two will be the blue team."

Foxface's lip twitched in a suppressed snicker, while his teammates looked relieved. To Jin's surprise, Bean wore a smug, toothy grin.

As they left the building, the red team gave them contemptuous waves. "Outnumbered! Give up now and we'll bring you something back from our day off," Westie crowed.

Bean spat, the glob landing just shy of Westie's foot. "What a laugh. The closest you'll get to a day off in the city is when you beg us to fart in your faces after eating our fill at the best inns!"

Jin looked at him, eyebrows raised.

"I'm not changing my language because of you," Bean scowled.

"I didn't ask you to," Jin replied. "But we do have to get moving. The eastern market is at least several wards from here."

Bean motioned toward the main avenue of Vermillion Birds, only a few streets away. "Not if we travel by main thoroughfare."

She followed him, confused, until they broke out onto the bustling north-south artery. Here, the avenue was a good arrow's flight across, so wide that one could barely see the other side. This was not just because of distance, but because of the throngs of people on either side, along with the thick flow of horses, camels, and donkey carts at the center.

Bean gestured at a passing horse cart. "That one!"

He wove through the pedestrians with an expertise that even a thief would envy, then expertly hopped on the back ledge. Jin joined him, admiring his thinking. A cart traveling along the central avenue would move faster, unencumbered by the foot traffic that clogged every other alley and street in the city. Here, vehicles kept to the middle, while foot traffic stayed on either side, allowing carts and merchants to move their wares quickly.

Jin eyed the tall clay vats of wine in the cart that hid them from the driver's view. "How do you know this is going to the eastern market?"

Bean grunted. "Taverns like to label their vats, to keep inventory. The vats are unmarked, so they haven't been sold to a tavern yet. Which means it's headed for the market. And the wine's cheap, you can tell by the containers. Western market only sells the fine stuff, so this is going to the eastern market."

Jin regarded him. "You learn this in the Veil?"

"No. I was in love with this girl who worked at a wine seller's. Figured I'd learn everything I could to try and earn her favor." He scrunched his face. "Didn't work."

Jin sat in silence for a moment. "You looked glad to be teamed with me. Why?"

"You used to be a thief, plus you're blood bonded. Girl or not, you have some advantages." He paused and looked at her, as if trying to decide how much to say. "Remember, there's no such thing as a Veil exercise."

"Meaning?"

"Meaning this is to weed out the non-Veil material."

"So if we fail . . . they kick us out?" Jin asked.

He gave her a pointed look. "Don't fail."

They rolled briskly by several streets before Bean elbowed her.

"This is us." He jumped down and would have dissolved into the crowd if she hadn't been right on his heels. They dove through the throng, and a few turns later found themselves before the market gates. The dark-robed market guards reminded Jin of her thieving days in Kwannay, but she gave no hint as she followed Bean forward. The guards here were more shabbily dressed than the ones at the western market, where luxury goods abounded. Here, where the average Changan citizen came for their foods, linen, pottery, and inks or dyes, the guards were relaxed, almost bored.

Jin scanned the people beyond the gates as she and Bean passed through with shoppers. No sign of Foxface or the others, which boded well.

Once they were past the gates, Bean scratched one cheek. "I say we start with the tea houses where the musicians play," he said.

In a market, there wouldn't be too many tea houses. People came to shop, not dine, and most of the food vendors were stalls, with no place to sit, much less host a performing musician. "I doubt it would be that easy."

Bean raised an eyebrow. "You have a better idea?"

"You start at the north end," she conceded. "From the tea house, work your way east and south. I'll start at the south end and work my way north and west."

"We shouldn't split."

"We'll be faster, which means winning," Jin said.

Bean nodded. "Fine. If you think that works."

They parted ways, and Jin found her teahouse without too much trouble. It had a tattered sun-beaten flag at the top, beckoning the thirsty and hungry. The place had two stories, but a quick sweep told her there was no one she was looking for. A few calligraphers tried to ply their services, and trinket sellers roamed the edges of the tavern's grounds, tempting the clientele. But there were no musicians.

Jin re-emerged onto the street and glanced up and down the milling alley. Time to do the footwork.

She combed street after street, doubling back at times when she thought she saw someone who didn't fit the landscape. She spotted plenty of thieves, her own past making them obvious to her at once. But she was not here for cutpurses.

Stalls selling spices, dried goods, and hand-woven baskets crowded the entire length, and the clink of weights punctuated the sound of haggling.

Jin's ears pricked. Sound. Wouldn't a musician be playing music?

She focused, using her blood bond to dig down beneath the layers of everyday market noise to the ones that were more rhythmic and melodic: the regular hammering of a blacksmith, the ringing of a bell as the inspectors examined each vendor's weights and coin to ensure no one was cheating their customers.

And there it was . . . the thin, reedy plucking of strings. A thought occurred to her then. They had been looking in all the wrong places. They were in a market where few musicians wandered the streets, and there were few taverns. But a market sold everything—including musical instruments.

She followed the sounds, passing lane after lane, circling back when the musical twangs faded. She turned a corner and grinned.

Every stall lining this lane sold instruments. There were pear-shaped pipas, flutes of every length and make, mouth organs, drums of deer skin and red lacquer, as well as long, heavy zithers that would have needed four men to carry.

Jin walked slowly amongst the stalls, analyzing every face, every robe. She wanted the day off for herself and Rayshan, not just for a reprieve from the training but also, if she was honest, because she relished paying Foxface back. Now she just had to find the spy before he did.

It was somewhere between the twentieth and thirtieth stall that she paused. Something had sparked a memory in her mind, and she retraced her steps, looking over every shop and every face to find what it was.

And that's when she saw him.

He wore a felt hat in the Tibetan style, and one eye was covered by a patch. He sat on a frayed woolen mat hunched over a *dranyen*, a Tibetan lute with a head carved in the shape of a dragon. And though he was tuning the lute with his head turned, Jin still recognized him.

He was the towering man who had brought her into the Veil that first day, the one with dead eyes.

She began making her way through the crowd, her hand on the sword at her waist, when two meaty fists descended on her shoulders, spinning her around. Her knee was up in a heartbeat, and Westie doubled over, clutching his midsection, his lips curled.

"Curse your mother!"

Jin turned around, ready to confront the "spy," when she saw Foxface smiling at her while Mushroom leaned against the stall with a semi-apologetic look on his face. "Better luck next time, eh?"

Foxface stepped into the shop and pushed past a customer before sauntering up to Dead Eyes. The younger man snatched the dranyen out of the brute's hands. He broke the instrument across his knee, revealing a scroll. He held it aloft, triumphant.

"We won!"

Jin seethed, but then a flash of steel drew her eye. The move was so fast, even she barely registered it, and Foxface didn't seem aware of what was happening until he noticed the damp staining his coat.

He looked down, confused, at the blood seeping from his side. The man stood and pulled the eyepatch away. Westie and Mushroom lunged at him, and soon instruments screeched and splintered as they crashed from the walls.

Jin stood, unsure what was going on, until a hand shook her roughly.

"Come on!"

She turned to see Bean's hand on her arm, and he yanked her with him, the scroll in his other hand as he pulled them through the crowd.

"Where are you going?" she hissed.

"To finish the assignment!" he said.

"They're getting killed back there!" she protested.

Bean licked his lips, clearly scared. "Maybe. But that's Veil training. Nothing matters but the target." He held up the scroll, the paper flecked with Foxface's blood. "Now come on."

She shook free. "We can't let them die there!"

"Listen—" Bean's gaze was fierce as he pulled her into an alleyway, avoiding a rush of shouting market soldiers who muscled their way through the disoriented crowds "—if you go back, you'll be disobeying Veil instructions."

"This is an exercise!" Jin protested.

"Nothing in the Veil is an exercise," Bean hissed. "Forget your precious Dragon Class training. This is not about loyalty to your team or wing mates. Mission first, life last, empire always, remember? Now come, or I'll have to kill you here."

She took a step back. "You can't kill me, remember?"

Bean swallowed, hesitating for a breath before saying, "Don't say I didn't warn you."

With that, he slid the scroll into his robes and strode out into the crowd, disappearing within a blink.

Jin stood, digesting his words, then raced back to the stall. What was once a luxurious music store was now a mess of wood and string. The market soldiers had formed a ring around the stall and were keeping onlookers back, but through their shoulders, Jin saw that Dead Eyes was gone. She also didn't see Westie or Mushroom, which meant that they had either escaped or had already been arrested.

But she did catch a glimpse of Foxface's lifeless hand, lying splayed open on the carpet like an overturned turtle.

Jin turned and stalked, numb and hot at the same time.

She had no love for Foxface, but the shock of his death still made her hand shake. Somehow, she had forgotten her first lesson in the Veil: that everyone was expendable. As Bean had said, this was not the Dragon Class. If a rider died, they lost the dragon as well—unless they decided to risk an unbonding and a rebonding to a new rider. But what was a person in the Veil? An insignificant life, to be replaced with a nameless other. Her situation came into sharp clarity in that moment, and Rayshan's hum across the bond both comforted and saddened her. For she would never endanger him, never put him in that situation, if she could help it. But Bean was right. Maybe she already had.

She wasn't sure where she was going until she was outside the market gates, where the guards had abandoned their posts at the commotion. When she had walked a few paces, a horse-drawn carriage drew up and the door flew open. She barely had time to recognize Dead Eyes, now without his eyepatch or Tibetan hat, before his burly hand pulled her into the carriage. She prepared to fight but then spied the other occupant. Or rather, occupants.

"I am glad we found you," Sanjin said smoothly.

Bean was sitting next to him and sweating so profusely that his face gleamed even in the dim light of the shuttered carriage. The vehicle swayed as they traveled through the streets, while Dead Eyes sat impassively on the other side of her, blocking the carriage door.

"Why did you not return with your team member?"

Jin was about to say she had gone back for Foxface when Bean's eyes caught hers. In that moment she remembered his words: the Veil only cared about completing the mission. They didn't care about loyalty, or morals, or whether she and Bean had worked well together. Only that they had both performed in the best interests of the Veil. And Bean's perspiration meant he was at risk.

Jin couldn't die. But Bean could. And Jin had had enough of death today. She would be seeing Foxface's ghost soon enough, she imagined.

"We felt it would be best to create a diversion, Master Sanjin," Jin said.

"A diversion?" Sanjin's eyebrows rose.

Jin nodded. "In the confusion, the other team couldn't know which one of us had the scroll. They would have to chase both of us, giving our team the better chance of delivering the goal."

Bean quickly blinked back tears, and Jin's heartbeat quickened. Were they tears of relief, or fear?

Silence stretched.

"That is truly clever," Sanjin said at last. "However, it doesn't quite match what your teammate says."

Jin tried to hide the rigidity in her. "Oh?"

Sanjin turned to Bean. "No. He says it was his idea to create the diversion, not a mutual decision."

"Things can be murky upon recollection of a stressful situation, Master Sanjin," Jin said tightly.

Sanjin tutted. "We train you for stressful situations. We have no room in the Veil for faulty memories. And certainly no place for those who lie to us. Therefore, for your lies and for not being able to debrief properly, we will reduce your prize to a half-day's holiday."

Bean's eyes found hers, and she realized he had risked much to defend her. He could have told Sanjin she had run back to help, and left her to her punishment, but clearly, he had worked her actions into something acceptable to the Veil. She didn't dare acknowledge it now, but throughout the ride back to the palace, the knot of gratitude in her grew. The man who feared death had risked his life to save her pain.

That night she returned to her bed bruised and aching, hoping sleep might help her escape the brutality of the day.

There was no mention of a funeral, or where Foxface's body had been taken. Foxface's dorm was wordlessly cleaned out by a silent Veil servant, and though Mushroom and Westie had only minor injuries, they seemed to withdraw into invisible shells and avoided eye contact with Jin. She wondered if they blamed her for Foxface's death. Well, what was done was done.

But just as she began twisting her hair into a braid, gongs sounded. Initiates suppressed their groans and rushed from the dorms to stand at attention outside.

She chanced a glance at Bean next to her, but he stared straight ahead, giving no hint as to whether he knew what was going on. Mushroom and Westie were even less readable, though part of it might have been Mushroom's swollen nose and Westie's split lip.

Ah-Ming strode down the line of Veil initiates, accompanied by two servants who bore brushes, combs, and vials of tonic on trays.

"Listen well!" Ah-Ming barked. "There are reports of a lice infestation! Everyone will be examined, and anyone with lice will be taken for treatment immediately. Bow your heads until I say you can go."

As one, the initiates bent over, allowing the examiners to comb through their hair and examine the napes of their necks. At the last moment, Jin caught sight of Sanjin entering the courtyard. His eyes surveyed the crowd and then landed on Jin.

Jin quickly looked at the ground. Lice? This late in the season? It was not unheard of, but given the close quarters in the dorms, Jin doubted anyone here would be infested without everyone knowing already.

Fingers dug into Jin's hair, pulling at the roots and flipping from side to side. The examiner combed her hair from the nape of her neck, first one way, and then another.

Jin saw Sanjin's boots stop before her.

"Any sign of lice?"

"No, Master Sanjin," the man murmured.

"Let me see."

A shiver of revulsion passed through Jin as Sanjin's hands brushed back a lock of hair from her neck.

Another thumb and forefinger bent her left ear to one side, then did the same with her other ear.

Was it her imagination, or did Sanjin pause over her scar? She braced herself for his question, but it never came.

"Continue," Sanjin said, and the servant rushed to obey. The boots continued down the line, until Ah-Ming barked for them all to return to their dorms.

Jin glanced at the moon gate leading out of the initiates' courtyard, but Sanjin was nowhere in sight, nor were the examiners. As she had expected, no one in the Veil had lice.

Not even bugs could survive the Veil uninvited.

THE SUMMONS CONFUSED JIN, and she had to read it twice to make sure she had understood.

But, yes, it was a summons to the baths. And when Ah-Ming reluctantly canceled her afternoon training, a servant led her to Meipin's to choose an appropriate gown.

Meipin pursed her lips when she heard. "That is quite an honor. One even I have not had."

Jin looked up, trying to decipher whether her friend was jealous. But Meipin smiled, the delicate silver birds on her hairpiece bobbing as she stood. "Only the immediate family are given access to the royal baths."

Jin hadn't known that the empress had social baths,

as she thought that was purely a custom amongst the middle class, who would come together to bathe, gossip, and trade information. But, she supposed, a palace was even more of a locale for such things, given how lives were won and lost based on information.

"Who usually goes, then?"

Meipin shrugged. "Some of the empress's sisters, who no doubt keep her informed of goings on amongst the royal princes they are married to." She lowered her voice. "And of course there are the rumors that the empress entertains her lovers at the baths."

Jin frowned. She had never considered the empress having lovers, though she supposed it made sense. She just couldn't think of who.

As if reading her thoughts, Meipin leaned forward. "They say Marquis Sanjin is one of them."

Sanjin being anyone's lover was sickening, and Jin found it hard to believe.

Meipin smiled wickedly. "Perhaps your trip to the baths will tell us whether the rumor is true."

This was one truth she didn't need. When night came, she followed the imperial servant sent to fetch her.

She tried to quash the unease at the thought of being naked with a group of strangers. It didn't matter that they were all women. She knew she would be different, her body a tapestry of scars and burns from her thieving, and dragonriding, days. From the time she and Lu had robbed the jeweler, who had thrown a hot crucible at them and clipped her on the calf, she had a half-moon scar. Not to mention the kiss of whips across her back courtesy of Haitao and the slice over one breast that a rival gang member had gifted her during a fight. That had bled much, but she had made him bleed more.

Jin had asked Meipin multiple questions about etiquette in the baths, and thankfully, Meipin seemed to know all the rules.

"Don't enter until the empress does," Meipin said. "You should rinse yourself in the buckets provided first, then enter the baths. Don't put your hair in."

The bathhouse was warm, heated by underground pipes that ran under the thin marble tiles. Columns studded with jade and pearl held up the high ceiling, where carved phoenixes and dragons flew amongst sculpted clouds.

The baths themselves were marvels in luxury, sunken pools that steamed from the fires beneath them. There were three in all—two small and one longer pool with paintings of lilies, exotic goldfish, and river fronds on the bottom, which created the impression of swimming in an exotic pond.

Despite her apprehension at bathing with strangers, she found the unexpected emptiness of the baths more disconcerting. The servant who had escorted her here had disappeared, leaving her alone.

Jin smelled the empress before she arrived at the far

corridor, several maids in attendance. A cloud of jasmine, incense, and pomegranate preceded them.

"The waters are from a spring, you know."

Jin bowed, even more aware of her own nakedness beneath her robe as two of the maids disrobed the empress. Though Jin averted her eyes, she caught sight of a body so smooth and pale as to rival the marble at their feet, the limbs perfectly proportioned. Not a scar to be seen.

Jin pulled her robe from her and placed it on a bench. "Will there not be anyone else joining us then, Your Majesty?"

The empress stepped into the pool, the water rippling. "No. I wanted to speak alone."

Jin shook her head. "I did not know you bathed privately with only one other, Your Majesty."

"I see you are asking around," the empress said. "Good. It is useful to know what you are walking into. I wanted to have a private discussion. Come into the water."

Taking a deep breath, Jin entered the pool.

"I heard you took swimming lessons. The prince says you are very good."

"I wouldn't say good, Your Majesty," Jin replied. Tai had given her private lessons before the Battle at Bohai, and she had to admit that without his help, she would have likely sunk to the bottom of the sea.

The empress looked pointedly at Jin's breast. "I see you fought much before you stole a dragon."

Jin self-consciously pulled at a robe that wasn't there. There was no hiding anything, not here, not naked, and she wondered if that was the empress's intent. She couldn't imagine two bodies more dissimilar, though perhaps the empress's resembled one of half her age. The smooth, supple skin and the elegant neck, everything unmarred, told only a tale of warmth and comfort every day, with the finest of oils. Jin's told an uglier story, every beating etched clearly on her skin like a sign of her ill birth, her past.

"Tell me, what do you know of your parents?"

The question took Jin by surprise. "I thought we weren't to speak of it, Your Majesty. I mean, Your Divine Majesty." Sanjin had in no uncertain terms told her that any hint at her criminal past would be a stain on the empress. For the empress had been the one to decide they keep Jin in Dagon Class—a decision that indirectly, if not directly, led to Gao's coup.

"I like to speak of things fully and put them to rest. What do you know of your parents?"

"That I was born to a criminal who was executed for murdering her husband, Your Divine Majesty," Jin replied.

The empress motioned at a servant, who hastened over with a large bowl. Inside were several balls of soap, their perfumes of lily, orange, and sandalwood more overpowering than soothing.

The empress took one and motioned for Jin to do

the same. The empress wet her ball and ran it around her neck and chest.

"Did your . . . adopted father, was it, tell you that?"

The thought of Haitao brought on an onslaught of conflicting thoughts, as it always did, and wasn't helped when Jin noticed his phantasm in the shadows of the pools, no doubt summoned by her whirlwind emotions.

The empress turned, but by then Haitao had dissolved like ash. "I'd rather you not summon while we are in the baths."

Jin shivered. She sometimes still lost control of whom she summoned and when. "Yes, Your Majesty."

"Your adopted father told you that you were the child of a criminal?" the empress repeated.

"No, Your Majesty," Jin said. "He told me he found me in the streets of the capital."

"A common enough story," the empress said. "It must be hard, having no idea who your parents are, where you came from." She paused. "Do you resent your parents?"

"Sometimes, Your Majesty."

"Do you wish you knew who they were?"

"No." This was partially true. For years she had managed to push her desire to know into a corner of her mind, but ever since Gao's accusation, she had felt torn. Torn between accepting the likelihood of his theory and hoping desperately that he was wrong.

"Curiosity can be a dangerous thing," the empress

said, and for once Jin had the sense that the empress was not just speaking of Jin, but of herself. "Once you know something, you cannot erase the knowledge and how it shapes you, sometimes for the worse. Would you choose that?"

"At least it would be my choice, Your Majesty." She expected Haitao to appear again, but he didn't. "All my life I have had knowledge withheld from me, by people who hope to control me by it. I am tired of it."

The empress rubbed the soap suds from herself. "I can understand. I often feel that there is a proper time for the truth." She stepped out of the bath, the water running from her, and Jin picked up on some hidden cue that she was meant to follow. She did, and immediately missed the water's protection, acutely aware of her nakedness as the two stood facing each other.

Maids hurried forward with soft robes and draped them over the empress's and Jin's shoulders. The material was thick linen, but Jin was simply grateful to regain dignity over her body. She wasn't sure whether the empress's intent was to shame her, but she refused to compare herself. The empress was a thing of beauty. She of blades and the streets and now dragon fire.

The maids took out combs and began brushing their hair.

"Here, may I?" the empress held out a hand, and the maid didn't even wait for a reply from Jin before handing it over. The empress motioned for Jin to turn around and then began brushing the younger woman's hair into a bun.

"You are lucky, Rider Jin. You don't have classic beauty, but you have something even more intoxicating." She pulled the hair back from Jin's neck, and her hands seemed to tense around Jin's hair.

Jin waited. When no answer came, she asked hesitantly, "And what is that, Your Majesty?"

"That's . . . mystery, Rider Jin. You have mystery." She pinned Jin's hair in a simple bun, and the point of it jabbed Jin's scalp. She winced.

"Forgive me," the empress said, "I have not done another's hair for a very long time." Jin thought her voice shook.

The empress turned abruptly and left, her robes billowing and her maids hurrying to keep up. If Jin didn't know better, she would have said the empress was fleeing.

CHAPTER 25

"**J**ust one more," Aadan promised.

Wanli huffed but obliged. The dragon was growing increasingly impatient with their project, and Aadan empathized. Pulling water out of these desert sands was like milking rock.

They had managed to create five wells thus far, spaced at regular intervals outside Samarkand. With soldiers guarding the wells, Samarkand would have an enviable source of income from all the traders coming and going with their thirsty camels and horses.

Wanli arched his neck and spread his wings, making the ground shiver. The sand next to him darkened, then glistened, then disappeared as water slowly took its place. Aadan patted Wanli's flank in encouragement, then jumped when his great silver tail swept past.

He commented on how irritable Wanli had become,

and the dragon gave a mental sigh. The Song of Scales was intensifying, and Aadan knew he could not put it off much longer. His dragon would have to return to China.

Aadan retreated to where his men were knee-deep, digging a square hole, along with dozens of Samarkand workers. A simple inn and toll collection office would be built here, along with basic accommodations for a small garrison.

Gah'med was waiting for him, having just ridden in from Samarkand. He held a cloth satchel, which he tossed to Aadan. "The latest."

Aadan entered a ramshackle tent that offered shelter from the sun, and sat down on a dusty carpet. He upturned the satchel and let the scrolls fall, sorting through them. Gah'med had followed him in, and sat down heavily opposite him, reaching for a pitcher of watered wine and serving a generous portion.

"This is everything?" Aadan asked.

Gah'med grunted. "You expected more?" He eyed Aadan shrewdly. "There's no response to the letter you sent with that dragonrider, if that's what you're searching for."

Aadan hid his disappointment. Composing even the shortest letter took him weeks, and he recognized the irony. He knew a dozen languages, and yet none had the words to express what he wanted to say to Jin.

He had tasked Gah'med to take that single letter to the dragonrider Mao, who occasionally made trips to the outermost posts of the empire. He could trust Mao to deliver it safely. Mao had once taken Jin's secret message to her thief clan and would know who Aadan meant by the addressee "a friend from Gaozho."

"If it's any comfort," Gah'med said, "I think the rider Mao is dead."

Aadan looked at him, shocked. "Dead?"

Gah'med nodded. "Heard it was some dragon mating accident."

Aadan closed his eyes and said a short prayer for Mao. He had been a friend, and though everyone in Dragon Class knew friendships were often cut short, it never seemed to numb the loss.

"And the letter?"

Gah'med spread his palms. "I haven't any idea. In enemy hands, for all I know."

He had made sure there was nothing that could be traced to his whereabouts or that might endanger Jin. But even so, Aadan cursed himself for the folly. Writing her was dangerous. Hoping for a reply was even more so.

Aadan sorted through the scrolls, trying to take his mind off Mao, Jin, his exile. Most were official letters from tiny surrounding countries and tribes, proposing alliances or offering to sell him information on the Arabs. None were worth considering. But others were messages from Persian informants within China and other countries, who secretly kept Aadan abreast of developments.

A roar sounded from outside, along with shouts. Gah'med turned, eyebrows raised.

"That beast will take someone's arm off one of these days."

"Wanli is the gentlest of his kind."

Gah'med snorted. "Then will he survive the mating? I have heard many do not."

Aadan pushed away his own nagging worries. "Do not mistake gentle for weak, Cousin."

Gah'med poured himself more wine. "Will you go with him? When the time comes?"

Aadan rolled up a letter he had been perusing and tossed it back into the bag. "No. Humans are not allowed on Nine Claw Mountain."

"I meant go to China."

Aadan paused. He wondered if his cousin knew how tempting the thought was. "No."

Gah'med nodded. "A wise choice." He slapped his knees and stood. "I'd best get back to Samarkand. We have much to prepare for our return to Persia once we have strangled the Arabs' trade."

But Aadan was only half listening. He was re-reading the scroll in his hands, the implications racing through his mind. "By the Wise Lord. The empress is declaring herself divine."

His cousin made a look of distaste, hooking thick thumbs in his sash. "Isn't there a Chinese expression? When the hen crows at daybreak, disaster follows."

But Aadan wasn't concerned with whether the

empress was subverting norms. With her elevation in status, no doubt it would be harder to convince her to help an underdog prince. If he was to win dragons from her, he'd have to offer something truly remarkable.

Wise Lord, there must be something valuable I can trade. But what?

AADAN HAD ONLY JUST SAT down to a quick flatbread meal after a morning of correspondence when a shout sounded from outside his tent. Jahmid appeared at the tent flap, his face pale under the dust. "Prince Aadan, you may want to see this."

Pulling on his coat and boots, Aadan stood and followed him outside. Work had begun at sunup, though Wanli was still resting from the previous days' water drawing, his hulking form visible off to the east.

Jahmid led him to where the workers had gathered around a hole as deep as two men. The crowd parted to let Aadan through, and when he looked down, he spied an ivory box half submerged in the wet sand beneath.

"What is it?" he asked.

"No one's sure," Jahmid answered. "Shall I have it brought up?"

Aadan nodded, frowning. He spied what looked like calligraphy along one side, and when the box made its way over the hole's lip after much wrangling, Aadan recognized the language.

Sanskrit.

The men gathered around as Jahmid pulled out a knife and worked the lid edge. Aadan squatted next to him, reading the writing.

"This box is from Lumbini," Aadan said, mind working.

Jahmid barely looked up from his work. "*Where?*"

"Lumbini," Aadan said. "The Buddha's birthplace."

Gah'med had reached him by then and stood squinting down at the box. "Perhaps the box is worth something, then?"

The lid gave way with a shower of sand, and Jahmid opened the lid. When Aadan lifted out the scrolls inside, he scanned the contents briefly, his brows furrowed.

"Solid elephant ivory, that's rare," Gah'med said, putting his three-fingered hand on the box and rubbing its sides. "A treasure."

Aadan shook his head. "That's not the treasure."

Gah'med squinted at him, amused. "You saying those bits of old paper are worth more?"

"Much more." Aadan scanned the documents again, wondering whether the Wise Lord had truly heard him last night. "Gah'med, these bits of old paper, as you call them, may just earn us our dragons from the Tang empire."

Gah'med and his brother simply looked at each other, then at Aadan. "How?"

Aadan grinned. "These are original sutras from Buddha's birthplace. Many monasteries and rich abbots in Changan, likely even the empress, will fight over possession for this."

Gah'med eyed him thoughtfully. "You're not suggesting you go to Changan, are you?"

Aadan didn't bother to hide his excitement. Such a find could change their fortunes, the entire fortunes of the kingdom. "No, Gah'med. I'm not suggesting. I'm ordering. I shall leave as soon as the last well is dug." He turned to Jahmid. "Please see that the box is cleaned and cared for. We'll need it for the empress."

Gah'med followed Aadan back to the tent, the scrolls still cradled in Aadan's arms.

"I will go with you."

Aadan glanced at his cousin. "The men here need you."

"*You* need me," Gah'med replied.

"Not to be unappreciative, Cousin, but for what?"

"To make sure you come back."

Aadan stilled, the scrolls still in his hands. "You think I wouldn't?"

Gah'med shrugged. "You have many ties to the Tang. You may not be able to extricate yourself, shall we say, without help."

Aadan bristled at his cousin's insinuation. "My first

duty is to the Persian people. That's why I am doing this."

Gah'med nodded. "And you need help on the way." At Aadan's look of protest, he held up a palm. "Jahmid can take care of things here. He's a good man and well-liked." He grinned slyly. "Besides, if you really are bringing dragons back with you, you'll need assistance."

Aadan sighed in exasperation. Of course. Gah'med wished to bolster his own image among the men, and share in the one advantage Aadan had: his status as the bringer of dragons.

There was no diplomatic way of leaving his cousin behind, and though Aadan had nothing to hide, he didn't relish a long journey to the Tang court with Gah'med either.

"Very well. But we will only take the bare minimum of men." Aadan didn't want to travel any slower than he had to. "We'll have to ask the king of Samarkand for a diplomatic seal so you and I can cross the border."

Gah'med nodded. "I'll see to it. And in the meantime . . . try not to let your excitement about going back to China show too much around the men. It's unbecoming."

CHAPTER 26

T he day of the deification ceremony dawned with a light rain, which the fortune tellers were quick to announce was a favorable omen of new beginnings and growth.

Tai rode with his mother in the ornate carriage built especially for the day, a golden contraption studded with carved jade, silver, and strings of beads that made music in time to the horses' gait, a six-steed affair with bridles threaded with gold. The empress had ordered the horses' hooves to be painted gold, and for gold silk to be threaded through the manes and tails. Above, dragons breathed a halo of fire in the sky, like the entrance to Heaven itself.

The roar of the crowds chanting Ten Thousand Years could, Tai thought, be heard from thousands of *li* away. It seemed the whole city was here—as they should be, for announcements had been posted across all wards that coins would be tossed to the throngs.

Even now, he could hear the sounds of raining metal and the excited shouts of the crowd as coins clattered on the attendees infiltrated the carriage. There had already been several deaths, he was sure, for the stampede for money had been feral.

The procession wound its way through the cleared streets, and Tai turned to his mother. He noticed new lines around her eyes and a deep groove around her "kway" ring. She seemed to have been fiddling with it far more of late.

"I hope all this helps ward off Mengkhis."

"It will," she assured him. "When he strikes, we will be ready."

Tai noticed she didn't say "if" and fought off a ripple of fear. His thoughts drifted to mage Situ Han.

"You have skipped two of our weekly dinners. Is the Ministry of War keeping you that busy?"

"As a matter of fact, it is." The war mongers had grown increasingly strident for a Khitan offensive, and it was becoming harder to hold them at bay. He looked back at her. "Have you thought more on having Princess Nobu rule Khitan as queen?"

The empress gave a disbelieving laugh. "What's there to think about? She will have to kill all her brothers first. Surely you are not spending all your free time with a disabled princess?"

He knew his mother was trying to bait him, but the remark felt uncalled for. Nobu was about as good-hearted and honest a person as he had ever met, fragile in her innocence despite having been widowed and orphaned in one day, with a family who only cared for her as a political tool. He felt a stab of sympathy for her —how long had it taken him to accept his role serving as the empire's chess piece? In that sense, she was about as strong as any bamboo, able to withstand the harshest of life lessons while still miraculously remaining unjaded. She likely would make a good queen for Khitan, in his opinion, if only her brothers would let her.

"I have other duties as well. The Ministry of War hungers for war with Khitan. It's all I can do to keep them in check, not to mention that we have no funds to train the soldiers, so I have some very prickly conversations with the heads of the navy and cavalry, not to mention the equerry departments."

"I put you in the position where we needed the most charm," his mother said lightly. "And hopefully the War Ministry will need less funds once we embolden the soldiers with faith in our throne."

Tai followed his mother's gaze and glimpsed in the distance a towering structure encased in yellow cloth. Even from here, he could see it was taller than most of the pagodas in the city and was being pulled into place by great thick ropes attached to four giant bronze dragons, tripled in size to better handle the statue's weight.

"You never came with me to view the statue," his mother admonished.

"I had a few pressing issues," Tai replied, not without some harshness. His last priority was seeing the monument his mother had paid a ransom to erect in the middle of Changan. But judging by its size, it was impressive. He just baulked at the idea of the cost. How many horses might they have bought? How many arrows and bows could they have outfitted their soldiers with to defend themselves against Mengkhis? Against the Khitans?

When they arrived at the square, the servants announced their presence after a great drum symphony, and the doors opened.

Tai stepped down first, and a deafening cheer went up, though he also detected cries of disappointment that Jin was not there.

You're not the only ones, he thought wryly.

His mother stepped from the carriage, a blinding vision of gold. The crowd seemed genuinely awed into silence, and Tai saw why. The empress had had her tailors working late into the nights to design a costume that would radiate light, and even on such a cloudy, leaden-sky day, her gold cast a halo about her, pushing back the darkness like a living thing.

For the first time, Tai understood his mother's point about faith and awe, for the people silently sank to their knees as one, putting down mats to bow in the mud, despite the rain and dirt soaking their finery.

Tai looked around, noting that all the top officials were there: the Minister of Law, Meipin's uncle. The Minister of Rites, as well as the Ministers of Transport, the Interior, and Agriculture, and Finance. Other nobles were also gathered in a special seated section reserved for them away from the common crowds, who were kept back at a distance of over one hundred paces. Tai spied the head mage Yao next to the Minister of Rites, and mage Situ Han behind him, his usual affable face visible and looking for all the world as if he and Tai were still on good terms.

Three gongs rang out, and the Minister of Rites walked stiffly forward. He pulled out a scroll.

"In this twenty-second year of our Divine Majesty, the Empress of Celestial Light, Wu Ze-Tian, we the Ministry of Rites dedicate this statue of the Boddhisattva to she who rules over us all, the Divine Empress Wu Ze-Tian, the Celestial Ruler of the Heavens and of the Earth, of the great China, and with thanks and humble gratitude we ask that she watches over us for the years to come. May she rule for ten thousand years."

"Ten thousand years!" the nobles echoed, and the chant grew among the crowd.

The rain eased, pattering a few moments more before the sun crept out from behind a cloud.

"Behold!" the Minister of Rites cried in a thunderous voice, pointing. "Heaven beams upon this great new statue of our protector and high savior, the Divine Majesty Wu Ze-Tian, the Boddhisattva reincarnated. She has come to ease our suffering and shield us from want! May the statue stand for ten thousand years!"

Drums sounded, and the dragons circling blasted three gusts of flame in a choreographed move.

As one, the men holding the ropes to the silk covering pulled, and the silk dropped like a dress, falling to the ground before being rolled up by the men.

Tai was, like most there, speechless. The glittering statue was the height of ten dragons, towering over the square. The feet of the statue were twice Tai's height, and the entire surface was covered in glittering gold. The face was unmistakably his mother's, whereas previous statues had all only borne a resemblance. This was, line by line, his mother's face, except for the long earlobes nearly touching the shoulders to symbolize infinite wisdom, and the tapered fingers gripping a single lotus bloom. The halo around the head was made of white jade and laced with gold, so that even the little sunlight hitting it now was refracted all around, creating a shimmering underwater ripple effect.

The crowd sighed in admiration, and even Tai had to admit it was an amazing work of art. The statue was visible from every corner of the city, he was sure, a new landmark that stood above all others. It was a clear statement: his mother oversaw the city, presiding over it like a goddess.

The crowds pushed forward, and the Minister of Rites invited people forth to touch the statue for blessings.

"Look at them," his mother murmured, practically drinking the fervor in their eyes, the pride. The city that had been gripped by fear just months ago when Baikalan was loose was now safe, happy that Mengkhis Lai and his dragon were dead, that their ruler was not just mighty, but divine.

Would anyone care that it was a lie?

If it brought peace, would it matter?

Tai believed that it did.

He watched in silence as the crowd came forward, hands clasped, murmuring prayers to Buddha. The monks moved among the crowds, chanting Buddhist mantras and taking donations from rich and poor alike.

Tai wasn't sure what made him look up, thinking the sun had disappeared once more behind a rain cloud. Yet when he looked, he blinked in confusion, for what he was seeing was impossible.

The sun was no longer where it should be, and neither was the statue. It took his mind a split breath to recognize what was happening, and by then the crowd had begun to realize as well.

The statue was falling.

Cries of surprise, then fear, rippled through the

gathering. Several onlookers at the front of the statue snatched children and turned to run but found a wall of people instead. The advancing crush made retreat impossible, so that a river of citizens was directly in the statue's path, with nowhere to go.

Tai's body reacted before his mind did. He dove forward and evened his breath. Would he be able to do it? He hoped his mother was right, that it had been made of wood instead of solid gold. Even then, he wasn't sure he had the power, and there wasn't time to unite all the mages together to pool their strength in a concerted effort.

Time seemed to slow. The statue listed and then fell, the head of his smiling mother blocking the sun as the weight of it tipped past the point of no return, the ropes snapping as the pedestal separated from mud with a great sucking sound.

Tai doubled his concentration and stretched out his arms, as if that could magically make his power more concentrated. Yet as the screams intensified around him, that seemed to be exactly what it did. The statue slowed, then halted, though the strain on his powers was like a physical assault.

"Back! Everyone, fall back!" he cried.

They didn't need to be told twice. Officials and commoners alike scattered, pushing back at the stunned crowd that at first resisted, confused. But then as they spied the hovering statue, the people retreated, pulling crying children and elderly to safety.

Tai felt as if his arms were being ripped from him, yet still he held for a few breaths before he let go, unable to hold on. The other mages had overcome their shock enough to act, chanting as they moved forward. Tai felt the weight ease from him as they helped lower the statue a hand's breath, then another, before letting it fall with a heavy crash to the ground. Half of the statue's face was still visible in the mud, the serene smile smeared with dirt, grime, and rainwater as the clouds cracked open and sunlight beamed down.

"The Prince of Dragons saved us."

The whisper started somewhere, and soon it was everywhere. The empress came to his side, her shoes muddied, and her hand found his shoulder.

"I am unharmed," he said, looking up at her, but when his eyes met her face, he saw she wasn't looking at him at all, but instead gazing in grief at her statue, then at the crowds.

With one wave of her hand she motioned to the attendants, who hauled Tai to his feet. Which proved necessary, for his limbs had gone soft and a deep ache in his bones made it impossible to stand without help.

The crowd pushed forward once more, trying to touch Tai.

"A miracle! The Prince of Dragons performed a miracle!"

The new cry took hold, and soon the crowd was like a tide, swarming the carriage. The soldiers tried to hold them back, and in the end only a warning burst of fire from a bronze dragon in the sky made the crowd collect themselves.

Tai slumped in the carriage, a marrow-deep exhaustion setting in, but laced with a strange, heady sense of power. The empress was looking at him as if he were a stranger.

"You have been lying to me." The fury in her eyes was both terrifying and, in a strange way, welcome.

"Just not entirely truthful, Mother." His voice was hoarse but firm.

"Where have you been learning the mage arts?"

"Does it matter?"

She sat forward and struck him, her long golden nails raking his face. He was too shocked to even touch his cheek but could feel the welts ripening. No blood, but the venom was unmistakable.

"Do you know what you have done?"

He stared, confused. "I did what I had to," he said tersely. "Those people would have died!"

"Do you even still have your manhood?" She made a grab for his groin, but this time he clenched her wrist so hard she winced.

"I am intact."

"Then how?" she hissed.

"Do you really think I'd tell you right now?"

This seemed to strike her as much as her blow had shocked him. Her eyes narrowed, and her lips turned a shade of purple that might have made violets envious.

She sat back, and Tai saw the effort she exerted to control herself.

"Is this part of a larger plan?"

Tai frowned. "What larger plan? Those people would have died under your statue if I hadn't intervened!"

"And now they chant your name," the empress murmured, looking out the window with a snarl.

"They were already chanting my name," Tai said, "and Jin's."

At this the empress snapped her head around to study him again. "You plan to take the throne from me." There was shock and hurt in her voice.

Tai suppressed a laugh. The reaction would only worsen things, he knew, and he likely needed to play contrite Confucian child at this point, if only to make his mother see reason. "Why would I plan that?"

"Because you have turned against me since Gao's coup," she said bitterly, and there was the threat of tears in her voice. "You don't trust me, and now you want the throne, and no doubt people will line up to help you."

"There have always been those wanting to usurp you," Tai answered. "You and I both know that. But as you said, this distrust will topple you if you let it."

She searched his face. "Then tell me, who taught you the mage arts?"

Tai hesitated. Regardless of his anger toward Situ

Han, he wasn't about to endanger him. "I do not wish to see someone punished wrongly."

The empress raised an eyebrow. "You think I would do such a thing?"

"I know you would," he said. "Throne above all."

"And you do not trust me to decide what is best for the throne?"

"Sometimes we have differing opinions."

This drew a silence from his mother. She took a deep breath. "To be honest, I am happy. It is reassuring to know that you will likely be able to hold the throne once you are ready. But I am not yielding the throne, for a very, very long time, my son. The mages have been very good to me and my health, and I intend to rule as I see fit."

Tai bowed his head. He had never craved the throne, as he had genuinely believed his mother was a good ruler, overall. "Of course, I as everyone wish you ten thousand years of life." He hadn't meant his tone to be so flippant, yet he didn't bother to soften it. After all, his mother hadn't softened the clear underlying threat in her words: that she didn't want to see him on the throne for years, and that if he tried anything, she would bury him rather than relent.

"And remember to whom you owe your title, your status," she said quietly. "I made you a crown prince. You haven't any idea how much I have done for you."

"Are you threatening me?" he asked quietly.

"Advising you," she said smoothly. "Some ducklings

get it into their heads that they can fly before they can walk. Don't make the same mistake, my son. I love you too much to see you do that."

He kept silent. The air hung, oppressive and poisonous between them, and he longed to escape the carriage.

Despite his mother's words, Tai knew a threat when he heard it.

CHAPTER 27

Sanjin granted her and Bean their half day off, though both were still shaken by Foxface's death and the market day exercise.

Jin used her day off to visit Rayshan and fly. She took her books about Mengkhis Lai with her, for over the last days Jin burned candles at night to read the forbidden book from the bookshop, clearing everything else from her mind. With no news as to whether she could take the test, this seemed her best use of time while she waited.

She swore she had been over every book on Mengkhis Lai by now. The evenings were a blur of scrolls and ink by candlelight, as she read of Mengkhis Lai's history and personal record, trying to find some clue of where he might go to hide and lay low. Of these, there were precious little. So much had been destroyed, though truth be told, she wasn't sure whether there was much to begin with.

How someone so infamous can be so mysterious is baffling, she admitted to Rayshan as he took care of an itch against a boulder near where she sat under a willow reading.

They clearly erased what they could. What do we know so far?

He was the son of a foreign princess, Jin said, scanning the parchment, *captured in war and brought back by the emperor of the time, Tai's grandfather Kangwen. Mengkhis grew up with Tai's father, Kangming, but then the two quarreled over the throne, and that's what brought them into war and the Year of Chaos.*

In the Firesong, Rayshan said, *I sense Baikalan's grief over something life-changing. Have you felt it?*

You mean that scene of the birth? Yes, there is an overwhelming anger and loss. Every time they had entered the Firesong to try to find information on Baikalan or Mengkhis, this scene kept reappearing, no matter how hard they tried to find others. When she had been hunting Baikalan and they had stopped at Jimo, the scene from the Jimo massacre had appeared, but this time they seemed unable to escape the vision of Tai's birth, the arrival of the emperor to see his new son.

What do you think it means? she asked.

I think it means that whatever caused that grief and loss will be the key to finding and defeating Mengkhis, Rayshan said.

What would Tai's birth mean to Mengkhis that he would feel such loss?

Rayshan hummed. *Perhaps the loss of the throne. Tai's birth would have meant the throne passed to him.*

But Mengkhis wasn't in direct line anyway, Jin reasoned. *He was already battling the emperor. He wouldn't hesitate to kill a newborn.* The thought sent a shiver through her.

And yet he didn't. Rayshan mused.

You mean he killed the emperor but not Tai? Jin thought on this. *Perhaps he didn't have time or didn't find them. I heard the empress hid with her son. Emar fought him and lost, but perhaps that is why the blood-bonded riders came in then.*

Jin sighed in frustration. *I've read every book on Mengkhis Lai. We've tried to search for anyone connected to him who might be dead.*

You haven't read every book.

Jin frowned, then snorted. *The gossip book about him and the empress? You really think that drivel has any worth?*

Rayshan flicked his tail. *Do you know a story about the great dragon queen Ma-shen?*

I barely know any of your legends, Jin said.

Ma-shen had a great treasure that she took from a sea god, a giant pearl that foretold the future. The sea god, angry, came to take it back, but Ma-shen denied having it. She even invited him to search her things to see for himself.

And did he?

Yes, he searched everywhere but found nothing, and so he left, reluctantly convinced that she had not stolen it.

But she had, Jin guessed.

Yes. She hid it in the refuse pile on Nine Claw Mountain, where the dragons leave their droppings and the bones of their prey. The sea god never looked there, for why would anything so precious as a magic pearl be hidden in a pile of dung?

Jin thought on this. *You think there might be such a pearl in the story of the empress and Mengkhis Lai?*

Is it not worth trying?

Yes, she admitted. *It is.*

She rolled up the scroll she had been reading and reached into her satchel to fetch the second scroll from a concealed pouch she had sewn inside. The book's author was named Bi Jian, but she suspected it was a pseudonym, for the characters were a homonym for "ink brush" and "sword." No doubt the author intended to skewer his subjects.

She leaned against the willow tree and began to read. The book was a salacious story about concubine Wu, who couldn't beget a child from the emperor, and so decided to seduce the brother, Mengkhis Lai. Chapters of sorcery and various medical tests followed, and then Wu was declared to be pregnant, which pleased the emperor but not the concubines, of whom only Concubine Liang had produced a child. Wu quickly became the new favorite.

Jin put the scroll down, thinking. Tai had no

siblings. And as far as she knew, the emperor did not have any other children, besides Concubine Liang's son, Ruzong, who died young.

She decided to ask Meipin about it at the next opportunity, which didn't come until two days later, when Jin convinced Ah-Ming she needed an ointment from her apartment.

At her question, Meipin at first didn't answer as she finished wrapping up the medicine Jin needed to take back to make her absence convincing. "There were many rumors about the emperor being infertile," she said finally. "But then Ruizong was born."

"Was there any suspicion over whether Tai was the emperor's son?"

Meipin snorted. "There always is. But at the time, the concubines were the ones to come up with most of the rumors. There were two of them, not including the former empress, and all worked hard to discredit Wu to Emperor Kangming."

Jin thought on this. "But if he wasn't the emperor's, whose would he be?"

Meipin shrugged. "Who wouldn't he be? The stories are more numerous than the hairs on my head. A visiting jeweler's son, her own brother. There was a rumor that Emar was his father, but just look at Tai. He's no huren; otherwise he'd look like you."

That was true. "Do you believe any of it?" Jin asked.

Meipin stilled. "I used to wonder, but I've realized there's no point. Prince Tai is the heir to the throne, whether he's truly the emperor's son or not." Meipin paused. "You haven't heard, have you?"

"About Tai saving those people from the statue?" Jin replied. "I heard." The stories had swept through the palace and even the Veil. Tai had become a hero overnight. "Though . . . it's hard to believe. Mage skills?"

"Well, the prince is more popular now with the people than ever," Meipin said.

"So if any of this about Tai's father is true—"

"Then you'd better be careful where you step," Meipin said softly. "Jin, I enjoy court gossip as much as anyone. But even I don't want to know the answer to that puzzle. That would be like reaching into a viper's hole expecting no fangs." She handed Jin the silk-wrapped medicine. "Don't dig too much, Jin."

CHAPTER 28

Tai paused at the audience hall doors, bracing himself for the onslaught. He had insisted he was well enough for this, though he now regretted giving up the luxury of one more day of rest.

The doors swung open, and the assembled mages, law officials, and representatives of the Minister of Rites all bowed low as he entered. He took his seat as the crown prince rather than the Minister of War, as today's decisions involved his actions as prince.

He spied the aged head mage Yao, who nodded deferentially to him, though he seemed decidedly more stressed than when Tai had last spoken to him in the hunting grounds.

The heralds announced the empress, and everyone knelt. "Ten thousand years, may the empress live ten thousand years!"

When the formalities of her title had been dealt with, Empress Wu entered the room on graceful feet, sweeping down onto her throne with a tinkling of gold hairpins.

"Ministers, I believe we all know of the statue incident," the empress said. "I am currently not interested in how, or why, but I will see that anyone illegally teaching the mage arts is punished. For now, let's deal only with what to tell the people."

"Your Majesty," Mage Yao began, climbing to his feet. "The Ministry is ever loyal to you and the crown prince. We had no inkling about this ... unprecedented use of magic."

"I appreciate your saying so, Head Mage," the empress said coldly, "but as I stated, we will deal with your involvement and responsibility later."

The head mage bowed. "Yes, Your Majesty."

"This incident has created a great deal of chaos," Sanjin said. "When the novelty of the miracle wears off, we will have to explain that a man who has not undergone the knife wielded magic."

"Clearly," the head mage said reverently, "Heaven favors the crown prince. That is the only explanation. No one in the ministry would teach an uncastrated man the arts."

"Then how do you explain this?" the empress snapped. She turned to Tai. "Someone taught you."

"I studied texts, Your Majesty," Tai said. "Out of curiosity."

Mage Yao tapped his chin. "Your Majesty, there is one other possibility."

"Yes, we know your opinion that Heaven favors him," the empress said impatiently.

"Quite," the mage answered. "But it is said that in ancient times, mages were naturally born, not trained. The ancient annals of mage arts mention this, and though it hasn't been seen for centuries, perhaps the crown prince is one such Heaven-ordained mage."

"Or perhaps," Tai said slowly, "the ministry might reconsider its admittance rules. The removal of one's manhood is a painful and unnecessary practice. What if we tried training without this procedure?"

The head mage glanced at the empress, then fixed a surprised look on the prince. "Your Highness, Heaven and Earth would have to reverse places."

"Yet Heaven and Earth seem to be in their rightful spots," Tai pointed out. "Despite my having used magic."

Mage Yao chuckled, "The crown prince is clearly favored by Heaven, as I said, but going against tradition would be unwise."

"How so?" Tai asked.

Mage Yao straightened, frowning. "Already some of the young initiates are murmuring as to whether their initiation was for naught, whether the throne and Heaven mock their sacrifice. We risk tarnishing the ministry and the whole mage community."

"You would continue to destroy these young men needlessly?" Tai asked.

"Not needlessly, Your Highness," the head mage sputtered. "It's tradition. Let us not confuse a one-time miracle, for you are the exception, not the rule."

"Is it not worth trying?" Tai said.

"Your Highness," the mage replied, "the men are happy to offer this in exchange for greater power, for the privilege of working and moving freely in the inner palace. They can serve their vocation without the distractions of family or physical wants."

"He speaks wisely, Your Majesty," the Minister of Rites interjected. "We risk offending the gods and spirits if we go against tradition and flout the writings of the sages before us."

Tai tried to keep his tone diplomatic. "It might behoove us to determine whether it's the gods we offend, or our own set beliefs."

"With respect, Your Highness, what would this gain?" the head mage protested. "Think of it. We will be made fools, if those who have given up their manhoods think they did it for nothing! A man unwilling to endure hardship and sacrifice is unfit for the Ministry of Mages."

"This practice must end," Tai said.

A strange look crossed the mage's face. "Your Majesty, I beg you. Do not abolish this. The ministry's traditions are sacred. If you change them, you will have a revolt. The best mages will be most distressed."

Tai was about to give a retort weighing their distress with those of new initiates undergoing the knife, when Sanjin cleared his throat.

"As you so wisely said, Minister, the crown prince is clearly favored by Heaven," the head of the Veil said. "I see this not as a sign that any man can wield magic without making the proper sacrifices, but more as a divine miracle. And divine miracles are signs from Heaven. Your Divine Majesty, I am by no means a sage, but I cannot see this as anything but further proving Your Divine Majesty's mandate to rule."

Tai glanced at his mother, suddenly sure that she and Sanjin had rehearsed this. His mother nodded her head once.

"That had not occurred to me. But your explanation makes sense, Marquis Sanjin. Minister, let your mages know that this was a one-time divine incident where the crown prince, as my son, was given the power to save the people and avert disaster. This does not mean he has this power normally, or that others wishing to enter the ministry's service do not need to be initiated in the traditional manner." She turned to the Minister of Rites. "Send a proclamation to every district office. I wish every governor and citizen to know of the crown prince's actions, and that the throne is humbled and honored by Heaven's favor."

"A wise decision as always, Your Divine Majesty," Head Mage Yao murmured.

"Will the governors not ask why Heaven chose to

give powers to your son, rather than you directly, as the divine ruler?" Tai's words seemed to shroud the audience hall in thick silence, and fear seeped from the ministers like a fog. He had just flouted his mother publicly, and in the heavy pall he wondered if his mother would smite him again, as she had in the carriage.

"Because my son acts on my behalf," the empress said smoothly. "A hand wields the knife not because it decides to, but because the head told it to." She smiled, but her eyes carried a warning. She stood. "Thank you for your time, Ministers. That is all for today."

As the heralds announced her titles and the end of the session, the empress gave Tai a curt nod. He knew it was not an ask, but a command to follow.

Once safely out of the audience hall and within the outer chambers of her apartments, she bade the servants retreat, shutting the doors behind them.

"You test my patience," she said as soon as they were alone.

Tai stood his ground, tense. "I simply ask what others will ask."

"Others will not because they know enough to keep silent," she snapped. "Unlike my son. What were you thinking, suggesting we abolish the initiation rituals of the mages?"

"It's cruel. And unnecessary," he said.

She raised an eyebrow. "If you admit that you were taught, and this wasn't a miracle, then I suppose that does prove it's unnecessary." She waited, but Tai stayed silent. She spread her palms. "So your argument fails. Besides, the entire ritual is a bedrock of mage culture. Even if you are right, to get rid of it would jeopardize the ministry. And you don't help a shoot grow by pulling on it."

Tai folded his hands in his sleeves. "Then you agree with me that we should abolish the practice?"

"All I know is that my son continually challenges me," she said coldly. "First in private, but now in public. Who is goading you into this?"

"My thoughts are my own."

His mother came closer, her eyes searching his. "I don't know if that is comforting or more distressing. Take care, my son. There are vipers in this court who would use you to see us both fall."

"Sanjin, for one?" Tai asked.

The empress frowned. "His loyalty is above question. But the mages have always resented my Buddhist leanings. The traditionalists hate the fact that a woman is on the throne. Meipin's family is all subservience, but once they secure her position, they'll lose no time getting me to abdicate in favor of you."

"You fear even the shadows, Mother."

Her lip curled. "Just because I suspect everyone, doesn't mean everyone isn't guilty."

"Including me?" Tai asked softly.

"Especially you," she answered, face stony.

Tai decided to break his resolve.

When the mage answered his summons to meet him at the ancestral temple in the imperial quarters, he bore his usual affable grin and a pouch full of melon seeds.

He waited to one side while Tai lit three sticks of incense and bowed toward the ancestral tablet, then fell into step as Tai walked by him to stroll the grounds. No one would think much of the prince walking and thinking around the imperial temple.

"I am happy that Your Highness is speaking to me again. I was growing bored having no one to train."

"You should be worried about your safety," Tai said.

"Why?" The mage looked unconcerned. "Is my brute of a mother in town?"

Tai raised an eyebrow. "The ministry is not happy with my having learned magic. If they find out it's you, which is highly likely, they may take drastic measures."

Situ Han chuckled. "That would be entertaining."

Tai stopped walking and faced him, all pretense gone. "You could be accused of treason, of subverting the ministry and my mother. If you landed in the tea rooms, even I would be hard-pressed to free you. So tell me, why did you decide to teach me magic?"

The mage cocked his head. "Perhaps I'm a romantic. I believe that one person can make a difference." He smiled. "And you have. You certainly surprised everyone with your demands of abolishing castration for mages."

"Well, it didn't work," Tai sighed. He glanced at Situ Han. "How . . . how did you enter the ministry?"

"I am not the first mage in my family. My parents sent my older brother to become a mage."

Tai caught the slight hitch in Situ Han's voice. "He died?"

The mage shook his head. "No, Your Highness. He didn't. He suffered through his initiation without any relief, for the operating mage had been drinking during the moon festival and forgot to administer the proper medicine. Then his wounds became infected, and he screamed for days. And when he finally healed, he was but a husk of himself." Mage Situ Han's voice was steady, but he avoided Tai's eyes. "And a week after he climbed out of bed, he bought a beautiful silk scarf. He looped it over our bedroom roof beam and made a noose, stood on a stool, put his head through, and stepped off a bench." Mage Situ Han took out his bag of melon seeds and cracked one between his teeth, but this time Tai felt it was to distract himself. "*Then* he died."

Tai let the silence stretch, his anger at the mage blunted as he imagined the mental scars Situ Han carried. "Yet you still wanted to join the ministry?"

The mage chuckled, though this time the sound was edged. "My parents wanted me to. And what filial son denies their parents? Though I had medication, and an experienced mage to wield the knife, I kept thinking, if this was my pain, how much more did my brother suffer under that drunken man?"

"Yet you survived."

"Oh, I assure you, Your Highness, I thought of killing myself." The mage spat a melon seed into his palm. "The scarf was tempting. I stood on the bench for a time. I almost did it. Except at the last moment, with sudden clarity, I decided that dying wouldn't achieve anything. Besides, my parents would have sent my next brother to become a mage if I failed, so here I am. The family's mage." He beamed.

"And what does this all have to do with teaching me the mage arts?" Tai asked quietly. "Did you teach me magic so I would abolish the practice?"

"I've said it before, but I think you can do great good," Situ Han said. "In more ways than just abolishing castration. You have the makings of a great emperor."

Tai stopped in front of the temple and faced the mage. They had walked a full circle. "Some would say you sound treasonous," Tai commented, "teaching a prince powers behind his mother's back."

"If I was truly treasonous," mage Situ Han chuckled, "then I would be trying to kill you or your mother. I am only trying to help the next in line, for whenever that time comes." He spat another melon seed into his palm.

"Why did you lie to me about the ministry when we

first met? What if I had told my mother about your teaching me?"

The mage shrugged. "I knew you wouldn't. Only a select few in the ministry know, and the ministry considers me half crazed anyway. Would you have agreed to my teaching you if you knew the ministry hadn't sanctioned it?" He clasped his hands together and leaned closer. "I still believe you can make great change, Your Highness. Become a great mage emperor. But only if you are willing."

Tai left the temple mulling over the mage's words. His explanation of why the ministry hadn't told Tai made sense—but it had also positioned Tai as openly defying his mother, in what looked like highly treasonous acts.

CHAPTER 29

Rain drizzled through the morning into noon, and Jin shivered in her thin tunic even as she and her squadmates sat inside a large hall where two meager braziers tried to heat the room.

They likely did less to warm the space than the body heat of the gathered fifty Veil students kneeling on the hard floor in rows of ten. Jin didn't know any of them besides those in her squad, but like them, she was grateful for these afternoons when they had text and code training.

Ah-Ming stood at the front of the room, hands clasped behind him. A large piece of slate leaned against the wall, where the Veil's motto was written across the top: "Mission First. Life Last. Empire Always."

"Last week, you learned hand signals to help you and your team in times when you cannot hear each other, or perhaps you need to signal each other without the enemy's knowledge. You—" he nodded at a broad-shouldered man at the front—"how do we signal that an enemy is nearby?"

The man gave a seated bow and then said crisply, "By folding our right sleeve with our left hand."

Ah-Ming grunted approval. "And what of the command to flee?" He nodded toward someone at the back, who clearly felt uncomfortable being chosen.

"By flicking our thumb against a forefinger," he mumbled.

"Correct," Ah-Ming said. "But you sound unsure. Are you unsure?"

"No, Master Ah-Ming," the man replied, louder and clearer this time.

"Good," Ah-Ming swept them with a cool gaze. "In the field, there is no chance to be unsure. Being right might save you. Being wrong might kill you. Being indecisive will doom you." Ah-Ming paced across to the other side of the room, closer to the brazier. He plucked out a piece of charred wood and strode back to the front of the room, to the large slate slab propped against the wall.

"In the Veil, we must convey information in a manner only we would recognize." He ground out the ember of the kindling and turned to the room. "Who here knows how we do that?"

Mushroom stood up. "By using code phrases, Master Ah-Ming?"

Certainly, that's how Jin had done it back in her thieving days. Haitao had never taught her to read, but she knew the phrases her clan brother Lu had used in written letters.

Ah-Ming's jaw worked, tightening the scars along his neck. "Code phrases must be changed and sometimes take up too much space. What happens when you're locked in a prison cell and haven't even a scrap of paper to write on? What if your only tool is a piece of your own clothing? How long will it take you to write a phrase on it?" Ah-Ming waved the stick in his hand. "But misspelled words are easy to place in a letter, or on a wall, or on the smallest scrap of material." He turned to the slab and began writing in long, flowing script. "The character for wine has this crucial horizontal in the middle." He stepped back to let them see the black word against the slate. "But if I rub this out—" he wiped a thumb across the horizontal line, erasing it "—then it becomes what word?"

There was only confused silence, though Jin sensed what Ah-Ming was trying to prove.

"It becomes a common mistake," Ah-Ming said, "slovenly writing by any drunkard not thinking straight. No cause for alarm or suspicion. But what it means, if you see this in an unexpected letter to you, is that you should flee, and immediately. Now what other situations might you be in where someone needs to communicate with you?" His gaze landed on Jin. "You, girl."

Though no one dared move to turn around, Jin felt their unwanted curiosity all the same. Being the center of attention had always made her more uncomfortable than any formal silk dress. She thought back to her thieving days.

"A mission might need to be aborted."

Ah-Ming nodded. "Yes. For that, we use this word, the word for *crow*, but missing one of the four dots. It means something has been compromised." He wrote the character on the slate, then turned back to the students. "There may also be situations where an embedded Veil agent will communicate with you via letter, but neither of you know the other. In these cases, they will indicate they are your ally by misspelling the word for *prevention*. The word for *prevention*—" he brushed a few quick strokes on the slate—"becomes a whole different word if we do one simple thing." He ground a single dot in the character's flowing right hook. "What word is it now?"

Rabbit.

Despite herself, she had to admit the system was clever. To an untrained eye, it might seem like a simple mistake, the confusion of nearly identical words, and thereby draw no notice—unlike phrases that Haitao had used, like inquiries about a non-existent relative, which no doubt the Veil or other spies could easily work out.

"If you see the word *rabbit* where only the word *prevention* makes sense," Ah-Ming continued, "this is the way another Veil agent is identifying themselves to you and telling you they are your friend. This is a sign to trust them and that they wish to establish a line of communication."

The side door creaked open, and she spied a messenger step in from the rain. Ah-Ming turned and dismissed them all, but as Jin stood, she watched the messenger murmur to Ah-Ming. Ah-Ming's face pulled into a displeased scowl before he looked in Jin's direction and strode over.

"Clean yourself up, person of no worth. Sanjin wishes to see you."

Jin's pulse quickened. She followed the messenger to Sanjin's office.

The bird fluttered in its corner cage, chirping at her, and Sanjin sat at his desk, finishing a letter. He glanced up as she entered.

"The empress has granted your wish. You will undergo the Iron Mind test tomorrow."

"Tomorrow?"

Sanjin leaned back. "Yes. I was under the impression you wanted to get this over with quickly."

"Is there—anything I can do to train?"

A snide smile grew. "I think we are past those questions. As I told you, you will be given a set code which you are not to give up under any circumstances. You will be interrogated for a day, and if you do not divulge the code until that time, then you will pass and graduate."

She nodded. "Will I undergo physical interrogation?"

"No. This is called Iron Mind for a reason. It will
require resolve, stamina, and clear thinking."

This she could do.

Mengkhis had undergone this, and she would too.
And then she would go after Mengkhis and end all of
this.

"You will need all your strength for tomorrow," he
said, a wicked little smile on his lips. "I advise you rest
and use your time wisely. I have taken the liberty of
letting the prince know you will be unavailable today
and tomorrow for your weekly interview."

Jin hated that he had made the decision for her, but
deep down admitted it might be for the best. She
needed to focus, without the pressure of having to
reassure Tai, whose worry for her always seemed to
skim just below his easy jests. She retreated to Rayshan
instead and did the best thing possible to rest her mind
and heart: fly.

Rayshan happily obliged, winging through the
clouds and cool air. He even performed his signature
dive, climbing so high that Jin thought the air itself
would pierce her lungs, and then turning upside down
and wrapping his wings around her until they were
shooting toward the ground like an arrow, plummeting
until Jin thought she would rip apart.

He pulled up at the last moment, his tail slapping
the ground and sending a spray of dirt into the air

before he leveled out, skimming over the lush rice paddies and wheat fields that stretched between the capital and the distant hills of the western tombs, where emperors were buried. The thought of the tombs brought a shiver of unease, but Jin shrugged it off as nerves due to the Iron Mind test.

Are you ready for tomorrow?

I am ready to do everything I can to end my Veil training and find Mengkhis.

Rayshan hummed, though she detected some unease.

You are worried about me? Jin asked.

No. Not you.

Jin placed a hand on one of his ridges, feeling the Song of Scales flickering through him. *We'll get through this, together.* She paused. *The Princess Nobu says she has a medicine that will take away the Song's pull, but . . .*

But what? he growled.

It also dims your powers for a while.

No medicine! It came as a roar, not only of anger but of fear.

Rayshan, I'm not saying—

No. Medicine.

Understanding dawned. *You are thinking of what happened in the Singing Sands.*

His silence answered for him. Every rider had been forced to take opium before their final Dragon Class test so they wouldn't know their destination, and Gao had secretly increased Rayshan's and her dose to get them far from the capital and leave them for dead.

If Rayshan had not driven the poison from Jin's body, Gao would have succeeded. And even then, he had had to resort to the blood bond to save her. Jin saw with crystal clarity why Rayshan now had an aversion to medicines of any kind.

No medicine, she agreed.

THE INTERROGATION ROOM for the Iron Mind test was bare except for the chair Jin was tied to and a small brazier that crackled in the middle of the room, with floors and walls painted white.

The white paint hid a thick layer of lead, she knew, blocking her bond with Rayshan, and Sanjin had ordered her wrists and ankles bound to the chair with ropes so tight they bit her every time she shifted.

She had already been sitting here for what felt like hours, the fire from the brazier making the air in the windowless room uncomfortably warm and stale. Every time she tried to move, the rope cut into her, and she resigned herself to shifting without moving her ankles or forearms.

Would the entire test be this silent, dreaded waiting? Clearly, Sanjin was making her sweat, giving her time to imagine the interrogation and break herself down before he even started. It seemed like a mind game the head of the Veil would relish. Already her throat was scratchy with thirst, and little flutters of panic worked their way through her stomach.

The worst was her sense of time, which began to fray.

How long had she been sitting here? Ten, twelve hours? Hunger had started to truly set in, and her thighs grew numb, then sore, then excruciating. She could think of nothing else. The few times Jin called out, no one answered.

Without warning, the door flew open, and Sanjin entered with a reedy-looking assistant Jin had never seen before. He was dressed in plain cotton robes and carried a bamboo tube.

"Peace upon your morning, person of no worth," Sanjin said. "Are you ready to commence?"

Morning? I've been sitting here for the day! she wanted to scream. Instead, she licked her dry lips, her voice pushing past her thirst. "Yes, Marquis. Mission first, life last. Empire always."

He nodded. "Good. Here is the code that you must protect. Let us know once you have memorized it."

The assistant came forward and opened the scroll, then pulled out a thin sheet of paper, which he held out to Jin to read.

The stork strikes at the hour of the snake.

She read it several times before nodding. The assistant tossed the paper and bamboo scroll as one into the flames and retreated to a corner of the room.

Sanjin smiled. "Would you like anything? Water? Something to eat?"

Her throat worked, tempted despite herself.

"As I said, this is mainly a mental test," Sanjin said. "You may have water if you wish."

Jin shook her head. She knew the dangers of ingesting anything, after what Gao had subjected her to in the Singing Sands.

Sanjin looked approving. "Then let's get started." He nodded to the assistant, who moved to the brazier, his back to Jin. He prodded the fire a few times with a set of metal tongs, before following Sanjin out, the door slamming behind them.

Jin stared, on edge. Why had they left?

She listened for footsteps but heard nothing. She was alone once more.

Jin leaned her head back and closed her eyes, willing the thirst away. She wanted water so badly that she could smell it.

Yes, she smelled water and wet sage. She breathed it in, then gasped as she choked on thick liquid.

Dirty fluid was rushing up her nose. The room was flooding, and she didn't even have time to figure out where it was coming from, for it was already up to her neck, her mouth. She was drowning, back in that cage that Haitao had put her in to test her.

As suddenly as it appeared, the water was gone. Jin sat gasping in her chair, hands clutching the arms, but the room was as it had been.

No. Not as it had been.

Someone was standing in the corner.

Someone with sandy hair and features she had last seen underground.

Mengkhis looked at her and grinned. His lips moved, but no voice came out.

He took a step, then another, until he was standing right before her. His face expanded like dough in an oven, then shrank into a narrow mask, while one hand reached for her.

None of it is real, fledgling.

She shrank back, wanting to scream, but her throat had closed.

Mengkhis's face morphed again, this time into that of a narrow-faced man with a cloth over his nose and mouth.

Sanjin.

Something connected in her mind.

"What did you put in the fire?" she snapped. Or at least, she thought she did. Why did her voice sound calm? Happy, even?

"Ah, the Root of Faraway," Sanjin said, smiling. "It helps with honesty."

"That's . . . not allowed, is it?" Jin asked. She sounded merely curious, which was wrong. A part of her knew that wasn't what she was feeling, and yet . . .

"When your enemies capture you, do you think they will be interested in what is allowed and what is not?" Sanjin's eyes crinkled behind his veil. "Now let us begin. What is the code?"

Jin closed her eyes. Something in her wanted to tell him, needed to. But she couldn't. It was important that she didn't tell him, though she couldn't quite remember why.

Sanjin circled her. "I currently have your squad mates available to kill at my leisure. Tell me what the paper says, and I won't harm them."

Jin shook her head of the little voice telling her to give him what he wanted. What had he said? This was to test her, wasn't it? Not the others? But her mind kept seeing that severed hand, Ah-Kun's willingness to drive his knife into himself. It was so clear in her mind that it took her a moment to remember she wasn't back in that courtyard.

"Ah, you think I'm bluffing," Sanjin said. "I suppose if I was truly the enemy, I would have to prove myself to you." He nodded. "Good point." He rapped on the locked door, which opened.

Jin stared, at first uncomprehending. Bean entered, his wrists bound and his mouth gagged, Dead Eyes pushing him in. The guard also wore a kerchief around his nose and mouth, while Bean's eyes held raw fear.

She blinked. Was he real? Or also her imagination?

Dead Eyes shoved Bean onto the floor, then stood back, awaiting Sanjin's order. All three of them swam before Jin's eyes, and the shadows in the corners seemed to writhe like smoke.

It's not real, Jin thought desperately, gripping the chair arm.

On the floor, Bean groaned, drawing Jin's attention back to him.

"You said this would not be physical," Jin accused Sanjin.

She couldn't see his smile, but she sensed his relish all the same. "Not for you, it wouldn't."

Sanjin chose a thin pole, examined it, and brought it hard across Bean's back. Bean flinched but didn't cry out.

"The code, person of no worth."

Jin shook her head, as much to deny Sanjin as to try and rid herself of the sluggishness in her veins.

The pole whistled again, and this one drew blood, the spatter staining the white floor. Jin looked at Bean, willing him to be a figment of her imagination.

"You cannot win against the Royal Veil."

Jin turned to see Haitao himself standing next to her. She blinked, and he was gone.

She looked back at Bean, doubt gnawing her. Was this real? Or was everything the Faraway Root?

She had to pass this test; it was important. Despite the fog pressing in on her mind, the mission, she knew, was above all.

"The code, person of no worth!" Sanjin shouted.

Should she give him the code? No. It was important. Don't give the code. Mission first.

Jin shook her head.

Sanjin looked pleased. He gestured to Dead Eyes, who pulled out a short, wicked-looking dagger.

Jin's clouded mind rejoiced. He was going to free Bean. *She had passed the test.*

But then Dead Eyes plunged the knife in, and reality singed through her like fire. This was real.

Bean was dying.

Jin wasn't sure whether she screamed aloud or not, but when Bean sagged in Dead Eyes's arms and was dragged out the door, something ripped inside Jin, and she let loose an angry roar that might have made Rayshan proud.

The anger seemed to burn away the last traces of the Faraway Root, and Jin wrapped herself tightly around the rage, letting it anchor her while the drug nibbled at the edges of her consciousness, trying to coax her back.

Sanjin carefully stepped around the blood on the floor until he was only an arm's length from Jin. "I'm glad you held out. Physical pain is very limited in its results. There are many more efficient ways of gaining information."

Jin forced herself to breathe, her eyes watching his hands for any signs of weapons or tools he would use on her, despite his words.

He held out his palms. "You have nothing to fear from my hands. I am unarmed." He paused. "You know, you're not the only one with information to give."

"Meaning?"

"Meaning I can offer a trade."

"No."

"You haven't heard the terms of the trade," Sanjin said, clasping his hands behind his back. "I want the code. And you want . . . hm, what do I have that you might want?"

"I don't want anything from you except your seal on my graduation paper," Jin said.

Sanjin nodded. "Ah, I have it. What about the truth of your parents?"

Jin smirked. "I already know the truth of my parentage."

"Ah, the murderess we executed," Sanjin said. "Yes, I forged the documents myself."

Jin stilled. Forged? He was lying. This was part of the test.

"You were not born to a criminal we executed. I know who you really are, who your parents are." She searched for a clue in his face, but by the eight levels of hell, he was not the head of the Royal Veil for nothing. "They are still alive, and I can tell you their names. In exchange for the code, of course."

She shook her head. Mission first. She would not give in now. Not after Bean had—she shut the memory down. "You're bluffing. No code."

Sanjin seemed to not hear her. "I wasn't sure about selling you to that thug—Haitao, I think it was? But options were slim, and time was short."

A cold foreboding settled on Jin. "How do you

know about Haitao?" He might have found out that she was sold, but he could not possibly know the name.

"I am the head of the Veil, person of no worth." He seemed amused. "It is my business to know everything, and every criminal in the capital."

He must have read Gao's documents, all his questioning of Haitao before Gao had Haitao executed. That was the only explanation. Her throat dried again, tightening.

"Give me the code, and I will tell you the truth," he said again.

The rope bit deeper into her, and she realized it was because she was leaning so far forward. She was surprised the chair hadn't toppled. Sanjin knew something, she saw it in his eyes, but she also saw his eagerness. He wanted her to fail.

This was a test of her willpower. This was a test of whether she'd fall for simple temptation.

"No."

Sanjin leaned closer. "I can assure you this is not a bluff. I know the truth, and all you must do is trade your information for mine. I'll even let you graduate."

Jin's resolve hardened. "No."

The head of the Veil nodded. "Don't say I didn't give you an out." He stood and left the room.

Doubt crushed in on her. What if he was telling the truth? But even if he was, could she risk failing the Veil, just to face this test again? Worse, how could she know that Bean had died during this, only for her to fail?

She slumped back, the thirst and heat of the room returning in full force. Jin had lost all sense of time. She wasn't sure how much longer she sat, thinking of Bean's slack body, her muscles cramping, guilt and self-loathing eating at her.

Jin almost wished for the hallucinations to begin again, for without them she was truly alone with her thoughts. Time seemed to become a weighted thing, pulling her down into an abyss of delirium.

In her imagination the door opened once again, and Dead Eyes came in, followed by Sanjin.

The head of the Veil stood before her, hands clasped, then motioned. The thickset man came forward, wielding a giant pair of shears, and Jin recoiled, despite telling herself none of this was real.

Dead Eyes leaned over her, and Jin braced herself. He slid the shears under the ropes and snipped.

"Congratulations, Wang Kway Jin," Sanjin said. "You have passed the Iron Mind test."

CHAPTER 30

Tai was working late in the War Ministry office, the air heavy with the smell of oil lamps kept burning for hours. Besides the mess of thoughts that mage Situ Han had brought up, along with the heated argument with his mother the day before, it seemed that rumors of Mengkhis Lai's escape were leaking despite their best efforts.

Tai regarded the reports on his desk of restless neighbors bolder in their demands and skirmishes. If they didn't capture and kill Mengkhis Lai soon, many would start assuming the Tang had lost its hold on power.

Tai rubbed his temples, sleep pulling at him. Even with all the hours he spent poring over documents and proposals and budgets, he often felt he was on the back foot with the war department and officers, all of whom respected him but doubted his suitability for office.

Added to this was the knowledge that Jin must be experiencing some rigorous exercise with the Veil, for they only said she was unavailable when she was injured, or about to be injured.

When his study door opened, he expected his valet had come to refill the lamps, but when he looked up, he found his mother. He stood, wary.

She motioned for the two private maids with her to retreat. She had only brought her bedchamber maids, which meant she had already retired for the night.

"Is everything alright, Mother?"

"That remains to be seen." She passed by his desk and sat down in one of the wide chairs opposite.

"I hope you've stopped practicing mage arts."

"I'm taking a short time away from it." He wasn't about to tell her about mage Situ Han's stories, nor that he himself was unsure whether to continue training.

His mother nodded, then sighed. "I realize angry words were spoken yesterday."

"Not just yesterday," Tai said, thinking of the week past.

The empress looked away. "We both said things we didn't mean."

"I meant what I said," Tai replied.

She studied his face. "I want to heal this rift between us. We need to be a family again. I want to prove that I care for you and that despite what I said, I do not resent you or Jin."

"You simply think we're plotting against you."

His mother sighed. "Even if you are, you are still my son." She paused and rubbed the ring on her finger with one thumb. "Do you remember the nursemaid you had when you were five?"

"Of course." He was surprised she remembered her, and just when he had recently visited the woman's mother with Jin. His nursemaid had been everything his mother was not: warm, gentle, always sneaking him his favorite foods and gushing about what a handsome child he was.

She tapped her fingernails. "I'll admit, I was jealous of her. You ran to her whenever you fell, you gave her all your first calligraphy attempts."

"Not all," he protested, though there was a measure of truth in it. Auntie Hwang, as he called her, always made sure to present his best work to his mother. But he knew that anything he made for Auntie Hwang, no matter how trivial, would garner that unconditional smile, the fluttering of her soft hands and her quiet praise. His mother, in contrast, picked out every flaw and wobbly stroke in his calligraphy, always asked why he had missed that one word in his poem recital.

"I grieved at her death, my son. Admittedly not because I cared for her, but because you cared. Part of me also recognized that I had let someone else mother you, and her death was a chance for me to do better."

Tai swallowed. Though he had never really tried to put a date on it, it was true that his mother had been much more involved after Auntie Hwang's death. She had comforted him when he sobbed openly in the confusing aftermath of the nursemaid's passing, never admonishing him for being weak. And she had never replaced Auntie Hwang. Instead, she took up his education herself and oversaw every detail of his upbringing, binding them ever closer as not just mother and son, but ruler and heir.

"You have been a good mother," he conceded softly, and though resentment still burned, he knew he owed much of his strength, charm, and resilience to her.

"I wish to see you happy, my son. And the throne safe after I'm gone." She appraised him. "I heard you asked to see Jin daily."

Though Tai knew Sanjin would report all this to his mother, it still irked him. "The training, as he calls it, is not fit for humans."

"Then you'll be glad to know she has graduated from the Veil."

Tai stared. Veil training usually took two years, and though he suspected it would be shortened for Jin, he hadn't expected it to be this short. Though Jin had mentioned she would get through the Veil, she hadn't mentioned when. "How?"

She raised an eyebrow. "I thought you'd be glad."

"I am, but she wouldn't be finished without your permission, and I want to know why you gave it." Tai crossed his arms. His mother always had reasons for showing mercy.

"I agree with you that we may have overlooked the

possibility that she would come to hate us. I also have reason to think that Sanjin . . . enjoys her training a little too much."

Tai snorted. "He is a monster in courtier's clothing."

"No one is all monster, my son," she said quietly. "If you ever forget that, you'll become one." She smoothed her gown. "Speaking of, you know that Gao and Sanjin both believe Jin is the child of an executed murderer."

"Yes."

"Does that affect how you feel about her?"

He had difficulty admitting his feelings for Jin to himself, never mind to his mother. But in this, as with many things, she seemed to see right through him. "I try to see people for their merit, not their blood."

"I will take that as a no, then," the empress said, folding her hands in her lap. "You are clearly fond of her, to say the least. I thought it a phase, but it seems to have persisted."

"Are you trying to warn me that someone might have her killed?"

His mother grimaced at the barb about his infatuation with Peilah and the implication that she was involved. "No."

Tai inclined his head. "Then why are you so interested in my views of Jin?"

"I am simply trying to think through the options of your marriage."

That was certainly not the answer he was expecting. "Marry Jin?"

"You object?"

"It's just—unexpected," Tai said. Regardless of his feelings about the idea, he knew better than to charge into something, especially if he didn't understand why his mother was suggesting it in the first place.

"You both seem to get along well, you're of similar age."

"I'm known to get along with even the most obnoxious at court," Tai argued. "Why are you really considering this?"

"The political reason is that she is powerful."

"And the best way to control someone is to make them family," Tai guessed aloud.

She said nothing, and strangely, he was comforted. Base as this reason was, it at least sounded more like his mother. "She is loyal; you don't have to make her family. Besides, since when do you shy away from threats and betrayal?" he asked. Thoughts of Aadan's exile quickly raised other questions, of what a marriage to Jin would do to their friendship, if Aadan ever returned. Not to mention, he still hadn't found the strength to contemplate the possibility that she was his sibling. "She would do anything to save her wing mates. You could just as easily threaten to kill them to make her do your bidding." He certainly didn't want to put ideas into his mother's head, but he needed to find out what her motives were.

"My son, just because I use a cleaver to solve one problem doesn't mean I need use it for all problems.

This gives us a double win." She held out her fingers as she counted off. "We keep the most powerful dragonrider besides Mengkhis Lai on our side. You marry someone you favor and have strong, healthy children, and none of the noble families can complain that we favor one over the other."

"I can't tell anymore when you're jesting."

The empress sighed. "Perhaps because you aren't spending enough time with your mother." She rose to her feet. "As you say, it comes with risks. She's half huren. The nobles would have to be appeased. I simply wanted to hear your mind." She studied him. "What is it? I can tell when something is bothering you."

Tai took a deep breath. This was the time. "Is she my sister?"

She frowned. "Is this about the ring?" At his expression, she let out a frustrated breath. "I told you, many concubines have those rings. She is not your sister."

"You swear it?" Tai stood very still, alert to any trace of deceit in her expression.

Every word came out slowly, and her eyes never left his face. "May my ancestors punish me in the afterlife if I am lying."

Relief flooded him, welcome and pure. She was telling the truth. A sly inside voice asked whether he was relieved because he didn't have a half-sibling, or that a relationship with Jin was possible.

"I am simply trying to make amends by giving you a

say. If you don't wish to marry her," his mother said, "simply tell me."

Tai picked up an inkstone, moving it thoughtfully. "I didn't say that." At his mother's knowing smile, he added, "But not without her consent. And I mean true consent, not just because you'd threaten her."

The empress laughed. "Since when would anyone need to be threatened into marrying the crown prince? She's a street rat. Do you really think she'd refuse an offer of becoming empress?"

"She's not a street rat," Tai said.

"You're right," the empress said quietly, "not anymore. She's the Princess of Dragons, slayer of Mengkhis Lai."

She seemed about to say something else, but then turned abruptly and swept out, leaving him restless from the unexpected proposal.

His mother was hiding something. What?

CHAPTER 31

That night, Jin returned to the dorms with a churning stomach. The thought of seeing Bean's rooms being emptied sickened her, yet a part of her needed to go.

When she reached the dorm door, however, Westie was squatting by the entrance, washing his headscarf in a basin of water.

"Congratulations," Westie grunted.

"I didn't think they'd kill him," Jin said softly.

Westie squinted up at her. "You don't know?"

"Know what?"

"He's alive," Westie said. "In the infirmary."

She stood rooted in disbelief before rushing through the dorm courtyards toward the far side where the infirmary wards lay, isolated from the rest of the Veil.

Though the doctor tried to turn her away, she

stayed until he relented to fifteen minutes.

The small room held a plain *kang* bed, a low platform with a stove underneath that was kept heated in winter. Next to it was a sideboard with an oil lamp and a basin of water. The latticed windows had been left open, but the air still smelled of ginseng, licorice, and a medley of other herbs Jin didn't recognize.

Jin tried to suppress her intake of breath at the sight of Bean, chest bandaged and face sallow.

"Think it'll scar?"

She hadn't even noticed he was awake. She stood next to his bed. "How are you—I saw him stab you!"

Bean nodded. "They gave me the shade blade."

"The what?"

"Shade blade. Top Veil members learn it," Bean rasped. Talking clearly hurt, yet he grinned. "Stab at just the right angle, and you miss the heart. They told me I could skip the Iron Mind test if I cooperated. Seemed like an easy shortcut to graduation."

Jin held a fist up in mock threat. "You're an idiot egg, you know that? You might have died! I thought you did die!"

He grimaced. "Alright, I lied. It wasn't all to skip the Iron Mind test. This was my punishment for the market exercise. Sanjin knew we were protecting each other. He just played along."

Jin's fists clenched. She should have known. This was not Bean's punishment, it was hers. "He's . . . sick."

Bean seemed about to laugh, but the movement made him hiss in pain.

"Anything I can do, just ask," she said.

"Sneak me a wine?" he grimaced. At her look, he closed his eyes. "It's more enjoyable than the healers' methods."

With her thieving background and blood-bond senses, Jin easily found a way past the servants into the cellars and made sure to take the finest they had. Once she had delivered the jar to Bean and watched him drink himself into slumber, she took the jar and retreated to her own dorms, where she fell into a dark sleep full of demons, and women marking their children with red-hot brands.

She awoke the next morning to the knocking of an imperial messenger, who informed her that the empress requested her presence.

He escorted her onto a horse and led her at a gallop through the Veil's courtyards. They passed the main gate, with its red emblazoned word of "zheng," or "righteousness," on the doors, and Jin was grateful to be in the regular palace again. Hopefully, she would never have to return to the Veil, and Rayshan's humming in her head echoed her wish.

When they reached the imperial quarters, Jin was surprised to find a carriage waiting for her. The messenger ushered her in, where the empress awaited, attired in her usual opulent gold.

"Sit," the empress said.

Jin obeyed, and the driver climbed into the driver's seat and slapped the horses with the reins.

"Congratulations on your passing the Iron Mind," the empress said. "Not everyone does."

"Not everyone has my need to, Your Majesty." She paused. "I would like permission to leave the palace and hunt for Mengkhis Lai."

"In good time," the empress said. "There are a few other things we must deal with first."

Jin wondered what could be more urgent than finding Mengkhis Lai but sensed the empress wasn't willing to say anything further.

And the woman indeed kept silent as they drove. But Jin felt her keen eyes during the entire trip, as if the empress was studying some fascinating new pet.

The carriage swayed to a stop, and a series of orders sounded before the curtain was swept aside. A bowing valet held out carved ivory steps for the empress and Jin to step down. Jin followed the empress, whose robes flowed behind her in a glittering gold cascade that made the sun look dull.

Jin gazed at the fields spread out before them. A long, low building squatted on the left, its blue tiles blinking in the sun. The field stretched far into the distance, with orderly rows of short mulberry trees planted. Workers in large conical hats bent between the rows, wide baskets full of a lumpy white substance.

"Have you ever seen how silk is made, Rider Jin?" the empress asked.

"No, Your Divine Majesty," Jin said. Her hometown of Gaozho was known for sand, dry barren soil, and more sand. Something so precious as silk passed through, but never originated from the harsh, barren terrain of Gaozho, which produced only the barest of foods and rustic pottery.

"There are millions of silkworms here," the empress said, motioning at a valet to lead them through the fields. The workers bowed low as they passed. "And this is just the farm for the imperial court. I have always loved silk. It's so strong it can hold a five-*jin* rock, yet so soft and delicate that its touch is like a cloud. This is what it is to be a woman, Jin. To the outside, all anyone sees is beauty and delicacy, but really test it, and it will hold under enormous pressure. I am like silk, Jin. And something tells me you are too."

"Your Divine Majesty honors me." Jin decided the rote and expected answer was best.

The empress reached out with long, slender fingers, her gold-painted nails plucking a silkworm from a leaf. She watched it wiggle, and Jin wondered what silk had to do with graduating from the Veil.

They entered the building. A long row of clay vats, each large enough to hold twenty full-grown men, lined the back wall, with wooden steps leading up to the edge of each one. Men in light tunics, their chests and arms bare, stood at the top of the steps, stirring the vats with giant wooden staffs, the sweat gleaming on their faces and backs. Steam rose toward slits in the ceiling, and overseers shouted orders and motioned at workers bearing large flat baskets piled high with fluffy white balls. These were handed up and tipped into the vats.

They walked to the end, where women were pulling out great long swathes of grey gauze-like material, unrolling it into large wooden trays of cold water. Another army of women pulled the silk toward them and began plucking out small black pods from the silk.

Not pods, Jin realized. Worms.

"The worms are boiled alive," the empress said. "It takes roughly five thousand worms to make the silk for one handkerchief, so you can imagine how many we must go through to clothe the court." The empress turned to Jin. "Beauty comes at a price. Sometimes an unfathomable one. But tell me, do you find the silk less beautiful now that you know how it's made?"

"Yes."

"You see, that's where you and I are different," the empress said. "I make myself understand that it is more beautiful, knowing that every thread in my scarf took all this to create. The empire is even mightier, for countless people must sacrifice themselves to keep it healthy. A worm is just a worm. At best it can become some dull-colored moth that dies within days. But its sacrifice with thousands of others means that it will make something beautiful, and strong. Silk built our empire. As empress, I must decide every day whether to be an insignificant moth, or part of the silk that makes the empire strong."

Jin thought the empress's eyes looked red-rimmed.

"It means I have made some very hard decisions in my life," the empress said softly. "Decisions I didn't want to make. And you must as well."

"I am afraid I don't understand, Your Divine Majesty."

An emotion in the empress's eyes flitted away almost before Jin pinned it down: tenderness.

"You have acquitted yourself very well in the Veil," the empress said. "Sanjin is most impressed, as am I."

Jin swallowed her surprise and simply bowed her head.

"You showed courage, initiative, and incredible strength. The empire needs you, and it may need you in ways that you didn't expect." She paused. "But I am getting ahead of myself. For now, it is only proper that you are rewarded for graduating faster than anyone else."

Jin's heart quickened. Was the empress about to grant her a request? She knew what she would ask for: Aadan's pardon, for him to return without any retribution.

"I have decided to make you nobility."

Jin simply stared, uncomprehending. The idea of her becoming nobility was laughable, possibly more ludicrous than the idea of becoming a dragonrider had first been. Dragons involved fighting and survival, and

Jin spoke both of those languages. Nobility and its rules were as foreign to her as the shores of Nihhon.

"Are you not pleased?" the empress asked. "This will open doors for you. Doors closed to you as a dragonrider."

And why would I want to open those doors? Jin wondered. All she wanted was to find Mengkhis Lai and earn her freedom. "Your Divine Majesty is too kind; this is not necessary. And I am sure you have better recipients."

"Sanjin and I are in agreement. You will graduate from the Veil immediately and be given a title, and therefore you must be adopted."

Jin's mind tried to keep pace with this blistering series of events. How was this more important than finding Mengkhis Lai? But questioning it would be questioning the empress's generosity, not to mention her decision, which would be unacceptable. She thought of Emar and his adoption into the empress's family at the time. "Adopted by a noble family, Your Majesty?"

"Yes," the empress said. "And we have the perfect family in mind."

A glimmer of hope sparked. "Meipin's?"

The empress laughed, as if this was the silliest thing anyone had said. "Oh no, Jin, that would not work at all. No, a much better family."

Jin frowned. What family was better than Meipin's? Or more influential? Meipin's uncle was the Minister of Laws, and she knew her friend had other family members in high places.

"Who, Your Majesty?"

"Someone you know well already, and who will protect you with his life."

A cold fear crawled through Jin's stomach, for something in the empress's tone warned her of the answer.

"The Marquis Sanjin has agreed to make you his daughter." The empress beamed as if she were conferring the most wondrous gift. "You will become his heir, Lady Jin."

CHAPTER 32

Jin was still fuming, and if she admitted it, terrified, when she re-entered the dorms at the Veil. Even Rayshan's humming at the edges of her mind didn't calm her.

The whole concept of Sanjin becoming her father was enough to make her want to throw herself in the nearest river and not come up for air. She had meant to free herself from the Veil—how had she somehow become the daughter of the head of the Veil?

She tried to think it through, for she knew her survival depended on her understanding the web that was closing around her, and why.

For all the empress made it sound like an honor and a kindness, her upbringing as a thief, and Haitao's teachings, had taught her to take all gifts with a healthy dose of skepticism.

She raced to her room as soon as the carriage

taking her back had deposited her and locked her door. Leaning against it, she let Rayshan into her mind.

There's some sort of trap here.

I sense it as well, Rayshan agreed, *but perhaps it's not as dire as you think.*

Sanjin? My adopted father? Why would he volunteer such a thing? Was it to further control her? It was hard to imagine him having more control over her than he did now—though the empress was pulling her out of the Veil. Why would Sanjin want to adopt anyone, much less her? It made no sense.

There must be a reason, Rayshan growled. *They have something planned.*

Rayshan was right. But no matter how Jin looked at it, she couldn't figure out what. Sanjin had his choice of anyone. He had riches enough to have an army of concubines, a palace full of children.

And yet he didn't.

She frowned. A rich man with no concubines was not just strange—it bordered on eerie. She had never thought to ask any questions as to why he wasn't married. In China, bloodline was paramount. One honored one's parents by having children, and the inability to have them was shame enough, but to deliberately not have children? That was an affront to Heaven, the worst insult to one's parents. Why had Sanjin never married?

Perhaps no one is willing to give their daughter to him, Rayshan suggested.

Jin almost laughed. *People would give him all their children for the right price, or if threatened.* If anyone would know the answer, it would be Meipin, for she knew of all the families and all their deepest, darkest secrets.

But in the meantime, her thoughts were in such a furor that she did the only thing she could think of: she wrote a letter to Aadan. She had no idea whether it would reach him, but he was the only one she wanted to tell, the only one who might understand why this adoption was like eating bile. He would understand her fears about family, her parentage, and her hatred of the Veil. Writing such a long letter pained her, for even after a year or more, writing was not one of her natural gifts, and she thought wistfully of Aadan's smooth, flowing script.

Not that she'd seen it at all of late.

And why was that? Why didn't he write? Meipin had told her that her last letter had been safely delivered to a trusted Persian emissary at one of the empire's westernmost posts. He had likely never received it. But even so, he was the smartest man she knew. How could he not think of a way to communicate with her? The thought was painfully raw. When she had finished the letter, she read through her disjointed sentences, her rambling words, and her outpouring of rage and confusion, and tore up the paper slowly.

Aadan didn't write because he didn't want to hear from her.

"The boy has other fields to tend," came a familiar voice behind her. "He is doing what he does best, and here you are, running to him for help. It's pathetic."

She turned to look at Haitao. He was still bloodied, as if he had just walked off his execution ground, but his head was where it should be.

"Why do you look different every time you appear?"

He grinned. "You're the summoner—you tell me. I guess you must have something to do with how I appear."

She stiffened, trying to put space between them. "Why do you come back?"

"Now that I am dead, you no longer call me master?" he said. "And all this time, you were like a daughter to me, the only thing I cared about in this world."

"Save your breath." She felt as if she had too many men claiming a father title. She mulled over a thought. "You didn't really find me in the streets, did you?"

"No," he said gruffly.

"Then where did you find me? Why did you tell Gao that you bought me at the prison?"

"Because it was the truth," Haitao said.

"You were in the tea rooms, you'd say anything."

Haitao held out his palms. "But as it happens, that was the truth."

Jin steeled herself. "So I was the child of a criminal."

"Seems so," Haitao said. "But I always doubted it."

"Why?"

"The official who handed you to me was not the ordinary midwife or soldier."

"Who was he?"

"Someone high up. He wore plain clothing, but judging from one of the rings on his finger and his soft hands, he was no prison guard. Hadn't done a day of work in his life."

Jin's mind raced. "Do you know what the head of the Veil looks like?"

Haitao scoffed. "How would I?" He reached up to touch his neck where the blade had sliced clean through. "I was tortured, but it was always by that man's orders, and he was an official but no Veil member. He didn't have the stomach to watch."

Jin's own insides soured at the thought. Gao had been a cruel bastard, but compared to Sanjin, he truly was nothing more than a kitten.

"Then who do you think gave me to you? Or sold me to you?"

"No idea. And besides, it's not my problem now, is it?" His grin was malicious as he turned to dust before her, collapsing into a pile on the ground.

Jin unclenched her palms, unaware that she had crushed the paper. She brushed the ink-stained shreds off, then sat down again.

Was Sanjin possibly her actual father? Had he sold her that night to Haitao? But if so, why? Why would a powerful man go to such lengths to pretend his daughter was born to a criminal and sell her off, when he had means and money to keep her and a thousand like her? Especially if she was his own blood.

Sleep, Rayshan advised. *A blood-bonded rider still needs sleep.*

She wasn't sure she wanted that either. Dreams that mixed with Rayshan's pull toward Nine Claw Mountain only made her wake exhausted.

I will try to control my thoughts, he growled.

Jin promised she would find Rayshan the next day, and they would fly. Only flying seemed to alleviate both her emotions and his wildly growing attraction to Nine Claw Mountain. A pull that was strengthening.

WHEN SANJIN CAME after the morning meal, Jin steeled herself. This was uncharted territory, and she half expected her adoption to mean he would treat her even more harshly.

But instead, he simply said, "Come," as if she were a dog, and at Ah-Ming's nod of assent, she left to follow Sanjin to his private office.

Once inside, she stood, stiff and unnerved.

He seemed to sense her discomfort and gave her a bemused look before settling himself behind his desk.

"The empress informs me that you have agreed to the adoption," he said.

"I believe I was commanded, Master Sanjin," Jin replied, trying to keep her voice even and free of revulsion.

"So was I," Sanjin said, "But the empress wishes to make a noble of you, and I live to serve the empress. I expect you to do your filial duty, and I will do mine. We will have a formal adoption ceremony, to be witnessed by the entire court, where you will go on to my family ancestral tablet." He said this slowly, as if still coming to grips with the prospect. "And, of course, that brings us to the question of your name."

"My name?" Jin repeated, though she began to understand where he was heading.

"I cannot have a Wang Kway Jin on my ancestral tablet," Sanjin said smoothly. "Besides, both the empress and I agree that it would be fitting to have a new name, to give you a new beginning as a noble."

"You honor me, Master Sanjin," Jin said carefully. "But why am I to be made a noble?"

"You don't need to know the why," Sanjin said. "You are nobody within these walls, have you forgotten?"

"No, Master Sanjin."

"Good. So I think you should be grateful, as we are not asking you to harm yourself or kill someone. This is commanding you to accept a greater honor than you deserve, and you are being given a chance to serve the empire."

Like a pig should be grateful for its last fattening meal before it is put to the knife, Jin thought darkly. She was up for some sort of slaughter—she just didn't know why, and by whom. And not knowing those two things meant defending herself against an unseen, unknown enemy.

I won't let them harm you, Rayshan reassured her in her head.

But we may not have a choice. When she had contemplated fleeing last time, she had realized how bleak her prospects looked if she went on the run with Rayshan. They would have to rely on the will of foreign rulers, who would no doubt yoke them with their own demands, possibly even worse than the empress's. Even the prospect of finding refuge with Aadan was just a dream. She had no idea what situation he was in, whether her seeking him out would endanger him with the Persians, especially as he hadn't even answered her letter. What made her think he even wanted her to find him?

"I have decided on a name for you, after consulting with the fortune tellers and the court astrologers," Sanjin said. "You will be officially renamed Fang Hwayping. Fang being my formal family name, and 'wise peace.' A fitting name for my daughter and heir to all that I own."

Jin knew better than to buy into his bait of wealth. She doubted she would get to see it, even if she had wanted a single *fen* from Sanjin. But worse was the change of name, for even though Wang Kway Jin was an arbitrary name, given to her by a man whom she had loathed and grudgingly depended on all her life, it still felt hers. It felt like it belonged to a past that she owned, that was all she owned. Now that little part of her life she knew to be true was being stripped away from her as well.

But there was no fighting the name change, for such resistance would not only be disrespectful but futile. Still, she struggled with the words in her throat as she said only, "Very well. Am I free to hunt down Mengkhis now?"

Sanjin looked amused. "You are not to leave the capital yet. I will notify you as soon as I have any news of his whereabouts."

"With all respect, Marquis Sanjin, I would like to go out and find him, rather than waiting for his attack."

"The man has vanished without a trace, like the invisible menace he is," Sanjin said. "If my network of top Veil officers hasn't found him, what makes you think you can?"

"You said yourself, you trained me to think like Mengkhis and have his strengths," she answered. "If anyone can find him, it's me."

"Patience," Sanjin said.

But Jin chafed, for she felt that if she had already found and killed Mengkhis, she would not be in this current trap.

CHAPTER 33

Over the following days, Sanjin removed Jin from the Veil, her scant possessions transferred to a private wing in his apartments. And though the suites were tasteful and luxurious by anyone's standards, Jin loathed the rooms simply for being Sanjin's. She also felt an instant wariness when she met her personal maid, Linlin—a short woman in her late twenties with a classic melon-seed face and apricot eyes. Though she seemed pleasant, Jin knew who paid her keep, and therefore mistrusted her.

Sanjin held a hasty Veil graduation ceremony, and as per tradition, it was a low-key affair with only Ah-Ming and the other initiates from her squad. Jin submitted to it all in a daze, for the more she watched Sanjin, the more his words during the Iron Mind haunted her: did he genuinely know her parentage?

She had no chance to say goodbye to Bean, for they had moved him, and Sanjin refused to tell her where.

In place of her Veil training, Sanjin and a new etiquette tutor, Madame Luo, devised daily lessons in court manners, imperial history, and dance.

Though Jin didn't think these would be painful, they were. Meipin had been assigned to assist her outside of lessons, and despite appreciating the extra time with Meipin, she loathed the actual exercises.

"I'm so sorry," Meipin said, voice stifled, "about your adoption. It was decided behind closed doors. Otherwise I would have asked Uncle to put in a request to adopt you."

"Why do you think they're doing this?"

Meipin sighed and seemed to think something over.

"Tell me, Meipin," Jin said, harder than she meant to.

Meipin rubbed at a piece of flaking paint on the teapot. "I think they intend to marry you off."

Jin tried to digest this, tried to make links but failed. "Marry me off? To whom? Why?"

Meipin shrugged. "You've grown powerful. The people admire you, as do the women in Dragon Class. Some would see you as a very prized marriage bargain that the empress could use to win the favor and loyalty of some of the nobles. You have support, and you would come with Sanjin's wealth as a dowry. The only thing missing is your bloodline. Which they are trying to fix."

Jin gave a sharp glance at Meipin. "It's not Tai. You know that, right?"

Meipin nodded. "That would make the empress too many enemies."

Jin realized with a start why Meipin had been a little warmer toward her. With the belief that Jin would be married to another noble family and not to Tai, her tension had eased, safe in her knowledge that her aspirations were still intact.

As if sensing her thoughts, Meipin gave a guilty sigh. "I'm sorry, Jin. But it might not be that bad. Whoever the empress chooses, she'll want someone to treat you well. After all, no one wants to offend Rayshan, and the empress probably feels it's easier to keep you loyal with gifts rather than punishments."

Jin tried to absorb some of Meipin's positivity but failed. She didn't want to marry anyone. And she certainly didn't want to be a pawn in a game. In addition, something about Meipin's explanation still didn't quite fit.

Which left her with fear—because just because she didn't see the trap set for her, didn't mean it wasn't there.

~

SHE WENT to Rayshan's cave, despite the late hour. The guards were familiar with her and waved her in without asking for her pass, and she climbed the steep mix of steps and inclines past the other dragons' caves, where riders staying late were leaving, and even the grooms were cleaning out their tools and hanging up their smocks for the day, washing their faces in the basins at the foot of the caves.

The stars had already bled into bright dots in the dark sky, a skein of white washing over them. The temperature dropped, but Jin barely noticed. Her blood bond meant she didn't feel the cold as much.

Rayshan hummed at the sight of her. *No rest for summoning the dead?*

Jin placed a hand on his neck, feeling the warmth of the scales there. *Not tonight.*

Who are we summoning?

Jin took a deep breath. *Master Emar.*

Rayshan huffed. *Is that wise?*

Summoning the dead had its own consequences besides ageing, especially when one was looking for answers. Jin had seen this happen with Oyang Kang, who had summoned his dead brother. The resulting guilt had racked Oyang Kang mercilessly. She still wasn't sure he had fully recovered.

No. But I think he's the only one who can give us answers.

Rayshan bent his head and blew out a stream of heat. *Then let us flare.*

He began to glow gently, then more.

Jin bore down harder. She knew this would age her, as it always did. This gift, unlike the gifts that the other dragons had, took as well as gave, and there was a price to be paid. But it would be worth it.

What was the one thing she thought of when she thought of Emar?

Compassion.

Emar had been compassionate, and perhaps that was always his downfall. He had been compassionate toward her, and known when she had been weak and needed help. He had known when demons had haunted her and had given her the tools to fight those demons. He had stood up for her when Madu, Gao's nephew, had tried to bully her into leaving Dragon Class. And he had always believed in the good of others, no matter how gruff or abrasive a face he showed.

Jin concentrated. Slowly but surely, the motes around her flickered, then began to gather, circling like fireflies, sometimes breaking apart but then coalescing again, as she forced them to stay together and take the shape they once had.

Was it moments or an hour? Jin wasn't sure except that she was beginning to ache. But then Emar was before her, flesh and blood. His eyes were whole, not the white marbled look she had remembered, and the side of his face was no longer white, but the same color as the rest of him, and it took her a while to recognize him.

"Jin?"

"Master Emar," Jin bowed, the old habit still

ingrained. "It is good to see your face." And she meant it. An unexpected raw lump formed in her throat. Of all the male mentors in her life, he had been the closest to being a real father to her, giving her guidance while remaining fair.

"You . . ." He paused. "Something must be very wrong."

"I need your help," Jin said. "I have been assigned to kill Mengkhis Lai."

Emar let out a surprised breath. "The empress agreed?"

"She sent me to kill him in the Well of Fire, but the mission failed. Mengkhis Lai is loose."

Emar sighed, eyeing her. "And now you want to know how to defeat him."

Jin nodded. "But first I have to find him. He has not appeared at Jimo. I thought you might have an idea of where else he would go."

Emar walked a few paces, hands behind his back, before turning and regarding her. "Tell me something. If you made it to the Well of Fire, clearly you survived. How?"

"I don't know," Jin said, and told him what had happened. "And . . . I can see through his eyes in the Firesong." She swallowed. "I see his memories."

Emar's face grew darker, and at one point she thought his eyes flickered with fear, but then it was tamped out. He ran a hand over his beard. "Perhaps the blood bond affects you differently. I was never able to see his memories. What troubles me is his sparing you. It makes no sense."

"He spared *you*, didn't he?"

Emar shook his head. "The only reason he didn't kill me is that he didn't get the chance. Besides, he figured I was a dead man anyway, having killed my dragon Yalongma."

"Do you have any idea where he might go?"

Emar's eyes clouded. "He was trained as a Veil agent. One of the best. With his invisibility, he is a master at disappearing. Knowing Mengkhis, he is hiding somewhere in plain sight, somewhere obvious yet unwatched."

Ice slithered down her neck. She remembered the Firesong, the images of the empress just after birth. How often had Mengkhis moved unseen in the palace then? Could he be doing so now?

"Watch yourself, Jin," Emar said. "And don't underestimate him."

Jin's energy gave way, and Emar faded until he was but an outline, before disintegrating to ash.

CHAPTER 34

The day of the naming and adoption ceremony was a blustery one, mirroring Jin's internal turmoil.

The actual ceremony was short, and unlike the weather, dry as a desert wind. The court gathered in the main audience hall as the Minister of Rites read out the proclamation that Jin was to be adopted by the marquis Fang Sanjin, and that she would henceforth be named the honorable lady Fang Hwayping.

Jin tried to read Tai's expression but saw only a nod of silent encouragement. Did he know why all this was happening? She longed for a chance to ask him. But the ritual swept her forward, where she bowed to the empress and then bowed to the marquis, and he named her his daughter and heir. Jin even caught some smug looks, as if people thought she would no doubt die under Sanjin's guardianship. Some clearly hoped she would, and others, she saw, had more calculating expressions, as if already weighing what a marriage to her might mean in terms of royal favor and gifts.

Jin now had a title, which was much more attractive to potential suitors.

She tried not to think of Aadan, but it was no use. If he were here, he'd likely be able to unravel the political implications of all this, maybe even advise her.

But he wasn't here. He needed to fight his own battles, fulfill his own destiny. And if she were honest with herself, his destiny really didn't include some street thief who had, by a strange twist of fate, become a dragonrider and now an adopted lady. She herself wasn't sure what danger lurked ahead. Involving Aadan might put him in a similar peril.

Jin followed the marquis out to his private quarters, where a separate ceremony awaited them. All her things had been moved from Meipin's to a small wing in Sanjin's courtyard home.

She changed into the traditional female robes of a noblewoman, with layers of silk over a bodice, and shoes that curled at the end, so as to not trip over the long skirts. Her hair was unbound from its rider braids and coiled into an elaborate creation, though Sanjin's austerity had dictated they abandon usual Tang traditions of fancy gold and silver hairpins. Instead, everything in her hair was jade, no doubt to remind everyone of her dragon's status.

She bowed the traditional three times to the ancestral tablet in Sanjin's great hall, a cold, marbled room that smelled of incense and ash. A bowl held a medley of fruit offerings to the ancestors, whose names were etched on a stone tablet mounted on the wall.

The empress herself attended, along with Tai, a great show of face that set the nobles murmuring. It was the ultimate honor, a clear stamp of favor. Jin almost smelled them scheming.

She lifted the incense sticks and placed them in the burner by the altar, then drank from the cup that Sanjin gave her. She wondered if it was poisoned, but then what would be the point of adopting her and trying to kill her?

I doubt poison would work, Rayshan agreed. *Unless it came from Mengkhis's hand.*

She sipped the tea, which, even sugared, tasted bitter. Joining Sanjin, even as his daughter, was vile. The empress smiled, looking triumphant, and suddenly Jin hated her. Why was the empress doing this? She couldn't think of a single reason that was for Jin's good.

The ceremony ended in a short feast, where the guests were ushered into the banquet hall and plied with roast duck, exotic fish steamed with scallions and ginger and ginseng for long life, mutton with chili and garlic, and chestnut-stuffed quail, along with spicy eggs and simmered river eel. Great pitchers of honeyed teas, wine, and baijiu flavored with hawthorn flowed endlessly, until the nobles were bawdily singing slurred poetry.

She was about to excuse herself when a familiar voice spoke next to her.

"You don't look like you wish to be congratulated on your new name, Lady Fang." The crown prince had his usual expression of easy charm trying to hide an underlying concern.

"I'd rather Your Highness still call me Jin, if possible."

His eyebrows shot up. "Very well. Stop calling me Your Highness, like I asked last year."

"What would I call you then?" Jin asked. Chinese custom was that a ruler or crown heir's name was reserved for that person alone, never to be used by others. Tai's name, Jin knew, had been changed to a specially composed character to prevent anyone from accidentally offending Heaven by using it. "It is forbidden for me to speak your name."

"That is what makes it so appealing."

Jin decided to ignore this and ask what she really wanted to know. "Meipin thinks your mother is doing all this to marry me off. Is that true?"

Tai stiffened almost imperceptibly. "Did she say who?"

Jin shook her head. "But I thought you might know."

Tai hesitated. "I don't think she's decided anything.

But I think she considered your joining nobility an honor for you. You don't agree?"

Jin darted a glance around, unwilling to speak against the head of the secret police in the heart of his own home. "Let's just say it was a surprise."

His mouth twisted in annoyance. "To me as well. My mother seems full of surprises of late."

THE DAY AFTER, Meipin showed Jin one of the public notices, where a center article declared the Marquis Sanjin as adopting the talented heroine Jin to be part of the Fang household. Jin knew these proclamations were posted up in the city boards, just as they were in Gaozho. The empress and Sanjin clearly wanted the whole population to know as well.

Everyone would know her as Sanjin's daughter. The thought still made her mouth dry.

THE FLIGHT over the mountain passes had them bickering constantly, until Jin told Rayshan in exasperation to land. Her one respite from her etiquette and history lessons was souring day by day as Rayshan's primal drive and yearning took hold, making him snappish.

Not to mention, the strain of Emar's words to her—that Mengkhis might be hiding in plain sight—was taking its toll on her. She had become jumpy at shadows, scattering crushed walnut shells around her bed to prevent a surprise guest in the night.

Though she had graduated the Veil and was therefore as ready as she would ever be to fight the man, the fact remained that no one knew where to find him. The only lead they had was to wait for Mengkhis at the ghost port of Jimo, where he would surely try to raise his dragon from the sea.

They arrived back at Dragon City, where Rayshan blew a wall of flame in the air to vent his frustration, nearly torching the saddle Jin had just hung. Jin cleaned him in silence, wiping down his sides and paring the dirt from his claws. His scales were molting, leaving a fine carpet on the floor.

Is this normal?

Yes. I am shedding skin for a new coat for the mating cycle.

She smiled. *Vain things, you lot.*

She had meant it as a jest, but it only sent Rayshan into a grumpy simmer.

Just as well, Jin thought testily. She wasn't sure she had anything nice to say, and that thought hurt her almost more than anything else.

He was the center of her life, and knowing they were at odds created a deep discomfort in her that nothing dispelled. He had even lost interest in oranges, instead tracking prey with a chilling vigor. A discordant buzz became ever present in their bond, making communication uncomfortable.

Still brooding over Rayshan's moodiness, she was unprepared for the sight that greeted her when she passed the mess hall on the way to Dragon City.

Standing in the courtyard was a familiar figure. At first, she wondered if she was imagining him, but then the scent of sandalwood reached her, and something inside her turned giddy.

No phantasm had a smell.

As if sensing her, he turned, and for one long moment she feasted on the sight of Aadan's face. He had aged, and a new scar ran along one temple, while his beard had grown as long as a sage's. But he was the same. And when he saw her, he broke into a slow smile that seemed to warm the very air.

She wanted to run and pull him into a hug, or more. She forced her legs to walk, and then she was before him, drinking in the sight and smell of him. Tears threatened, for she hadn't realized until this moment that a part of her had been frozen in time, carefully folded and put away in a corner, just like the pain of Ah-Ming's bamboo rods, for she worried she would never see him again.

They stood for a moment, words failing them.

"I don't want to eat here," he said. "You?"

She shook her head. She had lost her appetite anyway.

"Shall we walk to Dragon City?"

THE DUSK WRAPPED around them like a warm hand as they walked. Jin treasured the silence of just being together before she let out the flood of words that threatened.

"You shouldn't have come back. The empress may punish you." Jin remembered how the empress had accused Aadan of breaking Dragon Class law by fleeing the empire.

"Officially, I'm here as Samarkand's ambassador, so I am protected under law."

"How long can you stay?"

Aadan's smile faltered. "I'm not sure. As long as it takes to gain Her Majesty's—" he paused "—Her Divine Majesty's help in fighting the Arabs." From his tone, she knew he felt the title was awkward as well.

"How is Wanli?"

"He is cranky," Aadan smiled wryly, then held her gaze. "He blames it on the Song of Scales, but in reality, he misses you and Rayshan."

Jin found him studying her intently, as if memorizing her face. Self-consciousness knifed her.

"I know I look different," she said tensely. "I have aged."

He stopped walking. "I noticed."

She winced. "The summoning, it's . . . ageing me. I will turn uglier by the day."

"You will become many things, Jin," Aadan said quietly. "But you'll never be ugly."

She tried to believe him. But she had stepped on this path; there was no going back now. "Regardless, I don't know what the summoning is doing to me. I may not be able to die by anyone's hand but Mengkhis's, but this . . . this is something new. I don't think Emar has answers either."

Aadan gripped her hand, the unexpected touch making Jin's breath hitch. "Then stop."

She shook her head. "Once I've killed Mengkhis Lai, then I can stop."

His fingers squeezed hers. "I heard you were made to join the Veil." The anger in his voice was searing. "And that you're now Sanjin's daughter."

She nodded. "I still haven't figured out why."

"To marry you off," Aadan said tightly. "The empress sees you as a bargaining chip."

Jin spied a swarthy man in armor striding toward them. There was a faint family resemblance to Aadan in the curly hair and the jawline, but otherwise the two were night and day. One was rotund and square, with eyes that assessed everything in a calculating way, whereas Aadan was tall, his expression open.

"Ah, Cousin, you're working your alliances already," the man said. "Aren't you going to introduce me to the one I assume is the famed dragonrider?"

Aadan's expression grew guarded, and Jin sensed an undercurrent of tension between the two.

"Cousin Gah'med, this is Wang Kway Jin, dragonrider."

Gah'med bowed and took her right hand in his in the traditional Zoroastrian greeting. "May the Wise Lord protect you, my lady. I understand your name is no longer Wang Kway Jin, however. Should I address you as Lady Fang? Or Hwayping?"

"I will always be known to friends as Jin," Jin replied.

Gah'med smiled easily. "Well, I am definitely a friend, so Jin it shall be." He turned to Aadan. "The local Persian elders have asked for an audience to pay their respects, so I came to fetch you."

Aadan glanced at Jin. "I'm sorry. I have to meet them. But I'll come find you tomorrow."

Jin nodded.

Gah'med gave Aadan a critical look. "You won't have time tomorrow. It's the wedding."

"Wedding?" Jin asked.

"A cousin's," Aadan explained quickly. He cleared his throat. "Not mine."

Jin noted Gah'med's impatient look. "Come, we're late as it is."

Aadan turned to Jin. "Why don't you come with us?"

Jin felt as surprised as Gah'med looked. "Me?"

"Yes. You." Aadan seemed to warm to the idea. "My

cousin would be delighted to have the honorable Rider Jin at his wedding. Please?"

Jin didn't think she had the willpower to refuse those sage green eyes even if she wanted to.

Gah'med looked about to say something, but Aadan cut him off, suddenly cheerful. "Have one of the lads fetch her tomorrow. Hour of the rooster. Now let's go. As you said, we're late."

CHAPTER 35

Adan thought tomorrow would never arrive. There were meetings with the Changan Persian elders to hold, visits to temples and dinners by the wealthy families to attend. Gah'med made sure he attended all of them and stayed long after protocol demanded.

By the end of the night, he was thoroughly looking forward to the next day, when he would see Tai on the archery field and attend his cousin's wedding with Jin.

"I hear you have a friendship with the crown prince," Gah'med said over an early breakfast at Aadan's guest rooms in the eastern side of the imperial palace.

Aadan's friendship was no secret, but he knew where Gah'med was going with this. "I've already arranged to meet him. Alone."

Gah'med's mouth set in a line, but he said nothing.

Perhaps he realized that this was one meeting where Aadan would work best in private.

~

TAI'S FACE broke into a warm smile when the two met at the archery field where they often practiced together. Few except the prince and Aadan came here after a newer, fancier oval had been built closer to the military barracks, and a sense of nostalgia came over Aadan. When had life become so much more complicated?

The scar on Tai's neck, Aadan saw, had faded but was still visible. Tai no longer tried to cover it, however, and Aadan hadn't heard the moniker "Scarred Prince" even once. Instead, Tai seemed to be known widely as the Prince of Dragons.

"It is good to have you back, Aadan," Tai said.

"I worried I'd never see the day, Your Highness," Aadan replied.

Tai clapped Aadan on the shoulder as they walked over to the rack where the bows were stored. "I hear you are making progress against the Arabs."

"Progress, yes, but not final victory," Aadan said. "I have Samarkand's support, but I still need a few dragons to bring the Arabs down."

Tai nodded, and Aadan sensed the weight of this familiar conversation on him. Over the years, Aadan had been clear, if not overly aggressive, in his campaigning for the empire's support of the Persian cause. And though Tai had been cautiously open to such moves, the empress and her War Minister had always opposed. Now, however, Tai was the war minister, and Aadan hoped this would tip the balance. And if not, then he had the Sanskrit sutra from Samarkand.

The straw targets, he noticed, bore distinct Khitan characteristics: each had braids of hair crudely stuck to the sides of the head, in imitation of the popular Khitan hairstyle.

"Not forgiven nor forgotten, I see," Aadan commented.

"Not close. Everyone is still bloodthirsty toward the Khitan," Tai said. "But we can barely afford a war now. I'll need to think of something to persuade the War Ministry to your side."

Aadan thought on this as he lined up his shot and loosed. The arrow hit an arm. "They are still cash-strapped, I take it?"

"Gao siphoned enough gold to line two emperor's pockets." Tai stepped to the mark, stretched his bowstring back, and loosed. The arrow struck much more to mark.

Aadan rummaged for another arrow. "I haven't much to offer. Certainly not the amount Gao took."

The other prince smiled. "I know. And I would never ask it. I'm just trying to tell you the obstacles I'm facing."

Aadan remembered a conversation with Gah'med.

"What of the princess? Cannot her brothers be persuaded to pay a ransom?"

The prince looked like he had just bitten into an unripe plum. "Her brothers are stingier than a Wusong merchant in winter. They'd haggle over every fen until we were old men. And we need a capable army sooner than that."

Something in Tai's voice alerted Aadan, and he straightened from the basket of arrows. "Mengkhis isn't dead, is he?"

Tai sighed. "You believe the rumors?"

"No. But you have that same haunted expression you had whenever you had a nightmare about him when we were children," Aadan said. "Maybe more so. If he was dead, you'd look carefree." On more than one morning during their trainings, Tai had appeared with bags under his eyes and confessed to nightmares about his uncle returning to the palace to finish what he had started. And though Mengkhis was a true monster, Aadan sometimes wondered if the empress deliberately fanned the prince's fears to bind her son to her.

His friend ran a hand over his face. "Jin says he was somehow awake when she confronted him, that the mages' timing was off. She tried to kill him, but he escaped. And the empress doesn't want the people to know." He nocked his arrow, drew, and loosed, skewering the target through one eye.

Aadan wondered at how the mages could have been so careless with something so pivotal. Jin might have died. And having Mengkhis loose, with no idea of his whereabouts, was possibly more terrifying than having him at the gates. An unseen enemy, especially one such as Mengkhis Lai, was a wickedly dangerous thing. Aadan worried for his friend, but also for all the Persians left in Changan. This was a deadly time in the empire, and Aadan reluctantly admitted that Tai had reason to keep Jin close.

"And they have no idea where he is? Baikalan is still under the sea in Jimo?"

Tai rejected one arrow in favor of another, and Aadan noted the way his stance changed. The prince was agitated.

"The waiting is worse than facing his attack," Tai muttered.

"The empress will do everything she can to keep you safe," Aadan said, trying to be reassuring.

Tai's expression faltered, and Aadan realized his stumble. Tai was thinking to when Tai had a sword to his throat and his mother had done nothing. "It's natural for people to freeze from fear when panicked," Aadan assured.

Tai loosed another arrow that went straight through his target's neck. "Regardless, it's a foolish gamble to lie about Mengkhis, if you ask me. But even the War Minister has less say with Her Divine Majesty."

"How is being War Minister treating you, anyway?"

Aadan asked, sensing his friend would rather change the subject. "You never did like dragons."

Tai smiled, some of his easy charm returning. "They are starting to grow on me."

"True?" Aadan didn't bother hiding his skepticism. Much of the empress's decision to appoint Tai head of Dragon Class was to overcome his fear of heights and his aversion to dragons. "I thought perhaps the title Prince of Dragons was simply in jest."

"Well, I've found some of the advisers in the war room have tempers that rival any dragon in Dragon Class. Not to mention their breath."

Aadan gave a short laugh. "You should meet my Persian ones."

It was Tai's turn to chuckle. "Maybe I will. Maybe I'll visit you when you take back Persia."

"You know you'd be welcome any time," Aadan said. "Though I'll admit, you'd be even more welcome if you brought dragons."

Tai grinned. "As long as I don't have to ride one."

Aadan shook his head. "You'd get us both killed."

The two laughed as they retrieved their arrows from the targets, and Aadan let himself revel in his friend's company. He realized it was the first evening in months when he hadn't spoken Persian at all, which suited him just fine. The thought brought him back to his present predicament.

"I may have something that will help sway your

mother, if not the war cabinet," Aadan said, picking up a long bow and testing its bowstring.

"Oh?" Tai readjusted his archery ring, a fine jade piece that fit over his thumb.

"I uncovered a Sanskrit relic," Aadan said. "I suspect it was left by the monk Xuanzang on his way back from the holy lands of Lumbini."

"Xuanzang? It's true my mother always admired him."

The old monk had been a revered figure in Buddhist circles, having traveled to numerous western regions to obtain scriptures and translate them.

Tai paused in lining up his shot, brow furrowed. "But what kind of relic?"

"A sutra," Aadan said slowly.

"Not to pour cold water on you, my friend," Tai remarked, "but the palace is inundated with sutras. The monasteries have purchased Buddhist scriptures from abroad, and by now many of the monastic libraries rival mine."

Aadan nodded. "True. But this one foretells of a female ruler being the reincarnated Boddhisattva and bringing a thousand years of peace."

Tai lowered his bow, the target momentarily forgotten. "That is indeed an unusual sutra."

Aadan nodded. "I felt your mother might want such a document."

"She would," Tai said, then frowned, tapping an arrow against his thigh. "Would you consider not giving it to her if I promised to obtain your dragons instead?"

Aadan had suspected Tai wouldn't welcome the empress's calling herself divine, but he hadn't realized the prince felt so strongly. "I'm listening, Your Highness."

Tai glanced around, but they were alone. "Keep the sutra to yourself. As Minister of War, I have greater say over our dragons and who we align with."

"I thought you said there are obstacles."

"There are," Tai agreed, "but I will find ways to overcome them. She will use that sutra in ways that . . . that I disagree with." Tai paused. "Do you trust me?"

Aadan wrestled with himself. This find was priceless, and he had brought it here to win his kingdom its dragons. But he knew Tai's fears were well-founded—the empress would use such a holy document to cement her grip on power and crush her enemies, deserving and undeserving alike. Was that why he had told Tai about the sutra first? Had he unconsciously been worried about exactly what Tai feared?

"I trust you, Your Highness," Aadan said, and realized he meant it.

Tai nodded. "Good. I'll see to your dragons. I have a few candidates in mind."

"I do as well."

The prince glanced at him.

They chose new bows and replenished their goose-feather arrows provided in leather buckets nearby.

As they walked toward the targets, Tai added, "Jin will have to stay."

Aadan's neck twitched. "Because you wish her to?"

"Because the empire needs her here."

Aadan nodded, gazing at the field before them. "I've heard the talk. The Prince and Princess of Dragons."

Tai didn't glance at him. "People enjoy rumors."

"But you don't deny them, Your Highness."

At the archer line, Tai stopped and faced him. "You jealous, Aadan?"

The direct question hit harder than he expected. "Should I be?"

Tai held his gaze. Aadan searched for guilt, anger, or denial. But there was none. Just a flicker of quiet hurt, and then it too disappeared.

"No, Aadan. There's no reason to be."

The knot in Aadan's shoulders loosened but didn't vanish.

Tai waved toward the targets and found his stance. "Come, I want to shoot something."

Aadan shared the sentiment.

They shot arrows in silence for a time, but the easy companionship of before had dimmed.

CHAPTER 36

Jin berated her own nerves as she surveyed the dresses the maid had laid out from her new wardrobe.

Sanjin's stinginess and lack of knowledge about female court fashions showed, for whoever he had appointed to secure her clothing had bought colors that not only clashed with Jin's mixed skin tone, but even to Jin's untrained eye looked suspiciously like last year's fashions.

Normally this wouldn't have bothered her. She didn't even want to wear a dress, truth be told.

But you want Aadan to be attracted, Rayshan butted in crankily.

Jin sighed. *I thought you were asleep.*

I can't sleep with your pulse the way it is, not to mention the Song of Scales.

I'm sorry. It's just tonight. Shall I bring you more oranges?

She nearly flinched from the force of his scorn across the bond. *You think oranges are a substitute?*

She left him to his grumbling, knowing there was nothing to be done. She settled on a pleated skirt the color of ripe pomegranate, with a cream under blouse and a light blue jacket embroidered with birds and peonies. It was not the latest fashion, but at least it suited her slim frame a bit better than what was in style now.

She glanced at the water clock. Aadan's servant would be there soon. She wryly thought back to Lady Yang's words from her days with Haitao: "People will notice your eyes and your mouth first. Forget the rouge or the combs, but never forget your lips and eyes."

She brushed crimson on her lips, then lined her brows and eyes with only a few strokes before a servant appeared at the door to announce the arrival of a carriage.

The driver took her through the palace and out to the city, where the capital was already awakening for the night. Lanterns glowed from every eave, their sides painted with the words for *wine, song,* or *dice,* depending on what their offerings were. Other shops were closing, the streets abuzz with the chatter of people heading back to their wards before curfew.

The carriage rolled under the gates marking the

western ward and the Persian precinct beyond. Here, the number of huren increased, along with children of mixed blood. The signs bore Persian and Turkish words, and even some of the Tibetan language. Traders pulled carts and camels behind them, and the air smelled of incense and sandalwood, both of which made Jin think of Aadan.

The house they stopped at was a wealthy, sprawling mansion on the far side of the western market, its gates newly painted and pots of fresh flowers placed at the doors.

Jin disembarked, feeling suddenly alone and exposed in her Chinese silks, whereas everyone walking through the doors wore the traditional garb of Persia: loose baggy pants for the men, flowing robes and veils for the women. Many, she saw, wore white, a color Chinese wore only to funerals.

She followed the small crowd and stopped near the door, where an old Persian man was taking names.

"Good evening, esteemed lady," the servant bowed. "Your name?"

Jin hesitated, looking about. Aadan was nowhere to be found. "Wang Kway Jin."

The man surveyed his list, frowning. "I have no such name here. Perhaps you are at the wrong—"

"Jin!"

Jin looked over to see Aadan, wearing a cream long jacket over bright red trousers and shoes, a milk-white shawl over his broad shoulders. But the most beautiful thing he wore was the smile that could melt stone. The sight of him set off something warm and fluttering in her chest.

He stepped past the parting crowd and nodded to the servant taking names. "Jin—or Lady Fang, is my guest."

The servant bowed. "Ah! My apologies, Your Highness." He turned to the next guests as Jin followed Aadan under the arch and into the home.

"I'm not used to hearing you called Your Highness."

"I'm not used to calling you Lady Fang."

Inside the first rooms, lanterns had been hung and intricate carpets laid down, the rooms smelling of sandalwood, honey, and simmering sugar.

She glanced at the sea of head coverings, all brightly patterned silk and linen. "I didn't bring a headscarf. Is that a problem?"

Aadan smiled. He lifted the white cotton shawl from around his shoulders, shook it out, and in one deft move flew it around Jin to settle over her hair. He tugged it into place, pulling her to him as he did so. "Problem solved."

Just then a group of men pressed in, all of them bowing as they murmured excuses while jostling her aside to reach Aadan.

She gave him her best understanding nod as the men surrounded him, eager to convey their greetings.

"The people have great hopes in my cousin."

She turned to find Gah'med at her elbow. He smiled, but it held no friendship.

"Come, let me show you the home and welcome you properly. As you can see, Aadan has much on his plate."

With a last look at Aadan, who was engrossed in an animated discussion with a short man in flowing saffron robes edged with jewels, Jin reluctantly followed Gah'med into the home.

"I trust you have never been to a Persian wedding?"

She said nothing, unwilling to admit that the only weddings she had ever attended in her life were those where she had been stealing for Haitao. He allowed none of his thieves to marry, or have children, though some secretly did. And paid the price.

Gah'med led her into an ornate courtyard where guests milled over tables laden with honeyed pastries, candied nuts, aromatic spiced rice, date puddings, and loaves of sweet bread. Serving girls in long Persian gowns offered generous pourings of wine from copper pitchers. On a table in the middle of the courtyard, a great golden bowl studded with emeralds held several knots of flaming sandalwood.

"Do you know the significance of the *atash dan?*" Gah'med indicated the bowl and its flames.

"A sacred fire?" Jin guessed.

Gah'med smiled, as if praising a child for trying but failing. "Yes. It represents the purity of our god and Ahura Mazda. The marriage ceremony must have fire."

"Who is getting married?" she asked, realizing that things had happened so fast she hadn't had any time to ask.

"A distant cousin of mine—of ours, I should say, as he is also Aadan's cousin. He will be marrying another cousin of ours."

Jin tried to sound polite. "Cousins are allowed to marry one another?"

Gah'med raised his eyebrows. "Ah! Of course. You do not know our customs." He took a goblet from a serving girl and offered it to Jin, who shook her head. "Marriage within the family is considered pure. It is best to marry within the clan, and we, the Sasanids, pride ourselves on following tradition. Has Aadan not mentioned this?"

Jin swallowed, refusing to allow Gah'med the satisfaction of seeing her mood. "Why would he?"

Gah'med took a swallow of wine. "You two seem close. I thought he might have told you much of our culture, his heritage, what is expected of him?"

The rebuke was clear. Gah'med was trying to make her feel insignificant, far removed from Aadan's world. And worse, it was working.

"Another cultural pointer, if I may?"

She looked at him, seeing from his expression that this was the second time he was asking. "Please."

He made a thoughtful noise, as if debating the choice of words. "Lady Fang, anything to do with the dead is considered very unlucky in our culture, especially at a wedding. I hope you can make sure we do not have any unwanted guests, or appearances, tonight?"

She gave him her sweetest smile, though something bitter settled inside. "Some things are common to all cultures, Persian or Chinese. I would not invite the dead to a wedding."

Gah'med nodded. "Good. Ah! Here is my cousin!"

Jin turned to find Aadan at her side. "I thought you had disappeared. Let's take our places before I am waylaid again."

Jin followed Aadan into a second courtyard, glad to be rid of Gah'med.

"Your cousin doesn't like me."

Aadan sighed. "He doesn't like anyone I care for."

The words warmed Jin, but not as much as the hand on hers as Aadan drew her down to sit on a carpet with him.

This courtyard featured perimeter cushions and rugs. In the center, a gold-threaded carpet showcased a mirror and bowls of candied nuts. Some of the guests were already taking seats, while a boy in flowing white robes struck a gong to summon those in the outer courtyard.

"There's something else I should tell you," Aadan said softly, not looking at her. "He wants me to marry his sister. Which is why he is barbed with you."

"He told me it's tradition for you to marry your cousin," Jin said.

"It is," Aadan replied. "But I can't do that."

Jin looked away, worried of the emotions on her face. "Because of the blood tie?"

"No." He paused, and she looked at him. "Because there's only one woman I wish to marry."

Time itself seemed to hold its breath. A hundred thoughts raced through her, but none passed her lips.

"Am I interrupting?" Gah'med sat down on Aadan's other side, a smile doing nothing to hide his disapproval. Aadan and Jin subtly pulled away, though Jin swore the air itself still crackled.

Several men with thick black beards, ornate headdresses, and flowing red robes entered and took their seats, before a gong announced the arrival of a tall, lanky man in pristine white robes and a matching cap and veil across his nose and mouth.

The guests chanted a greeting, and the priest took his place at the central carpet before an assistant in white also entered with the bowl of fire. He reverently laid it on the short table before the priest.

Jin tried to avoid glancing at Aadan, but felt it every time his eyes slid to her. The priest finished his prayer, and a man in clean cotton trousers and jacket entered, his head covered in an ornate cloth cap. He took his seat, where the priest murmured more prayers in Persian before summoning the bride.

The bride entered with several girls in attendance, all dressed in white. The bride's head was covered in a white veil, and small bells sewn into her gown tinkled as she approached the central carpet and the fire.

"The fire is for purity," Aadan whispered. "While the mirror represents truth and clarity between the couple."

The bride sat opposite the groom, and the gathered crowd sighed happily at the sight.

As the priest launched into a rapid string of Persian, Aadan leaned close to interpret. "He is giving the traditional prayer and now asking for the father of the bride to come forward to present her and give his blessing."

A portly man with a neatly trimmed beard stood. He kissed the bride, gripping her hands in his, then retreated.

Jin felt an unexpected pang. There would never be that moment for her—unless it was Sanjin, and the idea of Sanjin presenting her at her wedding was enough to bring on nausea.

"Are you alright?" Aadan's concerned whisper brought her back.

She nodded. "What are they saying now?" She didn't need to share her ridiculous imaginings.

"The priest is asking the bride and groom if they consent."

Jin watched as the priest turned from the groom to the bride and asked a question three times. Each time, the bride bowed and answered with what Jin assumed was assent. At the third time, four female relatives rose and carried a white cloth, holding it over the couple while the priest pulled out a red-and-white thread from his pocket.

At some unseen signal, the bride and groom placed their right hands together.

"This is where they are bound together," Aadan explained softly. "A symbolic tying of the hands in partnership."

The bride and groom clasped hands, and then the priest wound the thread around their wrists, once, twice, three times, before a triumphant cheer rose from the crowd, along with a burst of music from the musicians waiting in the outer courtyard.

Jin joined in the shouts of congratulations, until a touch on her hand made her look down. Aadan's fingers had found hers, but when she looked up, she caught Gah'med's scowling face behind Aadan's shoulder.

"Lady Fang," Gah'med said, "might I ride back to the palace with you?"

Jin wanted to tell him to get lost, but bit back her words. He seemed to take this as assent as he climbed into the carriage and settled down opposite her.

"Ready, my lady?" the driver shouted back.

"Yes," Jin answered tersely, and the horse stepped into a trot. She cursed herself now for not accepting Aadan's offer to take her home, but she didn't want

Sanjin able to accuse her of unchaperoned time with Aadan, thereby giving him an excuse to restrict her movements.

"I love weddings," Gah'med said. "I imagine there are many who would like nothing more than to wed the famed dragonrider?"

"Dragonriders don't wed," Jin replied curtly.

Gah'med raised an eyebrow. "Oh? A pity. Though does your noblewoman status change that?"

"All the dragonriders are noble," Jin said. "So I don't imagine it does."

"Ah, well I am sure Aadan is very aware of that." Gah'med seemed to relax. "Well, then perhaps this conversation is pointless, but I feel obligated to have it all the same."

Jin reined in a reply about pointless conversations, knowing that learning Gah'med's agenda was better than driving it into hiding.

"Aadan is an idealist, which is refreshing," Gah'med said. "The young are full of ideas of how to change things. And I sense you two have a close friendship."

"We have battled together, and saved each other's lives," Jin said. "I would count that as friendship, yes."

Gah'med smiled indulgently. "Friendships are wonderful. We do things for those we love, even if those things don't benefit ourselves. Am I right?"

Again, Jin remained silent, refusing to be side-tracked by the word "love," and let Gah'med follow his own momentum.

"Aadan is in a unique position in that he is seen as a savior, a king of kings. His people have waited a long time to return home, and we have waited a long time for our returning prince. But some have concerns." Gah'med paused. "Do you understand what I am saying?"

Jin forced herself to look Gah'med in the face with a neutral expression. "You want him to marry your sister. I know."

Gah'med raised his eyebrows but then laughed. "I was told Tang women are forthright. I hadn't realized how forthright. Yes, Aadan and my sister have been betrothed for some time."

Jin tried not to show how the word punched her. "Betrothed?"

"Well, in all honesty, it was more of a discussion between his father and me. But Aadan will come to see reason, I think, because Aadan's wise enough to understand."

"Understand that you're trying to make decisions for him?" Jin contested.

Gah'med sighed. "Understand that if he is going to lead, then he needs to convince the people he is Persian. A prince who has grown up at the Tang court, riding Tang dragons, wearing Tang clothes, and eating Tang foods—such a man cannot hold the throne easily, even if we weren't having to fight the Arabs."

"He is a good leader," Jin insisted, "whether he's Persian or Chinese."

Gah'med leaned forward, his face impatient. "I am not arguing that. But people won't follow him if they think he's Chinese. And what happens when he marries a Chinese wife? Not even a Chinese wife, but a half blood?"

"Get out of my carriage," Jin said.

Gah'med held up his palms. "I mean no disrespect. But even if you were of noble blood and had parents to attend your ceremony, you came to a Persian wedding without even a head covering. How much of our customs do you know? You can aspire to be his mistress, but don't think you can be queen."

"Driver!" Jin called, knocking on the roof. "Stop the carriage please."

The vehicle rolled to a halt, and a servant pulled the door open, bowing. Gah'med gazed at her. "Hate me as you will, but I have Aadan's best interests at heart. Do you?"

"Get. Out."

Rage boiled in Jin. All the warmth of the evening, the looks and words of the night that she had burned in her mind to cherish later, withered under Gah'med's arguments. No matter that deep down, perhaps in her deepest darkest of hearts, she had always known these immovable mountains existed. But to have them pushed in her face, and to have her feelings laid so bare and trampled on by a total stranger, crushed her soul.

Gah'med stiffened. "I have worked for years to help his family regain the throne, but if you do this, Aadan will pay the price. Think on it, I beg you. Peace upon your evening, Lady Fang."

She watched him step off the carriage and walk away, struggling between the desire to throttle him for insulting Aadan, and throttling the little voice inside. Because even if her heart protested Gah'med's words, her head knew he was right.

CHAPTER 37

The announcement of the banquet came on delicate bamboo paper scrolls delivered to every noble's house.

Even in the heart of Sanjin's apartments, Jin over-heard whispers in the servants' quarters, the excited rumors leaking through the walls like water.

". . . surprise guests."

"I hear over three thousand invitations went out. That's more than any other banquet I've ever heard of."

"My cousin said there's to be an announcement."

Jin returned from an etiquette session to find Sanjin's maid waiting for her.

"Your invitation to the banquet, Lady Fang," the maid said, bowing. "I have been told to come tonight to help you prepare and escort you."

Where should we fly today? Jin asked after the maid had left, eager for an escape.

Only a growl came back.

She sensed his restlessness, and her own muscles rippled as she felt him pacing his cave. *This will pass, won't it?*

The snarled reply was half protest, half reassurance. *Yes. In a week.*

Jin tried to suppress her next thought but knew it had slipped through: *There's no guarantee that this will end then, no.*

We must find a way for this to stop, Jin said. *You cannot go on like this. I cannot go on like this. We'll take you hunting.*

This seemed to calm him a little, and she tried to persuade herself that with time, Rayshan's restlessness would lessen. It was like a woman's monthly bloods—it would pass, along with the symptoms.

At the hunting grounds, they discovered Aadan and Wanli not far from the gates. Jin and Wanli greeted each other, the dragon's thoughts loud in her head.

"You knew I would be here," Jin said to Aadan. She was still smarting from Gah'med's conversation, and tried to keep her tone light.

A hint of a smile appeared. "I might have spent some time near the Veil and bribed the keepers here to tell me when you came for Rayshan's hunting."

She raised an eyebrow. "Bribing? That's not the Aadan I remember."

He laughed softly, though sadness flickered underneath, and they watched Wanli and Rayshan fly off toward the trees.

"I heard about your time in the Veil," he said. "I'm sorry I wasn't here."

She swallowed, unable to jest too long about the Veil without touching memories of blood and corpses. "I can't be killed. So there was that."

"But you can feel pain," Aadan said tightly. "The marquis is . . . sick."

She said nothing, for there was no argument against that.

Aadan took her other hand in his, looking down as if she had a fascinating book written on the palms of her hands. "What of the flaring? You can't continue if this is killing you."

"It's not, it's just making me look older."

"You don't know that," he said quietly. "No one knows. It's safest to stop. Maybe there's a way to . . ."

But the words died, and he didn't need to say them. "I can't leave, Aadan."

"Can't, or don't want to?"

"Sometimes the two are the same," Jin said finally. "The empress would never let me leave, not without killing Mengkhis first. And it's something I need to do, for myself."

"Then after," Aadan said. "Come with me after."

Jin's insides fluttered, but cold reality froze it over. "It won't work, Aadan. A strange land where I don't speak the language? And you need allies, not someone with no dowry and no connections."

Aadan's hand squeezed her harder, as if to physically reshape the truth into something different. "You would bring something far greater than wealth or connections."

His kiss was feather-light, yet somehow also heavy.

"What if I gave it all up?" he whispered.

"You'd be a fool."

"But I'd be a happy one."

Jin screamed inside. He was making this harder, not easier. "For how long?"

"Until my heart stops."

She let out a breath. "I cannot let you do that to yourself. You'll end up hating me for what happens."

"Why?" he asked quietly. "Would you ever hate me?"

She knew the trap he was setting and almost resented him more for it. "I could never hate you."

"Then why do you think that of me?"

Jin swallowed. "Because you have more to lose. And not just you, your people have more to lose. Sanjin would never let me go with you. Neither would the empress. You need her help now more than ever. You can't make her an enemy."

She knew the words had hit home, especially when he drew her in and pressed her forehead to him. She sensed he didn't want her to see his eyes, and heard the erratic protest of his heartbeat.

He pulled back, as if suddenly aware there might be

other riders in the vicinity. "I'm sure there are many vying for the Lady Fang now."

She scoffed. "Yes, no doubt Sanjin sees me as a lamb for market."

"Anyone take your fancy?" His tone was light, but a scowl hovered.

Jin grimaced. "No."

"You're sure?"

He was worried, she realized. "You think I don't want to go to Persia because of some brat at court?"

Aadan didn't look away. "There have been rumors."

Jin snorted. "The Prince and Princess of Dragons is something His Highness came up with to please the people."

At this Aadan's expression softened. "So there's no truth in them?"

"None."

An animal's scream broke into their conversation, and Jin immediately reached out to Rayshan.

When there was nothing but enraged roaring in reply, she broke into a sprint, Aadan close behind her.

It took her a while to reach the jade, for the sounds came from a small ravine.

Rayshan was hunched over something, his tail thrashing and his wings spread over the ground like some dome, hiding his prey.

Rayshan!

The dragon didn't respond. Jin heard the cracking of bone and the tearing of flesh.

She scrabbled down the embankment, jumping from rock to rock.

Rayshan!

The silence disturbed her more than anything else. Rayshan not responding was not normal. And the enraged snarling only grew rather than eased.

When Jin reached the bottom of the canyon, she skid to a halt. But it was not Rayshan's turning around and baring bloody teeth at her that froze her. Nor was it the ear-cracking roar that blasted her, dotting her face with spittle and flesh.

It was the sight of the bloodbath before her. A herd of deer—or what she thought was a herd of deer—lay in a bloodied, pulped mess across the ravine. Bones and hide and flesh and horn had all been ripped asunder, and Jin recognized this was less of a feeding and more of a massacre.

Rayshan! What have you done?

The dragon roared again and then beat his wings as he took to the sky, leaving Jin and Aadan, who had caught up, standing ankle deep in the carnage. A cry behind them made them turn to see Wanli landing on the canyon edge nearby.

Anxiety rippled from him, and Jin sensed his worry that Rayshan's mating drive was becoming uncontrollable, that perhaps Rayshan should go with him when he left.

Jin turned back to the carcasses.

"Have you ever seen anything like this?"

Aadan shook his head. "Why does he not answer the call?"

Wanli explained that Rayshan feared the punishment for being blood bonded.

Aadan looked to Jin. "How long?"

"A while now."

Jin was no stranger to the killing of animals, but this was different. Something about Rayshan's behavior at the royal hunting grounds disturbed her. It was volatile, and mindless, a pure channeling of rage that meant the deer was essentially unfit to eat. Rayshan's eyes had seemed manic, and Jin remembered what she had felt: that she was looking at a stranger rather than her most trusted partner and friend.

When she finally found him at dusk, well beyond the palace curfew and hidden in a copse of trees in a far corner of the hunting grounds, he had calmed, his guilt and self-loathing thick and tangible as fog.

She took his great scaled head in her hands, gazing deep into his pain-clouded eyes. *Let's go home.*

He seemed grateful that she didn't ask questions and stayed still while she climbed on.

But as Jin rode Rayshan back to Dragon City, she felt something she'd never felt toward Rayshan.

Fear.

CHAPTER 38

Back in his cave at Dragon City, Rayshan submitted to her grooming the blood from him, the fight seemingly locked away and only the occasional burst of steam from his nostrils betraying any frustration. The cave at Dragon City had been his home since they had first arrived, but now it felt too small to hold him, much less his emotions.

This cannot go on. You know that, right?

Rayshan blasted her with a gust of steam. *I know!* he growled. *I apologize. It's . . . it's difficult.*

She tentatively placed a hand on his flank. He had nearly finished molting, the shiny new scales gleaming like polished glass.

And you will seek out the queen then?

I am not going.

If you were going. You would seek out the queen?

The queen chooses a male, not the other way around. If I

did go and I were rejected, then I'd try for one of her daughters.

Jin rubbed at a patch of flaking scales, sending it sloughing to the ground to join the thousands of others that formed an ash-like layer.

You want to go, don't you?

A protest formed in his throat, then died. *Yes. And no. But I'm a danger if I don't.*

Jin's heart constricted from the warring sorrow and guilt in his emotions. And the steady pull of the dragon queen's song, which was intensifying. She berated herself for not trying to do more about it sooner. With all her training and preoccupation with her own heritage, she had barely asked Rayshan how he was coping with the steady pull, how hard it must have been to resist.

You told me yourself, dragons aren't sentimental. You don't raise your young, you don't bond with another dragon for life. Why go?

Because I am a dragon, he replied. *It's in my blood, and I have to go.*

She should have understood it, and in a way she did. But it didn't mean she liked it. She decided to voice her fear. *Even if some dragons die during the mating cycle?*

He didn't answer, and her throat tightened. She put a hand on his snout and pulled his head toward hers. *Don't you dare die.* It came out fiercer than she intended. But she couldn't lose Rayshan. And not just because she would physically die of the white disease if he was killed. It was because she just couldn't imagine her heart continuing.

At his hesitant questioning, she took in a breath. *If you must go, then go freely, with my love. But don't die.*

I won't, he reassured her. *It's not very common.*

Liar.

A tenth only.

Her throat constricted again. *A tenth is . . . a lot.*

But not the majority. Remember that.

What of the blood bond? They might punish you.

His body shuddered, and his tail curled around her. *Or perhaps they'll see that blood bonding is not as bad a thing as they fear. Especially if it was to save a life. A worthy life.*

Her throat grew raw. He had bonded her that day in the desert, without hesitation, and she hadn't known what he had sacrificed. To deny him this chance at his own instincts was unfair.

I wish I could come with you.

Bittersweet gratitude flooded the bond, but also an undercurrent of relief that she had accepted his decision.

He lowered his nose and nudged her. *You do not want to be around dragons at this time.* He raised his head and rose to his feet, neck arching and ridges raised. *Let's fly,* he suggested.

She was only too happy to obey.

He nearly exploded off the ledge after she had gained the saddle, and the force of his wings sent several grooms scrabbling for handholds in the side of the cliff faces that housed Dragon City. They soared up into the crisp blue sky, where the clouds had been scraped away by a brisk autumn wind that promised rain.

But for now, they were free and flying, and Jin wished she could freeze time. She didn't want to go back to hunting Mengkhis. Here, she convinced herself that Mengkhis had truly disappeared, that he wouldn't come back and seek Baikalan, that he was gone from her life, along with all the uncomfortable questions he raised. Perhaps the empress was overly fearful. Perhaps their last encounter had convinced him to leave. Up here, in the world of "perhaps," she entertained those illogical fantasies and let them be true.

They dipped over the city and out past the giant outer gates, where carriages rolled on the wide boulevards atop the city walls. People pointed, and some even waved. She didn't bother telling Rayshan where to go, instead letting him loose his energy and restlessness, his circles bringing him ever more westward in what she knew to be Nine Claw Mountain.

When will you go?

The sooner I go, the sooner I return to help you fight Mengkhis. Stronger. Clearheaded.

And though it pained her, she agreed. Sanjin and the empress might be furious, but she would deal with that later. *Leave tomorrow, so that you'll return sooner.*

She had but hours with him. And then he would be

gone. Driven toward some primal instinct that she could not control or share. But for now, they enjoyed the isolation and the comfort of flying, of having possibly their last ride together before he left, perhaps to never return.

THE POWDER PROVED essential at hiding the dark circles, for worry shadowed her after knowing that Rayshan would leave.

The maid Linlin did the last of Jin's makeup and bit her lip. "Your huren features make this shade difficult, but I think we've done it."

Jin looked at herself in the mirror. Her hair was in an ornate pile of twists and coils, pinned with enough jade ornaments, Jin felt, to snap her neck. Her cheeks had been rouged, and her lips shone scarlet in the two spots the maid had dabbed on, while the rest of her lips were a rice white. Linlin had thinned her eyebrows and pasted a delicate paper phoenix over her forehead, which Jin examined.

"A phoenix?" She frowned, perplexed. "Phoenixes are for royal women only."

The maid nodded. "Her Divine Majesty chose it."

Sanjin was noble. Was he royal as well? Jin realized that though Sanjin had adopted her, he had given her no clue as to the family's lineage or background, and she had been too preoccupied to ask.

Once she was wrapped in the robes and silks, all shades of pale egg yolk, plum, and pure snow, soft and delicate as clouds on her skin, Linlin helped her into the curved silk shoes before passing her to the valet, who bowed and ushered her before him.

When she was announced at the banquet hall, Jin was astounded to find the chamber nearly bursting, a sea of people already gathered at the low tables and cushions. Sanjin was waiting for her in his official garb, looking even more imposing, his smooth hands making Jin think of snake flesh. She bowed to him, as was customary.

He led her into the banquet hall, where both received nods. Jin caught Meipin's eye and gave a brief smile. She knew Meipin would be dressed at her best, but even so, Jin thought her friend mesmerizing. She wore her usual favorite peach and bamboo-shoot green, but her earrings caught the light, and her low, tight bodice emphasized the smoothness of her neck and skin. Only the twisting of her fan's ribbon told Jin how nervous she was.

Jin took her seat by Sanjin, trying to ignore the stares and whispers of the other nobles. Most were focused on Meipin, but some were clearly watching Jin, and she even caught one of the nobles snapping at his son. She overheard him tell his wayward offspring to make an excuse to speak to Jin after the formalities.

She searched for Aadan, and gave herself a moment to luxuriate in the sight of him. He wore formal Persian attire, though this time a rich blue. The clothes suited him. He caught her glance, and his smile seemed to make his whole expression glow. She looked away toward the stage, worried that her feelings were painted plainly on her face.

Tai was already seated at one of the tables closest to the empress's on the dais, surrounded by his advisors. He leaned to one side, listening to someone urgently whispering to him. He looked concerned, and Jin wondered if he was nervous about the announcement. Something about his posture, the way his shoulders were squared, told her he was ill at ease.

The empress stood, a glittering tower of gold and silk and jade. The room immediately fell silent, and the empress clasped her gold fingernailed hands together. "Welcome, esteemed members of the imperial court. We are here to feast at the solstice during the year of the dragon. And as it is such an auspicious day, the throne has decided to make an auspicious announcement. One concerning the throne and the empire's future, its security. Its continuation."

She paused, and Jin heard the pulses of hundreds of nobles—men and women—quicken. She glanced at Meipin, trying to give her an encouraging smile. She also noticed Nobu, looking slightly green.

Poor girl, Jin thought. She was clearly besotted with Tai, but the chances of a hostage princess marrying the heir to the Dragon Throne were about as likely as Jin marrying him, despite Jin's suggesting Tai make the match.

And no wonder Tai looked on edge. Clearly, whoever had been chosen was not his favorite. Her eyes narrowed. Actually, she decided, he looked too nervous for that. If it was not his favorite, he would be stoic, resigned, or angry. But not nervous.

She stole a glance at Sanjin. He seemed not just calm, but smug. To others he appeared neutral, but she now knew her adopted father enough to know when he had won some plum prize. She sensed there was a piece of this puzzle just out of reach, and she was moving the parts in her mind when she caught the word "adopted" in the empress's speech.

". . . finest example of what makes our empire strong, united in this one esteemed person. Therefore, the throne has named lady Fang Hwayping as the designated wife of crown prince Wu Tai Shen, to be formally recognized immediately."

It took Jin a moment to understand that she was lady Fang Hwayping, and for the full weight of the words to sink in, along with the sudden abrupt stares of everyone in the room.

Everyone but Meipin, Jin noticed, who was still staring at the empress, her smile slipping into barely contained shock.

"Does Marquis Sanjin accept?"

Next to Jin, Sanjin stood and bowed to the empress. "This unworthy servant is humbled and honored, Your

Divine Majesty, and I, as father of lady Fang Hwayping, accept this with gratitude and humility. Our unworthy daughter will serve the crown prince to the full of her abilities."

Jin snapped her gaze to Tai and caught the guilty flinch. He had known.

He had known and not told her.

Everything slotted into place with a horrible clarity.

Why Sanjin had adopted her, why this whole charade. As an orphan, she would have been ineligible for the position of empress. With no royal blood and no family to speak for her, she was not only ineligible but also possibly free to refuse if she wished. But being part of Sanjin's household, being his daughter, meant she was beholden, and he had all legal rights to her, including who she married. The answers locked into place around her like the stocks prisoners in public squares wore, but none of that hurt as much as the stunned look on Aadan's face.

It was the same look she had just given Tai, a look of betrayal and anger. Before she could mouth words to Aadan, Sanjin was pulling her firmly to her feet and pushing her into a bow.

"We will await Your Divine Majesty's pleasure as to a wedding date," Sanjin said.

As polite congratulations resounded, Jin screamed silently in protest. Most were looking at her as if she had just gained the world. But in truth, the empress and Sanjin had just taken almost everything that mattered.

CHAPTER 39

The banquet had been a blur of nobles and congratulations, drinks pushed upon her and speeches from various ministers, where Jin was clearly meant to stay silent. There had been no chance to speak to Tai or Aadan, and at the gong marking curfew, Sanjin had virtually dragged her back to her new apartments in his residence.

She decided to wait until the entire household was asleep and then sneak out. She had to speak to Aadan.

Jin paced to control the nervous rage in her, but when that didn't seem enough, she took a melon from the fruit bowl that was kept filled on the table and began throwing a blade at it to kill time.

Just when she was about to pull herself through a window and sneak away after the last bell, she heard footsteps approaching, and so she quickly latched the shutters closed. Linlin entered and announced a visitor.

The scent of agarwood entered before the prince did, and soon he was standing in her rooms, the maid discreetly closing the doors behind him.

Rage choked her.

He cleared his throat. "I know it's late, but I worried you were angry."

"Why would I be angry, Your Highness?" She flung the knife, its edge kissing Tai's hair to land in the bedpost behind him.

He swallowed. "Your aim is still impeccable."

"No, this humble servant missed her target." Jin closed the distance between them in three strides. "Tell me why."

Tai cleared his throat. "First, I knew nothing of this."

"Your skills at lying have worsened, Your Highness," Jin said.

"My mother hinted," Tai conceded, eyes searching her hands as if afraid of another knife. "But she didn't say it in so many words. I specifically asked her to consult you first."

"Why didn't you tell me yourself, Your Highness?"

"As I said, she mentioned the idea, but I didn't think she would ambush you. Us. I didn't want to alarm you."

"Well, I'm alarmed, Your Highness," Jin said. Saying the words made the full weight of her having thrown a knife at him crash on her like a dead dragon's carcass.

She had hit him when they first met, and now she had nearly killed him. She drew a breath, working at calm. "Why? Why are you doing this?"

"I told you, it's not me."

"Very well, Your Highness," Jin made herself icily polite. "Why is your mother doing this?" Her survival was tied to these moves, she was sure. She had to know. Something was going on, something she didn't understand, and every minute that she didn't under-stand was a step closer to a trap she couldn't fathom.

"I think she fears your popularity," Tai said. "And mine. She's trying to harness us."

Jin absorbed this, grappling with how absurd it was, and yet how it did make a twisted sense. "She's jealous?"

"That's another word for it," Tai said. "May I move without fearing a knife in the back?"

Jin hesitated, then retreated a step, and Tai nodded his thanks. He turned toward the knife buried in the bedpost, making Jin lunge. She stopped midway when Tai held it out to her, hilt out.

"You bested me once," Tai said. "I don't care to repeat it."

She took the knife, but hefted it in her hand, needing to grip something solid. "So that's what this is for your mother? Control?"

He sighed. "It's always about control. She's angry at me for the statue incident, for learning magic behind her back."

"She didn't know?" Jin asked in surprise.

Tai shook his head. "It's silly, but . . . it was *my* way of keeping some control."

"So she marries you to a low-born orphan for revenge?"

"Revenge and control are not the same thing. Besides, I don't believe you qualify as a low-born orphan anymore."

"Sometimes I wish I did," she admitted honestly. "I preferred being a murderer's child to being Sanjin's."

Tai grimaced. "I sympathize."

Jin paced to the other side of the room. "There must be a way out of this. Surely you have a say, Your Highness?"

"I do," he said slowly.

"But?" Jin prompted.

He took a breath, eyes on hers. "This certainly didn't happen the way I thought it would. And my mother sprang this on both of us. But do you really feel this is a bad thing?"

Jin stared. "Yes."

Tai raised his eyebrows and circled the table. "Why?"

Jin frowned, wondering if he was being deliberately dense. "For obvious reasons, Your Highness."

"Then convince me."

Jin debated throwing the knife again but knew that was a death wish. "You yourself said this is your mother's plan to control me, and you."

"Just because that's her plan doesn't mean it will work. I have a mind of my own, and last time I checked, so do you. We are not helpless, and we can make this work to our advantage, remember."

"What advantage?" Jin nearly snapped. "Your Highness."

He counted on his fingers as he spoke. "We are known as the Prince and Princess of Dragons. We are well-liked. Together we'd do a lot of good, change things for the better. The empire would benefit."

"Even if that's what I wanted to do, Your Highness," she said, "there are far better choices. Choices that won't create a rebellion."

"Your choice won't create a rebellion," Tai countered. "In fact, it will prevent one."

"That makes no sense," Jin asked. "Meipin has been groomed her whole life for this!"

Tai nodded. "I know. But that doesn't necessarily mean she's the best choice."

"You seriously agree with your mother, Your Highness?" The thought was ludicrous.

"I do, actually." She waited for a smirk, some sign he was joking. She found none.

"And Sanjin wanted this because it makes him father to the future empress," Jin said bitterly.

"I'll admit, I doubt Sanjin is capable of even a shred of paternal love," Tai said. "But if it makes any difference, I don't think it's as outlandish as you think, once you consider it."

"Really, Your Highness?" she countered, face hard. "Now it's *your* turn to convince *me*."

She sensed one of his disarming smiles forming, but he seemed to think better of it. "I'll give you four. One, you are not part of the nobility, so you don't have the same obligations that others have. Meipin, as wonderful as she is, has a lifetime of favors she owes people, and as soon as she becomes empress, she'll be working night and day to repay them."

Jin opened her mouth to protest, but Tai held up a hand. "You are close to her, I know. But this is court, and she wouldn't be worth her reputation if she didn't have complex alliances. You are free of all those. Two, you have the people's love, at a time when they are becoming less content with my mother's support of the monks and the temples. She is having to deify herself, and there are many, like the mages, who resent her for it. Three, you are the only hope when Mengkhis surfaces, and the people are going to need that hope. If this lie my mother has chosen to build crumbles at any point, the throne is in peril. Unless you are there and seen as part of it, defending it."

Jin growled in frustration. "This wouldn't even be an issue if the people knew. And besides, they won't follow if they know I failed."

"We won't present it as a failure," Tai said.

Jin's thoughts spun. "You'll paint Mengkhis as a demon, resurrected."

"Is it such a stretch of the truth?"

This began to explain why the empress had insisted on the match, reversing completely from her earlier stance, when she had threatened Jin to stay away from Tai. Jin turned. "You said there were four reasons."

He cleared his throat. "Ah, yes. That." His voice turned soft, no hint of his usual flippancy. "I . . ." He seemed to change his mind. "I think we'd be good for each other. And not just politically."

Jin searched his face, trying to see if this was an attempt to influence her. The man was as adept at working heartstrings as the best shadow puppeteers in the city markets. She sometimes wondered why the whole of Dragon Class wasn't forced to take diplomacy lessons from him. *A key only opens one door. A skilled tongue opens all doors*, as Haitao used to say.

"Best of all, I don't have to worry that my favor will get you killed," he said. He gestured at her knife. "I can sleep at night knowing that even I wouldn't be able to touch you without fearing for my life."

The jest cost him, she saw. He was trying his best to put her at ease. And suddenly she sensed the undercurrent of nervousness in him. Much of what he had said was pragmatic, and she almost believed that his motives were all political. Yet hidden in there, buried but real, was a genuine emotional truth.

"A wise man once told me," she said slowly, "that those with great wealth can't afford some of the simplest choices."

He arched an eyebrow. "There you go being wise

again. Whereas I'm beginning to think that sometimes the foolish choice is also the right one."

She turned and looked out the window. "I need to tell your mother that I will kill Mengkhis for my own reasons. I want my freedom when I'm done, and I can swear whatever oath she wants me to take, but I want freedom from this, from Sanjin, from all of it."

Tai walked to stand beside her. "Sanjin will be hard to persuade, as will my mother."

"I'll deal with them. Which leaves you." She turned. "Would you oppose me?"

"No," he answered after a pause. "But can you give it some thought? Sometimes we fear opportunity because it's so large it's intimidating."

"If it's not what we want, Your Highness," Jin answered, "then opportunity is just another word for trap."

SHE FOUND Aadan in Dragon City.

Wanli's cave had been reassigned upon Aadan's fleeing the empire, and so Jin searched the quarters kept for guest messengers and warrior dragons on assignment from their permanent posts.

She reached out to Wanli, who guided her to one of the topmost caves, where Aadan stood silently cleaning the dragon's scales. Wanli gave her a gentle warning in her head.

He glanced up but didn't stop what he was doing. "Sorry I didn't offer my congratulations. May the Wise Lord protect your union."

She wanted to shake him, knock sense into him. But she inhaled and counted instead. "Aadan, I didn't know."

He said nothing, simply cleaning his dragon's scales in regular motions.

"Did you hear me? Say something."

Aadan paused and turned. "I wondered why you refused me, but at least now it makes sense. No woman in her right mind would refuse the opportunity to be empress."

Jin wanted to never hear the word "opportunity" again. "Then I'm not in my right mind. I had no idea that was the empress's plan."

Aadan looked at her. "So what did you think when Sanjin adopted you?"

"You said it yourself, she was planning to marry me off. I just didn't realize . . ."

Aadan turned back to Wanli, letting his brush fall into a pail of water with a loud splash. "Is this what you want?"

"Of course not!" She wanted to hit him.

"Then what do you want?"

Jin spied a flash of red in Aadan's pocket and reached for it, but Aadan stepped away and pushed the bit of thread out of sight.

Anger and hurt condensed into a hard, venomous

knot within her belly. "Will you marry Gah'med's sister, then?"

The wounded look on his face twisted her.

"I am sorry," she whispered. "I have no right to ask."

Jin slid down the wall to sit on the floor, and Aadan joined her. After a moment, his fingers found hers. "I know he told you about the betrothal. But technically, they cannot force me."

She warred with herself. Some words were so hard to say, she would have given anything to swallow them.

"I told you to be careful of Tai." The anger in his voice surprised her. "I've always thought him a friend, but he has his agenda."

"It's not all Tai's fault," Jin replied, exasperated. "As I said before, there are other reasons this wouldn't work."

"Well, those all seem surmountable compared to this," he said bitterly.

She took his hand, tracing the new scars, a burn on the palm, a thickness in his right thumbnail where something had ripped into him and forced the new nail to grow back differently. Her own body had countless new marks, evidence of the life she had been living since he left.

"You are not the same man who left after Jimo," Jin said.

"Are you the same woman?" Aadan countered.

Jin shook her head. "But . . . my feelings are the same."

His eyes darkened. "As are mine."

Jin leaned into him, wrapping her arms around him, and immediately felt his arms circle her. She rested her head under his collarbone, relishing the sound of his heartbeat, the smell of sandalwood and dragon scales, the whiff of saffron and aniseed.

"Do you remember that last night on the cliff? Before you left?" she murmured.

He nodded against the top of her head. "Every day."

"We should have taken our chance then."

His pulse jumped beneath her ear. "Time is like a river; it cannot flow backward."

She reached into his pocket and plucked the red string from it. She pulled slowly, until the entire length was in her palm.

"Give me your hand."

His eyes darkened. "Why?"

"I'm asking for your hand," she said quietly.

His breathing seemed to change, but he leaned in and held out his right hand. She held it in hers, then lifted them together, wrist to wrist. She began winding the thread around them, once, twice, three times.

"This is not marriage." His voice came out thick, a storm of emotions crossing his face.

"I know," she answered. "But it's love. Remember that. No matter what, it's love."

He pulled her to him, his lips pressed to her hair. She slipped the thread off their hands and placed it in his palm, folding his fingers over it before leaning in to kiss him.

He smelled of sandalwood and smoke, longing and loss. Something inside her was breaking, and it took all her willpower to spare him her tears.

"I can't stay," he said softly. "It would kill me."

Jin leaned her forehead against his. "I know."

They held on to each other until the sound of a guard's shout to another reminded them: the consequences of discovery would be brutal.

"You have to go," he said softly.

He was right, she was making this harder for them both.

Yet as she left, Jin wondered whether the consequences of giving up on themselves would be worse than any punishment from the empress, a white disease of the heart that would kill her even more slowly than the Veil.

JIN WALKED BACK to Meipin's without thinking.

She felt frozen, numb in parts and hollow in her core, where even Rayshan's attempts to comfort her didn't dull the sense of injustice and nausea. And beneath it all, a bottomless sea of grief.

She wondered if this was how Emar had felt, with some of his limbs affected by the white disease. Would she feel this way forever, like a part of her was dying inside?

She knocked on the doors but realized something wasn't right as soon as Ahlu slid the lock, a lantern in hand and a taut frown on her face.

"Lady Jin—I mean Fang," Ahlu murmured. "Linlin has been looking for you."

"Please, I don't want to spend the night there. Surely Meipin will let me stay?"

Ahlu pulled a scroll from her robe. "I don't think you'll be staying. She said to give you this."

She handed it to Jin. The imperial seal, along with that of the Veil, blazed across it. She used her fingernail to loosen the thin band of silk holding it closed, and tilted it to read it by the light of the lantern Ahlu held.

Her breath caught.

Mengkhis had surfaced.

By the time Sanjin's servant came to fetch her, Jin had already changed into her dragonrider leathers and was calling out to Rayshan.

Go to Nine Claw Mountain! I'll be fine.

All the dragon queens in the world couldn't make me leave you now, Rayshan roared back at her.

She knew her arguments would be half-hearted at best. Perhaps they would control his emotions long enough to hunt down Mengkhis. Perhaps Mengkhis hadn't really surfaced. Perhaps Nobu's medicine would solve this . . .

Jin shook away worries about Rayshan's state and followed Sanjin's servant to the imperial quarters, where lights blazed in the Minister of War's offices. Tai's offices. She refused to think of him as her future husband, and rubbed the spot on her wrist where the thread had been earlier.

Now, she didn't even know whether she had a future to plan, much less change.

"The prince and the empress await," the servant said, bowing low.

Jin ascended the steps to the courtyard doors, where guards let her through. Rayshan was alert and on tenterhooks.

I'm guessing he's with the Parhae kingdom, Rayshan growled.

Or the Khitans, Jin answered.

She was ushered into the meeting room and bowed low, avoiding looking at Tai. She needed to shut out all her anger and the complications of the court over the last weeks. Deal with Mengkhis. Then deal with her wants.

"Rider Fang," the empress said. "Better late than never. We have news that Mengkhis has raised Baikalan."

Jin's thoughts swam. Before she formed the question, Oyang Kang said, "All the mages and guards at Jimo were slaughtered four days ago. Only one rider escaped alive, so we received the word mere hours ago."

Jin cursed. Jimo was two days' travel from Changan. "Then he has a two-day start. He could be here already."

"We believe he is headed to join the Khitans," Sanjin said. "The border has sent word that their forces are on the move, and there have been sightings of Mengkhis heading north on the coast."

"Once the Khitans have Mengkhis," Tai said, "they may decide that Nobu and her dragons are expendable."

"What is the plan?" Jin asked. "Where is Mengkhis now?"

"We don't know," Sanjin replied. "We have sent soldiers to search every household or dignitary with Khitan ties, as they will likely be sympathetic."

Jin sensed the frustration in the room. "I can try to find him in the Firesong. But if it doesn't work, then we are no closer to killing him."

"But if we can launch a surprise attack on the Khitan capital," Tai said, "we eliminate his one refuge. They may give up their sister and her dragons, but they won't give up their own lives and the seat of their power."

"How do you know Mengkhis isn't already at the Khitan capital?" Jin asked. "He can move quickly."

"He might be," Tai admitted. "But we have the advantage of surprise."

Jin digested this. "We lure him out."

"With what?"

"Me." Jin wasn't sure what made her positive he would come for her, just that the chance to kill the only other blood-bonded rider would be seen as an opportunity. After all, if he could eliminate the only one who could kill him, wouldn't he take that up?

Tai seemed to follow her thoughts. "It's too dangerous."

"I've been brutally trained for this moment," Jin said drily. "It would be a pity for all that to go to waste. Whether I lure him to me or I go to him makes no difference. In fact, setting our own stage on our own turf might be better."

The empress and Sanjin exchanged looks.

"You'd be left exposed and alone," Tai protested. "That's the difference."

The empress raised a finger. "Unless . . . she wasn't alone."

"I'm the only blood-bonded rider, Your Divine Majesty," Jin said.

"But what if you weren't?"

The words sank into the silence, and everyone looked as stunned as Jin felt. Except Sanjin, whose mouth only thinned ever so slightly.

"You have other blood-bonded riders?" Jin asked, incredulous.

"No. But we will." The empress came down and approached Jin. "Emar already told you that I made a squadron of blood-bonded riders."

"All of whom died, Your Divine Majesty," Jin responded.

The empress didn't flinch. "This time we will better the odds."

Jin stared. "Your Divine Majesty, you're not thinking of repeating the blood bond?"

"It remains, as always, our best chance to defeat Mengkhis," the empress replied.

"You would force the riders to volunteer?" Tai asked.

Sanjin stepped forward. "Those in the Veil would gladly give their lives."

The empress nodded. "That gives us ten? I would suggest we ask for ten more."

Jin's stomach fell, and Rayshan growled in similar unease. *They don't know what they're doing.*

"Your Divine Majesty," Jin said, willing her voice to steady. "Most of them will die. Emar said half in his wing didn't survive."

"You can't make silk without boiling a few worms," the empress said. "What are twenty people, compared to an empire?"

Jin turned to Tai, whose expression looked torn. "She's right."

Jin didn't bother asking Sanjin. He would go forth just to study the effects of blood bonding, no doubt hungry for more pain-sensitive victims to abuse in the Veil. "Please don't do this."

"We must. We cannot risk Mengkhis surviving again," the empress said. "Besides, you are my son's betrothed. There is too much riding on your survival, and your future role in the empire." She turned to Tai. "My son, you agree? We cannot send your future bride out to Mengkhis. And I know many in the Dragon Class would gladly take up this duty."

Jin willed Tai to refuse, but when he looked at her, his eyes darkened.

"Volunteers only," he said. "We will not force anyone to take the blood bond."

The empress's lips pressed in disapproval. "Very well. We will let them choose."

"There is no glory in blood bonding, Your Highness." Jin turned back to Tai. "There's a reason it's forbidden, but it's not what you think. It's not because the rider becomes too powerful, it's because of the risks. To rider and dragon. Think what you will lose— half of your riders, half of your dragons."

"If it's to defeat Mengkhis and save the Princess of Dragons, then it's a risk we shall take," the empress said. "What says the Minister of War? And the head of the Veil?"

Tai swallowed, but his glance at Jin was unapologetic. "I agree. Those who wish to take the risk, take it of their own choice."

"Marquis?" the empress prompted.

Sanjin bowed. "No price is too great for defeating Mengkhis Lai."

"Then we are agreed," the empress said. "They shall have one day to decide. By nightfall I expect twenty volunteers to be ready and waiting to be blood bonded."

~

As Jin headed to the Blood Oval, she comforted herself that at least she didn't have to worry about Jao and Panshalar volunteering. Their faraway posting meant they couldn't arrive before nightfall. She reached out to Rayshan as she arrived at the weapons masters' quarters to submit her swords for treatment.

What of Nine Claw Mountain and the Song of Scales?

I cannot leave you now, Rayshan answered, and she sensed him tamping down the pull of the song.

Do you think you can resist until we see this through? She worried he was fighting on two fronts. Especially as he had already decided to go and had therefore let the Song of Scales roar through him unchallenged. Even now she heard the scattered threads of his thoughts, the distraction of the call.

I have to, he growled back. *Do what you need to do. I will control the Song of Scales.*

Jin certainly hoped so. The Song coursed through him, stronger than ever, even at this distance.

After she had retrieved her weapons, Jin stole a detour to the western side of the palace, where the nobles and royal families lived, knowing there was one other goodbye she had to make.

Meipin was already awake and having her hair brushed. Ahlu darted an inquisitive look at Jin but at Meipin's gesture slid out on quiet feet, making sure to close the door behind her.

"None of this was my planning," Jin said.

"No one plans on Mengkhis," Meipin pointed out.

"You know what I mean. I didn't plan the engagement to Tai."

Meipin sighed. "You're a terrible politician, you know. With no idea of how to play the court."

"I've been told that before," Jin said, remembering how Tai had snapped at her for the same reason when she'd defied Ulagan on his official visit. "And soon I might be a dead one."

Meipin's face crumbled. "You know I do not want that. I would never want it."

"I know," Jin said, coming to sit opposite Meipin. "I don't know what happens after. I just know that I must stop Mengkhis. If I survive, I will speak to the prince, and the empress."

Meipin held Jin's hands in her soft, plump ones. "Don't think of that right now. I have grown disgustingly sentimental, but I want you as a friend much more than I want the phoenix crown."

Jin gave a lopsided grin. "Careful, Meipin, the fate of many girls rests on your ambition."

Meipin shrugged. "There are many paths to Mount Huashan, for anyone resourceful enough to think of them. Go and kill Mengkhis so that we can fight tooth and claw over the throne, and the crown prince, like two proper court women."

They embraced, and Jin swore that if she survived, she would do everything in her power to help Meipin in her agenda to put more women in government, for Meipin's leadership and forgiveness were a refreshing change.

CHAPTER 41

That night, drums heralded the fall of dusk, and the imperial mages, officials, and Dragon Class volunteers filled the palace's largest courtyard, including Jin. Oyang Kang stood, face stony, next to Sanjin and Prince Tai, who flanked the empress. Foreboding collected in Jin's belly.

Dragon Class initiates lined the courtyard in five rows of four, and Jin's breath caught. Nearly half standing next to their dragons were women.

"They're too young," Jin argued.

"They're only a year younger than you," the empress pointed out. "And they wanted to support their inspiration."

Jin wished the empress hadn't said those words. She didn't want to have anything to do with these women and the horrible risk they were taking.

Just as bad, if not worse, was her recognizing two of

the men, someone tall and broad next to a familiar short figure.

When they caught her eye, Jao gave the briefest of defiant smiles, but she saw through Panshalar's bravery right away.

"What are they doing here?" Jin said.

"You are to be commended, Rider," the empress said. "Your wing mates were the first to volunteer when we sent the messages."

"But messengers only went out today," Jin said. "They couldn't have known in time to come back."

"I took the liberty of sending out initial calls a week ago," the empress said.

"You didn't know about Mengkhis then," Jin pointed out.

"I like to be prepared," the empress replied. "Especially as this is the Song of Scales year. Many dragons are at Nine Claw Mountain."

"This was always your plan," Tai accused.

"No, I planned for this possibility," the empress corrected him. "In case it came to this, I wanted us to be ready."

Jin felt sick. Emar's face flashed through her mind, the image of him telling her about being blood bonded, and how his wing mates had volunteered when they had heard he was going against Mengkhis Lai.

History haunts us, Rayshan growled in her head, and Jin had to agree. All of Emar's wing mates died, and she bucked against the same fate befalling her remaining comrades. They had once been bastards to her, yes, but she liked them nonetheless. They had fought with her before, and they were there now, risking their lives.

"I can do this myself," Jin said. "There's no need to make them do it."

Tai looked like he would grip her shoulder but held back. "This isn't a moment for pride, Rider. Mengkhis bested you once. Let's not make the same mistake."

"But we're not, Your Highness," she hissed. Sanjin and the empress had tried to kill her along with Mengkhis, and that was how they were here.

Tai's expression told her he knew what she meant. He stepped close, until he was looking down at her, only breaths away, and his eyes held a fierceness that stunned her. "Why risk it?"

"If you're doing this because you're afraid of Mengkhis, Your Highness—"

"I'm doing this," he snapped, "because the only thing I fear more than Mengkhis Lai is your not coming back."

The silence between them sounded even more deafening than the shouts and boot falls from the courtyard.

"By the eight levels of hell," Tai muttered, taking a breath.

The empress's clearing of her throat broke through. "We are about to begin."

Jin pulled herself back to the bonding. Tai and his emotions, real or otherwise, would have to wait. "What of their dragons?" Jin said. Surely their dragons wouldn't agree.

"They were consulted, and they follow their riders," the empress said smoothly. "They know the risks."

"You would overturn this taboo? What does the rest of Dragon Class say about this? The Minister of Laws?" Jin asked.

She caught the telltale tightening of the empress's brows. Not everyone agreed, and perhaps not everyone knew.

The empress was ignoring significant opposition.

"Laws are to protect the empire," the empress said. "The empire is not here to protect the laws."

The dragons came flying in then, and Jin watched as they blocked out the sky. They landed next to their riders, a mix of ebony, silver, gold, and bronze, their roars and flames singeing stone and brick.

Jin had lost all words, knowing that nothing would stop this. Some of the riders held no fear, it was true, only anticipation.

Jin spotted Bo Tan amongst them and steeled herself.

"Don't do this," she murmured.

His expression was firm, and he gave her a slight nod. It hit her why he had volunteered. He was doing this because he felt he owed her for Ice Beard Mountain.

She tried one last time, using the only method she had left. She reached out to the dragons as one.

Don't do this. It's not too late!

But then a gong sounded, and each dragon sank their teeth into their forelegs, unleashing rivulets of blood. Servants stepped forward with bronze vessels to catch the crimson flow, before bowing and offering them to the riders.

Each rider took the vessel, and when all had full cups, they raised them to the empress.

"Ten thousand years! Ten thousand years! May the empress and the Princess of Dragons live ten thousand years!"

As one, they drank.

The next moments seemed to trickle to a stop for Jin. She dared to think that they had all been untouched, but then the first rider, a tall, robust oxen of a man she had never met, fell to his knees, clutching his sides. His dragon screamed and thrust a snout against the rider to try to breathe life back into him, but it was too late. The man was already growing stiff on the stones, his eyes wide and his fingers curled in on themselves like a dead crow's.

The empress watched, stone-faced, while Jin turned, horrified, to Panshalar and Jao.

Jao tossed the vessel away and put one hand on his dragon, while Panshalar belched and gave a wobbly smile. He's fine, Jin told herself, until his face contorted.

Jin swallowed down her helplessness, unable to look away.

Panshalar sank to his knees, then his hands, and curled into a ball. Jao moved toward him, but a general barked for him to keep his distance.

By now, half the Veil riders had fallen, writhing. Some had blood coming from their mouths, while others seemed to have been simply struck where they stood. They lay on the ground, straight-backed and staring at the sky, while their dragons keened into the clouds. The baleful cries cut Jin, and she wanted to wash the sound from her ears.

But she would hear it for as long as she lived, the cry of dozens of dragons mourning their fallen riders.

Jin forced herself to look at Bo Tan, who stood with his hands on his knees. A slick pool of vomit lay at his feet, but Jin saw no blood. His bronze was growling but otherwise seemed unscathed.

"Get healers to them," Jin said. "They need healers."

Oyang Kang shook his head. "There's little the mages or healers can do. The blood bond takes its course. Some will fall and some will stand. We will only know by tomorrow morning who is left."

Hope surged in her. Panshalar and Bo Tan were not lost. Perhaps it would pass. Unfortunately, Madu was also still holding on, grinning as if he were enjoying a bath instead of a cursed blood bonding.

"Come," Sanjin said, "the survivors will be given what comforts we can give. There is no use in your staying here."

"They have given me their lives," Jin said. "I will stay until the end."

The empress, Jin thought, looked approving. Not that Jin cared. The empress was doing this to protect herself, and Jin would have liked nothing better than to hurl her from the courtyard steps.

Guards came in to take the deceased away, and Tai turned, grim, to Oyang Kang. "We will give them honorary funerals and posthumous titles. May their families mourn with honor."

Oyang Kang bowed, face unreadable. "It shall be done."

Jin shut her eyes, thinking of all those who would be in mourning white, the dragons who were already taking to the skies, their cries of grief echoing out over the city.

Rayshan keened in sympathy for them.

Where will they go? Jin asked.

Each is different, Rayshan said. *They will go to a private place. To grieve. And die.*

The empress and Sanjin also watched the skies, and Jin suspected their sadness was likely only for the loss of their precious dragons.

Now only half the field remained, and Jin was gratified to see that Bo Tan, Jao, and Panshalar were still alive, though Panshalar only just. His great swarthy face was so ashen it made the wisps of his beard look like coal against snow. Sweat shone on his brow, and he kept holding one arm, as if it pained him. Another woman was scratching madly at her face, as if ants crawled there, while her dragon roared, rubbing his own snout against the courtyard stone as if he, too, felt the itch and burn. The woman's hands came away long enough for Jin to recognize her. Bo Tan's friend in the mess hall. Wei Ru. Jin's gut twisted.

The healers wrestled Wei Ru to the ground and bound her hands so she wouldn't gouge her eyes, and Wei Ru screamed all the way out.

Jin sent up a silent prayer for her, that she would live, though she knew chances were slim.

"Well," the empress said crisply. "The worst of that is over. Welcome to your new team."

THE NEXT DAY, the whole of the palace seemed on edge as Dragon Class and the infantry coordinated to press back against what the Veil had warned of: Khitan forces gathering along the border to the Tang empire, ready to invade.

Of the riders who had chosen to take the blood bond, only eleven had survived, including Panshalar, Jao, Bo Tan, and Madu, though Panshalar still looked ill, and his dragon was not faring much better. Rei Wu was nowhere to be seen.

Jin took the first opportunity to see Jao and Panshalar but knew that words of thanks were inadequate.

"Emar would have done the same," Jao muttered. He lifted a cup of plum wine. "To his memory."

"To his memory," Jin murmured, and thought she saw the man appear briefly behind Jao before he faded away. She looked at each of the blood-bonded riders and silently toasted them in turn. There were five women, the rest men. Some sat stunned, and others seemed grim, while a few were clearly coming to terms with their newfound senses.

She went to find Aadan in the guest wing of the palace, her heart and mind a mess of what she would say if he was there.

This would be goodbye for a while.

But she found the guest chambers empty, devoid of any belongings of the Persians except the faintest ghost of sandalwood in the air, clinging to the cushions in the foyer.

"They left, Rider Jin—I mean, Lady Fang," the servant said.

"When?"

The servant shrugged. "I cannot say. I was asked to clean the chambers this morning."

A crushing sadness settled in, making itself at home where her heart should be. He had said he would go. She just didn't realize it would be that soon.

She pulled herself away and sought out Rayshan and the other blood bonds in the oval. Rayshan's drive was like a raging torrent in him, barely controlled. And the other blood bonds all smelled different, she realized, along with their dragons. Not to mention Madu, who tracked her with eyes made even more predatory by his blood bond.

Oyang Kang and Sanjin stood at the forefront, along with Tai, who looked inquiringly at Jin.

She nodded subtly to reassure him. There was no point in both of them being emotionally distraught. She felt she carried enough turmoil for the entire wing.

"We fly at the hour of the snake," Oyang Kang barked. "Every rider will be responsible for their own gear, tack, and dragons. You have been assigned your wings; we fly to Luoyang tonight and then on to the wall bordering Khitan. Your mission is to find Mengkhis Lai and destroy him, nothing else. Our forces will engage the Khitans at the border, to distract them and draw them, but we want you to track down and hunt Baikalan. You'll be doing so in groups of five. Jin and her team, Panshalar, Jao, Bo Tan, and Madu, will take the capital."

Jin didn't have to look over to sense Madu's cold glare, and her stomach coiled. Madu could now kill her, as he was blood-bonded, and she cursed whoever had put them together.

"The empress promised me my title and lands back," Madu said softly, "if I made sure you came back alive. So my plan is, kill Mengkhis, bring you back, and then kill you slowly."

"I appreciate your warning me," Jin said. "But I doubt you'll survive Mengkhis, much less me."

Madu shrugged. "We'll see. I intend to gut you for what you did to my uncle, just debating whether to do it before your wedding to the Scarred Prince or after."

Jin nearly leaped on him, but Oyang Kang was there between them with a speed Jin didn't think possible without the blood bond.

"You have a common enemy right now," Oyang Kang barked, "and by the eight levels of hell, it's not each other!"

Madu glared murder at her but backed down.

"Anyone who threatens this mission will have the mages to answer to," Oyang Kang continued. "Am I clear?"

Jin knew what he meant. They'd be imprisoned like Mengkhis was, in a permanent sleep until another blood-bonded rider was sent to kill them. Jin wondered if Madu had secretly fantasized about that exact situation.

Jin forced her anger aside and joined the others. Unlike their previous attack on Mengkhis, this time there was no fanfare, no public celebration to see them off.

The utmost secrecy shrouded this mission, and Jin had to laugh that she once again felt like a thief, stealing off into the night while the city slept.

Only this time, Mengkhis was not helpless and locked in a lead cave.

And this time, she knew at least one on her team wanted her dead.

CHAPTER 42

The dawn light had barely broken the horizon, but Aadan was already awake and in the far paddock, readying Wanli for his trip to Nine Claw Mountain.

The dragon's reproaches had started as almost a constant trickle in Aadan's head from the time they'd left Changan, but after the second day, Aadan told him in no uncertain terms to leave the subject of Jin alone. To Aadan's mind, if he thought about her and her engagement any more, he'd lose himself. Gah'med and the others had already commented on how quiet he'd become.

"You're worrying about me when you should be worried about surviving Nine Claw Mountain."

Wanli snorted steam, but the warning had its intended effect. Wanli scented the air, his tail thrashing, and Aadan knew the pull of the Song of Scales was almost at its peak for the silver dragon.

Aadan rubbed the beast's snout. They'd agreed that Wanli would accompany the Persians this far, before heading northeast toward Nine Claw Mountain. The traditional home of the dragons was unsafe for humans at the best of times, never mind during the Song of Scales, so Aadan and his men would wait for Wanli at the northern city of Tongguan, which lay on the route back to Persia.

Wanli's shoulders rippled as he butted Aadan in the chest.

"Stay alive. I can't lose both of you." Aadan's light-heartedness was clearly unconvincing, as Wanli gave a series of worried clicks in the back of his throat.

Aadan rubbed a spot above Wanli's eye, looking into the blue orb that always reminded him of a late summer sky. "Go. Before we disgrace ourselves with tears."

Wanli blinked once, then gusted Aadan's face before springing into the air.

Aadan shaded his eyes against the rising sun, watching the silver's wings slice the air, growing ever higher. A bellow reached him below. Not a farewell, but a promise, and then Wanli was disappearing into the morning clouds flushed with dawn.

A loud belch made him turn to see Gah'med exit the inn they had chosen in this small Silk Road town. His cousin's hair was loose, and his trousers untied, as if he had just come from the privy.

"A beautiful day for travel," Gah'med commented. "Stop looking so morose. I've saved you the best horse."

"You slept in," Aadan said instead of answering. "Keep this up and we won't make Tongguan in a week at this rate."

"I see you're even grumpier now the dragon's gone," Gah'med remarked.

Aadan gave one last glance at the sky before joining his cousin and the other men in the inn's common room for breakfast. Gah'med kept up a jovial chatter with the waiting staff, who brought bowls of steaming rice porridge peppered with spring onions and thin slices of salted pork. Everything tasted bland to Aadan, and he tuned out Gah'med's constant talking, but this only allowed his thoughts to stray to Jin.

If he ever saw her again, she'd be empress. And Tai's wife. His hand strayed to the pocket where he kept the red thread and clenched it. His parting with Tai had been less than civil, for though his friend had denied knowing the engagement plans, Aadan had a hard time believing him. He had never thought the prince capable of lying outright to Aadan, but now he wasn't so sure. And the thought of accepting Tai's help in obtaining his three dragons felt like a bitter and underhanded trade, like Tai had agreed to his request only to win Jin. Aadan would win against the Arabs, even without the dragons.

At some point Aadan realized that Gah'med was no longer talking to the waiting staff, but someone sitting at their table. All the other men in his travel group had finished eating and left, Aadan noted.

"Greetings, friend," the stranger said when Aadan looked over. The man was tall, a northern huren with long sandy hair and angular features. The eyes were friendly, a shade of greenish brown that reminded Aadan of Jin.

By the Wise Lord. Would everything remind him of her?

"Merchant on his way traveling to Changan," Gah'med explained to Aadan before turning back. "I didn't catch your name?"

The man waved off the apology. "Foreign names are strange and hard to remember, I know. Name's Viktar. Though I go by Wei Kaito here amongst the Chinese."

Aadan understood how most would not remember the name. Chinese had no words with the "v" sound.

"Viktar was just asking about news in the capital," Gah'med explained.

"I hope to sell some furs to the merchants who supply the palace," Viktar said. "You wouldn't happen to have any connections?" He leaned in conspiratorially. "I notice you're traveling with a dragon, friends. I thought you might have some gossip, as I find that always helps with sales, to know what's going on and who is in favor."

"Like any court, it shifts with the winds," Gah'med

said, spooning a large mouthful of rice porridge and sipping a bowl of warmed soy milk.

Viktar nodded. "Naturally. Though I hope this girl dragonrider rises to the top, myself, this one who killed Mengkhis Lai. I owe half my business to her, since orders of furs for the Dragon Class have increased after women were allowed to join."

Aadan looked away. The last thing he wanted to discuss with anyone was Jin. How was it that even in such a small town as this, he couldn't escape it?

". . . mind him." Gah'med cast a reproving glance at Aadan. "He's a bit lovesick, can't think of anything at the moment."

Aadan gave Gah'med a gaze meant to freeze fire.

Viktar chuckled, swirling his bowl of what smelled like spiced chai. "Ah, I understand. But in my experience, women are as plentiful as water in the ocean. It's not like this one is the empress, is it?"

Gah'med pressed a fist to his mouth but then seemed to decide on tact over laughing at Aadan's expense. "No, but the heart wants what the heart wants, doesn't it?"

Aadan frowned at Gah'med, surprised at his attempt at sympathy. His cousin shrugged.

"Leave him alone," Viktar said, smiling. "The young are entitled to their heartbreaks. So, if you don't mind my asking, what is a dragonrider doing out here without a wing? I don't know much about them, but I thought everyone was called back to the capital."

"A personal pilgrimage," Gah'med said lightly, and Aadan caught the shift in tone. Gah'med didn't want to give details of their true identities, and Aadan was grateful for his cousin finally showing some discretion.

Viktar nodded. "Ah. I see. Well then, I wish you a safe journey." He groaned as he stood, stretching out long limbs. "I should be on my own way, before someone else beats me to that cutthroat of a dog son that buys for Dragon Class."

He nodded to Aadan in greeting, then to Gah'med, and left the inn. It was only after Viktar had left that Aadan realized the man had drunk none of his morning chai.

THE TRAFFIC on the road thinned beneath them as they drew further away from the town, and Aadan's irritation only deepened.

They had ridden for just over half a day, but already Aadan missed Wanli. The best horse Gah'med mentioned was indeed a fine mare, but she was no dragon. With Gah'med riding a tan gelding beside him, Aadan was subjected to the man's lengthy talks about lineages and what they would do when they were back in Persia.

They crossed wide fields of wheat and sorghum, with the odd hamlet scattered on the roads offering meager food for travelers. The dozen men in Aadan's entourage sang songs of home and laughed at tales they would retell their loved ones. Aadan tried to smile and share their enthusiasm. There was nothing left for him in China, after all, yet that didn't make the future seem any less bleak. Perhaps he wouldn't even be alive to see it, if Wanli didn't return from Nine Claw Mountain.

He buried the ominous misgivings and goaded his horse into a canter to rid himself of Gah'med and his morose thoughts.

As they crested a hill and neared the river Qingyu, Aadan noticed a figure by the bank, waving wildly at them. A downed horse lay on the ground, but otherwise there was no one else in sight.

Gah'med pulled up alongside and squinted. "That looks like . . ."

"Viktar," Aadan agreed.

The man's face lit up at the sight of them as they drew closer, and Aadan's men slowed behind him.

The horse lay unmoving in the dirt, eyes open and already caked with flies.

"Well met, I can't believe my luck," Viktar cried out, rushing to them as Gah'med dismounted.

"What happened?" Aadan asked, taking in the dead horse and surveying the area. No one else was in sight, which struck him as odd. This part of the road was not necessarily busy, but even the river crossing ferry was unattended.

"Where are your supply horses?" Gah'med asked.

Viktar grimaced. "Stolen. I'll tell you the story in a moment. Help me, please." He gestured at the horse.

Aadan's senses prickled, but Gah'med was already moving forward.

"Can your men give me a hand?" Viktar cried. "I can't move the horse with just the two of us,"

"He's dead," Aadan said. "Why move him?"

"That's what I need to show you. Come!" Viktar motioned impatiently, his hands already on the horse's bridle.

Aadan glanced around once more, then slid down and approached. Something struck him as wrong about meeting Viktar here, about the corpse. What was it? The men's horses shifted nervously at the blood, and two of them had to murmur encouragement when their steeds reared.

Gah'med was bending over the horse's carcass, peering at the belly, where a mess of entrails lay on the ground. "By the Wise Lord."

Viktar nodded. "Brutal."

"You're going the wrong way." Both men turned to look at Aadan. "Changan is the opposite direction," he said to the huren. "What are you doing here?"

Viktar looked at him, a slow smile curving his face.

And then he vanished.

Aadan's men sputtered curses before drawing their swords.

"What in the Wise Lord's . . ." Gah'med muttered.

The truth hit Aadan just as something growled

behind him, and a primal part of him already knew what was there.

A great jade dragon, scarred but very much intact, stood on splayed legs, jaws open. One clawed foot was smaller than the others, but looked smooth and unlined. A new limb, Aadan realized with macabre fascination.

Aadan pulled his sword, but three things happened even before he had it free.

Viktar magically appeared behind Gah'med, sword drawn. A vicious thrust sent the tip clean through his chest, and the Persian crumpled with a surprised grunt.

At the same time, a great river of flame rolled from Baikalan's mouth and over the mounted soldiers. The steeds screamed as fire licked their manes and hides, and the panicked animals galloped while their riders fell thrashing, breaking necks and limbs on impact.

Aadan didn't even have time to rally his men, for none were left.

Aadan charged Viktar, screaming across his bond to Wanli.

But before he landed a single blow, spots of light exploded in his head and darkness swallowed everything.

CHAPTER 43

Jin surveyed the wall, remembering the last time she had stood here with her wing. A different wing, when Ezho was still alive. And Emar.

And Aadan had been here with them.

This will be different, Rayshan growled.

Will it? This time they knew they were facing Mengkhis and his dragon, whereas last time they had only had to face Khitan's king, King Ulagan.

Panshalar and Jao joined her, and again Jin was struck by how different this was. Last time, they stood here and Panshalar joked. Now, all humor seemed to have left him. The blood bond had made him quieter, harder, and Jin wondered if she'd ever see the old Panshalar back. Jao, for his part, seemed unchanged, except for occasionally complaining about everything he now smelled.

"This reeks," Jao muttered.

"You get used to it," Jin said.

"No, I mean this situation reeks," Jao said. "We're fishing for a needle in an ocean. Mengkhis could be anywhere."

"Then it's good you're both more powerful now," Jin remarked. She looked around. "Is Nakkalan hiding again?"

Jao motioned with his chin. "He's inside Bo Tan's ear canal."

Jin frowned as she spied Bo Tan absently scratching his head as he cleaned a saddle down by the tack room. Jao's bronze had developed the blood-bonded ability to shrink down to the size of a seed when Jin had last checked, but apparently he had practiced until he learned to enter much tighter spaces.

Jin shuddered. "You're a son of a turtle, you know that?"

Panshalar snorted. "Good you didn't see where Nakkalan went last night. Bayan's still laughing about it."

Jin crossed her arms but was also glad to see Panshalar's humor return. "You're both disgusting."

The gold dragon Bayan was practicing his metal skills with two other blood-bonded golds in an adjacent pasture, liquefying the metal in the earth and then drawing it up to form instant shields. It was like watching Wanli pull and shape water, but Jin instantly snuffed the thought. Thinking of Wanli led her to Aadan.

"Who do you think gets to kill him?" Panshalar asked Jin, his tone serious again as he watched his dragon defend himself against another's practice fire. "Mengkhis, I mean?"

"I only care about who gets to survive," she said.

Scouts had already reported the Khitan army gathering near the border, led by the eldest Khitan prince. Jin glanced behind her at the garrison, where she knew Nobu was being kept, brought along as the bargaining chip. She wasn't sure how much the girl had been told, but the princess no doubt knew where they were, and the dragons certainly had grown more agitated near Khitan, where they likely had memories of their lives while bonded to the Khitan king.

As if conjured, the girl appeared on the wall, and cast regal, if hesitant, looks toward Jao and Panshalar.

"I was hoping for a word alone with Rider Jin."

The two frowned, but at a nod from Jin, they descended the steps, leaving the battlements to the women. The princess walked over, her shorter leg giving her a rocking gait as she came to Jin's side.

"I read your message. You wanted to see me, Rider Jin? I mean, Lady Fang," Nobu corrected.

"I prefer my old name," Jin said. "If you're willing."

Nobu nodded. "Of course." She turned to look out. "I'd never been this far south when my father was king," Nobu said. "It's ugly."

"The wall, or the land?"

"Both." Nobu surveyed the area and sighed. "My

father always said the Tang were smarter than the previous dynasties. They didn't bother with the upkeep of the wall like the others."

"How is that smarter?" Jin asked.

"A wall makes everyone curious about what's inside, what is so precious that it has to be defended," Nobu said. "The nomads have no walls, because true wealth is not something to be hoarded behind structures."

"I didn't think your father admired the Tang for anything," Jin said. "Besides, most wealth is guarded behind doors, locks, walls. Including Khitan's."

Nobu didn't answer right away. "I think my wealth doesn't need walls, and cannot be held by them. That's something my father and I agreed on." She looked to the sky, where Shafeng and Satu wheeled overhead. "They are all I need. Speaking of, here."

She fumbled in her pocket and pulled out a thin clay jar, unremarkable except for the walnut stopper carved in the shape of a curled dragon. She held it out. "You wanted this?"

Jin glanced from Nobu to the jar, and took it, hesitant. "You knew what I was going to ask?"

"I heard about the slaughter at the hunting grounds," Nobu said softly. "And I had a feeling you'd be worried about Rayshan in the upcoming battle with Mengkhis."

Jin hefted the jar. It felt both light and heavy at the same time, and she still debated its use, even though Rayshan was the one to suggest it.

"How much of his powers does it dim?"

Nobu shrugged. "Almost all. He'll have his usual strength, his fire, but he just won't be able to flare—as you call it? Certainly not like what he did in Bohai."

Jin searched for words. She realized she had never fully apologized for what happened, for killing Nobu's father. A horrible man, to be sure, but Nobu's father all the same. "Princess Nobu, I hope time erases your grief."

Nobu gave a bow of the head. "Thank you for your concern."

Jin tried to discern whether the girl held any anger, but as if deliberately masking those emotions, Nobu drew a breath and spoke before Jin could ask.

"I wanted to raise a suggestion. If Prince Tai lets me go to talk to my brothers, I can persuade them to join us against Mengkhis. It's worth a try."

"That's . . . not my decision to make," Jin said.

"He will listen to his future bride," Nobu said, and pressed on when Jin's expression darkened. "At worst, won't a meeting between the two sides buy you and the riders some time to find Mengkhis Lai? If there's a choice between bloodshed and negotiation, isn't nego-tiation better?"

Jin was surprised at how much sense Nobu was making, once again.

"I will try," Jin promised. She watched the princess walk away toward the wall steps.

"Princess Nobu!"

The girl turned.

"You would make a fine queen for Khitan, in my opinion."

The girl looked down shyly, then beamed. "Your opinion counts for a lot, Rider Jin."

She watched the girl descend one step at a time due to her leg, but Jin's words seemed to have buoyed her. Jin then made her own way down the other side, the jar in her pocket.

Jin approached Rayshan where he was staying with the other dragons in a paddock by the wall.

He lashed his tail but said nothing as she showed him the vial.

You don't have to do this, Rayshan. Taking away his powers felt wrong, somehow, and not just because of what they might find ahead.

I want to, he growled. *The Song of Scales is growing so strong that I may lose control. Better to weaken my flaring powers for a time, than to lose myself during the fight.*

It made sense, yet Jin still wished there was another way.

Give it to me, Rayshan said. *It's for the best.*

She pulled the jar from her pocket and uncorked it. Rayshan opened his great maw, exposing his tongue and teeth. Jin reached in and poured the jar's contents, a dull grey powder, on Rayshan's tongue, then stepped back as he closed his mouth and eyes. A shudder ran through him from his nose to his tail.

How do you feel?

I need a short rest, Rayshan said, placing his giant head against his front claws and exhaling a great blast of steam.

She leaned against his neck, feeling the warm scales beneath her as his breathing evened out. His heartbeat steadied, the insistent thrum of the Song of Scales easing to a distant tempo.

THE PRINCE LOOKED haggard when she approached his quarters, the guard letting her in without a word.

"Have you slept, Your Highness?" she asked.

He glanced at her. "Have you?"

"I don't need as much sleep," she answered. "The Khitan princess has a suggestion."

The prince smiled wryly. "That girl certainly tries all avenues."

"You know?"

"Yes. Arrange a meeting between her and her brothers. I admit it's worth considering."

"Then why not do it, Your Highness?"

"There's the risk it's a ploy. What's to stop her from leaving with her brothers and killing us at the parlay?"

"She won't do that." Jin didn't know how she knew, but it was like the girl's honesty was a scent. Nobu would keep her promise.

"That's my feeling. But I can't persuade the generals based on my feelings," Tai said. "They are itching for blood, a chance to prove themselves." He paused. "You leave this morning?"

Jin nodded and bowed. "I'd best prepare, Your Highness."

She turned to go, but stopped when Tai said, "Jin, wait."

She stopped and stood for what seemed a long silence.

"You're angry with me. I know."

"Those blood-bonded riders shouldn't be here, Your Highness."

"And who decides that?" he countered. "For once, it's not me. They chose."

"They had no choice," Jin said tightly. "No one defies the empress when she 'asks' for volunteers. Just as I don't have a choice in marrying you."

He winced. "I think I prefer your punches to the face."

"You know what I mean to say, Your Highness. It's not completely voluntary."

"I more than anyone know that," Tai said. "But this was different. Besides, do you really think the empress would only select twenty riders if it was up to her? These riders did it because they wanted to. And I'm glad they wanted to, if it gives you an edge against Mengkhis. These people are here because they believe in you and want to help you. As I do. Accept it."

"I will try, Your Highness," Jin said.

Jin reached Rayshan a few moments later, where

the dragons were all stabled in the leeward side of the wall.

Riders were preparing for departure, and everywhere she heard the rush of boots and the cinching of leather, the snorts of dragons testing the air.

Rayshan was tense to her touch, but the Song of Scales had noticeably faded.

How do you feel?

Strange, Rayshan growled. *But I'll be fine.*

It won't be like last time, she reassured him. *We won't need to flare and bring back a whole village. And we have the other bonded riders.*

Are you ready? he asked instead of answering.

She nodded. They had agreed they would try one last time to find Mengkhis in the Firesong. It was the only lead they had, and though Jin didn't hold much hope, she knew she'd be remiss to not try.

She placed another hand on Rayshan and leaned into him, closing her eyes and actively ignoring the Song of Scales. Rayshan cocooned them in the Firesong's familiar colorful web, and Jin pressed through the various shapes and shades, the snippets of sound and music that came to her.

Previous journeys into the Firesong had always involved slow progress, so she was surprised when a shriek came to her across her bond with Rayshan, and all the colors fled, as if sucked into a whirlpool.

She half expected to see the same memory of Tai's birth, or a scene from Jimo, but instead she saw walls of camel hide, where the setting sun bled through canvas like a wound through a bandage.

Her excitement at potentially having found Mengkhis gave way to disquiet.

Something felt wrong.

The air stank of blood, horseflesh, and something else. Sandalwood. Quiet triumph thrummed through her, and Jin recoiled. The emotion was wrong, somehow.

Because it was not hers.

Her skin crawled with a feeling that was eerily familiar. A feeling she had felt once before, when she was in the coastal ghost city of Jimo.

A face came into focus.

No. No no no—

Aadan's blood-streaked face stared back at her, the glare chilling in its hatred. His hands were tied, and his head and beard were wet, as if he had been doused in water.

"I have made a new friend," Jin said. But it was not her voice, and not her.

It was Mengkhis. She was seeing a memory through Mengkhis's eyes.

"Aadan Sasanid, heir to the Persian crown and exiled prince fighting for his kingdom," Mengkhis continued. "Though I care nothing for your titles, or your wealth. Do you know what I do care about?"

Jin's heart nearly stopped.

"I care only that he is worth something to you. Is he not, Jin?"

The hatred in Aadan's face deepened, but he didn't bother to struggle against his bonds.

He's speaking to me, Jin realized with dawning horror. *Mengkhis knows I am seeing this . . .*

"Bring the empress to the western tombs, and come by yourself," Mengkhis said, and though he spoke to Aadan, Jin knew the words were for her. "I'll know when you're there. A fair trade. What's the expression? A liver for a liver."

Jin reached out to pull him to her, to hold him safe. But Aadan disappeared into darkness. When the world came back into images that made sense, she was on her back, with Tai on top of her, her hand clutching his robe where she'd pulled him. A loose circle of riders, including Madu, surrounded them, biting back snickers.

"It's alright," Tai said, pulling himself to his feet. "I tripped."

The guards exchanged sly looks, but Jin didn't care what they thought she and the prince had been doing. She needed space. She sat up and leaned against Rayshan, trying to collect her breath and hold on to some vestiges of calm. Their audience dissipated at the prince's pointed looks, including Madu.

Tai squatted next to her, his voice low. "I'd like to be wrong, but I'm guessing that wasn't some fit of passion."

"Mengkhis has Aadan," she said quietly.

Tai stilled. "What? How do you—?"

"The Firesong. I saw a memory. I don't even know if he's still alive."

Tai took her arm and dragged her to a secluded spot by a tree, while Rayshan stretched his wings to shield them.

"Tell me exactly what you saw."

"There's no time. I just know he has him," Jin said tonelessly. Rage enveloped her. "I have to go. I have to find—"

"Calm yourself," Tai said, gripping her by the shoulders. "Look at me. What did he say?"

"He—" Jin hesitated. Tai mustn't know that the price of Aadan's freedom was the empress. Not that she could trade the empress for Aadan—could she? Tai would stop her. "He wants me to meet him. Alone."

"What are you not telling me?"

Jin knew she'd have to give something up. "He told me he'd trade Aadan for me."

"It's a trap."

"Of course it is," Jin argued, "but that doesn't mean I can stay here. And you can't make me stay here."

"Aadan's my friend as well, remember, but I can't let you walk into a trap," Tai said, tense. He paused. "Let me help you."

Jin shook her head. "He wants me. There's no reason for anyone else to risk themselves."

"He only wants you because you're a blood-bonded

rider and he thinks you're the only one," Tai said. "If he knew there were others, he wouldn't be fixed on only you."

"The team here needs you, Your Highness. Rayshan and I can handle this. If need be, send me with another blood-bonded rider."

He sighed, a wistfulness in his voice. "You never do that unless you want something."

"Do what?" she asked.

He glanced at where her hand rested on his arm. "That. You're trying to distract me. What aren't you telling me?"

She slid her hand away, suddenly shamed. The panic of saving Aadan had overridden everything else, making her lie to Tai. Whatever Tai was, whatever complex entanglements the empress and Meipin had for him, the prince had become a friend. A very good one that sometimes Jin wondered if she deserved.

"He wants me to bring him your mother. In exchange for Aadan."

Tai's throat worked as he thought on this. "Then let's bring her to him."

It was Jin's turn to stare. "You can't mean that."

Tai began to pace. "We can make a decoy. Make him think we're bringing her to him, and once Aadan is safe, we can finish him."

"This is Mengkhis Lai," Jin said. "You really think you can outwit him?"

"He wants my mother for revenge, and revenge

clouds judgment," Tai said. "That's our advantage. If he thinks he's getting her, he's likely to slip."

"Then who will be the decoy?" Jin asked.

"Me," Tai said.

Jin snorted. "If he captures you, he'll have your mother right where he wants her. It'll be as good as having her. Let me take a blood bonded instead."

"Your confidence in my mother's love for me is greatly unfounded," Tai said. "Besides, I'm not some helpless princeling. I'm a mage. Mengkhis won't be expecting that."

He has a point, Rayshan cut in.

Jin had to admit it made more sense than her own initial gut reactions of charging in on Rayshan and pulverizing Mengkhis and his dragon into the ground. Especially as Rayshan would have reduced flaring abilities, they wouldn't be able to summon an army of dead as they had at Bohai.

"I have to leave. As soon as tonight," Jin said.

Tai spread his palms. "Then I'll leave with you."

His easy agreement to accompany her comforted her more than she wanted to admit.

"What about the meeting with the Khitans?" Jin argued. "You'll be expected to head the negotiations."

"I'll send the princess Nobu."

"I thought you said that was a bad idea?" Jin said. "You don't trust her."

"We'll keep one of her dragons as a hostage. If she can't negotiate terms with the Khitans, we'll kill the dragon." At Jin's look, he sighed. "We'll threaten to kill the dragon. She'll never risk that, and to be honest, her brothers don't want to risk it either. The beast is worth more to them than she is."

This was sadly true. And though her throat was still tight and raw from knowing Aadan was a hostage, Jin felt infinitely better, and knew why.

She had Tai on her side.

CHAPTER 44

The nights were colder than Jin had expected, but it wasn't the winds that chilled her.

She would have traded places with Aadan in a breath. Aadan didn't deserve whatever he was suffering through, and each time she thought of him, she forced her mind somewhere else. Sometimes she even sought the haven that she had with Rayshan.

Though Tai never complained, she knew he suffered from the cold, unlike Jin, whose blood bond gave her Rayshan's powers to stave off the chill. They had left in such a hurry that Tai had only been able to bring a few layers of clothing and the necessary piece for his disguise, for Oyang Kang had been told they were doing a preliminary scout and would be back in a few days. Her wing mates had scowled when she told them she and Tai were going to scout together, and she knew the rumors would fly thicker than locusts in summer. But it was the only way that people would not ask other pointed questions that Jin didn't want to answer.

If they knew she and Tai were going after Mengkhis, then they would insist on coming too. And Mengkhis was too smart to be ambushed by a group of newly blood-bonded riders.

And so, they had left, promising to be back in three nights. Which meant hard riding through cold, barren territory back to the western regions of Changan, where the imperial tombs lay.

And where Mengkhis awaited them, with Aadan.

Jin sensed Tai shivering through the cloak, though he used his mage skills to keep warm. When they stopped for a quick sleep outside a small hamlet, though, Jin motioned for him to join her in the crook of Rayshan's belly.

"I am fine," he said.

"You're using up your energy," she replied. "And you'll need to save it for Mengkhis. Rayshan will keep us warm."

Rayshan rumbled, *I can feel his desire from here.*

Though the medication had all but silenced the Song of Scales, its side effects clearly included irritability.

Just because it's your Song of Scales time doesn't mean it's everyone else's.

True, he grumbled. *It must be exhausting, enduring mating season all the time.*

Tai hesitated.

"I'm not wanting something from you," she said, "besides your being fully able to combat Mengkhis."

He let out a breath, and from his shivering Jin presumed the warmth went away with it, as he rose to his feet and walked over.

He stepped over Rayshan's tail, glancing at the dragon apprehensively, but the great jade simply blew steam in his direction.

"I'm already warmer."

He sat down next her, then after a moment's hesitation, lay down, his back to her as Rayshan folded a wing over them both like a roof.

Soon their body heat, combined with the dragon's, warmed the space. But Jin's insides still felt like ice.

None of this would be happening if not for her.

If she had only acted quicker, killed Mengkhis as soon as she laid eyes on him.

If only she had agreed to leave with Aadan, or at least asked him not to leave, anything to have persuaded him to stay.

Regret is like rust, Rayshan said. *It will eat you.*

Jin squeezed her eyes shut.

"Are you ... crying?"

She didn't answer him, not even when he turned around and placed a hand on hers. And though the old Jin would have pushed Tai away, the new one was too scarred, and scared, to care.

"When I first met Aadan, he barely uttered a word,"

Tai said. "He was always so quiet, unlike the other boys. I thought he was mute, and I teased him about it."

Jin dug the heel of one hand into her eye. Talking about Aadan was painful. But talking about past Aadan was easier than thinking about a dead Aadan.

"This continued for months. I was a bit of a pain, really, but I would try to get him to talk. And eventually he did." Tai paused. "We became friends. I helped him. He helped me. Especially when my mother ordered me into the hatchery."

Jin frowned. "Princes aren't allowed to bond to dragons, are they?"

"My mother wanted me to, so there I was. Aadan and I couldn't have been more different. He so badly wanted to bond, and that was the last thing I wanted."

Rayshan shifted, the contempt needing no translation.

"Oh, dragons are fine creatures," Tai added. "But I've never been an animal person. Not to mention, I hate heights. So I was dreading this bonding. What if a dragon chose me? What if I bonded and became a dragonrider, tied to some beast for the rest of eternity?"

Rayshan's tail slammed the floor.

"Again, nothing against dragons. I have the utmost respect. Just not what I wanted. And Aadan . . . well, Aadan had the solution. He knew that lead repulses dragons, and he said, 'Why don't you wear a lead vest?'

So I made him help me steal one from the nursery master."

Jin half laughed, half choked through the tears. The ever-clever Aadan. The nursery masters always had lead vests on hand to keep the dragon hatchlings from bonding to them.

"I can't imagine Aadan agreeing to steal," she murmured.

"I think I termed it 'borrowing for a just cause.'" He smiled. "Aadan was my best friend after that. He never judged me for not wanting to bond with a dragon, just accepted it wasn't my path." Tai paused, his voice pained. "I love him like a brother."

And I . . . Jin shut the thought away. Admitting it would only make fighting Mengkhis harder.

"When it's time," she said slowly, "and as soon as we have Aadan, I want you to take him and run. There's no guarantee Wanli will be there." She didn't voice what they both knew: Wanli might not have gone to Nine Claw Mountain, or Mengkhis might have killed Wanli. They might be rescuing a man already dead in spirit. But they had to try.

"I'm not going to leave without you," Tai said, shifting. "And last I checked, I was your commander."

Jin turned around to face him, his lips only a hand's breadth from hers, the pulse beneath his scar audible to her blood-bonded ears. "Then I will kill you and leave you here. Promise me you'll get him out. That's the only reason I'm letting you come with me."

"Should have thought of that before you left," Tai said, yawning. "Now I'm your only option for a decoy."

Her expression never faltered. They were so close she could see each eyelash, the ribbed scar on his neck from the day Gao had almost killed him. "I can't fight him if I know there's a chance he'll capture one of you. He'll use you against me. So promise me you'll flee."

"I'm stronger than you think," Tai answered, eyes closed. "And I've saved your skin before."

She tensed at the memory of the seas in Bohai, when Baikalan had nearly dragged her to her death. Perhaps she should have died then.

Rayshan's mental roar of disapproval drowned those thoughts. She turned to Tai, but his breathing had slowed, and somehow her fingers had entangled in his.

CHAPTER 45

The Tombs of Heaven, the final resting place of all Tang emperors, lay to the northwest of Changan, on a high hill befitting royal status.

A light drizzle started as Rayshan's wings sliced through the clouds, their wet tendrils brushing Jin and Tai as they descended.

They landed near the towering gate that marked the long, wide avenue leading to the mausoleum itself. Trapezoidal walls surrounded the burial grounds, marked at intervals with stone guard towers.

If Tai was uneasy visiting his father's tomb, he didn't show it, instead lying still as they'd agreed, his wrists bound and the thick robe they'd brought covering every part of his face and body.

Jin and Rayshan walked cautiously down the paved road, the rain slicking everything in shiny rivulets. Jin opened her ears and nose, drinking in every scent and sound. Giant statues taller than Rayshan's shoulder lined the boulevard, their marble faces stoic. Jin saw roughly sixty, all evenly paced on either side of the avenue.

Like every thief, she had heard exaggerated tales of the imperial tombs: deep caverns carved into the hills held untold treasure, with myriad secret chambers, dead ends, and tunnels to deter grave robbers. Even without Rayshan's flaring, Jin sensed the flickering energy of dead souls everywhere.

Occasionally the human figures were interrupted by winged horses and foreign-looking giant birds carved of stone, their necks longer than Jin's arms and their heads bald.

"Ostriches," Tai murmured. "Horrible creatures with tempers."

But Jin had no heart for a discussion of foreign animals.

It's quiet.

But they are here, Rayshan growled. *Watching.*

Jin took a shaky breath. It was time to draw him out.

"I have the empress!"

Her voice bounced amongst the statues before the rain hammered it into silence. A moment passed. Two. As if on some hidden sign, the rain slowed, then stopped.

The silence pressed in, and Jin's neck prickled. She smelled sandalwood.

Ahead of her, near the mausoleum, a body lying on the ground appeared out of thin air.

Jin recognized Aadan immediately but resisted the urge to rush to him. Instead, her eyes roamed every corner, trying to spy Baikalan or Mengkhis.

"He's here," Jin whispered for Tai's benefit.

To his credit, Tai barely flinched, though she heard his heartbeat quicken. They had rubbed rosewater and frankincense into his skin, as Jin knew Mengkhis's keen nose would easily pick up Tai's scent.

Jin quickened her pace, eager to reach Aadan, but then he vanished again. The swoop of wings and a muffled cry reached her. She tried to track the dragon with her ears, but soon only the silence greeted her again.

"Show her to me," a voice right next to her whispered.

Jin whirled and came face-to-face with Mengkhis. His greying sandy hair was tied back in double plaits, as was his beard. He had gone back to his Rus ways, it appeared, as he was dressed in huren robes and boots. But the snarl on his face was familiar.

Rayshan bared his teeth, but Mengkhis simply smiled.

"A beautiful beast. Don't make me kill him."

Rayshan stepped forward, but Jin calmed him. *Remember the plan.*

"How do I know that Aadan is unharmed?" she asked.

Mengkhis sighed, as if weary of her petty demands, and glanced to their right.

A soft flash of wings and a thud, and Baikalan landed, dropping the trussed Aadan to the ground. One of the dragon's front feet was smaller than the others. The foot that Emar had hacked off on the ship that day near Jimo, Jin realized.

Jin forced a calming breath. She could not afford to act rashly. Neither could Tai. To his credit, he had lain motionless the entire time, though the whiff of fear was thick on him. A whiff that perhaps Mengkhis sensed as well.

"Where is Wanli?" Jin asked.

Mengkhis pointed toward the mausoleum, and Jin watched as the great silver dragon shimmered into view. Part of Mengkhis's power was the ability to not just turn himself invisible, but objects and living creatures around him. From what she knew of blood bonding and mage magic, the ease with which he made vast numbers of people and structures disappear took incredible skill.

The silver dragon thrashed against a chain tethering him to one of the mausoleum's great pillars, and Jin noticed the metal hood covering the dragon's head, without even an opening for eyes.

It was a lead hood, Jin realized, designed especially to sever a rider's connection with his or her dragon, and a metal chain bound Wanli's forelegs together.

"He returned from the Song of Scales to rescue his

rider, but he was no match for Baikalan. Give me the empress, and you'll have your Aadan and Wanli." Mengkhis's eyes slid to Tai's figure, and Jin tried to detect any suspicion in the man's expression.

Jin walked slowly to Rayshan's side and took her time pulling Tai's body down to her. Her blood bond meant she lifted him easily, though he had lightened himself to ensure she needn't struggle.

"What will you do with her?" Jin asked, carefully keeping the covering over Tai's face.

Mengkhis's face darkened. "That's my business. Now show me her face."

Jin looked down and gave Tai his cue. "If you want her, take her."

Jin heaved with all her might, throwing the lightened Tai at Mengkhis. She hoped Tai's skills really could work that fast, for he had mere seconds to change his body weight. Mengkhis looked puzzled, then enraged as Tai's body slammed into him, taking him down to the ground as if the prince weighed as much as a dragon.

Baikalan shrieked and lunged, but Rayshan was ready and leapt on him, snarling with open maw. Jin sprinted to Aadan, who lay on the ground by one of the giant winged horse statues. She immediately began tearing at his bonds.

"Jin . . ." Aadan breathed.

"Quiet," Jin said. "Let's get you gone." She cut

through his bonds and noted with dismay the dried blood caking his side.

"You shouldn't have come," Aadan said.

"I shouldn't have let you leave," Jin replied, hooking an arm under his shoulder. "Go now, free Wanli!"

Something slammed into the space between her shoulder blades, and she staggered forward, then turned around. Tai was on all fours, groaning.

"Jin!" Aadan shouted.

"Run! Free Wanli!" Jin screamed back, before an invisible hand clamped around her mouth. She instinctively reached up and gripped the arm around her as a voice tutted in her ear.

"You think you can outwit me, fledgling?" Mengkhis's chuckle made her skin go cold.

He was dragging her away, and from Tai and Aadan's desperate looks around them, Jin realized she and Mengkhis were invisible. She tried to call out, but Mengkhis's arm around her throat made it hard to even breathe.

The scuffing of her feet finally alerted them, however, and Tai's eyes almost seemed to connect with hers as he rushed them.

Mengkhis spun her to one side, and she managed to gasp in a lungful of air before whipping around and landing a heel to his ribs. Mengkhis grunted but delivered a hard chop downward that caught her in the knee, sending daggers of pain rippling through her. His other fist shot out, catching Tai in the throat like a mallet.

The prince went down, gulping air, and Jin's gaze turned to Aadan. If he freed Wanli, and they had another dragon on their side, they just might tip the scales. Aadan's outline was barely visible, sprinting up the steps to the mausoleum.

Near the steps, Rayshan and Baikalan were locked in combat, teeth and wings battering, each clawing and twisting for a chance to flame the other.

Rayshan!

Never mind me, the dragon snarled back. *Save Tai! He doesn't stand a chance against Mengkhis.*

Ignoring her knee, Jin drew her sword and stalked toward Mengkhis, whose back was to her.

Tai had regained his feet and darted behind one of the towering statues.

"You can't hide, boy!" Mengkhis roared.

"Who says I'm hiding?" Tai called out.

Jin guessed his plan. He would lighten the statue, allowing him to push it over, then return it to its usual weight as it fell, crushing Mengkhis.

But the statue didn't move. Jin heard Tai curse, before he ran to the next one.

"Looks like your powers were never as strong as you thought," Mengkhis grunted, and with blood-bonded speed he pulled a distraught Tai from behind the statue and drove the prince's head into the stone. Tai stumbled back, stunned.

Jin closed the distance in two steps and swung her blade in a vicious arc. In one motion, Mengkhis pushed Tai to the ground with one hand and deflected her with the other, then casually, in smooth practiced moves that seemed effortless, flicked Jin's sword to the side. Her throat tightened, and her hands went to the blades she kept at her thighs.

"I wouldn't do that, fledgling," Mengkhis said, and with a speed that made Jin's eyes water, Mengkhis delivered a right hook to Tai's face before pulling him to his feet and pressing the sword against the prince's throat, right where his scar was.

"Pity to open this up again, yes?" Mengkhis commented.

Tai struggled, but the movement only made Mengkhis press the blade harder. "Surrender, Jin, and he lives."

"You have me," Tai rasped, his jaw and throat clearly suffering from Mengkhis's blows. Blood trickled down one temple. "The empress will give you whatever you want."

Mengkhis laughed in genuine merriment. "You really think so, Prince? That is not what I hear, and certainly not the woman I know. She doesn't love her own children. What makes you think she will do anything for you?"

Jin saw the words hit Tai like arrows to a pressure point. She tried to spy Aadan, but he hadn't even reached the halfway mark up the mausoleum, and

Rayshan was weakening, unable to fight off Baikalan's lightning attacks from thin air. A sickening amount of blood covered Rayshan's back and neck.

Tai tried to say something, but Mengkhis's grip tightened in his hair, and the blade drew a ribbon of blood.

"I'm getting impatient," Mengkhis snapped.

"I submit," Jin said.

"Well chosen, fledgling."

She barely had time to give Tai what she hoped was a reassuring glance before something hard struck her in her forehead.

Sparks circled before her eyes, and a great black dragon appeared, a familiar figure in the saddle, swooping in on Mengkhis from behind.

Madu?

For once the thought of him was comforting. Madu had come to help.

But then all the light bled out of her vision.

CHAPTER 46

"Jin, wake up."

She burrowed away from the voice. She didn't know where she was, or when, but she instinctively knew that darkness was safe.

Close all the doors, shutter the windows, keep the sunlight out . . . out . . . out . . .

"Jin."

She darted and hid. She needed to find a place where the voice wouldn't find her.

"I know you're there."

Was she crying? Jin didn't know. She just knew that the voice was pulling her closer, and she could no longer resist it. It was tugging her, gently but firmly, away from the darkness, from safety.

A face appeared next to her, and then a body. Emar.

"There you are." He looked at her, somber. "I don't

blame you for being here. You've escaped the tiger only to battle a wolf."

She tried to push him away. But she had no body. Nothing happened, except for Emar leaning closer. "You must fight, Jin. Before it's too late."

She struggled, the darkness calling to her. She had to go. The other way was simply too painful.

"If you go, Rayshan goes too."

She stopped. Rayshan didn't deserve the darkness. Rayshan was the other way, back where agony and fire and people who would hurt her waited.

But Rayshan had saved her in the Singing Sands.

It was time to save him.

Jin reluctantly let go of the darkness, and felt it rip away from her like a scab from a wound.

THERE WAS nothing but light and pain. Though she tried to scream, Jin's lips wouldn't obey her. They were thick, and dry. Jin tried to lick them, but that only made them sting more.

She blinked, taking in her surroundings.

Two torches on the walls scattered light over the chamber, but most of it was lost in shadow. Stone walls painted with vivid murals but smelling of ancient earth, metal, and moss surrounded her, giving her the distinct impression she was underground.

A figure loomed just beyond the light, drinking from a chipped water horn.

Tai lay bound and gagged against one wall, his face lanced with blood but his eyes full of bittersweet relief when Jin met them.

"You said you'd let him go," she managed to whisper.

"Did I?" The figure turned to face her, and Jin sucked in a breath.

It was not Mengkhis.

Madu grinned. "Welcome back."

She tried to lunge forward, but pain in her wrists and hand seared her until she couldn't breathe. Her arms were horribly raw and on fire with pain—likely from the bonds—and her legs cramped. Her arms had been tied behind her back to the leg of a large, bronze tripod vessel used for incense and funeral offerings.

She reached out for Rayshan but heard only silence.

"Where's Rayshan?"

Madu shrugged. "Either dead or digging his way out of rubble."

Jin screamed across the bond, but again there was no answer. Did the tombs contain lead? Was that why she couldn't hear Rayshan?

"I took care of Mengkhis for you," Madu continued. "Blood bonding is incredible. No wonder you did it. I have never felt so alive, or so powerful. And Tian Pao can now suck the very air from a person's lungs; you should have seen Mengkhis's face." Madu's smile broadened at the memory.

"You killed him? And Baikalan?" Jin's disbelief almost overwhelmed her pain.

"I told you I would, didn't I?" Madu squatted before her. "That I'd kill him, and then I'd kill you."

Jin looked at him with pure loathing. She forced her breathing to even, remembering her Veil training. Haven. She had to think about her haven to push the unbearable pain to one side, figure out her options. Through the dim lighting of the torches, she made out a tunnel snaking off to the left.

If she freed herself, she'd have a chance to free Tai and escape. She just needed to undo the bonds, kill Madu, and . . .

"Thinking of escape?" Madu glanced at the tunnel. "It'll be hard for you to kill me with broken hands."

Jin stilled, his words sinking into her like poison, and she saw the sickening truth in Tai's eyes—the rage, the look of raw helplessness.

The pain in her hands was not because of lack of circulation, or the ropes. She flexed her left hand, which seemed unharmed. But her right hand, she understood now, was a mess of fire and bone, throbbing until her stomach heaved.

As if her recognition gave it a pathway, the agony came surging up her arms and howling into her head.

Fire seemed to burn in every nerve.

"I told you I'd break that hand," Madu said evenly. "And soon I'll break the other. But I wanted you to be awake when I do it. I want you to suffer like you made me suffer."

"Your uncle brought this on you, not me," Jin said.

Madu's fury made the spit fly from his mouth, some of it landing on Jin's shoulder. "Do *not* speak of my uncle! You took him away from me. You took away my future. You took away my cousin's future. Do you know she's now engaged to some lowly courtier who doesn't deserve to lick her shoes? When she should have been empress!"

Jin had heard that Gao intended his daughter to marry Prince Tai. "Gao tried to kill her groom, remember?"

Madu's lip curled as he glanced at Tai. "I don't think anyone expected the empress to love her son so little she wouldn't save him."

Jin didn't need to look at Tai to know the words had struck home.

"The only thing that kept me alive," Madu said, turning back to her, "was the goal of coming back and seeing your face now."

"You going to kill the prince too?" Jin asked, incredulous, indicating Tai with her chin. "You'd kill the Son of Heaven?"

Mengkhis gripped Tai's hair with one hand and hefted his dagger in the other. "Of course not. I'll say I followed you here, which is true. Tried to save you from Mengkhis, which is partially true. I'll say I was too late. He'd already had his way with you and killed the prince." Madu glanced at Tai, whose look of silent fury could have melted metal. "I'll be a bigger war hero than even Oyang Kang."

"I thought you were taking me back to the empress," Jin protested. "What about your lands and titles? You giving all that up?"

Madu scowled, shrugging. "Uncle always said my flaw was giving in to my urges. I'm sure the empress will reward me something, even if I fail to bring you back alive."

Jin floundered in the pain, trying to think of a way to reason with Madu. She held his eyes, struggling to keep the pain in her hand from overwhelming her. The throbbing, the stabbing pain . . .

You've trained for this, she told herself, nearly giggling in hysteria. *Pain is in your head . . .*

Think of something else. Locking the pain away would allow her to think clearly and plan. She focused on the pulse in Tai's neck, the fact that he was alive, the fact that Aadan must be alive somewhere . . . Haven. She needed to focus on her haven.

But then fingers closed around her left hand.

Jin froze, heart hammering. Something moved against her palm, and she instinctively jerked away, but whatever it was held her firm, making her gasp. The movement came again.

"Rabbit . . ." she whispered. Had she imagined it?

Madu grinned. "Lost your wits from the pain, girl?" He raised the blade, making Tai writhe. Jin screamed and pulled anew at her bonds.

Madu paused.

"Just curious," he said. "Do you actually have feelings for His Highness? It'd make his death more satisfying."

Jin spat, and enjoyed a momentary pleasure as the spittle hit true, sliding off Madu's cheek.

Madu scraped it off with the edge of his dagger before holding the blade to Tai's throat. "Goodbye, Prince."

A garbled cry broke out.

It took Jin a moment to realize it wasn't Tai's. Or hers.

Madu's dagger was half buried in his own throat, his shaking hand still on the hilt. His eyes darted to his blade in confused disbelief before he viciously pushed it all the way in, eyes swelling. His mouth moved, but only wet gurgles came forth, before Madu toppled face forward.

The blood pooled out from Madu's neck, widening in a circle before diverting, magically, into the shape of two feet.

Jin stared, dread setting in even as she knew who stood there before he flickered into visibility.

His wild hair held dust and caked blood, and he had a gash across the forehead and bloodshot eyes, but otherwise Mengkhis looked unscathed.

He kicked Madu's body for good measure, then pulled the dagger free, wiping the blood on Madu's leathers.

Tai struggled against his bonds, but they still held tight as Mengkhis took two slow steps to Jin and squatted before her, just where Madu had.

Jin braced herself, ready to fight with what little she had.

"Poor little fledgling," he said. He cupped her face in one hand, his eyes examining her intently. "Let's end this, shall we?"

Desperation erupted in Jin. She twisted like a snake and sank her teeth into his hand, feeling bone, sinew, and the salty rush of blood.

Before he could draw back, she twisted one leg around Mengkhis's, hooking her foot around his ankle to restrict his movement in any way possible.

He swore and jerked his hand away so hard, the flesh ripped in Jin's teeth. She spat the piece to the ground, while Mengkhis lunged for the blade.

She would only have one chance.

Jin worked her legs until they were underneath her. Bracing her shoulders against the large vessel, she focused all her energy, took a deep breath, and pushed with all her might.

The metal scraped against the stone floor, and then the vessel began to tip.

"Stop it!" Mengkhis snarled, and launched himself at her.

Jin heaved even harder. The force of Mengkhis barreling into her sent the vessel crashing to the ground, and Jin stumbled with it as the leg she was tied to levered up. The movement sent fire lancing through her broken hand in a sickening wave, and she fought off the blackness as she kicked Mengkhis in the chest, sending him to one knee and giving her precious moments to slide her bound hands off the vessel leg.

Mengkhis reached to grab her, but she twisted away from him. Spinning on her heel, she kicked him hard in the jaw, propelling him back against the tomb wall.

Jin fell toward Tai and knelt with her leg bent.

"Take the knife!" she snapped.

He reached up and closed his hand around the hilt before Mengkhis's hands closed around her throat and they both crashed to the floor.

"Stop fighting me, you witless girl!" Mengkhis snarled on top of her, and the backhand he delivered to her face sent a ringing through her ears that muted everything for several heartbeats. Tai had the blade positioned awkwardly in his bound hands and was desperately trying to saw at his bonds.

Jin!

Rayshan! Jin screamed in her mind, relief and fear mingling.

I'm coming!

Mengkhis was leaning close. "Do as I say, fledgling, if you want to live."

"I'd rather die."

The huren nodded, and Jin thought she detected something close to sadness, before it was snuffed out.

"I respect that, fledgling. But I'll be making the decisions for now."

CHAPTER 47

Mengkhis pulled her up by the arm to drag her toward the tunnel, and though it was her uninjured limb, pain continued to spiral through her.

Flare, Rayshan!

At first there was nothing, and her frustration made the pain flood back.

Rayshan had little power left. But after the medicine and the fight, and with her hands literally tied, she had no defenses except for summoning. She focused once more, until she felt a flicker of light.

A shape took form behind Mengkhis, a woman's shape, with long flowing hair. Jin recognized her as the huren who had appeared on the day she left for Champa. Jin cursed silently, tears of futility threatening.

Of all the people to summon, this was who came?

Jin tried desperately to summon someone else, but the energy wouldn't obey, and the woman stepped forward.

Mengkhis seemed to sense her presence, for his grip slackened, and he turned around.

Her light auburn hair and wide eyes were unmistakably from the northwest. There was still something familiar about those eyes, something haunting that was both familiar and foreign. And the face.

Mengkhis had frozen, as if mesmerized. Jin scrambled away from him, and he let her go. Mengkhis simply stared as the woman approached.

Jin picked up the blade at Tai's feet and cut his bonds. Tai scrambled to his feet, also disbelieving, before lunging for Jin and pulling her with him down the tunnel.

The woman, whoever she was, had bought them time. Jin stumbled after Tai, her hands still tied, nearly fainting from pain and exhaustion as he navigated the labyrinth of stone tunnels.

After a few dead ends that saw Tai cursing in frustration, Jin slid to the floor. "I can't. Leave me."

Tai knelt before her and worked at her bonds. She muffled her cries as white-hot pain shot through her. Her stomach heaved with it, and she leaned over to retch.

When he at last had the rope undone, he wiped her mouth with his sleeve and cradled her face. "I'm not leaving you. You hear me? Don't ask again."

He picked her up with a surprising strength, and she vaguely understood that he had made her lighter to carry her. They managed to follow the sound of dragon roars from outside and emerged into the dusk light.

They had come out on the west side of the mausoleum, Jin guessed, and through the waning light Rayshan came winging toward them, Wanli and Aadan just behind. The Persian leaped off Wanli. Before he landed, his face blanched at the sight of Jin's injuries, but Tai helped her stand. Aadan immediately encircled her waist with one arm and helped her onto Rayshan.

Can you ride? Rayshan asked worriedly.

I will, Jin said. Aadan was already strapping her in using an improvised leather from her saddle. *Besides, we have a monster to kill. You're going to have to be my sword and hands.* Of all the things the Veil had taught her, why had they never taught her to fight left-handed?

As soon as she was secured, they stood in a semi-circle around the entrance to the tomb, which had fallen deathly quiet.

"By the Wise Lord, where is he?" Aadan muttered as Tai sat behind him on a crouched Wanli, all taut trepidation.

Jin swallowed, every nerve in her raw.

She heard the rush of wings a moment too late. Baikalan appeared out of thin air and crashed into their side, sending Rayshan sliding across the paved stones. He recovered his footing, but not before Jin pitched out of the saddle, the leather snapping from the weight of her fall.

Rayshan shifted just in time to avoid crushing her under him, and she instinctively pushed herself to her knees, nearly screaming from the pain of her broken hand against the ground.

She ground her teeth as Mengkhis emerged from the tomb entrance, just as Aadan crashed into the ground next to her and tried to pull her upright.

"Give me your sword! And the leather strap!" she shouted.

Aadan looked at her in confusion, but then understanding dawned. He ripped the leather strap from its saddle and hacked the material with his sword. Jin gripped the blade in her left hand, then stretched out her right arm, still trying to not think about her broken bones. Aadan's hands shook, which made the buckle slip.

"We don't have time, just do it!" she snapped. Baikalan had already landed before Mengkhis, and the huren was climbing on.

Aadan's face contorted, but he tied the leather belt around her forearm, leaving the metal buckle swinging on the end.

There is no pain.

Pain is in the mind.

Pain is in the mind. In the mind. Pain is in the mind. Painisinthemindpainisinthe—

Jin swung her arm once to make sure the belt was

secure, then stood and sprinted toward Mengkhis and Baikalan, who were about to take to the air. She sensed Aadan and Tai behind her, but with her blood-bonded speed, she was far faster.

Rayshan and Wanli swooped in to harry Baikalan's rear, circling and snapping with their jaws to keep the dragon from flight. Baikalan blasted a vicious wave of fire at both dragons, making them fall back just long enough to allow him space to launch into the air.

Jin sprinted to Rayshan, who lowered himself. Jin leapt up on his foreleg and vaulted onto his back, gripping him with her legs. Even so, she slid crazily as he immediately rose in pursuit of Baikalan and Mengkhis, who were heading toward the tombs' northern wall.

Wanli! Circle back for Aadan and Tai! she called out.

Jin rallied her thoughts as Rayshan gained on the other jade dragon, whose tail lashed behind him.

Get me alongside!

Rayshan roared and put in a burst of speed, cutting just past Baikalan.

Tilt to the left!

Rayshan did, and she swung a leg over, sliding down his wing and onto Baikalan's back.

The dragon roared at the new weight and swerved toward the northeastern wall tower. It took all of Jin's concentration to stay astride with one broken hand and her good hand gripping a sword. Jin swung the leather belt over her head and lashed out with the buckle.

It was not a hard blow, but the metal struck Mengkhis's ear. It was not meant to wound, only throw him off balance. Jin immediately followed with another strike of the belt, this time whipping Baikalan on the back. The dragon instinctively twisted away from the pain, sending Mengkhis and Jin rolling off to hit the northern wall's boulevard.

The impact brought bile to Jin's throat, but she forced back the darkness and clambered to her feet. Ahead of her, Mengkhis was doing the same.

Baikalan circled up, roaring as Rayshan gave chase, before he flickered to nothingness. Rayshan spewed flame in a crackling circle around him but hit only empty air.

Jin chanced a quick glance to the south. She vaguely made out Wanli landing near Aadan and Tai at the southern gates where she had mounted Rayshan.

Their help would be too late. Mengkhis was about to reach the tower, and once he disappeared into that cramped space, she wouldn't have Rayshan's help if she needed it.

She sprinted for Mengkhis, ignoring the pain in her ribs and hand.

"Mengkhis!"

He turned.

"Give up, fledgling," he snarled. "You can't win."

Jin hefted her sword and leapt.

As she had hoped, he went to deflect the sword. This allowed her just enough time to brace herself for the pain before she smashed her broken hand with the buckle into his face.

He stepped back in surprise, and Jin landed her heel against his left knee and was rewarded with a crack. He crumpled for a split breath, but that was all she needed. She kicked him in the chest, but his hand whipped out to seize the strap still tied to her bad hand, yanking her to him.

The pain made the edges of her vision darken, but she forced it into a box. She rammed her knee into his cracked one, and immediately felt his arms loosen. She shoved him onto his back, then pressed her blade tip just under his breastbone above the heart.

He looked up at her and grinned through bloody lips.

"It ends," she whispered, as Rayshan landed on the tower above them, wings spread and eyes wary. They both feared Baikalan appearing out of nowhere, even more likely now that Mengkhis was in danger.

"You're just like your mother," he said.

Jin froze. "What did you say?" Her mind flashed back to a scene so vivid that she thought she had traveled in time. Her sword point to a man, his face looking up at her. Though Mengkhis's had less contempt than Gao's—in fact, Mengkhis's was downright—proud. She had killed Gao after he had told her she was just like her murderess mother.

"You're just like her in spirit," Mengkhis said. "But you have *mamushaka's* eyes."

"What are you talking about?" She pressed the sword point further, her whole body throbbing now from something more than just pain.

Jin, Rayshan growled above them in warning, for like her, he knew her control was slipping. In the distance, Jin heard, rather than saw, Wanli approaching with Aadan and Tai.

"Go ahead, kill me," Mengkhis said. "But then you'll never have the answers you seek. Like who your parents are."

Jin froze, every nerve in her thrumming on a knife's edge. A cold wind scuttled past, and it felt as if every finger of the air had found its way into her throat, so she had to think on every breath she drew in. "You lie."

But she saw again the huren woman who had appeared, the color of her eyes. And Jin realized, with a sickening punch to the stomach, why the woman looked so familiar.

She looked like Jin.

Mamushaka. The woman was Mengkhis's mother, the Rus princess captured in war.

"No," Jin whispered.

"What are you waiting for?" Tai called out as Wanli landed on the wall. The two men slid off Wanli.

"Go on, kill your father and marry your Chinese prince." Mengkhis's voice lowered to a whisper.

The rioting thoughts in her head wouldn't quiet. "You're lying to save yourself." But with every heartbeat, doubt shredded her a little more.

"This is not an Iron Mind test, Jin," Mengkhis snarled, his eyes never leaving her face. "I'm offering you the truth. I just saved you in the tomb, didn't I? I can save you from the ghosts that have haunted you all your life. I can answer every question you've always had. Who you are, why you have that precious scar, why the empress wants you to marry Tai. What the blood bond does to you." He swallowed. "Why do you think I asked you to come here? Why do you think I gave you the code for friend?"

Every word crumbled her defenses, and she dimly heard another cry from Rayshan. *Jin!*

She shut her eyes.

"Jin, what are you doing?" Aadan was striding toward her now, the panic in his voice unmistakable.

Suddenly, a wall of fire blazed behind Jin, cutting her off from Tai and Aadan. Rayshan roared and leapt off the tower, but Jin's eyes stayed locked on Mengkhis.

"It's really very simple, fledgling," Mengkhis said. "You'll have to decide what the truth is worth to you."

A pounding reached her, and she thought it was her head, until she heard the screeches on the horizon.

Mengkhis's hand came up to grip the sword blade. "Choose!"

Jin recognized the screeches now. Dragon Class. Aadan must have sent a message to the forces stationed at the wall. There was no time to wonder how they had made it here so quickly. In moments, they would be upon her, and even if she spared Mengkhis, there were a dozen other blood-bonded riders who could, and would, kill him. As Madu had tried.

"It won't be your choice for much longer," Mengkhis whispered. "Kill me now, or never."

No. No no no. He couldn't be her father. Yet what he said made horrifying, chilling sense.

She had been so intent on killing him, she hadn't asked why he had spelled the code for friend in her palm, why he had saved her from Madu.

And after they had fled the tomb, he hadn't tried to kill them—he had tried to flee.

Mengkhis Lai was her father.

With a cry that seemed to rip her in half, Jin took the sword and plunged it. Sparks flew as the blade bit into the cracks of the stone just next to Mengkhis's head.

They stared at each other, eyes hard.

"It will not be by my hand," she whispered.

Mengkhis cursed under his breath. "Oh, fledgling."

Before she realized he had even moved, his hand held a blade—the other one she had strapped to her thigh.

"This is for you," Mengkhis said, and the blade parted leather as it knifed into her chest.

Time disappeared as she folded to the stone floor, a sickly warmth pooling. She wasn't sure whether the rushing in her ears was Rayshan's bellowing or her own blood surging in her veins.

There was also shouting—hers? Aadan's? Tai's? And

then the air around them whipped into a frenzy as Baikalan appeared again, claws outstretched. They closed around Mengkhis, and then the two were airborne, vanishing like smoke.

The last thing Jin saw was Rayshan's jade wings as they blocked out the sky, his great bulk descending to her.

The dragon curled his body over her like a shroud, and this time she let the darkness take her.

CHAPTER 48

A pounding sound. Scraping. Jin could barely breathe.

Something gripped her chest tight.

She opened one eye and then the other, and light crashed in on her. The constriction around her ribs, along with the aching throb in her bandaged hand made her panic, before Rayshan's soothing hum stilled her. But even so, it all came rushing back: Mengkhis, the battle on the wall, her own knife sliding into her ribs. Aaden.

At the thought of Aaden she turned her head, grimacing.

Tent walls surrounded her. She recognized the make of imperial army canvas. She lay on a simple cloth pallet, and a low table held an assortment of salves, a pitcher of water, pots of ointment and a lantern. Slouched against one wall was Aaden himself, his bearded chin resting against his chest, an open scroll in his hand.

Jin shifted, a hissing groan escaping her.

Aaden's eyes snapped open as if he'd never been asleep.

"Hey," he said, and swallowed, as if something was stuck there. "For someone who can't die, you certainly try very hard."

Jin tried to sit up, but the agony ripping through her chest made her lie back, gasping a few times before she rallied enough breath to speak. "Where are we?"

"Just outside the tombs," Aaden said. He rose to his feet and came to her bedside, unabashedly staring as if he would never look away. The concern was evident on his face. He reached for a pitcher of water and a cup. As he poured, Jin glanced at the light limning the tent door. "How long have I been down?"

Aaden held out the cup of water. "Two days. Rayshan hasn't left the outside of this tent."

Rayshan's hum came again, along with a jolt on the canvas wall where a tail—Rayshan's—gently slapped it.

Jin tried to sit up to drink, but fell back. Seeing her struggle, Aadan gently worked an arm underneath her head and pulled her to a sitting position. Cold sweat broke out on Jin's forehead, and her face must have betrayed her pain, for Aadan grimaced. He raised the cup to her lips, and she drank gratefully.

Just then, the tent flap opened. Tai's cuts had been

cleaned, but his cheek and throat still bore ugly bruises from his fight with Mengkhis.

Aadan hesitated, then withdrew his arm from around Jin's back. A palpable tension descended.

"I leave for one hour over two days, and that's when you decide to wake up?" Tai asked. His voice sounded strained, and Jin wondered how much damage Mengkhis's fist had done.

"Timing hasn't been my friend lately," Jin said bitterly. Her memories snapped back to Mengkhis. How she had hesitated. How she had been such a fool, letting Mengkhis's lies get to her.

Only they weren't lies.

A nauseating wave threatened.

It felt like a nightmare, but she knew right down to her bones that it wasn't. Which made it hurt even more than the hole in her chest.

"Jin," Aaden said quietly, "are you alright?"

Jin squeezed her eyes shut. "How am I still alive?" Mengkhis had sunk his blade in her to the hilt. She'd felt it. He'd aimed for the heart. A fatal blow from a blood-bonded rider should have killed her. And not just any blood-bonded rider. Her own father.

"Either your luck is very good, or Mengkhis's is very bad," Tai said. "One finger width to the left and we'd be burning incense for you in the afterlife right now." His tone was light, but his expression was rigid.

Aadan nodded. "We left the knife in until the mage doctor arrived."

Something clicked in Jin's mind. The knife sliding in . . . one finger width to the left. What had Bean said? Top Veil members learned how to deliver the "shade blade." What if Mengkhis had never meant to kill her?

"Where is he? Mengkhis, I mean?" Jin asked.

"We don't know," Tai said. Talking still clearly hurt. "But he's a walking corpse. We'll find him. And kill him. You're not the only one who can do the deed now."

Aadan's hand moved toward hers, but then he seemed to remember himself. "We will find him, Jin. I promise." He paused. His eyes searched her face. "What exactly happened up there?"

Jin drew a deep breath. Her limbs trembled with the storm of emotions that assaulted her—rage, horror, confusion, shame. And self-doubt. Could she tell them what Mengkhis had said? Would she sound like a madwoman? She wasn't ready to face it yet. At least not in front of Tai and Aadan. She hardly knew what to think herself. And suddenly she was exhausted by the possibility of having to answer questions that she had no answers to.

It's safer to keep this to ourselves, Rayshan growled in her mind. *If people find out you're Mengkhis's daughter . . .*

He was right. No one could know. Not yet. Maybe not ever.

"I failed. Again," she said. "That's what happened."

That, at least, was true. She had failed to kill

Mengkhis. Failed to see the trap that she had stepped into.

"Mengkhis is notorious for twisting your thoughts," Tai said. "Don't blame yourself."

"What did he say to you?" Aadan asked softly.

Jin swallowed. "I—I don't remember. It's a blur."

Aadan didn't look convinced, but just then a flurry of footsteps sounded outside, followed by shouts and obsequious murmurs of, "Your Divine Majesty," before the tent flap opened.

The empress herself stepped in, followed by two soldiers. One carried an ornate stool, which he placed just behind his sovereign.

Despite no doubt having traveled half a day to reach the tombs and wearing a simpler riding robe rather than her usual court attire, the empress looked as dazzling and pristine as she did in the palace, a stark contrast to the military tent around her. Aadan and Tai both bowed.

"Your Divine Majesty," Aadan greeted her.

The empress turned to him. "Aadan Sasanid. It is good to see you. The throne thanks you for helping us battle Mengkhis. I will see to it that you are appropriately thanked, and of course all misconduct pardoned. Though I had my hesitations, I believe we can arrange for you to receive the dragons that you seek for your campaign against the Arabs. My son the War Minister will see to arrangements."

Aadan bowed. "You are most gracious, Your Divine

Majesty, though I wish to remain at court until Mengkhis Lai is found and destroyed."

Jin's breath hitched. She'd be grateful to have Aadan around, but she didn't relish that he was staying to kill her father.

The empress regarded him, seemingly debating. "Very well. My court will welcome you for as long as you'd like to stay. But in the meantime, leave us. I wish a moment alone with Jin."

Jin struggled to control the emotions on her face. Tai shot his mother a questioning glance before looking to Jin. Aadan seemed even more reluctant, but Jin nodded.

"We'll return soon," Aadan promised.

The two exited the tent, and the empress motioned at the soldiers, who bowed and backed out the tent flap, leaving Jin and the empress alone.

The empress approached, bringing the stool with her, and sat. Her silk dress whispered, then silence descended once again as the two women looked at each other.

"You are a hero yet again," the empress said. "The Dragon Class is saying you are truly immortal."

"Simply lucky, Your Divine Majesty," Jin replied.

"Hm," the empress said. "I heard what happened. To an untrained eye, it might seem like you and Mengkhis have a bond."

Jin swallowed, pulse racing. Did the empress know? If so, her life would be forfeit.

"Sanjin suspects Mengkhis spared you to make an ally of you, and plant you at court for his own ends."

"With all respect, that's ridiculous, Your Divine Majesty," Jin replied evenly, reining in her anger. "The man tried to kill me."

"Yet some say you hesitated in killing him. Why?"

Jin decided to test the empress's reaction. "He said he knew who my real parents were."

To her disappointment, there was absolutely no change in the empress's face. "And who are they?"

"I don't know." This was partially true. "He stabbed me when my attention was divided, Your Divine Majesty."

"A costly mistake."

"Yes. I won't make it again."

The empress's eyes bored into Jin's. "Can I trust you, child?"

She had never called Jin "child" before. Did she know what Mengkhis had said? No, Jin assured herself. That wasn't possible. "Why wouldn't you, Your Divine Majesty?"

The empress smiled. "One can never be too careful. Tai always worried that we might turn you against us. And though I constantly assured him you were very loyal and dependable, it always pays to be cautious."

"I believe all my actions have proven my loyalty," Jin said tightly.

"Quite," the empress said. "But I've learned the hard way that those with a sword in their hand often have honey on their lips. I need to protect the throne, but I also want to protect my son." She paused, her gaze never leaving Jin's face. "You know he loves you?"

Jin wondered if the empress was trying to guilt her. "His Highness is ever dutiful and would love whomever you wished him to marry."

"You are growing more diplomatic," the empress smiled. "But a mother knows these things. As you will when you have children."

Something about her near brush with death made her throw caution to the wind. "Why are you so concerned with me? Why are you so intent on my marrying the Son of Heaven?"

The empress smiled. "When you first arrived at court, I saw great potential in you. But I was gravely mistaken." She leaned close. "I thought you might become a decent dragonrider, at most take a minor wing command in Dragon Class. But I had no idea how much you are capable of. You defeated the Khitans. You passed the Veil. You survived Mengkhis. You have the support of the people. You are so much more powerful than you can imagine. You just need to embrace your destiny, one that I can help you achieve. But only if you trust me." Her expression darkened. "Besides, I need you. Now more than ever."

"Why?"

"It seems Mengkhis might not be acting alone."

Jin stilled. "What do you mean, Your Highness?"

"All this time we thought Mengkhis was lying low,

recovering," the empress said, "but he's been busy. Sanjin has uncovered evidence of traitors in the palace, and the princess Nobu told us her brothers hinted at it when she spoke with them. Mengkhis has been recruiting, and we now think there's a significant network of people working for him."

"To mount a coup?" Visions of Gao made Jin tense.

The empress shook her head. "I don't think Mengkhis wants the throne. He just wants revenge." The empress leaned forward. "And what better revenge than killing me and destabilizing the empire? I need to know whose side you're on. Because I need you and Sanjin to work together to weed out these traitors."

"You have an entire Veil. You have other blood-bonded riders."

"None of them knows Mengkhis the way you do. None of them has fought him twice and survived." She looked down. "They plan to kill the crown prince. If there's no heir, then the nobles will drag us into chaos fighting for the throne." At Jin's silence, the empress glanced up. "If you won't do it for me, then do it for the crown prince. I need to move him out of the palace until the threat is eliminated, and I want you to head an elite group of dragonrider bodyguards."

No matter what her feelings about marrying Tai, Jin knew she would never walk away from him if he was in danger. He had risked his own life to save hers—not just back in the tombs, but at Bohai, and he had come to help save Aadan. Even if she didn't love him the way she loved Aadan, she couldn't leave him vulnerable to Mengkhis. He was a friend. A good one. A good man who needed to live if only for the empire. In this, the empress was right. The nobles would drag the empire into a civil war trying to claim the Dragon Throne.

"So can I count on you to defend my son?" the empress asked.

"On one condition, Your Divine Majesty."

The empress raised an eyebrow. "I suppose you have earned the right. Name it."

"When we capture Mengkhis Lai," Jin said, "his life is mine to do with as I see fit."

"That's impossible."

"That's my ask, Your Divine Majesty."

The empress stilled. "You think he will tell you who your parents are? All he will give you is lies."

"I would still like to hear them, Your Divine Majesty." Mengkhis had, as far as Jin knew, never lied to her. His theory that they were both meant to die in the Well could have been true, and she knew in her bones he was her father. Whether he had really tried to kill her was uncertain. But he hadn't lied. Whereas the empress had always been spare with the truth at the best of times. Jin had many questions, and she wouldn't rest until she found the answers.

The empress nodded. "Very well. Mengkhis is yours. Just keep the crown prince alive."

Pre-order Book 4 in Riders of Jade & Fire, *releasing 2026!*

WHAT'S NEXT?

Thanks for reading! If you enjoyed this, why not join my readers' club? You'll get 10% off your first purchase in my store, plus be first to know about upcoming books in the *Riders of Jade and Fire* series. You'll also receive free:

- *Night of the Black Dragon* - the prequel to *Dragon Class,* with the events leading right up to Jin and Lu's heist;
- *The Queen and the Dagger,* the prequel to my other series, *Book of Theo;*
- exclusive previews and bonus stories. Join at www.melanieansley.com

Enjoyed *Dragon Rogue?* Please consider leaving a review on my store, Amazon, Bookbub or Goodreads. You'll ensure many more of Jin's stories follow!

FAQS

Why Tang China?

Tang China was considered a "golden age" and has always fascinated me!

Many of China's most famous stories and historical figures come from this period–including the Empress Wu, the Buddhist monk Xuanzang (whose travels to India inspired the book "Journey to the West" featuring the Monkey King), and Judge Di Renjie (a magistrate whose cases inspired multiple "detective" novels).

How much of the history in this third book is true?

A lot of this series has been inspired by fact, but I also believe in the old storytelling advice: "Never let the truth get in the way of a good yarn."

The Empress Wu did exist, and actually ruled in her own right as an emperor (not just through her husband or son) from 690 to 705. She was born in a wealthy family and she received a robust education, which was rare for girls at the time.

Her full history reads like a Shakespearean play gone wild, with enough intrigue to fill several novels. But in brief, she joined the emperor Taizong's harem at age 14, and when the emperor died, his son Gaozong brought her back from seclusion into the palace to become his wife. From there, she consolidated her power (at times ruthlessly) and was famous for keeping a harem of young men in her older years.

She also had a beloved youngest daughter, Taiping, whom she consulted on policy decisions, and for whom Wu orchestrated two political marriages.

Empress Wu was quite the feminist, and favoured Buddhism over Confucianism because it was less misogynistic.

The part about the Empress Wu portraying herself as a Bodhisattva from heaven is based in fact. The Great Cloud Sutra, brought by a famous monk named Xuanzang to China, was in fact used by Wu and her supporters to establish that she was a living god, for the texts suggested (or were translated to suggest) that a Buddhist god would be reborn as a woman and rule over a vast empire.

Aadan is loosely modeled on a real Iranian prince, Narsieh, who fled to China in the mid 650s with his father Peroz III when his kingdom was invaded by the Arabs. He was in China during Empress Wu's ascent to the throne, so it's quite probable they knew each other.

I drew some inspiration for Prince Tai from Wu Zetian's real son and Crown Prince, Li Hong. Li had a reputation for compassion and fairness, and even argued with his mother over her treatment of her political rivals. So when he died mysteriously at age 23, many suspected assassination. Will Tai meet the same end? We'll have to see…!

Sanjin is a fictional character, but based on the very real secret police force Empress Wu kept–and which I've renamed the Royal Veil for the ROJAF series. Many of the department officials were ruthless and corrupt, fabricating crimes and confessions when it suited them.

The capital city, Changan, which is near today's Xi'an, was the biggest in the world at the time, with a population of 1 million people–many of them huren like Emar and Aadan, or of mixed heritage like Jin. The empress actually moved the capital from Changan to Luoyang in 690 when she became emperor, but I've kept the capital in Changan for this story.

The tombs outside Changan do exist and are a tourist attraction today, with the statues and parts of the walls that I depict in the battle between Jin and Mengkhis still standing.

Where do you get all the traditional expressions/sayings?

Part of the fun of this series has been using real Chinese expressions/idioms. I used to be a translator for films and for producers working in China, and I love trying to bring the flavour of these words over to English.

Still have questions? Drop me a note on my website (www.melanieansley.com), I'd love to hear from you!

ACKNOWLEDGMENTS

Some say that every book gets easier.

I don't know whether that's true, but I do know that every book still takes a village. I don't need any less people the more books I write, and I'm so very grateful for everyone who has supported me from the beginning, or joined me along the way.

This book wouldn't have been possible without the help of my beta readers, Hannah Greer and Andrea Letourneau. You helped steer me off my darker storytelling tendencies! Those years making horror films have certainly influenced my writing.

Thank you to my editor, Stacey K (GrammarGal), for smoothing out the language and cleaning up the words--all 105,000 of them.

Thanks also to the community of independent authors I have had the pleasure of meeting this last year--Jasmine Young, who has been so supportive and generous with advice; Richard Fierce, Helen Garraway, RM Krogman, Eileen Mueller, Natalie Wright, Katrina Cope and Alexis Johnson, thanks for helping spread the word about this book.

Lyn Ducich and Cecilia Sutton, you have both been such staunch cheerleaders for so long. Thank you!

I also want to thank my wonderful and amazing ARC team, who read this book early and supported the release: Vicky Hopkins, Eric Herbaut, Tiffany Ewald, Lisa Hunt, Judith Jenkins, Sara Rosevear, Marcie Walters, Abigail Blesi, Janett Armstrong, Greg Selvitelli, Cathy Griffin, LolaJune Wayneg, Ina Aust, Emma D'Ambrosio, Mary Lou Repetti, Kez Shaw, Marten Persson, Tanvi Chandra, Renee Portnell, Melissa Steele, Heather Stewart-Williams, Yuan-Chia Wang, Kay Wisdom, Andie Letourneau, Cecilia Sutton, Prenscella Hardwell, plus others who wish to be anonymous.

And last but not least, thanks to Sam, Artemis, and Evander, for putting up with me when I'm off riding dragons.

ABOUT THE AUTHOR

Melanie was born in Canada but raised in China, and now lives in Ballarat, Australia with her husband and two children. She loves to read, write, and laugh. She also makes movies.